THE PAIRING

From the New York Times & USA Today Best Selling Author

KATIE ASHLEY

The Pairing (The Proposition #3)

Copyright © 2014 by Katie Ashley

Edited by Marrion Archer | Making Manuscripts

Marilyn Medina | Eagle Eye Reads

Cover Designed by Letitia Hasser | RBA Designs

Chapter One

With a shrill decibel ringing in his left ear, Alpesh, or Pesh Nadeen, as he was more commonly called, groped blindly along the nightstand before hitting the snooze button on the alarm. When the sound continued, his dark brown eyes popped open. Cutting his gaze to the nightstand, he realized it was not his alarm, but his hospital pager going off. Scrubbing the sleep from his eyes, he sat up in bed. After picking up the pager and peering at the screen, he groaned before pressing the OFF button. He knew the code all too well. One of the ER docs was unable to come in for his or her shift. As supervisor, he had to either find a replacement or take their place. Considering there wasn't much else exciting going on in his life, he grabbed his phone. He alerted the charge nurse that he would be filling in, and he would be there as soon as he could.

As he trudged into the bathroom, he didn't bother lamenting that one of his few days off was being taken. Most of the other doctors he worked with had wives or husbands along with children. They never called in unless it was a grave necessity. So why shouldn't he, as the only single and childless one among them, take up the slack? It was the honorable thing to do, and if there was one thing Pesh prided himself on, it was having an honorable character.

After a record breaking shower and shave, he hurried into the closet. He threw on one of his signature long-sleeved blue shirts and trademark khaki pants. Besides his white lab coat, it was his uniform. He never wore plain white shirts. Blue was a comforting color, and he always wanted to put his patients at ease and make them feel comfortable. Once he tightened his tie, he hurried out of the closet and over to the dresser.

When he grabbed his wallet and hospital authorization card, his gaze fell on the picture in the antique silver frame. His late wife's smile radiated from behind the glass. Jade was gazing up at him with her twinkling blue eyes—both of them wore brilliant smiles while being outfitted in the traditional Indian wedding attire. Her long blonde hair fell in waves and was adorned with various ribbons, charms, and beads, as were the custom.

His chest tightened as he thought of the day his American-as-apple-pie-wife embraced his heritage by partaking in the full Indian wedding ceremony. Although there were many happy days and good times in the course of their six-year marriage, he couldn't remember a happier day than his wedding day. It was the day they had finally come together as one—a uniting of two different people and cultures. The day had held such promise of a happy and long future together.

Turning away from the dresser, he also tried to turn away from the overwhelming grief that gripped him. Two years had passed since the horrible day when his thirty-five year old wife had been snatched away from him. Not a day went by when he didn't miss her, when he didn't dread coming home to an empty house not filled with her laughter or her sweet presence. No one could quite fathom the true agonizing turmoil he had been through—only a select few, who had also had their heart torn from their chest, fully understood the gaping hole of emptiness left behind.

With a heavy heart, he headed out the door. On the short drive in to work, Pesh didn't bother turning on the radio to drown out the voices of sorrow echoing through his head. He knew it was no use. No matter how hard he tried, he could not rid himself of his pain. Family and friends had afforded him one year of grieving before they had been on him to move on. Desperately, they tried to get him to realize that the last thing his Jade would want was for him to continue carrying a torch for her—to spend his life sad and alone. He'd tried to prove to them he had moved on, but that only resulted in projecting what he thought was love onto a woman who was just as confused about her life as he was. He'd vowed after that mistake that he wasn't going to let anyone dictate when it was time for him to move on from Jade's memory. If he was to love or marry again, he would be the one to take the steps.

He made the same rote pilgrimage from the staff parking lot into the hospital. Every day was just the same, one right after the other. He'd barely had time to ease on his white medical coat when he heard his name being paged over the intercom. Rushing over to the sink, he scrubbed up as quickly as he could before whirling around. Using his back to open the door to the doctor's lounge, he did his best speed walking down the hallway to the trauma area. The moment he swept through the glass doors, the staff pounced on him.

Two nurses were at the man's head. One held down the face mask as the other pumped air through the bag into his airways. Another was stationed at the man's side doing CPR compressions intervals on the chest.

After donning a pair of rubber gloves, Pesh glanced to the charge nurse as he hurried to the man's side. "Male, forty-five, collapsed at the jogging park during a run. No known medical history. Coded once on the trip over," she quickly informed him.

"BP is dropping," another nurse called behind him.

Machines began beeping on and off, a symphony of noise heralding impending doom. "Okay, we need to shock him again." The crash cart was rolled up to the gurney. Pesh grabbed the paddles. "Charging. Shocking at 260 joules."

"Clear," Pesh commanded. The nurses administering compressions to his chest and the intubation bag stepped back, holding their hands off the man. Pesh brought the gelled paddles to the man's chest. As the electrical charge raged through the man's body, his arms and legs flailed.

Pesh glanced at the heart monitor. "Still asystole. Again."

"Charging at 360 joules," a nurse replied.

"Clear." As he brought the paddles once again to the man's chest, Pesh muttered, "Come on, come on, beat, dammit," under his breath. It didn't matter how young or how old, he hated to lose a patient. Although the body shuddered and jerked in reaction to the electricity, the heart remained frozen. Although it was a losing battle, he called, "Clear!" once again.

When the man's vital signs didn't change, Pesh shook his head. "We need to open him up to massage the heart. Get me the rib spreader and the chest saw and page one of the residents," he ordered. He took a face mask from another nurse and slid it on.

After making a quick incision in the man's chest, Pesh took the saw from one of the nurses. Once he had sawed through the sternum, he shifted to the side to allow a nurse to move closer to work the crank on the rib spreader. Pushing aside the hard bone of the sternum, he gently took the man's still heart in his hands. No matter how many times he'd had to do it before, there was still something so humbling as holding the most important muscle in the human body in the palm of your hand. Squeezing it over and over, Pesh mimed the usual pumping the organ did.

Seconds ticked agonizingly by as they waited to see if the damaged heart would restart. When it remained still, Pesh sighed and closed his eyes for a moment. He eased back from the man. Glancing up at the clock on the wall, he said with regret, "Calling time of death: nine forty-seven a.m."

"Want me to handle the family?" the resident asked.

Pesh shook his head. "No. You get him closed back up. I'm sure they'll want to see him." He took off his bloody gloves and tossed them dejectedly into the hazardous materials trash can and then removed his mask. He walked over to the glass doors of the trauma area where a paramedic stood surveying the scene. "Do we have a name on him?"

The paramedic flashed the guy's driver's license. "Aaron Chapman."

"Thank you."

He walked down the long hallway before pushing open the button on the mechanical door that led out of the emergency area. In a room to the side of the waiting room, the man's wife and two teenage sons sat in hushed silence. As he opened the door, he said a silent prayer for strength. This was the most difficult aspect of his job. While he relished in the long hours of saving lives and diagnosing illnesses, this part drained him both emotionally and physically.

"Mrs. Chapman?"

The woman, who appeared to be in her late thirties or early forties, rose from the chair she was sitting in. "Yes?"

He held out his hand for her to shake. "I'm Dr. Nadeen. I was assigned your husband's case."

She bobbed her head and took a step forward. "How is he?"

"Your husband experienced a severe myocardial infarction." At her blank look, he replied, "A heart attack."

"Oh my God, I can't believe it. He's had some high cholesterol, but he's been running every day. I was only ten minutes from here dropping the boys off at school, and I told them I bet their dad had fallen and broken his ankle or something. Of course, I wondered why he wouldn't call instead of the hospital..." Realizing she was rambling, her voice cut off. Her hand hovered over her throat. "But he's okay now?"

Pesh shook his head. "I'm very sorry, but the heart attack caused too much damage to the heart. We were never able to revive him after he was brought in."

The woman's eyes widened to the size of dinner plates. "No, no, NO! Surely there is something you can do!"

"I'm so very sorry. We did everything we could to save him, including multiple attempts of resuscitation past what the paramedics originally did, but he did not respond to our attempts."

The woman's wail pierced through to Pesh's soul. She collapsed back against her sons, who now had tears in their eyes. Stoic on the outside, Pesh stood by her side as she sobbed uncontrollably. Most doctors when playing the Grim Reaper would deliver the bad news and then retreat. Pesh believed that part of a patient's care also meant the care of their family. That's why he ignored his pager going off in his pocket. It was only when his name was paged over the intercom that he took a step forward. He placed a hand on the widow's shoulder. "If you would like to be with him until the funeral home arrives, you can follow me."

"Y-Yes, please," she murmured.

With her sons flanking her, she followed Pesh out of the room and behind the mechanized doors. When they got to the exam room where her husband's body was, Pesh turned and once again touched her shoulder. "I'm so very sorry for your loss."

"Thank you," her son mumbled when his mother was unable to speak. Instead, she rushed forward to bury her head against her husband's chest. Her body shook with her sobs.

Pesh nodded and then finally turned away. With determined steps, he answered his page—some sort of consult on a diagnosis. After his input, this patient would pull through. It was the true embodiment of the dichotomy of his job.

Once he finished, Pesh went over to the office area of the emergency room. He eased down onto a stool, placing his head in his hands. As he rubbed his eyes, he swore they were moist from overuse, not from the potential tears welling behind them. If there was one thing he was, it was a professional. Doctors had to be emotionally detached when they were doing their job, or they would lose their minds. But it wasn't staying detached in the moment that was the issue—it was the aftermath. The agonizing moments when the adrenaline stores depleted, and his sagging body seemed to shoulder the hysteria, the panic, the grief, and the heartbreak of the family.

He didn't know how long he remained like that, head in his hands, tuning out the noises humming around him. When he felt a tap on his shoulder, he jerked around.

It was Kristi, a charge nurse and one of his most trusted coworkers. She smiled warmly at him as if she knew the inner turmoil he was in. "Dr. Nadeen, I hate to interrupt, but you have a visitor."

"Oh?"

Kristi nodded. "Exam room D."

"Thank you."

When Pesh pushed open the door, he couldn't help the surprise that filled him. With her auburn hair pulled into a loose knot and her emerald eyes glittering with happiness, Emma Harrison Fitzgerald, stood before him with her six-month-old son balanced on her hip. "Hi. I hope I'm not interrupting you."

A rush of pure love entered his chest at the sight of her. Nine months ago he would have confused the feeling with amorous love, but now he knew the difference. He loved her only as a friend. "Hello to you, too. It's so good to see you." His brows furrowed as his mind wondered why she was here in the ER. "You're okay, aren't you?"

"Oh, I'm perfectly well. It's just—"

Pesh's gaze dropped to the strawberry-blond haired boy sucking voraciously on a pacifier. "Noah's fine, isn't he?"

Emma smiled. "He's perfect."

Pesh exhaled the anxious breath he'd been holding. "I'm glad to hear that. You both look well."

"Thank you." Emma surveyed him and frowned. "I wish I could say the same for you. What's wrong?"

"Just a tough day." Even with Emma's expectant expression, he didn't want to elaborate. Gazing down at his hands, he finally responded, "I held a man's heart in my hands this morning ."

Emma's eyes widened, and she sucked in a breath. "Oh my God…"

He shook his head with regret. "But no matter how hard I tried, I still couldn't save him."

She reached out to rub his arm. "I'm so, so sorry."

"Thank you," he murmured. Since he was ready to change the subject before his emotions overcame him again, he motioned for her to have a seat. "So, what brings you here?"

"I have a favor to ask of you."

His brows rose in surprise. "You do? Another flight for Aidan perhaps?"

Emma laughed. "No. I think it'll be a long, long time before he ever gets in a small plane again." As Noah began to squirm, she shifted him from her lap to her shoulder. He spit out his pacifier and started to fuss.

"Here. Let me," Pesh suggested, bending over to take Noah into his arms. Noah's surprised blue eyes met his, and then he smiled at Pesh. "Hello, little one. My, how you've grown since I saw you last."

Noah cooed and reached for Pesh's stethoscope. "You were saying?" he questioned Emma.

"I know it's a lot to ask, considering you're not Catholic, but I was wondering if you would be Noah's godfather?"

Pesh couldn't hold back his surprise, and his mouth dropped open in shock. "You're serious?"

Emma nodded. "Since I'm not Catholic, I'm basically humoring Aidan's father by having a baptism for Noah. You remember him?"

Pesh laughed. "How could I ever forget Mr. Fitzgerald, the matchmaker?"

Emma smiled. "That's right. Well, you can understand how persistent he is."

"Oh yes, I do."

"We're allowed one Catholic and one non-Catholic godparent. We've chosen Aidan's niece as godmother, and then I wanted you."

"But what about your good friend?"

"Connor?"

"Yes, him."

Emma waved a dismissive hand. "Besides the fact that Connor is a non-practicing Baptist, he's refused on the grounds he doesn't want to have any moral or religious responsibility for Noah." She grinned and shook her head. "While he and Casey were obvious choices, let's just say they're looking forward to corrupting Noah, rather than guiding him on a spiritual path."

Pesh smiled. "I see."

Emma's auburn brows knitted together in worry. "I hope you're not offended that I told you that. I don't want you to think you were a second best choice. When I thought of someone to protect and guide Noah, you were one of the first people to pop into my mind."

Pesh worked to free his stethoscope from Noah's mouth. "And what does Aidan say about this?" He knew that although he and Aidan had come to some sort of friendship on the night of Noah's birth, he couldn't imagine, as possessive as Aidan was, that he would want a potential ex-flame of Emma's having a major part in his son's life.

"He's fine with it," Emma replied, as she toyed with the strap on her purse.

"Emma," Pesh pressed.

She threw up her hands as she met his gaze. "Okay, so he wasn't thrilled with the idea at first. It took some convincing on my part, but he's totally onboard now."

"As honored as I am, I would not cause contention between you two for anything in the world."

"And you won't. I promise." Emma reached out and took his hand. Months ago, that touch would have electrified him from his head to his feet. Now it was nothing more than the caring touch of a friend. "In this day and age, it is so hard to find a truly honorable man. You have such a kind heart and a caring spirit. Coupled with your integrity, I couldn't ask for a better person in my son's life, and Aidan agreed." She squeezed his hand. "Please say yes."

Pesh brought his gaze from Emma's intense one to Noah's inquisitive one. How could he say no? He loved children, and he wanted nothing more than to have a house full of them one day. The fact that Emma thought so highly of him truly melted his heart. As he stared into Noah's sweet face, he wanted to be a part of his life. "Emma, it would be a privilege."

Emma's green eyes widened as she bounded out of her chair. "Really?"

He smiled at her excitement. "Of course, it is an honor and a pleasure."

"Thank you, Pesh. Thank you so, so much!" she cried, throwing her arms around his neck.

Noah squealed happily between them and kicked his legs against Pesh's chest. When Emma pulled away, Noah grinned at the two of them, which caused Emma to smile. "I think Noah approves of his new godfather."

Pesh returned her smile. "I think he does, too. Or he realizes his mother's talents for manipulating any man within a mile radius."

"You're terrible," she replied, swatting his arm playfully.

Kristi poked her head in the room. "Sorry to interrupt, Dr. Nadeen. But you have a patient in exam room A."

"Thank you. I'll be right there." He shook his head at Emma. "I'm sorry, but I have to go."

"No, it's fine. I understand." She reached for Noah and took him back into her arms. "The baptism is in two weeks. I'll send you all the details. It'll be at Transfiguration in Marietta since it's closer to our house. Afterwards, we're going to have a big party."

"I'll make sure to clear my schedule."

"Wonderful."

Pesh leaned over to kiss Noah's cheek. "Goodbye my godson. Be good for your mother." He pulled Emma to him and hugged her. "Goodbye to you as well."

She squeezed him tight. "Thank you again. You can't imagine how happy you've made me. And Aidan."

He imagined that Emma's elation was far greater than Aidan's, but he kept that to himself. Instead, he walked to her the door. Just as he went for the doorknob, Emma shocked him with her next statement. "Oh, if you're seeing someone, please feel free to bring her with you."

Pesh couldn't help the burst of nervous laughter that escaped his lips. "That wasn't obvious at all."

Emma frowned. "But I thought…at least I hoped you would be dating someone by now."

"Well, I'm not."

Shifting Noah to her other hip, Emma shook her head. "How is that possible? Do you walk around with a bag over your head? Live as a hermit?"

"No to the bag, and I guess yes to a hermit." He glanced around. "I'm always here."

Emma's gaze left his and took in some of the nurses passing by them. He could imagine from the looks they were giving him, and more particularly the envious daggers they were shooting Emma, that she knew what was on their minds. "Do you have any idea what effect you have on women?"

He crossed his arms over his chest. "No, but I suppose you're going to remind me again."

Emma sighed. "I just want you to be happy, and I know that deep down you aren't."

"Please, just let it go for now, okay?"

Although she nodded, Pesh could tell she was far from agreeing. Somewhere within that pretty head of hers the wheels of matchmaking were turning hard and fast. "See you soon," she said, before starting down the hall.

As he watched Emma and Noah walk through the mechanized double doors into the waiting room, a pang of sadness reverberated through him as he wondered what his child might have been like. In the months before her death, his late wife, Jade, had been on fertility medication. She'd miscarried once, but she had great hopes that their latest baby making attempts would be successful. She died never knowing if she was pregnant or not. When the autopsy had come back, Pesh refused to read whether she had been. It would have been too difficult to bear.

Shaking off his morbid thoughts once again, he went into the room where a patient needed him.

Chapter Two

"Where the hell is my dress?" Megan McKenzie demanded, as she rifled through her closet. The one formal and demure dress she owned had been dropped off at the cleaners earlier in the week to prepare for her godson, Noah's, baptism. As the godmother, she wanted to look mature and responsible. Most of the dresses in her closet were from her former life—in other words, her life before her son was born. That meant they were too short, too tight, and too revealing.

She cut her eyes over to the couch to check on Mason. Sitting stock still, he was enraptured by the cartoon on the TV. "Be right back, sweetie."

"Awight, Mommy."

She pounded up the basement stairs and into her parent's kitchen. She hoped she would find the dress hanging in the hall closet. If not, she was totally screwed. As she started into the living room, the mere sound of a voice on the television caused her to freeze. Her stomach churned, and her heart raced. She knew that voice all too well. It belonged to the man who had shredded her heart, crushed her spirit, and left her broken almost beyond repair.

Her nineteen-year-old-brother, Sean, lounged on the couch, watching ESPN. On the screen, her ex-boyfriend, Davis Durello, gave an interview outfitted in his Falcons jersey and pads. Becoming enraged that he was invading her home, Megan stalked across the room and snatched the remote out of Sean's hand. She flicked off the television and tossed the remote at him, smacking him in the chest. He glowered at her. "What the hell, Meg? I was watching that."

"Are you that big of an insensitive asshole that you even have to ask?"

"I'm an asshole because you're getting pissed I'm watching some old interview of Davis'?"

"Aren't you perceptive?" Megan snapped sarcastically.

"I thought you were over him," Sean countered.

Megan didn't even bother trying to explain to Sean that even after two years, it was hard getting over the man who left you knocked up and refused to have anything to do with his son besides signing a check. As a teenage male, Sean just didn't have that much emotional depth to understand that a wound like that may look like it has healed, but it was always festering just below the surface.

"I am," she lied. "But that doesn't mean I want to see him. Most people get to leave their ex-boyfriends behind, but I have to have mine thrust into my face during football season. But even when that's over, he still seems to be creeping around." Crossing her arms over her chest, she shot a death glare at Sean. "It would be nice if you cared enough about me not to want to watch him."

"Can I help that your douchebag ex happens to play for the Falcons, and ESPN is doing an interview?"

"You don't have to be watching it in my presence!"

At her outburst, Sean held up his hands in defeat. "Sorry. I didn't know it got to you that bad. I'll turn the channel next time, okay?"

"Fine," she muttered. Feeling slightly psychotic after her outburst, she kept her head down as she headed for the hall closet. Thankfully, her navy blue dress hung on the rack still in the plastic from the dry cleaners. When she turned around, she found her mother outfitted in her finest pale pink suit. She eyed Megan's robe-clad form disdainfully. "Megan, we leave in half an hour. Why aren't you dressed yet?"

Closing her eyes, Megan counted to ten so she wouldn't bite her mother's head off. "I left my dress up here after I picked it up at the dry cleaners. I'll be ready on time. I promise."

"Would you like me to get Mason dressed?"

"I've already taken care of him. It's just me that needs to get her act together." Without another word, she brushed past her mother and went into the kitchen. Wearing his best suit and tie, her father stood at the bar, putting on his cufflinks.

At his expectant look, she held up her hand. "I know we leave in half an hour. I'll be ready. I swear." She then threw open the basement door. Pounding down the steps, she tried calming down. She didn't know what it was about her parents' seemingly good intentions that grated on her last nerve. Of course, they hadn't bothered her as much when she had lived alone. Now that she was back under their roof, they seemed to forget she was twenty-five, a mother, and not their little girl to boss around anymore.

With clinicals looming to enable her to finish her nursing degree, she'd known she wouldn't be able to work fulltime. Although she loved the freedom and independence of having her own apartment, there was no way she could afford it and daycare for Mason. So, she'd packed up, tucked her tail between her legs, and moved back home to her parents' finished basement.

It wasn't all bad. She had her own kitchen and bathroom, not to mention she and Mason still had their own rooms. With her father recently retired, she had a great male role model on site for Mason.

She found him exactly as she had left him, lounging on the couch watching his favorite movie, *Despicable Me*. She smiled at the sight of him in his khaki pants, black, button down dress shirt, and red clip-on tie. He looked just like a little man sitting there, even though he had just turned seventeen months the day before. Usually, he would be tearing around the living room, playing with his toys. But just one look at a minion sent him practically catatonic. That had been Megan's plan when she got him dressed earlier. He'd seen the movie almost by mistake, considering he was a little young for the PG cartoon, but with older cousins, along with her brothers, Mason was often exposed to things that were older. She liked to think being surrounded by adults and older kids was one reason why he was a such a good talker for his age.

"Aren't you being a good boy?" she said.

Mason barely acknowledged her. Instead, his baby blues remained focused on the television. Since the movie was almost over, Megan knew she better slip into the bedroom and finish getting ready.

Each time she looked into Mason's face, she was grateful that he looked nothing like his father. His platinum blond hair and blue eyes were completely hers. It was only his build that he was taking after his father. Where Megan was a diminutive 5'3", Davis was 6'1" and two hundred pounds. Mason was already registering off the charts in height and weight according to his pediatrician.

Davis had seen Mason only twice in his lifetime—the day he had been born and the day he came home from the hospital. After that, he hadn't been interested in any of the pictures and emails Megan sent. With his professional football career on the rise, Davis hadn't wanted to be shackled with the responsibilities of a baby.

Instead, he wanted to spend his time off the field partying until all hours of the night. He only paid child support when Megan threatened to have his wages garnished. She dreaded the day when Mason was old enough to ask about his father. She never wanted anything in the world to hurt him, and she knew that being rejected by his father would.

With a sigh, she stepped into the dress and slid it over her hips. Wrestling around to get the zipper all the way up caused her to huff and puff. Standing back from the mirror, she turned to and fro to take in her appearance. She'd always loved how the dress made her feel sexy, but at the same time was very respectable. While it boasted a sweetheart neckline, the hemline fell just below her knees. She put on her pearls—a high school graduation gift from her Uncle Aidan, or "Ankle", as she often called him.

Aidan was her mother's baby brother and only son of the family. When she was born, he was only eight and a half. As the first grandchild, Megan spent a lot of time with her grandparents, and that in turn, meant she spent a lot of time with Aidan. He had devoted hours to holding her and spoiling her rotten. When it came time for her to talk, she just couldn't seem to get "Uncle Aidan" out. Instead, she called him "Ankle." It was a nickname that had stuck with him even now that he was thirty-four and married.

While it had been no question that she wanted him as godfather for Mason, she had been extremely honored when he and his wife, Emma, had asked her to be their son, Noah's, godmother. She loved her newest cousin very much and planned to be the best godmother she could for him.

As she stepped out of the bedroom, she found that Mason had yet to move. "Okay buddy, time to go."

When he started to whine, she shook her head. "We have such a fun day ahead of us. It's Noah's baptism, and then there's a party at Uncle Aidan and Aunt Emma's house."

"Beau?" he asked.

She laughed. "Yes, you'll get to see and play with Beau, too." As she went to the couch and picked him up, she couldn't help finding it amusing that out of everyone he was going to see today, he was most excited about being with Aidan and Emma's black Lab, Beau. One day when they had their own place again, she would get him a dog. He loved them too much to be denied.

"Oomph," she muttered, as they started up the basement stairs.

"Heawy?" he asked.

"Yes, you're getting to be such a big, heavy boy."

When they made it to the kitchen, Megan paused to catch her breath. She only had a second before her mother breezed in with Sean, and her youngest brother, Gavin. "Ready?" she asked.

Megan nodded. Feeling like she was once again a teenager, she filed behind her parents as they headed into the garage. "I want to drive," Gavin said.

With a smirk, Sean replied, "Like I'm gonna let you drive my car." He then slid into the driver's seat as Gavin reluctantly walked around to the passenger's side.

"We'll see you there in just a few," her mother called.

Sean acknowledged her with a two finger salute before cranking up and pulling down the driveway. Megan worked to get Mason into the car seat in her parents' Land Rover. Once he was safely strapped and buckled in, she hopped in beside him.

Her parents rattled along to each other as they made their way through the tree-lined suburbs where Megan had grown up. While some might look on her as having a mark against her character being an unwed mother, she had lived a relatively non-rebellious life. Even though she'd been a cheerleader and ran with the popular crowd in school, she rarely partied to excess. Instead, she had focused on getting good grades. At that time, she had her heart set on going to medical school and becoming a doctor. From the time she was a little girl, she had wanted nothing more than to help people. She was always mending birds with broken wings or trying to resuscitate squirrels who had been hit by cars. She ditched playing princess for playing "hospital." Her desire to become a doctor was why she needed the best scores and best activities and why she generally shunned any temptations to lead her off the right path.

She had even managed to bypass the usual freshman craziness when she went off to the University of Georgia. It wasn't until she fell in love for the first time in her life that she threw everything away. Sadly, she couldn't say that her first love was Davis, Mason's father. Instead, it was another football player, this time a running back at UGA, who captured and later broke her heart a year later. Carsyn ran with the fast crowd, and when she was with him, she partied and drank too much. He was controlling and possessive, and he wanted all of her time. When she was with him, she had little time for studying. With her grades already in the toilet, she was unprepared for the emotional breakdown she experienced when Carsyn broke up with her. Devastated, she stopped going to class and ended up flunking the semester.

By the time she got back on track with her grades, she had abandoned any hope of medical school. Instead, she decided that she would become a nurse, which would fulfill her need to care for sick people. Of course, her relationship with Davis ended up derailing shortly before graduation when she got pregnant unexpectedly. She had to take several semesters off after Mason was born. She was a few years off from when she had originally planned on graduating, but she was excited after everything had that had happened, she was finally finishing.

Her mother's voice brought Megan out of her thoughts. "Here we are," she said pleasantly.

Leaning forward in her seat, Megan eyed the clock on the dashboard. She wasn't surprised to see they had arrived half an hour before the baptism started. One thing her mother prided herself on was being on time and lending a hand. As they started into the church, her mother reached for Mason. "We'll take him so you can go see if Emma needs any help."

Megan bent over to kiss Mason's cheek. "See you in a little while, sweetie."

He grinned and then happily dodged her mother's arms for her father's instead, which made Megan smile. He was such a man's man already. He loved sitting between her brothers on the couch and watching TV. While it was good that he had so many male role models, she only hoped he hadn't inherited too much of his father's personality.

After Megan watched them disappear in the crowd of family and friends waiting in the church alcove, she bypassed everyone by turning right and heading down the hallway. At the last door on the right, she knocked. "It's me, Megan."

Emma's best friend, Casey, answered the door. "Well, if it isn't the fairy godmother," she mused with a grin. After Megan stepped inside, Casey threw her arms around her. Megan had only met her a few times, but it was hard not liking Emma's vivacious and outgoing friend. Casey's long brown hair was pulled back in a lose knot, and she wore a demure black slip dress and heels.

"So how's it going?" Megan asked, gazing from Noah's diapered but naked form to Emma. She was feeding him a bottle while her upper body was draped in a towel. Peeking out from the covering, she saw Emma was wearing her signature color, green. As

Noah sucked on his bottle, he twirled a strand of Emma's auburn hair between his fingers. Both father and son were fans of Emma wearing her hair down.

Emma grinned. "Good, I guess. I mean, I don't have a lot of experience with baptisms."

Megan laughed and motioned to the towel and Noah. "It looks like you're taking all the proper precautions—nothing like spit-up on your dress or his."

With a nod, Emma replied, "Tell me about it. Especially since his gown is so old." Megan eyed the lacy baptismal gown hanging on the closet door. She recognized it from pictures of Ankle's baptism. He had worn it, and now it was being passed down to his son.

Casey snorted. "I'm sure Aidan wouldn't appreciate you alluding to the fact his gown is an antique, thus in turn saying he's old."

Emma laughed. "No, I'm sure he wouldn't. Of course, he'd probably argue that while the gown might not have held up, he still looks fabulous and much younger than his age."

Megan smiled. "That sounds just like him." She bent over Emma to rub one of Noah's hands. He grabbed her thumb in his fist and held on for dear life.

"Aw, you love your godmother, don't you Noah?" Emma asked.

Noah momentarily stopped sucking on the bottle to flash a quick smile, which warmed Megan's heart. "He's such a sweet boy," she mused.

"And a charmer, just like his old man," Casey mused.

"That too," Megan agreed. Thinking about her position, she cocked her head at Casey. "Are you sure you're fine with me being the godmother?"

Casey waved her hand dismissively. "Honey, the last thing I need is the responsibility. I plan on spoiling Noah rotten and corrupting him as only a good auntie can do!"

Emma rolled her eyes. "I'm very satisfied with both my choices, Megan. You don't have to worry."

"So who is the godfather again? I know he's not part of the family."

Casey gasped as her hand flew to her chest dramatically. "You mean, you've never met Dr. McDreamy Bollywood?"

Megan shrugged. "No, I haven't. I mean, I've heard about him and how he flew Aidan home in time for Noah's birth." She noticed the pleading look that Emma exchanged with Casey. "Why? What should I know about him?"

Casey tapped her chin with her index finger. "Hmm, what should you know about the good godfather?" She winked at Megan. "First off, he is seriously delectable. I mean, the man is like sex on a stick. Tall, jet-black hair, dark eyes, and he's built like a brick shithouse."

Megan suddenly felt her interest piquing. She hadn't imagined that the godfather would be good-looking. It had been such a long time since she had dated anyone. Scratch that—it had been a long time since she'd had *sex* with anyone. She'd spent the last two years completely dateless since she and Davis broke up. She could practically join one of the local parishes as a nun with how long she had abstained. "Really?"

"Mmm, hmm. He reminds me of that Bollywood actor John Abraham," Casey said.

Emma snorted. "Since when do you watch Bollywood movies?"

"Since one of Nate's friends asked us to an Indian film festival." Casey grinned at Megan. "Besides the fact that he's a serious looker, he's also kind, compassionate, and caring—an overall wonderful man."

"Really now?" Megan questioned.

"And he's loaded because he's a doctor."

This man was sounding better and better by the minute. "Is he single?"

Emma made a strangled noise before Casey replied, "Oh, yeah, he's single. He's a widower actually."

Megan pursed her lips at the prospect. Widowers usually fell into two categories—those who were still devastated by their wives' deaths or those who were ready to have fun and live a little. She certainly hoped this Pesh guy fell into the second category. More than anything, she wanted to have a little fun herself.

"Do you really think you might be interested in dating Pesh?" Emma asked, as she moved Noah to her shoulder to burp him.

With a shrug, Megan replied, "Dating him or just having some fun with him. Sounds like he could use some."

Emma grimaced as she wiped Noah's face off. "This is exactly why I told Aidan not to try and fix you two up."

"What do you mean?"

"Pesh needs a relationship, not a hook-up after all he's been through. Besides his wife's death, he hasn't had it easy on the dating front."

"What happened?"

When Casey snorted, Emma shot her a death glare. "Nothing. It's just he doesn't need to get involved with someone who isn't interested in a long-term relationship."

"Em, you might as well tell her," Casey urged.

Megan glanced between the two of them. "Tell me what?"

"Fine," Emma huffed resignedly. She handed Noah to Casey. "Make yourself useful by changing his diaper."

As Casey got busy cleaning up Noah, Emma turned to Megan. "When Aidan and I broke up—"

"What you meant to say is, after you left Aidan when he didn't show up for Noah's gender ultrasound because he was cheating on you?" Casey interrupted, waving around the wet wipe in her hand.

Emma closed her eyes for a moment before shaking her head. "Yes, that's right. Thank you so very much for bringing up that aspect of our break-up on today of all days."

Casey gripped Noah's ankles and hoisted up his little butt to slide on the new diaper. "You're welcome."

"Anyway, as you were saying," Megan pressed.

"Right. So it was when Aidan and I were broken up that I met Pesh. I was with your Papa Fitzgerald the day of his heart attack at the VFW, and Pesh was the doctor who treated him."

"So…you both struck up a friendship then?" Megan asked.

Emma grimaced. "Not exactly. You see, Patrick wanted to force Aidan to really fight for me, and he felt the best way to do it would be for him to have some competition."

Megan felt her eyes widening in surprise. "Papa wanted Pesh to date you?"

"Yeah."

"Did you?"

Emma was momentarily distracted by Casey blowing raspberries on Noah's stomach. A smile spread across her face as Noah kicked his legs and giggled at Casey. "Want me to get him in his dress?" Casey asked, as she glanced up.

"If you don't mind."

Bringing her hand to her hip, Megan huffed out an exasperated breath. "Um, could you please focus for just a minute considering the bomb you just dropped on me?"

"I'm sorry. I didn't want to tell you at all. I mean, whatever was between us is all in the past. Neither one of us really cared for each other like we thought we did."

"Did you…" Megan said. At Emma's confused expression, she wiggled her eyebrows suggestively.

Emma's face flushed. "No, of course not!"

Casey eyed Emma as she took the baptism gown off the hanger. "You did make out with him though."

"*One* time. And he certainly didn't get to second base," Emma argued.

With a wicked grin, Casey added, "Pity. Wish you could inform us on what he has going on below the waist."

Emma rolled her eyes. "You're impossible." She snatched the gown away from Casey and then started wrestling Noah into the yards of fabric. "It wasn't like we were in a relationship. We didn't really even go out together. He came to the house once to bring me dinner and check on me when I was on bed rest, and then he took me to the opera. That was it."

"Was there no chemistry between you two?" Megan asked.

Without responding, Emma pulled Noah up into a sitting position and started fastening the row of buttons down the back of the gown. "Em?" Megan pressed.

She gave a heavy sigh before picking Noah up. She stared into his face before she responded. "We had great chemistry together. He was an amazing kisser who got all my senses up and running in all the right ways. Besides the physical part, he is smart, kind, and intelligent—any woman's dream." She shook her head. "But it didn't matter because he wasn't Aidan. I could never, ever love another man like I do him." Giving Noah a kiss on the cheek, she added, "Neither one of us were really in a good place—I was trying to make sure that Aidan really was the one, and after being pressured by family and friends, he was trying to date for the first time after his wife's death."

Megan crossed her arms over her chest. "I get that he doesn't need to be hurt, but who is to say that having a fling is going to hurt him? Maybe it could give him the confidence he needs to go out and find the real woman of his dreams?"

Casey snorted. "How could a man that looks like that have any self-confidence issues?"

Megan shrugged. "You never know. If he was married a long time before his wife died, he might find it hard to get back into the dating world. Especially if the last woman he cared about loved someone else."

Emma shook her head. "Trust me, he isn't the fling kind of guy. He wants a wife and children."

Although Megan had a son, she wasn't quite ready for marriage. Maybe in a few years but right now she just wanted to date and have fun. She'd willingly sacrificed so much to ensure that Mason could have all of her attention since he was short a father. After all, he was the greatest hurdle in her having a committed relationship. She didn't want to open her son up to any hurt that might come from him getting attached to a man she dated only to have them disappear when they broke up.

"Ankle really wants to fix us up?" Megan questioned.

Emma nodded. "Regardless of what happened with Pesh when we were broken up, Aidan does respect and admire him. He wants Pesh to be happy." She gave Megan a pointed look. "Most of all, he wants that for you, too."

Megan wrinkled her nose. "But I'm really not ready for all of that yet."

"Then think long and hard before you agree to do anything about Pesh. He is unknowingly very persuasive, and in the moment, you might forget your resolve only to have it come back later to hurt you…or him."

Megan held up her hands in defeat. "Okay, okay, I promise."

Emma smiled. "Nothing would make me happier than if you were to fall in love with Pesh."

With a laugh, Megan said, "Did you just hear anything that I said? I'm anti-love."

"So was Aidan."

Just as Megan opened her mouth to protest, Aidan waltzed into the room. "Everything okay?"

"Fine. Just finished feeding and dressing him," Emma replied

"Good. The natives are getting restless to see the little man of the hour before the baptism." He strode over to them and took his son into his arms. "You ready to go work the crowd, Noah?" Noah's response was to grunt and reach for Aidan's tie. With a laugh, Aidan announced, "I'll take that as a yes." He then leaned in to kiss Emma's cheek. "Ready Mrs. Fitzgerald?"

She smiled before linking her arm through his. "Yes, Mr. Fitzgerald, I am."

Megan and Casey followed them out the door and down the hallway. They entered a noisy room crammed with family and friends. She left Aidan and Emma's side to seek out her parents to check on Mason. She found her parents, but their arms were empty. In a panic, she demanded, "Where's Mason?"

Her father smiled and pointed over to where a pile of her younger cousins were. Mason was on the lap of her Aunt Becky's oldest son, John. Mason was mesmerized with what whatever John was doing on his phone. Megan smiled as she walked up to them. "Everything okay?"

Without taking his eyes off the screen, John replied, "We're fine."

"Are you sure he's not bothering you?" What she wasn't asking was if John was actually keeping an eye on Mason between playing on his phone.

John glanced up. "Considering I have two younger brothers, I think I can handle him. Besides, he's really into this game."

"Okay then," Megan replied.

She spoke to John's brothers, Percy and Georgie, before making her way around the room. All her relatives were interested to hear how her schooling was going and how Mason was. She had just turned away from talking to her great aunt and uncle when someone pressed up against her back.

"Don't look now, but there's Dr. McDreamy Bollywood now," Casey whispered into her ear. Without hesitation, her eyes scanned the crowd. And then she saw him. Ankle was taking him around and making introductions.

Pesh was impossibly tall and wearing a tailor-made black suit. Even beneath the lines of the clothing, she could make out his large biceps and thick thighs. He obviously spent his downtime between hospital shifts working out. His wavy, jet-black hair was cut short, and his dark eyes took in all that Ankle was saying.

And while she may have been in a church about to stand up as a godmother, she couldn't help the nipples tightening and panties moistening reaction of seeing him. He was all the way across the room, but he had the same effect as if he were standing by her side, rubbing against her.

"See what I mean?" Casey questioned.

Megan licked her lips. "Oh my," she finally managed.

"Sure you don't want to give him a chance?"

Fighting the urge to fan herself, Megan quickly replied, "I'd like to give him many, many chances." *Chances at ripping off my clothes, chances at kissing and licking me all over my body, chances at allowing his hands, fingers, and the promising bulge in his pants to stroke me until I orgasm...yep, many, many chances.*

As if she could read Megan's mind, Casey laughed. "Oh girl, this has trouble written all over it."

Chapter Three

Pesh paced nervously around the back of the cathedral. The fact he was in a Catholic church wasn't the only reason he felt out of his element. As he eyed the massive statue of Jesus, he fidgeted absently with his tie. Although Emma had sworn Aidan was fine with the idea of him as godfather, he was still a little apprehensive about seeing Aidan again. The last time they'd been together, Pesh was the hero flying Aidan from North Carolina to Atlanta just in time for Noah's unexpected birth. But that was six months ago. The euphoria of the moment now had time to fade, and to Aidan, Pesh could still be the man who almost stole Emma away.

A side door opened, and Aidan stepped out. He immediately met Pesh's anxious gaze. When his lips curved into a wide smile, Pesh exhaled the nervous breath he'd been holding. "Well, there you are," Aidan said, as he strode up. He bypassed throwing out his hand, and instead, he pulled Pesh to him for a bear hug. "Emma was worried about you."

"She was?"

"Yeah, she asked me to come out and see if I could find you."

"I'm sorry. I wasn't sure where to go, and no one was out here."

"Don't worry about it." Aidan pulled away. "So how the hell are you?"

Pesh couldn't help laughing at Aidan's choice of words, especially in a church. "I'm good, thank you." He cocked his head at Aidan. "And what about you? Is fatherhood agreeing with you?"

A beaming smile lit Aidan's face. "I'm absolutely fantastic. I never could have imagined that being a father would be this…amazing."

Pesh nodded. "I want you to know what an honor it is for me to be Noah's godfather."

"We're glad to have you." Aidan patted Pesh's back. "And I do mean that."

"I hope you do. I have had my concerns…"

Aidan shook his head. "Well, don't. I'll admit I wasn't too thrilled with the prospect at first, but Em was able to make me see the light. You were there for us when we really needed you. I mean, besides my wedding day, I would've missed the most important days of my life—my son's birth. I can never thank you enough. So when it comes down to it, I don't think I could ask for a better godfather for my son."

Aidan's words touched Pesh. "Thank you. That means a lot. You have my word that I will always do what is right by Noah."

After giving him a hearty thump on the shoulder, Aidan said, "Come on back with me. I want to introduce you to everyone."

"Do they…" Pesh wasn't sure how to ask if Aidan's family knew the story of how he and Emma truly knew each other.

Aidan chuckled. "Let's just say that Pop's the only one who knows the truth. The others just think you met us when Pop had his heart attack."

Pesh couldn't help the relieved breath that whooshed out of him. It would have been a nightmare to have most of Aidan's family hating him for trying to steal Emma away. "I see."

He followed Aidan back into a large room filled with chattering people. As he craned his neck, he saw Emma in the corner with Noah in her arms. She looked radiant as ever in an emerald suit. Noah, however, didn't seem too thrilled to be outfitted in the lacy gown that flowed over Emma's arms and stopped mid-thigh. His tiny brows wrinkled as he waved his fists back and forth as if any moment he might let loose with a scream.

Taking him by the elbow, Aidan guided him over to a group of men and women. Aidan introduced him to his four sisters and their husbands. Pesh smiled, nodded, and shook their hands before being bombarded by a hoard of Aidan's nieces and nephews.

"Now I want you to meet my niece, Megan. She's the godmother."

"It would be my pleasure."

Aidan surprised Pesh by leaning in and whispering in his ear. "I'm pretty sure over half of the people here are gunning for you two to get together. You know, a real romantic story to tell future kids about how you two met being the godmother and godfather of this sweet and adorable kid."

Pesh gulped. Why was everyone he knew hell-bent on setting him up? Had Emma harbored some secret, ulterior motive in asking him to be Noah's godfather? "I'm flattered, but I don't know if that's such a good idea."

Pulling back, Aidan surmised him before winking. "Normally I would agree because she is, after all, my niece—my favorite one if I'm being honest. But as much as it pisses me off to admit it, you two would make a great couple."

"We would?"

"Hell yeah." Aidan swept his hand over his chin. "Megan needs someone strong and stable like you are, and then you need someone who is so full of life like she is. I can guaran-damn-tee you that you've never been out with a woman like her before. Emma is like, one tenths the sassiness that Megan is."

Pesh couldn't help giving Aidan a skeptical look.

"Just keep an open mind, okay?"

With a reluctant nod, Pesh replied, "I will."

"Megan," Aidan called.

When the tiny blonde turned around, Pesh fought to catch his breath. Everything about her from her sparkling blue eyes to her long blonde hair was just like Jade's. How was it possible for someone to remind him so much of what he had lost?

Aidan grinned as he glanced between the two of them. "I wanted to introduce you to Pesh Nadeen, the godfather."

Thrusting out her hand, Megan smiled warmly at him. "It's very nice to finally meet you."

He stared at it a moment before his good manners overrode his shock. He took her hand in his and shook it. "It's very nice meeting you, too."

"I'll leave you two to get to know each other," Aidan said. Before Pesh could protest, Aidan turned and disappeared into the crowd.

He turned to Megan and tried clearing his throat of what felt like a wad of sawdust. He knew he should try to make polite conversation, but he was still so shell-shocked by the way Megan looked.

Finally, she took pity on him. "So, Emma tells me you're a doctor."

Pesh smiled politely. "Yes, I am."

"What type of medicine?"

"Emergency Services."

Megan's face lit up. "Oh, how interesting. I'm about to finish nursing school, and I've asked for clinical placement in the ER."

Pesh widened his eyes in surprise. Aidan had failed to mention that they had the medical profession in common. "Really?"

Megan nodded. "I'm hoping to get placed at Grady, even though my parents would die a thousand deaths."

He cocked his brows at her. "I assume they're afraid for your safety?"

"Yes. They can't help worrying about the neighborhood. They sometimes forget I'm an adult, rather than a child."

"What is it about Grady that attracts you?"

"Besides the fact that it's nationally recognized for its ER?"

He smiled. "Yes, besides the accolades."

Megan tilted her head in thought. "I guess it's the fact I really want to feel like I'm making a difference and saving lives. I feel like at Grady I would be seeing some of the worst cases imaginable, and in turn some people who really don't have a lot of hope."

He was taken aback by her words and the passion with which she delivered them. While she possessed a beautiful exterior, she certainly seemed to have a greater depth of character than he had originally expected. He didn't often meet someone like her. Most of the women at the hospital who threw themselves at him possessed only surface beauty. He didn't have to be with them very long to perceive their true shallowness and self-centeredness. To them, he was a prize to be won. He couldn't ever imagine Megan feeling that way. She wasn't the type of woman to care about a trophy man on her arm—she wanted to make her own way in the world.

"It is so good to hear someone speak with such passion about nursing."

"Really?"

He nodded. "We desperately need more people like you. I know I would love to work alongside someone who had your passion."

She smiled at his compliments. He couldn't help noticing what a nice smile she had. The way it framed her heart shaped face made her appear much less like Jade than he had originally thought. "Thank you. Maybe we'll end up together." She licked her lips before adding, "You know, at the same hospital."

"I would like that. But I'm afraid that Wellstar pales in comparison to Grady."

"Surely the suburbs offer some interesting cases?"

"They do. I've been there since my residency, so I can't imagine working anywhere else. After all, I wouldn't be standing here today with you if it weren't for Wellstar and your grandfather."

"That's true." Tilting her head, she gave him a very alluring smile. "And what a pity that would be if our paths hadn't crossed."

He sucked in a breath at the directness of her statement. Could she really be interested in him? Sure, it was common knowledge that Aidan and others wanted them to get together, but he had imagined that she had not known their intentions. And while originally he had been turned off by Aidan's suggestion of fixing them up, he couldn't help but be intrigued now. There was something so refreshingly different about Megan, despite her physical similarities to Jade.

"Mommy!" a small voice cried. Pesh glanced over Megan's shoulder where a fair-haired toddler came bounding over. He wrapped his arms around Megan's thigh.

She gave him an apologetic look before bending over. "What's the matter, sweetie?"

He grinned up at her. "Miss you."

With a smile, she bent over and picked him up. When he sat on her hip, she turned her attention back to Pesh. "This is my son, Mason."

Pesh couldn't help noticing how Megan searched his face to see if there was any judgment or even disgust at her having a son. He felt neither of those emotions. He had to admit he was a little surprised. Aidan had failed to mention that fact as well. Not to mention, she seemed young to be a mother, considering she was just finishing her clinicals. "It's nice to meet you, Mason."

"Can you tell Pesh hi?" Megan urged.

"Hi, Esh," Mason said, with a grin.

Pesh couldn't help laughing, and he was thankful that Megan giggled as well. "How old are you?"

Mason held up two fingers to which Megan shook her head. "He's seventeen months."

Pesh smiled. "You must be very proud of him."

"I am." She snuggled Mason against her chest. "He's the sweetest and best boy I could ever hope for."

"You're very blessed."

"Thank you."

They were interrupted by Aidan's sister, Angie, who Pesh had met earlier. "Looks like it's time to start. Come on Mason. Mommy has to go be Noah's godmother now."

Mason reluctantly went to his grandmother. "Be good for Grammy," Megan instructed.

After Angie walked off with Mason, the other family members began filing out of the room. Pesh turned to Megan and gave her a sheepish smile. "I must admit that even though I attended a class with Emma, I'm a little unsure of what I'm supposed to do."

"It's okay. Just follow my lead, and you'll be fine."

"Thank you."

Once it was only the two of them and Aidan and Emma in the room, Aidan motioned for them. A priest in decorated golden robes appeared at the door with a gleaming crucifix in his hands. Pesh tried not to feel intimidated as the odd man out in the situation. Music struck up on the organ, and the priest motioned for them to follow.

Before they went out the door, Emma glanced down at Noah. "*Please, please*, do not scream in there and act like a demon baby. Be the angel I know you can be." He acknowledged her request by sticking his tongue out and flailing his fists.

Aidan chuckled at Emma's plea. "Relax, babe. If he feels you getting all tense, he's going to get fussy."

Emma sighed. "He's already fussy. He was fine until I put him in the gown."

"I guess he feels that wearing a dress is insulting to his manhood," Aidan reasoned with a smile.

When Emma shot Aidan a death glare, Megan and Pesh couldn't help laughing at the two of them. Aidan winked at Emma before starting out the door. At Megan's side, Pesh walked up the aisle. When they reached the baptismal font, the music ended, and the priest began speaking. He informed the crowd of what was about to take place and the significance of all the religious rites Noah was about to receive.

Aidan and Emma made the sign of the cross on Noah's forehead before Megan leaned in to do the same. When Megan elbowed him, Pesh reached over to clumsily follow their lead. After he finished, he glanced at Megan. She smiled and mouthed, "Good job."

He returned her smile. He followed through the rest of the proceedings as Aidan and Emma pledged to raise Noah in the faith. Then it came time for him and Megan to agree to stand by Noah as godparents. The priest took a fussing Noah from Emma's arms. When the first trickles of water hit the base of Noah's head, he cooed and kicked his arms and legs. Emma appeared relieved at how Noah wasn't behaving like a possessed baby as she had feared.

"Thank God he loves his baths," Aidan muttered beside Pesh.

Once the baptism part was finished, the priest made a final talk, and then it was over. Just as Pesh sighed with relief and was looking forward to making a quick exit, Aidan grabbed his arm. "Don't go anywhere. We have to do pictures."

Inwardly, he groaned. He wanted, no he *needed*, a moment alone to process his thoughts. Everything had been so overwhelming—being outside his usual world, meeting all of Aidan's family, and then having the prospect of Megan thrown in as well.

Awkwardly, he stood around as a photographer came forward and proceeded to take several pictures of Aidan, Emma, and Noah.

Then it was just Aidan and Noah or Emma and Noah. "Okay, I need the godparents now."

Pesh smoothed down his tie and allowed the photographer to pose him in the group shot. After they finished with the four of them, Noah was handed to Megan for pictures with just the godparents. As the photographer pushed Megan closer against Pesh's chest, he glanced down at her. Her reassuring smile caused his heartbeat to accelerate. For the first time, he noticed the sweet aroma of her hair as the long, blonde strands brushed against him. He could also make out the alluring scent of her perfume. He liked the feel of her against him a little too much. It made him want to draw her into his embrace...maybe do other things that he shouldn't be thinking when he was in a church.

Glancing over her shoulder at him, she joked, "Jeez, you're like a giant standing next to me."

"Am I?" He hadn't noticed the differences in their heights—he'd been focusing on her too much.

She laughed. "Just a little bit. Of course, it doesn't take much for someone to make me look short."

"You look perfect to me," he said sincerely.

Craning her neck back to look at him, she gave him a teasing grin. "Do I? Are you flirting with me, Dr. Nadeen?"

He stared down at his feet, trying to avoid the heat of her stare. He tried to hide the red flush he felt entering his cheeks. "Okay, now just with the godmother," the photographer ordered.

Reluctantly, Pesh stepped away from Megan. As the flashes went off, snapping hers and Noah's picture, he kept his gaze on her. As she focused on the camera, Megan's blue eyes sparkled as she stretched her face into a wide grin. Noah's tiny fingers wrapped around some of the strands of her hair, causing Megan to yelp in pain. "Easy now. I gotta keep that," she said to Noah.

"Okay, that should get it," the photographer said.

"Here godfather, it's your turn," Megan said, as she handed Noah to him.

By now, Noah was tired of being held and tired of being ensconced in yards of lace. He peered up at Pesh before howling. "I'm sorry, little guy," he cooed, trying to bounce Noah in his arms.

As Noah continued to cry, Pesh looked apologetically at the photographer. Just before he was ready to give up, Megan came up and started clapping her hands and making noises at Noah. The baby instantly stopped crying. "That's right, Noah. Give me a smile," Megan urged, as she backed up to stand by the photographer. She continued making the noises, and she even resorted to flashing one of the strands of her hair at him. Finally, Noah's quivering lips broke into a grin.

"There we go," the photographer said. Pesh quickly plastered a smile on his face. After several flashes went off, the photographer put down his camera. "Got it."

Both Noah and Pesh sighed in relief. Gazing down at him, Pesh asked, "Bet you're ready to get home and get out of that dress, huh?"

"It's a gown, not a dress," Megan countered with a smile.

He laughed. "Regardless of what it's called, I don't think he likes it very much."

Megan brought some of the lace between her fingers. "Probably a little itchy for him."

"Did your son wear this gown?"

"No, this is Aidan's gown. Mason wore my mother's, which my brothers and I also wore."

"I see."

"In your culture do they do anything special like this for a baby?"

Pesh nodded. "We have the Namakaran, or naming ceremony. It's sometimes held in a temple. And like this, it's all about offering blessings to the child—family and friends coming together in support of the new baby."

"I like it."

They were momentarily interrupted by Aidan and Emma walking up. Noah immediately reached out for Emma. "Such a mama's boy," Aidan muttered, which earned him a glare from Emma. He merely winked at her in response before starting down the aisle.

Pesh saw Megan's mother beckoning her with a wave. "Guess you need to go," he said.

"But I'll see you at Aidan and Emma's, right?" she asked.

He swallowed hard. "Um, yes, I'll be there."

"Good," she replied, with an alluring smile. She gave him a small wave before walking off to join her parents.

Shaking his head, he mumbled, "This is trouble."

Chapter

Four

When Megan arrived with her parents at Aidan and Emma's, she was surprised to see a catering truck outside in the driveway. Her surprise continued once she got inside the house. Gazing out into the backyard, she saw where tables were set up alongside the pool. The tables were adorned with blue and white tablecloths and glittering blue and white centerpieces.

A low whistle behind her got Megan's attention. Turning around, she saw Casey shaking her head. "Wow, this is one epic baptism party," she remarked.

"It's impressive. That's for sure," Megan agreed.

As Emma breezed into the kitchen with Noah in a more comfortable outfit, Casey cocked her head. "So, I was just wondering where the ice sculptures were?"

Pink tinged Emma's cheeks. "I kinda got carried away. With me not working anymore, the old marketing and PR side of me let loose. And with my connections, I was able to get everything ridiculously discounted."

Megan smiled. "Everything looks wonderful. You waited so long to have a baby that it makes sense you might go a little overboard."

Emma wrinkled her nose. "I never wanted to be one of those moms who threw the over-the-top parties."

While Casey started to open her mouth, Megan smacked her playfully. "It's just catered in food, right?"

Emma nodded. "They did the tables, too."

"Then I think you're safe from being a Momzilla Party Monster…for now."

Casey laughed. "I'll anxiously be awaiting Noah's first birthday party."

With a scowl, Emma mumbled, "Whatever."

Realizing she didn't see Mason, Megan quickly excused herself and went outside. She didn't like the idea of him being close to the pool. Even with everyone around, it was still too dangerous for her liking. Just as her chest started to tighten, she saw him on her papa's lap. The two of them sat at one of the tables underneath the shade of a massive umbrella. Several of her other younger cousins sat around them, playing on their PSPs and other hand-held devices. "Everything okay?" she asked.

"We're fine, honey," Papa replied.

"Let me know if he gets to be too much."

Cocking his head, Papa demanded, "Are you trying to say I'm old or something?"

"No, not at all. He's a handful even for me."

He waved her away with a hand gnarled with age and time. "Go on and enjoy yourself. I'll keep an eye on Mason."

She smiled and leaned down to kiss his weathered cheek. "Thanks, Papa."

He returned her smile. "You know, while you're enjoying yourself, you might go spend a little time with the godfather."

Megan's eyes widened. Was he trying to set her up with Pesh like he had with Emma? He gave her a knowing look. "Be good for both of you."

"Um, okay. Whatever, Papa," she murmured, before she turned away. Although she hated to admit it, she had been looking forward to talking to Pesh again. She had tried to kid herself that she hadn't secretly been searching the crowd for him when she was taking in all of Emma's decorations. When she did finally catch sight of him, her traitorous heart skipped a beat. She didn't mind if her body gave a reaction, but it pissed her off that her heart was affected by him as well.

He'd ditched his suit jacket along with his tie. With the first button of his shirt undone, she could see a tuft of dark chest hair. She bit her lip at the sight. She was a sucker for chest hair. Her eyes dipped down to take in how the sleeves of his white shirt had been rolled up to his elbows, giving just a glimpse of his defined biceps. Casey had been absolutely right—he was built like a brick shithouse. Megan wanted nothing more than to get better acquainted with his body, especially with fewer clothes on him.

At the sound of Emma's voice behind her, she jumped. "Ready to eat?" Emma asked.

"Um, sure."

Emma gave her a puzzled look before nodding in Pesh's direction. "Why don't you ask Pesh to join you at Aidan's and my table? He doesn't know a lot of people, and I would hate to have him end up with the kids."

Megan quirked her brows in surprise. "Are you sure?"

"Why wouldn't I be?"

With a shrug, Megan replied, "I don't know. Maybe because you didn't like the idea of me getting to know him."

Emma shook her head. "I never said I didn't want you two to get to know each other—I said I didn't want you using him for a fling."

Megan couldn't help rolling her eyes. "The day isn't over yet. I could still turn on my powers of seduction and lure Pesh into a night of seedy passion."

Emma stared at her in shock before busting out laughing. "*Seedy passion*? Those words and Pesh will never, ever go together in the same sentence."

"Are you saying that you and Aidan have never had seedy passion?"

"Aidan and Pesh are not in the same league of men. I love Aidan, but he's not necessarily a gentleman. Pesh is."

"Yeah, but you're a lady," Megan protested.

"Maybe in the street, but she's one hell of a freak in the bedroom," Aidan said behind them.

Emma squealed before whirling around to smack him. "People could hear you," she admonished.

As Aidan chuckled, Megan shook her head. "Forget other people. *Me* having to hear it was painful enough."

Crossing his arms over his chest, Aidan said, "I came over here to ask if we were going to eat or not? People are getting restless. I had no idea I was going to interrupt such an interesting conversation. Of course, I don't think I want to know why the two of you are discussing Emma's and my sex life right now."

Emma waved her hand dismissively. "We weren't. And yes, we're ready to eat. Let's round everyone up."

As Emma walked off to call people to sit down, Aidan grinned at Megan before saying, "Total freak."

Megan closed her eyes as if in pain. "Spare me. Please."

"Just saying. Because you never know if your gentleman might be a super freak too." And with a wink, he walked off to join Emma, leaving Megan to wonder why everyone seemed so concerned with hers and Pesh's love lives.

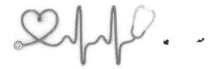

As the sunlight started fading, most of the party guests began to trickle out the door. By the time it was dark, it was only a few of Aidan and Emma's close friends left. Megan had let her parents take a sleepy Mason home, vowing she wanted to stay to help Emma clean up. The truth was she wanted to spend as much time as she could with Pesh.

Thankfully, she found herself sitting next to him at one of the poolside tables. Somehow they managed to end up by themselves after some of the other guests had left. Leaning forward in her chair, she asked, "Did you always want to be a doctor?"

Pesh nodded. "For my fifth birthday, my father bypassed the usual play doctor's kits by giving me a real medical bag with tools from the hospital. I examined everyone who would stand still long enough, including the two dogs."

Megan laughed. "I bet you were a cute little doctor."

"My mother has some embarrassing pictures," he replied, with a smile.

"So your father was also a doctor?"

"Yes, he had a general medicine practice for forty years. He just recently retired."

"Did he pressure you to follow in his footsteps?"

He grinned. "I'm starting to feel like I'm being interrogated."

She laughed. "I'm sorry if you feel that way. I'm just trying to get to know you."

"You're certainly a very attractive interrogator," he said.

"I think you're avoiding the question by flattering me."

"There's flattery and then there's the truth."

Cocking her brows, she replied, "And then there's not answering my question."

He held up his hands in defeat. "Fine, fine. No, I didn't feel pressure to become a doctor. My father would have never wanted me to pursue a profession where I didn't feel useful."

Megan smiled. "So you've always had a need to help people?"

"Pretty much. As the oldest, I always looked out for my two younger brothers and sister. My mother has always called me an old soul."

"I can see that about you."

Leaning forward, he rested his elbows on the table. "Now it is my turn to be the interrogator."

"Okay, I don't mind."

"What about you? Did you always see nursing in your future?"

"Yes and no. Originally, I wanted to be a doctor."

His brows shot up in surprise. "Really?" When she nodded, he asked, "What happened?"

There was no way she was going to tell him the truth about her past and why she had been forced to abandon medical school. Instead, she shrugged. "Life happened, I guess. I decided on the next best thing, which was nursing."

Pesh stared thoughtfully at her. "Was it your son?"

"Excuse me?"

"Was it your son who changed your plans about medical school?"

She shook her head. "No, it was before I had Mason."

"Does he…are you…?" Pesh shook his head. "Forgive me. I was being too forward."

"No, go ahead. I told you I wasn't afraid to answer your questions."

He grimaced. "But it's rude to pry, and it's not my business."

"Just ask your question," she replied.

After a resigned sigh, he finally asked, "Were you married?"

"No, I'm not divorced. And no, Mason's father doesn't have anything to do with him."

Anger flashed in Pesh's dark eyes. "Even though I know nothing of him, I know that he is not a man. A man does not abandon his children and his responsibilities."

"You would be right. He's just a boy playing at being a man," she replied, glancing down at the table.

When Pesh took her hand in his, she jerked her head up in surprise. In a soft voice that vibrated with empathy, he asked, "He hurt you very much, didn't he?"

As she shifted in her chair, she tried downplaying the moment by wagging her free finger at Pesh. "Now you're really turning the heated questions on me, aren't you?"

He quickly released her hand. "I apologize."

She sighed. "No, it's okay." She raked her fingers through her hair as she tried processing if she was really going to be honest with Pesh. Gazing into his eyes, she didn't detect any judgment or prying—there was only compassion. "Yes, he hurt me. He continues to hurt me each time I look at Mason and realize what he's being denied." She jerked her chin over to where Aidan cradled a sleeping Noah in his arms. As the others talked and laughed around him, Aidan stared down at his son with such love in his eyes and adoration on his face that it cut a jagged hole in Megan's chest. Her chin trembled as she replied, "I want *that* for my son."

Pesh's dark eyes pooled with empathy as he once again took her hand in his. "It isn't the same pain, but I do know how you feel. I experience it every time I see a husband and wife sharing a loving moment. It drives home what I do not have…what I have lost."

Megan wiped her eyes with the back of her hand. "Emma told me about your wife. I'm very sorry."

"Thank you," he murmured.

Nibbling her bottom lip, Megan then hesitantly asked, "What was she like?"

By his raised eyebrows, Pesh seemed surprised by her question. Megan hoped she hadn't stepped over a boundary in asking. He leaned back in his chair and drew in an agonized breath. "She was my world—the sun, the moon, and the stars." He met her intense gaze, checking to see if she really wanted him to continue. After she gave a brief nod, he began to talk. He told her how they had met and all the little attributes that Jade possessed that made her special. As Megan listened to him speak with such reverence and love about his late wife, she couldn't help feeling just a little bit jealous. She'd never had a man possess such intense feelings for her. She couldn't imagine ever being loved so completely by a man that not even death could lessen his feelings.

"What you had with Jade, what you still feel for her, it's really beautiful," she murmured when he finished.

Pesh jerked a hand through his thick hair. "It's interesting to hear you say that. I think most women are turned off by what they perceive is a man who can't let go of his dead wife."

Megan shook her head. "I don't think so. Who wouldn't be turned on by a man who feels so deeply that he didn't stop loving his wife just because she died?"

Pesh's eyes widened at her statement, and he sucked in a harsh breath. "Most women don't want to share your heart," he challenged softly.

"Then they're obviously insecure. All of us have the ability to love people in infinite capacities. I love my son with all my heart and soul, but there will still be room for a man…someday."

He stared at her for a moment, unblinking and unmoving. "I have to say that I find your reasoning absolutely fascinating."

"You do?"

"Yes."

The intensity of his gaze caused her to laugh nervously. "I don't think a man has ever called me fascinating."

"That's a pity."

Before she could try changing the subject, Aidan came by their table with Noah in his arms. "After I put him down, I'm going to make some drinks. Emma wants one of her margaritas. You game?" he asked Megan.

She nodded. A drink would certainly help cool her off after the conversation she'd been having with Pesh. "Sure. I don't think I've had one in forever."

"Neither has she. I may be peeling her off the ceiling tonight," he teased.

Megan laughed. "You have seriously got to stop with the innuendo. You are my uncle, and it is mortifying and disgusting to have to think of you in that capacity."

"I am so terribly sorry for scaring your sensitive mind." Grinning, Aidan turned to Pesh. "Beer okay with you, or would you like something fruity, too?"

"I'm fine with a beer," Pesh replied.

Aidan bobbed his head. "Be right back."

After Aidan headed in the house, Pesh caught her staring at him. "What?" he asked.

"Just surprised you wanted a beer, that's all."

"And why is that?"

She shrugged. "You just seemed a little too refined for beer."

He tilted his head at her. "What other preconceived notions do you have about me?"

"None really," she lied. In her mind, she couldn't help thinking how she wanted to make him be dirty just for her. She wondered what other surprises he might have up his sleeve.

"For some reason, I don't believe that." He crossed his arms over his broad chest. "Let me guess. You think that I'm a 'refined' man who drinks wine, would never think of cussing or have inappropriate thoughts, organizes his underwear drawer, and who considers doing the crossword puzzle a fun Friday night?"

Megan couldn't help snorting at his summation. It was a good distraction not to focus on how he had mentioned inappropriate thoughts and his underwear drawer. At the moment, she was having inappropriate thoughts about his underwear…or hopefully lack thereof. Of course, she couldn't help judging him as not being the commando type. "No, that's not what I think of you."

"I would hope not. I know that since I'm a little older than you—"

"Just a little?"

The corners of his lips turned up. "Obviously you think I'm an old man."

"No, I don't," she blurted.

"How old do you think I am? Just shy of adult diapers and a walker?"

She scowled at him. "I was not insinuating that at all. I think you're probably close to Ankle's age."

Pesh's brows furrowed in confusion. "Ankle?"

She laughed before explaining where the nickname came from.

"I see. So just how old is Ankle again?"

"Thirty-four."

"Hmm," Pesh murmured.

"Are you younger than that?"

"Older actually. I'm thirty-seven."

Damn, he was a lot older than her. Twelve years to be exact. "Did I shock you?" he asked, with a teasing lilt in his voice.

She shook her head. "I'd hardly call thirty-seven old."

"It's considerably older than you are, right?"

"I suppose," she lied.

He grinned at her as he leaned on the table with his elbows. "And just how old are you?"

"Twenty-five—I'll be twenty-six in a few months."

"Twenty-five going on twenty-six."

"Yes."

"I must be positively ancient to you." He held out his hand and examined it. "I might have a liver spot or two."

She smacked his hand playfully. "Shut up. Thirty-seven is *not* old."

"See any grey hairs?" he asked, bending over to where his delicious head of hair was in front of her face. Her fingers itched to run through the dark strands. Her mind ran straight to an illicit image of her fingers tugging on his hair as he went down on her, jerking too hard when he sucked and licked her until she came, and then stroking the damp hair back from his forehead as he rose up to cover her body with his.

She cleared her throat that had run dry. "No, of course not."

He jerked his head up to wink at her. "Then there's hope for me yet."

"I would think so."

Aidan appeared then, carrying all the drinks on a tray. "I expect a tip when you guys finish," he teased.

"I'll remember that," Megan replied.

After jerking his chin toward the table next to him, Aidan said, "Why don't you guys come over here with us?"

She fought the urge to slap him. She was enjoying having Pesh to herself. "Um, sure. Okay," she said, reluctantly rising out of her chair. When they changed tables, she was glad to see Pesh take the empty chair beside her, rather than across from her.

Once she got settled in, she wasn't lamenting her seat change too much. Between Casey, and Emma's other best friend, Connor, the table was kept in raucous laughter. It was good being with a group of friends. After she had gotten pregnant, she didn't have much in common with her sorority sisters anymore. Then when she became a mom, she rarely saw anyone from her old group. Her life moved in an entirely different orbit than theirs now.

The conversation and laughter flowed as easily as the drinks. Megan found herself halfway through her second margarita when she started feeling funny. A flush filled her cheeks at the same time she felt clammy. As Aidan came back with another beer, she asked, "Did you put something different in this one?"

"Yeah, we ran out of the tequila I got for the party, so I gave my favorite niece a good dose of Sierra Silver."

"What?" Megan demanded.

Aidan's brows furrowed behind his tipped back beer bottle. Once he swallowed, he asked, "Does it taste bad?"

Megan pinched her eyes shut. The room was beginning to spin around her a little. As she brought her hand to her forehead, she heard a smack across the room and Aidan cry, "Ow, dammit, Em!"

"That tequila is a hundred and fifty proof alcohol, Aidan," Emma chastised.

"Sorry. I didn't realize it. I just thought it was the better stuff because it was white tequila. That's your drink of choice, not mine."

Oh God, she was in so much trouble. She'd barely consumed any alcohol since she got pregnant and had Mason. Now she'd had one regular dosed margarita and almost a full one of straight alcohol.

A gentle hand landed on her thigh. "Are you all right?" Pesh asked.

She opened her eyes to see two blurry images of him staring at her with concern. "Not exactly."

"Would you like me to take you home?"

"Yes, please. While I can still walk."

As she rose out of her chair, she swayed a little in her heels. After taking two steps, Aidan's apologetic face appeared before her. "I'm sorry, Meggie."

"It's not your fault. And I'll be fine." She wagged a finger at him. "But when I get shit for coming home drunk, I'm so telling Mom it was your fault."

He smiled. "I'll gladly take the blame and fear Angie's wrath." He leaned in to hug her. "Thanks for today—you know, for being Noah's godmother."

"You're welcome. Thanks for me asking you." She shook her head. "I mean, thanks for asking me." God, this was bad.

After exchanging hugs with Emma and reassuring her at least twenty times that she would be fine and that she did need to go home, Pesh led Megan out the front door. He slid a strong arm around her waist to steady her as they went down the porch steps.

As she staggered to the car, she moaned. "I can't go home yet. Not like this." She stared up into his face. "I can't let Mason see me like this."

He pushed a strand of hair out of her face. "Don't worry. I'll take you to my house then."

"Just so I can sober up?" she questioned, although she really didn't mean it. She wanted to go to his house for a lot more, especially after being so close to his fabulously built body.

"Yes, of course. I'll make you some strong, black coffee."

"Thank you," she murmured, trying to still the spinning of her head.

"You're welcome." Always the gentleman, Pesh opened the door for her, and she collapsed onto the seat. Once he made sure she was comfortable, he closed the door and went around the front of the car. Megan gazed around at the plush interior of the Jaguar with its leather seats and sleek console.

After Pesh slid into his seat, he put the key in the ignition and cranked up. As they started backing out of the driveway, she glanced over at him. "Do you have to come to the rescue women of drunken." She shook her head. "I mean, drunken women a lot?" she asked. Wait, was she slurring?

He cut his eyes over at her and smiled. He seemed to be trying really hard not to laugh at her. "Not exactly. But I'm always happy to help a damsel in distress."

Megan giggled. Oh God, now she was giggling? She *never* giggled. She eyed Pesh suspiciously. "Got a hero complex, huh? Wanna be every woman's knight in shining armor?"

"Not every woman's," he murmured.

"Mmm, Pesh, you wanna be *my* knight in shining armor?" As soon as the words left her lips, she fought the urge to slap her hand over her mouth. Alcohol always had this effect on her—it left her completely without a sensor.

Pesh's jaw clenched, and he didn't reply. Pitching her upper body over the armrest, she got as close to him as she could. "You didn't answer my question."

Taking his eyes momentarily off the road, he pinned her with an intense gaze. "I'd be anything and everything you wanted me to be, if you would give me the chance."

Momentarily dumbfounded, she could only stare at him. "Oh wow," she replied, as she collapsed back onto the seat. The motion caused her to feel dizzy. Mumbling almost incoherently, she said, "Mmm, hot as fuck and anything I want. Lucky me."

"I have a feeling you wouldn't have asked the original question if you weren't intoxicated."

With a snort, she replied, "Drunk or sober that woulda been a helluva line to hear from a man."

"I'm glad you think so."

After spending a few moments in tense silence, Megan leaned forward to flick on the radio. "Do you mind?"

"Go ahead."

Humming along with one of the songs, she laid her head back on the seat. "I won't hurt your ears by singing."

"Do you not sing?"

"Oh, I sing, but I don't do it well. Emma's the one with the voice."

"So I've heard."

Turning to look at him, Megan asked, "Did she ever sing for you?"

"Sadly, no."

Megan harrumphed as she crossed her arms over her chest. "She made out with you, but she wouldn't sing for you? That's just rude."

Pesh made a strangled noise. "Emma told you...about us?"

"Mmm, hmm." She grinned at him. "I hear you're a *great* kisser."

Cutting his eyes over to her, he gave her a pained look. "It really wasn't like that for us. I mean, we weren't in love with each other."

"Yeah, that's what she said. Course, she did admit that you got her all hot and bothered."

"S-She did?" he stammered, embarrassment coloring his cheeks.

"Hey, the ability to get a woman hot is nothing to be ashamed of. Hell, I got turned on when I first saw you today. Like my panties got wet."

"Megan, don't," Pesh warned, gripping the steering wheel to where his knuckles turned white.

Turning in her seat, she eyed him before licking her lips. "You don't want me to say how you got me hot in a church? How you still get me hot acting all bashful about the sex talk?"

"Please. Just don't."

"Fine," she muttered, before flouncing back in her seat. She didn't speak to him for a long time. Instead, she closed her eyes and laid back with her head cushioned on the head rest. When the car started to slow, she snapped her eyes open. She didn't know if she fell asleep or passed out. Sitting up, she peered out the window at the posh houses of the subdivision they were in.

As they pulled into the driveway, Megan couldn't help staring up at the house. "Holy shit, this place is beautiful."

Pesh chuckled. "Thank you."

"I know you think it's just the alcohol talking, but I'm serious. You have great taste."

"I hope you'll like the inside just as much."

"I'm sure I will."

After he came around to open the door, she hopped out of the car a little too fast. Her wobbly legs wavered, and she ended up crashing into Pesh's chest. Staring up at him, she gave an apologetic smile. "Sorry about that."

"It's fine. Need some help?"

With the alcohol fueling her libido, she replied, "If it means having your hands on me, then sure."

Pesh grimaced, but his arm still came around her waist to steady her. She loped along beside him. After he unlocked the door and punched in the alarm code, she followed him inside. Her blurry vision took in the expansive kitchen with his gleaming stainless steel appliances. She followed him as he made his way into the living room.

Motioning toward the couch, he said, "Why don't you have a seat while I fix you some coffee?"

While it was a nice idea to sober herself up, she didn't want any coffee. She just wanted Pesh. Grabbing the lapels of his suit coat, she pulled herself flush against him. "When did you put this back on?" she wondered aloud. She felt so tiny against his massive chest. It was a good feeling though—one of safety and protection. It also lit her even more on fire with lust. Cocking her head, she glanced up at him to survey his expression. Even in the semi-darkness, she could see his dark eyes burning with desire. She ran her hands up his chest to his neck. She tugged him down to where his face was inches from hers. Fortified with liquid courage, she brought her lips to his.

She couldn't help the little moan that came from deep in her throat. Pesh's mouth was warm, soft, and inviting. The brief connection made her want him all the more—for him to devour her. Tentatively, she slid her tongue across his bottom lip, beckoning him to open for her. Almost instantaneously, the warmth of his tongue met hers. They slid against each other, tasting, searching, and seeking. He gripped her face in his hands, holding her captive as his tongue plunged in and out of her mouth. Emma had been right—the man could kiss like there was no tomorrow. He knew when to be gentle with his mouth and then when to switch to more demanding, almost conquering kisses. If he could practically make her soak her panties with just a kiss, what the hell could he do with his dick?

As she started to feel lightheaded and weak on her legs, they stumbled over to the couch before Pesh collapsed back, taking her with him. Straddling his lap, she gazed at him momentarily before his mouth attacked hers again. As his tongue once again invaded her mouth, she began to raise her hips and grind against him. Groaning, he broke the kiss by throwing his head back. He gulped in long breaths of air like he was a dying man deprived of his last breath. She felt the same way.

She kissed a trail over his chin and down his neck. "Pesh, I want you," she murmured into his skin.

His chest heaved up and down with her declaration as if he was finding it hard to breathe. She broke away to stare into his eyes. "Please."

Chapter Five

Pesh couldn't believe the delicious nightmare he found himself trapped in. A beautiful, sexy blonde writhed against him. The hem of Megan's dress had ridden up to her hips, and a tiny scrap of lace underwear was the only thing covering her core as she rubbed herself against his crotch. Her heat and her arousal scorched through the fabric of his pants to singe the skin of his growing erection. He wanted nothing more than to flip her on her back, tear away the underwear, and plunge himself deep inside her. It had been so, so long since he had been within the tight walls of a woman. While his conscious railed against him for even entertaining the thought, his body was onboard.

"Please," Megan whimpered, as she continued to rise and fall over his erection.

"We can't...we shouldn't."

She ran her hands up his chest before wrapping them around his neck. "But I could make you feel good."

"I'm sure you could."

"And I know you could make me feel good, too. I'm already drenched just kissing you." Her fingers raked through his hair, tugging desperately on the strands. "I need this, and you need this."

His body was completely onboard with how much he needed her. If she pressed any closer to him, she was going to set him off and make him do something he hadn't since he was a teenager, which was come in his pants. But his once hazy mind was starting to refocus and overpower the desire pumping through his body. He could not and would not take her when she was drunk. It was completely against his character. He'd never taken advantage of a woman, and he never would.

He gazed into her hooded eyes. "But it would be so very wrong."

Her lip trembled. "Don't you want me?"

"Yes, without a doubt."

"Then why won't you have sex with me?"

"Because you're inebriated."

She rolled her eyes in a huff. "You're sooo proper, aren't you? A proper gentleman."

He cupped her face in his hands. "If not taking advantage of you in your state of intoxication makes me a gentleman, then I suppose I am. What kind of man would I be to take you now only to have you wake up with regret and remorse?"

"The kind of man who wants to get laid!" Her hand dipped between them to grasp his erection, causing him to hiss. "I feel you against me—I know you want this as much as I do."

Although the devil on his shoulder raged at him, he quickly removed Megan's hand. "Believe me when I say I won't have sex with you like this. I would never disrespect you so much as to not make love to you like you deserve."

She blinked a few times as if she was having a hard time processing his words. "Regardless of what you have going on in that head of yours, you are better than this. You deserve a man who will take his time with you and show you what pleasure through making love really is."

"I've never had that," she whispered regretfully.

He gave her a sad smile. "I didn't think you had." He brushed the hair out of her face and cupped her cheek. "If I take you, I'll be making love to you. I'll have you begging and pleading, but you'll be coming so many times you'll lose count. You'll understand the difference between a quick tumble and the all-consuming power of a physical connection fueled by an emotional one."

She rapidly blinked her blue eyes in disbelief while her cheeks flushed. "Oh God, did you actually just say that?"

"I did." He gave her a teasing smile. "And you'll be calling out my name more than his."

"I…" she began before she quickly clamped her lips shut. Her eyes widened before she scrambled off of his lap. Before he could question her on what she was doing, she threw up all over the front of her dress.

When she wavered on her feet like she was going to collapse, Pesh tumbled off the couch, reaching out for her. Grabbing both of her shoulders, he steadied her. She glanced down at her dress before gazing back at him. Pesh's heart ached at the sight of tears pooling in her eyes. "Are you all right?"

Her chin trembled before big, fat tears slid down her cheeks. "Oh God," she whispered.

"Please don't cry."

"T-This is s-so embarrassing," she hiccupped.

"It's okay. You don't have to be embarrassed."

Moaning, she covered her face with her hands. "First, I made a fool out of myself coming on to you and now I've puked in front of you like some sorority girl who can't handle her liquor."

"Stop beating yourself up. Come, let's get you cleaned up."

He slid an arm around her waist to steady her on their way down the hall to the bedroom. She continued to weep softly as they made their way into the bathroom. Using his free hand, he flicked on the light. "Can you stand in the shower?"

With a weak nod, she replied, "I think so."

"If not, there's a ledge you can sit on. Let me turn on the water for you, and I'll get you a towel." He propped her up against the counter before striding over to the shower. Once he felt the water was a good enough temperature, he then went over to the closet. He pulled out a towel before returning to Megan who had her head in her hands.

With his free hand, he took one of her hands and pulled it away from her face. "Please stop beating yourself up. I hate to see you so upset."

"I can't help it. I'm such a fool."

"No, if you're a fool, then so am I. We both wanted each other."

"But I got drunk…I never get drunk anymore."

"It was an accident. Things like that happen." He cupped her chin and forced her to look at him. "You are none of the negative things your mind is calling you right now."

"Really?"

Her broken expression, coupled with her need for his reassurance, nearly crushed him. He had to fight from taking her in his arms. He knew if he did that, he would end up doing something he shouldn't with her. Finally, he nodded. "But you do smell, so go on and get in the shower."

The corners of her lips curved up in a half smile. "Do you have something I can change into? And maybe a toothbrush?"

He nodded. "One second." Leaving her in the bathroom, he went back into the bedroom to his closet. He took out a pair of scrubs he knew would be too big and too long for her and then coupled it with an Emory University T-shirt. When he got back to the bathroom, Megan was struggling with the zipper at the back of her dress.

With a defeated expression, she dropped her hands. "Could you please help me?"

"Of course." He sat the clothes down on the counter. He then reached up to tug down the zipper. The back of the dress gaped open, exposing her cream colored skin and navy blue lace bra and panties. He closed his eyes to try and block out the glaring images rocketing through his mind. His lips on her skin, his tongue licking up her spine, his hands curving around her ribcage to cup her breasts. He forced himself to step back. Clearing his throat, he replied, "Done."

Glancing at him over her shoulder, Megan gave him a weak smile. "Thank you."

He took out a spare toothbrush from underneath the counter and placed it next to the clothes he'd brought her. "Let me know if you need anything else."

"Okay."

Whirling around, he strode out of the bathroom. Not wanting to go too far in case Megan needed him, he began pacing around the bedroom. He momentarily faltered when he heard the shower turn off. He waited for her to appear, but she didn't. Just as he was about to knock on the door, the whirring hum of the hairdryer started. He continued his pacing as she dried her hair. Next, he heard the sink water turn on as she brushed her teeth. When it was quiet once again in the bathroom, his feet froze as he stared anxiously at the bathroom door.

When it opened, Pesh's breath caught. Appearing fresh-faced and clean, Megan looked so beautiful as she tentatively stepped into the bedroom. "Everything okay?" he asked.

She jumped at his voice. "Um, it's fine. Thank you again for the clothes and for letting me shower."

"You're more than welcome. And there's no need to thank me."

Chewing on her lip, she glanced from the bed to him. "I texted my mother to tell her I was staying the night at Emma's." Before he could say anything, she quickly added, "Thank you for putting my purse in the bathroom. That was very thoughtful of you."

"You're welcome," he replied. Then he thought of her text. "So you're staying at Aidan and Emma's?" After all, the last thing he needed was to have her here—a reminder of what he couldn't have. It would be enough to drive any man crazy.

Megan shook her head. "Do you mind if I stayed here instead?" When he started to open his mouth, she shook her head. "I promise no funny business. I just don't want to go home yet. If you don't want to me to stay, you can take me to Emma's."

"Of course you can stay."

"I can sleep on the couch or in the guest room."

He shook his head. "You'll sleep right here." He walked over to his massive king-sized bed. He turned down the covers before glancing back at her. "Come on. Getting some rest will make you feel better."

She eyed him hesitantly. "I really can't take your bed. That would be imposing."

"I don't mind. I promise."

"Only if you're sure?"

"I'm sure."

Tentatively, she started walking over to him, her eyes never leaving his. She eased down onto the mattress before sliding beneath the sheets. When she appeared comfortable, he covered her up. As he started to go, she reached out to grab his arm. "No, please don't go. Don't leave me alone."

His brows shot up in surprise. "You want me to stay with you?"

"Yes, please."

"In this bed...with you?" When she nodded, he exhaled a ragged breath. "Megan, I don't think that's a good idea."

"Don't overthink it; just stay with me."

Although his brain was raging war at him to make the sane and responsible decision, he replied, "Give me a few minutes."

"Okay," she replied softly.

Turning, he strode into the bathroom. He didn't bother glancing in the mirror because he was pretty sure he wouldn't like what he saw. Instead, he stripped off his suit and tie. Although he probably should have thrown on more clothes, he left his boxers on and grabbed a white shirt off the hamper. After pulling it over his head, he went back out into the bedroom.

Megan lay on her side in the bed, her face turned toward the bathroom. Her eyes were closed, but they popped open the moment he entered the bedroom. Without a word to her, he walked around the other side of the bed and climbed inside. Lying on his back, he propped one arm over his head. His other hand rested on his chest. He twisted his fingers into the fabric of his shirt over his heart. Somehow he wanted to still the erratic beating.

Just when he thought he might be comfortable, Megan turned over to face him. "You're so far away," she whispered.

"I thought it was for the best."

The corners of her mouth momentarily turned down in a pout. Then she inched closer to him. He sucked in a breath and tried not to hiss when he felt her head nuzzle against his chest. Before he could stop her, she had thrown an arm around him. Thankfully, she didn't try anything else. And within a few minutes, her labored breathing signaled she had fallen asleep. Pesh stared up at the ceiling and willed himself to be able to go to sleep as easily.

Surprisingly, as Megan's soft snores echoed against his side, his eyes grew heavy. For the first time in two years, he fell asleep with someone in his arms.

Chapter Six

Sunlight streamed across Megan's face, causing her to squint her eyes tighter closed against the bright invasion. She was warm and comfortable, and she didn't want to wake up. But the tranquility of her morning was shattered when a soft snore came from behind her. It was far too deep to be one of Mason's.

Panic prickled its way up her skin. *Where am I?* Her eyes frantically scanned the room. Overcome by both masculine décor and smells, she realized she was in a man's bedroom, or more importantly a man's bed. She hadn't woken up this dazed and confused since she got hammered for the first time. She couldn't even remember what day it was. This was bad. Very, very bad. She had to get out of there and get home to Mason. What kind of mother was she to wake up in a strange man's bed?

As she tried to roll over, she found herself entrapped by a strong arm wrapped around her waist. Her gaze flicked down to the tan, muscled arm. Who the hell did that belong to? A whimper escaped her lips. Oh God, had she actually slept with a man she had no memory of? Never in her life had she made such a mistake as that. Nausea overcame her, and she knew she needed to get out of bed and into the bathroom.

She shoved herself so hard away from the person that she ended up elbowing him in the ribs. He groaned. "Oh, I'm sorry. I didn't mean to hurt you," she quickly apologized.

"It's okay, Megan," he murmured drowsily.

That voice. It took only a second for her to register who she was in bed with. And with that realization, everything from the night before came crashing down on her. She had accidentally gotten drunk off her ass, Pesh had taken her to his house to sober up, and then…oh God, she had come on to him like a brazen floozy. She buried her head in her hands and moaned.

"Hey, how do you feel this morning?" he asked.

"Like I've been run over by a truck."

"Want me to fix you a good hangover cure?"

She peeked at him through her fingers. "You actually know a hangover cure?"

He smiled. "You think someone like me has never been drunk?" When she bobbed her head, he laughed. "I'm sorry to disappoint you, but there have been many, many times I've woken up just as you are now."

"That's hard to imagine." She gazed down at the scrubs and T-shirt she was in. Although she doubted it, she couldn't help but ask. "Did we…"

"No, we didn't."

She arched her brows in surprise. "If we didn't sleep together, then why did you…I mean, why are you in bed with me?"

"Because you begged me to stay."

She gasped in horror. Wasn't it enough that she had thrown herself so wantonly at him, but now she'd begged him to stay with her? "I did?"

He nodded. "You said you didn't want to be alone."

Vaguely she remembered pleading with him to lie close to her. What a nightmare. "I'm so sorry."

"Don't apologize." When she started to protest, he held up a hand. "I have to admit it was nice being in bed with someone again—feeling their warmth, the softness of their body as they lay beside you." He swallowed hard. "I've missed that more than I knew."

Overcome with the emotions threatening to overtake her, Megan didn't know what to say. All she knew is she needed to get out of there. "I need to get home…or to Emma's. I can't let my parents think I stayed out all night with a man I just met."

"I understand. I wouldn't dream of compromising your reputation."

She stared at him for a moment. Sometimes the way he spoke made it seem like he was from a different world or time period. "I, uh, I need to use the bathroom."

"Go ahead."

Tumbling out of the covers, she then streaked across the room. Once she closed the door behind her, she exhaled the breath she'd been holding. She made it to the toilet just in time to throw up again. She wondered after doing the same thing the night before how there was anything left in her stomach to empty. Once she finished, she leaned over the sink, pooling water in her hand before bringing it to her mouth. After gargling to rid herself of the nasty taste, she eventually dug under the counter for some mouthwash, and then brushed her teeth.

Without a hairbrush or comb, she did her best to tame her out-of-control hair. Once she surmised that she looked presentable enough to face the firing squad, aka Aidan and Emma, she left the bathroom. Pesh had thrown on some clothes and stood in the middle of the room. He raised his brows expectantly at her.

"I'm ready to go now."

"Of course."

When she started for the bedroom door, she abruptly stopped. "Wait, my dress?"

"I'll send it out to be dry cleaned."

"Oh," she murmured. "Thank you."

In silence, they made their way through the house. Megan tried not to be so obvious as she took in the high ceilings of the living room, the floor to ceiling windows that overlooked a large, spacious yard. Pesh had an amazing house—one that was far too big for just him. It certainly was made for a family—the one he sadly didn't have.

As he started to open the door leading out to the garage for her, Pesh stopped and turned around. Staring intently at her, he said, "I'd like to see you again."

Megan couldn't help the shocked gasp that escaped her lips. She'd made a repeated fool out of herself the night before, and he still wanted to see her? "You can't be serious."

"I am."

She gave a slight jerk of her head. "I don't think that is a good idea."

"But why?" he countered sincerely.

With a contemptuous snort, she replied, "Isn't it obvious?"

"If you're alluding to the fact you accidentally got drunk last night and then became ill, that has little relevance to me. Accidents happen, and I'm man enough to realize that." He closed the gap between them. "I liked being with you yesterday."

Remembering what Emma had said, Megan couldn't help asking, "You want to date me, don't you?"

"Yes of course. What else would I want to do?"

When she replied, "Have sex," a flush entered his cheeks.

"That is not what I meant."

"And that's a pity."

His brows furrowed. "Whatever do you mean?"

"You and I…we want different things. You want to date and get married again, right?"

"Yes, that is something I desire very much."

She shook her head. "But I don't want to be in a serious relationship right now with you or anyone for that matter. I'm certainly not ready to get married anytime soon. I just wanted to have some fun with someone."

Pesh frowned. "I don't think I understand."

"What I want from you is the same thing I wanted last night. Just *sex*," she answered honestly.

"You don't want to date me…you only want to have sex with me?"

If the situation hadn't been so dire, Megan might've laughed at the horrified expression on Pesh's face. He appeared absolutely floored that she could ever think of only using him as a sex toy.

Finally, when she gathered herself together, she shook her head. "I'm sorry, but that's the way I feel."

She braced herself for some sort of wrath out of him or even a lecture. What he did was even more surprising. He gave her a sad smile. "And I'm sorry you feel that way because I would have really enjoyed getting to know you better." Without another word, he opened the door. Always the gentleman, he waited for her to go through first.

Tucking her head to her chest, she bypassed him to walk to the car. Once again, he appeared to open the car door for her. "Thank you," she murmured.

He nodded before walking around the front of the car. Without another word to her, Pesh cranked up, and then began backing down the driveway.

The ride to Aidan and Emma's was only twenty minutes, but it seemed to take an eternity. The painful silence hung heavy around her. Pesh didn't look at her. Instead, he kept his gaze firmly on the road ahead of them.

When he pulled into Aidan and Emma's driveway, Megan felt her stomach clench. She wished there was some way to make things right between them. But she had a feeling she had gone too far and said too much. As he put the car in park, he turned to look at her. "Thank you for the ride," she said.

"You're welcome. It was my pleasure."

"Most of all, I want to thank you for taking care of me last night. You truly went above and beyond. I can never thank you enough."

"You don't have to thank me. I'm glad I was able to help you."

Nibbling on her bottom lip, she finally allowed herself to say what she was holding back on. "I wish things could be different," she said softly.

When she dared herself to look at him, she found him staring intently at her. "I'm sorry, too. Take care of yourself. Okay?"

She bobbed her head. "The same to you." With trembling hands, she fumbled for the door handle. When she was finally able to open the door, she stumbled out onto the pavement. As she made her way up the driveway, she could feel Pesh's eyes on her. The car remained parked as she climbed the porch steps and rang the doorbell. She hoped that Noah was already up, and she wasn't waking the household.

Aidan threw open the door. "Megan? What the hell?" he asked.

His question and concern caused her to burst into tears. "Why are you crying?" Aidan demanded.

"It's a long story."

He glanced from her out the door to Pesh's car. His expression darkened. "Did Pesh hurt you?"

"No! Of course not."

"If he's made you cry, I don't care whether he's Noah's godfather or not. I'll punch his lights out!"

She grabbed his arm. "Stop it, Ankle! It's not him, it's me. It's all my fault. Okay?"

He stared at her in surprise. "What happened?"

"Give me some coffee and a chance to calm down, and then I'll tell you everything."

Although his expression was skeptical, Aidan nodded, and then started to close the door. Megan stole one last glance of Pesh as his car started reversing down the driveway. She hoped for her sake and his it was the last time she would have to see him.

Chapter Seven

TWO MONTHS LATER

Megan nervously tapped her thumbs on the steering wheel of her car. Her clinical placement had come through, and she was now on her way to make her introductions to her preceptor, the nurse who would supervise her. Although she had initially been disappointed in not receiving Grady, she was still excited to be doing the last part of the journey to becoming a nurse. She was also grateful she hadn't received the night shift that some of her fellow nursing students had. She would have rarely been able to see Mason if she had to sleep during the day and work at night.

She pulled into the parking lot of the Wellstar ER and eased into the first space she found. After turning off the car, she grabbed her folder of paperwork along with her purse and headed inside. She stopped at the front desk. "I'm not a patient. I'm a clinical student here to see Kristi Parkman."

"Go on through," the receptionist said, before she buzzed open the Authorized Personnel Only door. Breezing inside the heart of the ER, Megan couldn't help feeling excited. She couldn't wait until she got her feet wet by working with patients.

Glancing around, she wasn't exactly sure how she was going to find the preceptor. She stopped at an area teaming with nurses. "Can I help you?" one of them asked.

"Yes, I'm here to see Kristi Parkman."

A tall blonde woman in her fifties came over to her with a beaming smile. "You must be Ms. McKenzie?"

"I am."

"It's so nice to meet you."

Megan smiled. "It's nice meeting you, too."

"We're so very glad to have you. I've taken a look at your transcript, and it's quite impressive."

"Thank you," Megan replied.

"Why don't I show you around today? That way you'll be ready to go with the flow tomorrow."

"Sounds good."

With a smile, Kristi led her around the maze of rooms. She pointed out where the medicine room was, the trauma area, and where she would find the break room. Each time they passed a nurse or a doctor, Kristi was quick to introduce Megan.

"Everyone seems very friendly," Megan mused.

"It really is a great place to work. Now, I'm not going to lie that some of the residents can be real assholes. But we're so lucky to have a supervisor who is such a sweetheart."

"That's wonderful."

"Yes, everyone loves Dr. Nadeen."

Megan's heartbeat slowed to a standstill. *Nadeen*. No, it couldn't be. Surely there were more doctors with that last name. Searching her mind, she tried desperately to remember where he said he worked.

"Oh good, he's just down the hall. Let me introduce you two."

"No, that's really isn't necessary," Megan protested feebly.

Ignoring her, Kristi called, "Dr. Nadeen, come meet our newest nursing candidate."

The moment he turned around, Megan felt like she was going to throw up. After spending two months trying hard to forget about her infamous night with Pesh Nadeen, there he was right in front of her. She couldn't help having the classic line from Casablanca flash in her head, "Out of all the gin joints in all the world, she had to walk into mine." She certainly felt that way about all the hospitals she could have possibly been assigned to, she had to be assigned to his.

The shock and surprise registered on his face as well. He was quick to mask it by smiling warmly at her. "Hello again, Megan."

Kristi's brows shot up at the familiarity of Pesh's greeting. "You know each other?"

"Um, well," Megan began. How was she going to explain? The last thing she needed was to get off on the wrong foot with her coworkers.

Pesh nodded. "She and I share a godson."

"Oh how wonderful." Kristi patted Megan's back. "What luck for you then ending up here out of all the hospitals?"

"Yes, what luck," Megan murmured.

Kristi smiled. "Well, I'll let you two catch up for a minute or two."

"No, that's okay. You don't have to do that," Megan protested.

Waving her hand dismissively, Kristi said, "It gives me a chance to go grab a snack and something to drink. Be back in a few, and we'll finish the tour."

Megan fought the urge to run after Kristi as she walked off. Instead, she turned back to Pesh who was staring expectantly at her.

"You don't exactly look happy to see me," Pesh said.

She shook her head wildly. "How could I be? The man, who I completely made an ass out of myself in front of, is at the hospital where I'm doing my clinicals. That doesn't exactly make my day."

"For the last time, you have nothing to be embarrassed about."

"Sorry, but that does not make me feel any better," she grumbled.

"What can I do to put you at ease about working with me?"

Rubbing her now aching head, she replied, "I don't know. If I thought it wouldn't make me look bad, I'd request a transfer."

"I offend you that much?" Pesh asked. As she gazed up at him, his expression was wounded.

"No, no, you don't offend me. It's just that…" She chewed mercilessly on her bottom lip before she continued. After taking a ragged breath, she replied, "It's just that for the past two years, I had pretty good control of my life. The night I was with you, I let all that control crumble. By getting drunk, I became someone else— someone I used to be. The girl, or woman, who would do anything to get a man's attention. I don't like that person very much, and I don't ever want to go back there. Seeing you just makes me remember all of that."

Megan couldn't help being surprised by how honest she'd been able to be with him. Pesh remained silent for a moment. His dark eyes bore into hers. "I am sorry that you reflect so negatively on the night we were together. For me, it was not marred by drinking or you getting sick. I enjoyed spending time with you and getting to know you." He swallowed hard. "I enjoyed waking up with you. I would give anything for you to be able to look at me without having to feel bad about yourself."

"You really enjoyed being with me that night?"

He nodded. "When I told you I wanted to see you again, I was serious."

She sighed. "That's very sweet of you, but I haven't changed my mind about dating."

"You haven't?"

With a shake of her head, she replied, "I have too much going on in my life right now to get involved with someone. It wouldn't be fair to them…to you. Especially since we still want very different things from each other."

"I see," he replied.

Megan noticed the sadness that darkened his expression. "I'm sorry," she murmured.

"You have nothing to regret. Any grief I'm experiencing is once again my fault." He gave her a rueful smile. "I seem to keep falling for women who aren't meant for me."

She sucked in a harsh breath at his words. "Falling? You are…you *were* falling for me?"

Pesh opened his mouth to reply, but at the sound of Kristi coming back from the break room, he shut it. Closing the gap between them, he whispered, "Don't worry about working with me, Megan. We'll always be friends, and I will respect your wishes and your distance."

For some reason, his words had the opposite effect they should have, and regret ricocheted through her. Finally, she managed to say, "Thank you. I appreciate that."

With a smile, he then turned and walked away. She heaved a painful breath as Kristi walked up to her. "Such a sweetheart, isn't he?"

"Yes, he is," Megan murmured.

"Not bad on the eyes either."

A nervous giggle escaped Megan's lips. "No, he's not."

"I swear that half of the women here in the ER act like they're in heat whenever he comes around." Kristi fanned herself. "I mean, that body, those eyes, and those dimples. Lord, if I wasn't a happily married woman, what I wouldn't want to do to that man!"

Megan knew exactly what Kristi meant. Unfortunately, she was never going to get the chance to experience it for herself. Somehow she'd managed to find the only man left in the world who wouldn't partake in just a sexual relationship. No, Pesh had to want more than she was willing to give.

"Did you hear what I said?" Kristi asked.

Megan snapped her gaze from Pesh's retreating form back to face Kristi. "I'm sorry what?"

Kristi laughed. "Oh no, I'm about to lose another one to Dr. Nadeen's charms, huh?"

Shaking her head wildly, Megan replied, "No, no, we're just friends—I don't feel anything like that for him."

Kristi winked. "Yeah, just keep telling yourself that, honey."

Chapter Eight

As Pesh exited one of the exam rooms, he saw Megan sitting on a stool at the counter, working on a chart. When the door shut behind him, she jerked her head up and caught him staring. He cleared his throat and walked over to her. "Hello," he said, pleasantly.

"Hi."

"So, are you settling in?"

She nodded. "Everyone has been so nice and helpful."

"Good. I'm glad to hear that. We usually have very good success rates with our clinical candidates." Megan smiled before her head dipped back down to work on the chart. Nervously, he scratched the back of his neck. Things were rolling along with them now that he knew he shouldn't try to rock the boat. After all, he had promised her he would keep his distance. But he couldn't help himself. In the two months since their first encounter, he hadn't stopped thinking about her. Now that she had shown back up in his life so out of the blue, he couldn't help feeling that it was fated.

Ask her to dinner, his mind shouted. He bit down on his lip to keep the question he was burning to ask from escaping his mouth. Finally, it rushed forth before he could stop himself. "Why don't you let me buy you dinner after work?"

Megan's scribbling pen stilled on the chart. She glanced up and cocked her head at him. "Dinner implies a date, and I thought we were clear on that."

He gave her a nervous smile. "Well, I was only offering some less palatable cafeteria food. I hardly think that constitutes a date."

"In my realm of dating consciousness, any time you sit down at a table while eating and drinking together, it is a date."

Crossing his arms over his chest, he countered, "If that were true, it would mean you were dating your father and brother every time you sat down together. I know your family is close, but I don't believe they're that close."

Megan's brows rose. "Oh, is the good doctor cracking jokes now?"

"Perhaps."

The corners of Megan's lips turned up. "Then what exactly would you consider a date?"

Pesh leaned back against the wall, surmising her teasing smile. "A mutually agreed upon event."

"You're so proper," Megan teased.

He rolled his eyes at her, something he rarely did until he began spending more and more time in her presence. "And you're avoiding the initial question."

Megan put down the pen and chart and crossed her arms over her chest. "So, if you could take me on a date, where would we go?"

Pesh rubbed his jaw in thought. "Well, if would have to be something you would want to do, but I would begin with dinner." When she started to protest, he held up his hand. "Somewhere that was romantic with candlelight and soft music—perhaps a place where we could dance in between courses."

Staring at him in surprise, Megan replied, "You're serious?"

"Of course."

She slowly shook her head back and forth. "Okay, go on."

"Once we finished wine and dessert, I would then want to take you somewhere you've never been—"

"Like your bedroom?" Megan interjected with a smirk.

"I do believe you've already been there before." The teasing faded from Megan's expression, and a flush entered her cheeks. "May I continue?"

"Yeah," she murmured.

"I would want to be with you to experience something you never have before—an art gallery, an opera, a musical. Anything that would bring wonderment and excitement to your face." He gave her a small smile. "And it would mean all the more that I was getting to share it with you."

He watched with almost mild amusement as she processed his words. Most likely she had never had a man speak to her the way he was, and it was certainly affecting her. Feeling like it was time to go in for the kill, he asked once again, "So, will you have dinner with me?"

Pesh leaned forward expectantly as Megan opened her mouth. They were interrupted by the sound of Emma's voice. "Oh thank God. I'm so glad you two are on   ."

Her anxious tone was the only thing that could have torn Pesh's attention away from Megan. He glanced from Emma to Aidan, who was grimacing and rubbing his head. "What happened?"

Emma replied, "He fell and hit his head," at the same time Aidan grunted, "Nothing."

Megan stepped forward and went over to Aidan. She gasped as she surveyed him. "Ankle, your pupils are huge!"

Pesh took his penlight out of his coat pocket and went to Aidan. As he flashed the light into Aidan's eyes, he grimaced. "Yeah, they are. What exactly happened?" He made sure to direct his question to Emma since she appeared to be the only one being honest.

"We were at my OB's for our first ultrasound."

Pesh's eyes widened. "Ultrasound…you're pregnant?"

"*Again?*" Megan questioned by his side.

The concern for Aidan on Emma's face washed away and was replaced with a beaming smile. "Yes, I'm eight weeks."

"Why didn't you say something at dinner Sunday?" Megan asked.

"Well, I only found out two weeks ago, and we wanted to wait to tell everyone until we had the first ultrasound."

Megan's blonde brows creased. "So what does the ultrasound have to do with Ankle hitting his head?"

Emma pursed her lips and cut her gaze over to Aidan. "Would you like to tell them?" When he shook his head and then winced, Emma sighed. "When they hooked me up to the fetal monitor, they thought they heard two heartbeats. At the word 'twins', Aidan passed out and hit his head on the counter and the floor."

While Pesh quickly turned a laugh into a cough, Megan wasn't so tactful. She burst out laughing. "You seriously passed out during the ultrasound?"

Aidan scowled at her. "In my defense, it wasn't quite the ultrasound yet." At Megan's continued laughter, he shrugged. "It was pretty mind-blowing news."

"Oh Ankle, honestly."

Aidan turned to Pesh. "So am I going to stand around all day getting shit, or are you going to examine me?"

Pesh nodded. "Of course. Your pupils are definitely a matter of concern."

Glancing at Emma, Aidan said, "Just wait for me here."

"Okay."

Pesh motioned for Aidan to go into the first examining room. As soon as the door closed behind him, Aidan lunged for him, grabbing the lapels of his white coat. "I need a vasectomy. *Today.*"

Pesh fought the urge to laugh at the absurdity of the situation as well as Aidan's desperation. "Okay, let's get you to sit down. You've obviously been through a lot of trauma in the last hour."

Aidan plopped onto the examining table. He buried his head in his hands and groaned. "What a fucking nightmare of a day."

"Does your head hurt?" Pesh asked.

"A little."

"Any nausea?"

"Maybe."

Pesh furrowed his brows. "What do you mean, *maybe?*"

Aidan raised his head. "If you're asking if I'm nauseated now, the answer would be no. I'm not. But on the other hand, if you're asking if I get nauseous thinking about the fact that Emma could have been pregnant with twins, and I would have had three kids under two and in diapers…" Aidan shuddered. "Then yeah, I get *really* fucking nauseous, and the room starts to spin a little."

Easing down on his stool, he rolled over to Aidan. "Take a deep breath for me, okay?" Aidan's chest expanded as he inhaled and exhaled. "Again," Pesh instructed. After a few cleansing breaths, Pesh cocked his head at Aidan. "Better?"

"Yeah, a little," Aidan croaked. He jerked his hand through his hair. "Are you going to get me a referral for a vasectomy?"

Pesh held up his hand. "I'm confused. If you know that Emma isn't having twins, why do you want to have a vasectomy?"

"Because twins run on both sides of our families. Pop was a twin, and Emma's uncles are twins. It's like we have a genetic bull's-eye hovering over us. We can barely be in the same room without conceiving, so it's just inevitable that she'll get pregnant again, and then I'll have four kids…maybe even five." Aidan swallowed hard as some of the color drained from his face. "I can't be a baby making machine."

"Actually, most recent studies still conclude that identical twins can happen to anyone, whereas, fraternal twins are the result of the mother producing two eggs in a single cycle. This tendency to create multiple eggs is passed from mother to child. Given that Emma doesn't have a non-identical twin, you are fairly safe."

Aidan tilted his head, his expression one of confusion. "So you're saying I don't have to worry about that?"

"Without knowing Emma's full genetic history, I couldn't say, but it sounds like a no—at least for fraternal twins."

After processing Pesh's words, Aidan shook his head. "Like it really matters about the twins. We're still way too fertile together. I need to stop this before it gets out of hand."

"And what does Emma think about all of this?"

A red flush entered Aidan's cheeks. "Um, well, I haven't actually mentioned it to her."

"You don't think your wife needs to know about such a life-altering decision?"

"Well, of course I'd tell her before I went in for the surgery."

As Pesh crossed his arms over his chest, he couldn't help wondering just how hard Aidan had been hit in the head. "You cannot seriously be sitting there saying that."

Aidan stared at Pesh for a moment before he groaned. "Oh man, I'm being a giant, selfish tool about this, aren't I?"

Pesh smiled. "Pretty much."

Aidan rubbed his hand over his eyes. "It's just…being a father is fucking scary sometimes. I worry about Noah constantly, and now there's another baby in the mix. Plus, another baby means more time taken away from Emma." He gave a weak smile. "I love her so much. Sometimes…I just can't get enough of her, and I don't want to share."

"I think that's a perfectly normal feeling."

Aidan shook his head. "It makes me sound like a selfish bastard. I mean, who is jealous of their kid for taking their wife's time?"

"A lot of men. So stop beating yourself up over what you're feeling. Most of all, don't bottle it up. Talk to Emma."

Aidan's blue eyes widened as he shook his head furiously back and forth. "Oh hell no, I don't want her thinking badly of me."

"She won't. Emma always appreciates honesty."

"About me being jealous of her time with our kids? I'm pretty sure she would not want me being honest about that."

"What has Emma always said is the most important thing in a relationship?"

"Trust."

Pesh nodded. "So how are you building her trust by lying to her about your feelings?"

Aidan's blonde brows furrowed. "So I should just tell her I'm afraid of losing her and that I want us to maximize our time together?"

"I would think so. I don't think any woman could get angry hearing her husband say how much he loves her and wants to be with her."

Aidan appeared thoughtful. "I guess you're right."

Pesh smiled as he patted Aidan's shoulder reassuringly. "You're doing a wonderful job being a father. I'm sure you'll do just as well with a second and maybe even a third child."

At the mention of a third child, Aidan swallowed hard, his Adam's apple bobbing up and down. "I don't mind a third kid…just not now. Maybe in a couple of years." He glanced up and smiled at Pesh. "But thanks for the vote of confidence on me being a father."

"I just call it as I see it."

"I appreciate that."

"How about I check on your head now?"

Aidan nodded. "Okay."

Pesh started feeling for unusual lumps and bumps on Aidan's head. "Hmm, I don't feel anything abnormal. But just to be on the safe side, I want you to have a CT scan to rule out concussion or any brain bleeds."

"Jesus, I could have all of that from just hitting my head?"

"You would be surprised. Let me go call in the order, and they'll come take you back. Hopefully you won't have too long a wait. We're usually slower during the afternoons when the doctors' offices and imaging centers are open."

As he started for the door, Aidan stopped him. "Hey, man, with all the craziness, I almost forgot to ask how is Megan doing with her placement?"

Pesh didn't have to think twice before responding, "She is going to make an incredible nurse."

Aidan grinned. "I'm glad to hear it. Not that I ever doubted her abilities. It's just good to hear her praises sung by a doctor." Popping Pesh on the chest teasingly with his hand, Aidan asked, "How's it going between you and Megan?"

Pesh almost laughed out loud at Aidan's forthrightness. It was not in his nature to be so blunt, and after Megan turning him down yet again, he wasn't really sure how to answer.

"I truly respect and admire Megan." He considered that the most diplomatic way to answer her uncle's enquiry. Despite feeling glad that he obviously had earned his friend's respect, he wouldn't say anything untoward about Megan in front of him. It is her business who she did or didn't date.

"That's not what I meant."

"I didn't imagine it was."

Aidan eyed him before saying, "Look I know you got off to a rocky start, but it's not hopeless. Are you planning on asking her out?"

"You're not letting this go, are you?"

"Nope. Not a chance."

Pesh shoved his hands into his lab coat. "I have asked Megan to accompany me on a date, but at this point, we are at a stalemate. But, I am not planning on giving up anytime soon. Does that satisfy your inquisition?"

Aidan laughed, but then his brows furrowed. "What do you mean? You two looked pretty cozy and comfortable together when we walked up."

With a regretful shake of his head, Pesh replied, "She doesn't want to date me."

"I call bullshit. I may have been bonked in the head, but no one could deny the way she was looking at you. Maybe if you—"

Although it was against his character, he let his anger override his better judgment. "She wants me for sex but not for a relationship, okay?"

Aidan's mouth gaped open. "You mean, she's acting like…a dude?"

"If you mean that she has pretty much refused to go to dinner with me or any other honorable event that a man and woman can partake in on a date, and instead, she would rather pursue a strictly physical relationship, then the answer is yes."

"My God, it's like she's turned into the old me," Aidan muttered. He ran his hand over his face before he looked at Pesh again. "I'm so sorry."

With a shrug, Pesh replied, "She's still very young. I suppose in her eyes, she's been deprived of fun the last two years. This is a way for her to make up for that. Regardless if we agree or understand it."

"Well, I still call bullshit on the whole thing." He gave Pesh a long, hard stare. "You have to keep trying, no matter what."

"I didn't say I was giving up, did I?"

"No, but I know from personal experience how hard it is to keep trying when it feels like you aren't winning."

"What occurred with you and Emma is totally different than with Megan and me."

"You still have to try." Aidan hopped off the examining table and wobbled for a moment on unsteady legs. "Megan has been hurt before, and I don't think she really knows what it is to be loved. Not deeply where her needs were considered. Hell, she was only twenty-three when she got knocked up. I want her to find someone who will cherish her, man. I want my girl cared for." He patted Pesh's shoulder. "I think that someone could be you."

"We'll see." When Aidan started to argue, Pesh shook his head. "Time to see about your head."

"Whatever," Aidan mumbled.

When Pesh opened the door for Aidan, Emma and Megan stared expectantly at them. "So what's the verdict?" Megan asked.

"I think he's going to be just fine, but to be on the safe side, I've ordered him a CT scan."

Emma's eyes widened in fear. "You think he has some brain injury from the fall?" she asked in a panicky voice.

Pesh smiled to try and put her at ease. "I don't think there's anything wrong besides a slight bump on the head, but I want to make sure there is nothing wrong with him."

"Okay then," Emma replied.

An orderly appeared with a wheelchair to escort Aidan to his scan. Before he sat down, Aidan leaned over to kiss Emma. "I'm fine, babe. Stop worrying. It isn't good for you or the baby."

She gave him a weak smile. "I'll try hard not to."

He winked at her before collapsing down in the wheelchair. "Nothing can keep me down—you should know that by now."

Megan snorted. "At least we know the bump didn't do anything to your ego."

"Of course not," Emma agreed.

Kristi poked her head out of one of the examining rooms. "Dr. Nadeen, I need you."

He nodded before turning to Megan. "Why don't you show Emma to one of the family waiting rooms?"

"Sure," Megan replied.

Emma reached up to hug him. "Thanks for taking care of Aidan."

"It was my pleasure." He gave them a final wave before disappearing into the waiting patient's room. But after talking to Aidan, he definitely had a little more determined bounce in his step.

Chapter
Nine

Two days later when Megan came in for a later shift, she found the emergency room in a state of chaos. "Whoa, what happened?" she asked Kristi, after she'd clocked in and put away her things.

Kristi rolled her eyes. "Every month or so we seem to have a day where everything is madness from start to finish. You can never anticipate it—you kinda just have to go with the flow." She grinned at Megan. "So get ready to be on your toes today."

Megan laughed. "Okay, sounds good."

As they started working their way through patients, things continued to escalate into overwhelming territory for Megan. Kristi seemed to be experiencing the same feeling since the tops of her cheeks had a shine of perspiration beads on them. The moment they finished with one patient and disinfected the room, another patient was waiting to enter it.

Megan followed behind Kristi as she went to poke her head in to the registration area. "Hey Janet, could you not call anyone else back? We're getting swamped."

Janet shook her head. "It's just as crazy out in the waiting room. Like we're almost overflowing."

Kristi rolled her eyes. "Fabulous. It's probably another full moon, which makes things absolutely insane." She turned back to Megan. "Listen, since we're so swamped, can you take the man in exam B?"

Megan couldn't help her eyes from widening. "Really? On my own?"

Kristi smiled before patting Megan's hand. "I've seen you in action the last week. I have faith in you."

"Okay, if you're sure."

"I'm positive."

Megan couldn't contain her smile. "Thank you."

Taking her iPad, she flipped open the registration details on the patient awaiting her. When she pushed open the door, she eyed the man on the examining table. "Good evening Mr. Robertson, I'm Megan. What—" Before she could even get out the standard "What seems to be the problem?" question, the man started shaking his head furiously. "No, no. I won't let you examine me. I want a doctor. *A male doctor*. You understand?"

"Sir, I understand, but I have to follow protocol, which is to ascertain your issues before the doctor comes in. I see on the chart that you're experiencing some abdominal swelling?"

He refused to meet her eye. Instead, he gazed over at the wall before holding up one finger to her. "I meant what I said. I demand to see a male doctor."

"Yes, but we're very backed up this afternoon. I'm not sure how long it will be before you are able to see a doctor, least of all a male doctor." When it appeared the man's resolve was fading a little, Megan took a tentative step forward. "Please, if you would just let me take a look at your abdomen."

"It isn't my stomach," he mumbled.

"Then what is it?" When he didn't respond, she sighed with frustration. "Mr. Robertson, you cannot ignore abdominal swelling. It can stem from many issues and have many repercussions."

He shifted uncomfortably on the table. Just when she thought she was making headway with him, he threw his head back and began screaming at the top of his lungs. "GET ME A MALE DOCTOR!"

Megan rolled her eyes. The first time she had the chance to see a patient on her own, and he had to be a stark raving lunatic. Refusing to give into him or accept defeat, she stalked over to him. She was going to exam his sexist ass if it was the last thing she did. "Keep screaming, and I'll call security," she warned before snatching the sheet off him.

His screams cut off to a shriek as he clawed for the sheet, but the damage was done. She had seen more than enough.

"Oh. My. God," she murmured. She gazed wide-eyed and open-mouthed at what had to be the poster child picture to go along with the warning labels on Viagra and Cialis for four-hour erections. "That's going to have to be aspirated."

"Excuse me?" he demanded.

She cocked her head at him. "The excessive blood in your penis?" He nodded. "It's not just going to go away on its own. It has to be aspirated, which means drained out."

Mr. Robertson swallowed hard. "Like with a needle?"

"Yes, with a very large needle." When he started to protest, she brought her hand up. "Lucky for you, I cannot do the procedure—it is to be handled strictly by a doctor."

"A male?"

"If it came to your penis exploding from the pressure by waiting for a male doctor, would you seriously be that picky?" His blue eyes widened in horror. "Yeah, I thought so. I'll be back."

When she whirled out of the room, she ran right into the last person she wanted to have to deal with at the moment.

"I'm so sorry. Are you all right?" Pesh asked.

"I'm fine."

He smiled down at her. "Doing some patient evaluations on your own? That's wonderful."

"Um, well, yes and no."

His brows knitted in concern. "What's wrong?"

She couldn't imagine telling Pesh about Mr. Robertson's condition. The last thing she was going to do was refer the case to him. Draining an engorged penis should be left to the interns, not an attending physician. "Oh, it's nothing. He's just a little demanding."

At that moment, the door to the exam room flew open. Mr. Robertson stood hunched over, his legs an almost painful distance apart. He took one look at Pesh and his white coat, and he lunged at him. "Help me. Please!"

Although it was strictly against the nursing code, she would have loved nothing more than to have throttled Mr. Robertson right then and there. Pesh grasped Mr. Robertson's hands on his coat and pulled them down. "Sir, you need to get back inside. As unsteady as you are, you certainly do not need to be on your feet."

As Pesh led Mr. Robertson back to the examining table, Megan reluctantly followed them inside the room and closed the door.

"What seems to be the problem?"

Mr. Robertson glanced from Pesh to Megan and then back to Pesh. With a sheepish expression, he replied. "Um, I seem to be having some lower abdominal swelling."

Megan had to fight from rolling her eyes. She stepped between Pesh and Mr. Robertson and looked Pesh full on in the eye. "While the patient refuses to acknowledge his condition, it appears after examination that he has an extreme priapism."

At the word, color flooded into Pesh's tan cheeks, and he broke eye contact to momentarily stare down at the floor. His reaction was exactly what Megan had feared she would experience in the moment. She had hardly imagined his level of professionalism would allow him to be embarrassed about a medical condition. But of course, their past interactions made anything of the sexual kind a little more mortifying than if she was dealing with one of the male interns.

It took Pesh only a few seconds to recover, and then he immediately turned his attention to Mr. Robertson. "Did you take any erectile dysfunction medication in the last four to six hours?" When Mr. Robertson started to look at Megan, Pesh shook his head. "My nurse will stay with me through the duration of your care. So I will repeat once again, did you take any medication?"

"Cialis."

"How many milligrams?" When Mr. Robertson shrugged, Pesh demanded, "Are you being purposefully evasive, or do you not know?"

"I don't know, okay? I got it off a buddy of mine."

"Do you normally take medication that isn't prescribed to you?"

"I just wanted to try it out."

Pesh glanced over at Megan. "I'm going to ask for a full blood work-up. Who knows what else he might've taken."

Megan nodded and punched in the code on the electronic chart to get a member of the Phlebotomy team up to draw the blood. After going over to the dispenser, Pesh slid a pair of rubber gloves on. "I'm going to have to examine you now."

With a resigned huff, Mr. Robertson threw the sheet back. Megan bit down on her lip to keep from laughing at the expression on Pesh's face. She was pretty sure he hadn't had to deal with a lot of penises that resembled enormous eggplants in his career. Of course, her amusement quickly faded when she realized how awkward it was being in the room with him while he held another man's penis in his hand.

She tried busying herself with the electronic chart in front of her. She wanted to do anything but look at the scene unfolding before her. Once Pesh finished that part of the exam, Mr. Robertson eased back down on the examining table, and Pesh once again eyed the eggplant-colored penis.

"Precisely how long have you had the erection?"

"Five and a half hours."

"There doesn't appear to be any artery rupture, so we won't need to perform surgery. I think the quickest form of treatment, as well as the least invasive, would be to try an injection to narrow the veins and reduce the blood flow to your penis. That should reduce the swelling."

Mr. Robertson's eyes narrowed suspiciously. "And where do you have to give me the shot?"

"In the penis, of course."

With a gulp, Mr. Robertson replied, "Fine. Do it."

Pesh nodded. "Can you grab a syringe of alpha-agonist please?"

"Sure," Megan replied. She gladly retreated from the room to head to the medicine closet. After checking the syringe dosage, she reluctantly returned to Mr. Robertson's room.

"Thank you," Pesh said, as he took the medication from her. She watched with mild disgust, as well as fascination, as he took Mr. Robertson's penis in his hand. "Take a deep breath," he instructed.

The moment the needle pricked the skin, Mr. Robertson howled uncontrollably. Megan couldn't help rolling her eyes at what a complete pansy he was being about the pain. Once Pesh finished, he dropped the empty syringe in the biohazard container and then glanced back at Mr. Robertson. "If the swelling hasn't begun to dissipate in the next ten to fifteen minutes, we're going to have to take another course of action."

"What's that?" Mr. Robertson questioned, with a grimace.

"Aspirating the penis of the blood."

Mr. Robertson paled considerably. "Oh God, she mentioned that." He said the word she like Megan was a swarm of locust.

Pesh turned to smile at Megan. "Then she made a good call." He then eyed his pager that was going off. "Keep an eye on him. I'll be back in fifteen."

"Okay, I will."

Time ticked by agonizingly slow as she worked on charts and kept an eye on Mr. Robertson. Every few minutes, he was lifting up the sheet to eye his erection. Each time he grimaced, Megan imagined that the shot wasn't working and the swelling hadn't gone down. When Pesh entered the room again, he glanced from her to Mr. Robertson. "So how are we doing?"

She shook her head. "No change."

"I see." He went over to a drawer and searched through it before producing a very large syringe with a very thick needle. "I'm sorry, Mr. Robertson, but it looks like this is our only choice."

Mr. Robertson seemed speechless for the first time all night. "Ms. McKenzie, can I get you to assist me?" Pesh asked.

"Of course."

"I need you to help restrain him. I need him to be as still as possible."

Megan fought the urge to roll her eyes at his suggestion. Mr. Robertson had to outweigh her by a hundred pounds, not to mention that when pain got your adrenaline pumping, you were even stronger. But she did as she was told.

As Pesh brought the needle to Mr. Robertson's penis, she gripped her hands tight into his shoulders. When the needle pierced the skin, it took everything within her to keep him on the table. Gritting her teeth, she held her ground. Finally, when the last of the blood had been withdrawn, she was able to loosen her grip.

Pesh tossed the syringe into the biohazard container and then turned around. "I advise you take some Ibuprofen for both the pain and for the anti-inflammatory benefits. I would also do a round or two of using an ice pack on your crotch. It would be my strongest advice that you never take anymore erectile dysfunction medication until you actually need it."

"Whatever," Mr. Robertson croaked, collapsing back onto the table.

"Give him about thirty minutes, and then he needs to head on home. We'll need the exam room," Pesh instructed.

"Okay, I will."

He gave her a quick smile before exiting the room. After thirty minutes, she saw Mr. Robertson to the door of the ER. As he staggered into the waiting room, she shook her head.

"Megan," Kristi called.

"Yes?"

"Go ahead and take your dinner break now."

"Are you sure? I mean, I can work through it since we're so busy."

Kristi shook her head. "We're fine. Besides, you're going to need all your strength. Things are probably going to get even crazier after the sun goes down."

Megan tried not to appear horrified at the prospect. Instead, she ducked into the break room to grab her purse. When she came out, Pesh was waiting for her. "Where are you going?"

"Oh, it's my dinner break."

Pesh gave an impish smile. "How fortunate. It's mine as well."

Realizing what he was intending, she slowly shook her head back and forth. "No dates."

After crossing his arms over his chest, Pesh asked, "And how would it be a date if we happened to go to the cafeteria at the same time and sit at the same table?"

"You're pushing it, and you know it."

"After what we both just endured, how can you deny me the pleasure of buying your dinner?" A teasing twinkle flashed in his dark eyes—one she wasn't used to seeing on him. For some reason, she found it completely irresistible. "Besides, how can I possibly have romance on my mind when I just held another man's penis in my hands?"

Her eyes widened in shock at his words. "D-Did you actually just say that?"

"Yes, I believe I did."

She shook her head. "I can't believe you sometimes."

"Don't try to pin me as one thing or the other. Just take me as I am," Pesh suggested.

"I'll try." As they started to the elevator, Megan chewed her lip with unease. Turning to Pesh she asked, "What will people say if they see the two of us together?"

"That we're two single people having dinner," he replied.

"You're a physician, and I'm a clinical student. Couldn't I get in trouble?"

"Doctors and nurses often have dinner together on their breaks. The cafeteria is a pretty inconspicuous place for us to be alone together. If someone came upon us in one of the medicine rooms or an empty patient room, then we might have a problem."

"If you say so," she mumbled, as he punched the down button on the elevator.

After they stepped on the car, Pesh eyed her. "You really are worried, aren't you?"

She nodded. "My career means everything to me. I don't want to do anything to jeopardize it."

"Then I'll make sure we don't sit by ourselves."

"Thank you. I really appreciate that."

As the car started its decent down, Pesh threw his head back and exhaled a long breath. "Well, that was…"

Megan grinned at him. "The good doctor seems speechless. Surely in all your years in the ER, you've seen crazier or more mortifying cases."

He cocked his head, appearing thoughtful. "A screwdriver lodged in a rectum is probably the tamest."

"The tamest?" Megan questioned incredulously, as the elevator door dinged open.

Pesh laughed. "A man high on meth walking into the ER with his penis in his hand is probably the craziest."

Megan's hand swept over her mouth. "He actually cut off his…" She gazed around to make sure no one was listening to their conversation.

"Is the good nurse speechless?" he teased.

She rolled her eyes at him. "So what happened?"

"We got him sedated and into surgery as soon as we could. I heard they were able to sew it back on. I'm not aware of whether or not it was ever…fully functional again."

"That is crazy."

"I know."

Pesh handed her a food tray. As they surmised their choices, Megan asked, "Was that your standard line of questioning in a situation like that?"

"I think we've established that I haven't been privy to many priapism cases, but yes, any time there is an issue with the penis that is not related to the urethra or bladder, you would ask those questions." After the food service worker gave them both an odd look, Pesh looked pointedly at her. "Why do you ask?"

She shrugged. "Just to be prepared for the next time."

He cocked his brows at her. "Do you want to practice your line of questioning? You know, show me what you've learned?"

"Let's get our food first, shall we?"

"Okay."

After deciding that the grilled chicken salad was about the most appealing item in the food line, she grabbed a drink and some of the freshly baked chocolate chip cookies. Just as she inched up to pay, Pesh put his tray next to hers. He had chosen some kind of stir-fry that didn't look appetizing to Megan. When she dug in her purse for her wallet, he handed a twenty to the cashier.

As he took his change, she shot him a look. "What?" he asked.

"You buying my dinner doesn't look very innocent," she hissed, as they started toward the tables.

Pesh shook his head with a smile. "I highly doubt she's keeping the gossip mill going on how Dr. Nadeen bought the lovely new clinical student a salad."

"You never know," Megan countered. Trailing Pesh, she watched as he made his way over to a table filled with doctors and nurses. While the bottom half was filled with people, the top was practically empty.

"Mind if we take these seats?" Pesh asked.

"Go right ahead, Nadeen," a bushy haired doctor replied.

"We're expecting a few more to join us," he said, before covertly winking at Megan.

"You play a good game," she said, softly.

"Thank you."

She'd just finished drizzling dressing over her salad when Pesh said, "Ready to prove yourself?"

"Are we really going to talk about this while we eat?"

"You'll learn that most lunches and dinners are spent either reviewing cases or getting input on cases."

"Fine then." Putting on a professional air, she asked, "Have you taken any erectile dysfunction medication?"

After swallowing a bite of stir-fry, he replied, "No, never."

"Do you have trouble obtaining an erection?"

The twinkle returned to his eyes. "I would think you wouldn't need to ask that question after our previous encounter."

A shiver went down her spine as she remembered her core rubbing against the hardened ridge in his pants. "Considering it is unlikely that I would have any previous knowledge of the patient, just answer the question."

He gave her a sly smile. "No, never."

"Do you have trouble maintaining an erection?"

"I could once again point out that you had personal knowledge of how well I was able to maintain myself once aroused, but I'll refrain. Instead, I'll say no."

"Ha, ha, nice way to get your point in."

"I had to try."

She cocked her head at him, giving him a teasing smile. "If a patient was trying to flirt as much as you are during my questioning, then I would have to remind him that I am a professional."

"I see. Then forgive me for trying to undermine your professionalism."

"You're forgiven...for now."

He took a long swig of his iced tea. "You did really well back there."

"Really?"

"Yes, you did. For that to be your first case on your own, you managed to keep yourself together and to give the patient the best level of diagnosis and care you could."

She couldn't help the warmth rushing to her cheeks that his compliments caused. "Thank you. I appreciate your confidence."

"I think you're going to make an amazing nurse. I know that there will be many hospitals vying to hire you."

Megan shook her head. "I don't know about that."

"Don't underestimate your talents."

"You think they would want to hire me here?" she asked.

His brows rose in surprise. "You wouldn't mind a permanent placement here?"

She shrugged. "It hasn't been long, but I have been happy here. I like the people I work with. I guess I wouldn't want to go into the unknown when I know what I have here."

He swallowed a bite of his rice. "That's understandable." After wiping his mouth, he smiled at her. "I think they would be crazy not to make you an offer."

"I hope so."

Leaning in over his plate, he held her gaze. The intensity in which he stared at her caused her to shudder. She didn't like the effect he was having on her in the middle of the hospital cafeteria. A mixture of emotions coursed through her—warmth, safety, lust, happiness. She hadn't experienced that range of feelings with a man in a long, long time.

Finally, he spoke. "I know it would make me very happy to have you here, and I would do everything within my power to ensure you stayed."

Before she could reply, a tray smacked down onto the table next to her. One of the residents, a young male named Dr. Morris, grinned at the two of them. "So, I hear you two just handled a priapism case."

"Yeah, we did," Megan replied. She didn't dare look back at Pesh to gage his expression on being interrupted.

Dr. Morris groaned. "Oh come on. Give me the juicy details. I haven't gotten to see one of those yet. The best groin swelling I've had is when some idiot tried to pierce his balls, and they got infected."

When Megan wrinkled her nose, Pesh's laughter surprised her. Her gaze flew to him, and he winked. "I told you that the conversations we had over dinner were not exactly appetizing."

"I'm starting to believe you," she replied, with a smile. Somehow she managed to devour the rest of her salad while Pesh told Dr. Morris the ins and outs of the case. After she finished, she rose out of her chair. "I guess I better head back. You know, with everything being so crazy."

Surprisingly, Pesh didn't get up nor did he offer to walk her back. Instead, she saw an acceptance on his face that told her he was letting her go so there would be no suspicion raised about the two of them. "Thank you for dinner," she said.

"You're welcome," he replied, with a smile.

His smiles were starting to do something to her that she didn't like. They were no longer igniting her panties on fire; instead, they were making her long to spend time with him. She quickly slung her purse over her shoulder and strode out of the cafeteria. With the chaos surrounding her, she thankfully put Pesh out of her mind for the rest of the evening.

Chapter Ten

After two exhausting weeks in her clinicals, Megan was ready for a little R&R. So she was thrilled when Emma called her asking if she wanted to join her for a girl's day. She was even more stoked when Emma said that Aidan was willing to keep Mason, so he and Noah could play together. Even though she was sure her parents would have watched him, she hated imposing on them so much.

An hour after the call, she was pulling into Aidan and Emma's driveway. When she opened the backseat to get Mason out, he was already bopping up and down in his car seat with excitement. He loved Aidan and Emma's house, and he especially loved playing with Noah, even though they were eleven months apart.

She grabbed him and his diaper bag and then made her way up the front walk. Emma answered the door with Noah on her hip. "Hey, I'm so excited you could make it."

Megan grinned. "You should know by now I have no life except for Mason and work."

"I feel the same way sometimes," Emma replied, as Megan stepped through the doorway. As she walked through the foyer and down the hall to the kitchen, Mason squirmed to get down. Once she set him on his feet, he ran into the living room.

That's where Aidan was lounging on the couch with Beau on the floor next to him. "Beau!" Mason cried. He leaned in to hug the massive Lab. Megan never had to worry about Beau and Mason; he was truly a gentle giant when it came to infants and kids. Beau thumped his tail heartily at the attention.

Aidan glanced up from the TV and smiled. "Hey, how are you?"

She grinned as she reached down to kiss his cheek. "Good thanks. And you?"

"Great. Looking forward to having a man's day with the boys."

Megan laughed. "Yeah, with two kids under two, let's see how much fun you'll have."

Aidan shrugged. "It's good practice for me when the new baby gets here."

"Baby or babies?" she teased.

With his eyes widening, he quickly replied, "*Baby* singular. That was confirmed, thank God."

Cocking her head, she teasingly asked, "And when is the ultrasound to confirm the youngest Fitzgerald granddaughter is on her way?"

Aidan huffed exasperatedly. "Not for a few more months, smart-ass."

She brought her hand to her chest in mock outrage. "It was just a question."

"Yeah and considering you've had a kid yourself, I'm sure you know all too well at what month the gender ultrasound is."

Megan grinned. "I just think it's cool that I'll be the oldest granddaughter, and she'll be the youngest."

With a pained expression, Aidan groaned, "Whatever."

She ruffled his still unkempt bed hair playfully. "Relax, Ankle. You're going to be an amazing father to that little girl. She'll undoubtedly have you wrapped around her finger before she's even out of the womb."

"A man like me, or I guess I should say, a man like I used to be, does not want to bring forth daughters into the world."

"Payback is a bitch," she mused.

"Don't I know it," he grumbled.

Emma came into the living room then. She handed Noah to Aidan along with a bottle. "You sure you'll be all right today?"

"I'll be fine—*we'll* be fine. Won't we Mason?"

Mason glanced up from lumbering around the room on Beau's back. "Yeah!"

"See. Stop worrying." He gave Emma a very pointed look before adding, "A promise is a promise after all."

She flushed a little at his words, but then gave him a shy smile. When he winked playfully at her, Megan couldn't help feeling her chest tighten at the exchange. Seeing her once man-whore uncle now a loving, devoted husband and father was always surprisingly unnerving. But deep down, it was how much she truly wanted what Aidan and Emma had. Love, companionship, and devotion within marriage while having someone else to parent with you.

If you weren't so stubborn you could probably have something just like Aidan and Emma have with Pesh! But no, you have to keep believing that you're too young to get married. You're probably throwing away happiness with both hands just because you're afraid.

Emma brought her out of her self-deprecating tirade. "So what should we do first?" she asked, as they walked into the garage.

"Nails and toes?" Megan suggested.

"Mmm, that sounds good."

They both slid into Emma's SUV. As Megan buckled up, Emma turned to her. "I hope you don't mind that Casey is meeting us for lunch?"

"Of course not. The more the merrier. Besides, Casey is a hoot."

Emma smiled and cranked up the car. "That she is."

Before long, they were pulling into Starbucks to grab some coffee for Megan and tea for Emma. Then they walked around the corner to the nail salon. After relaxing manicures and pedicures, they drove about twenty minutes to meet Casey at their favorite little local restaurant that was housed in an old train depot.

As they walked up, they saw Casey sitting outside in the sunshine texting. "Hey girl!" Emma called.

Casey waved to them before rising off the bench. "Hello, hello."

A round of hugs was exchanged between the three women. "I thought you two would never get here. *I'm starving.*"

Emma grinned. "Sorry. They were a little behind at the nail salon."

They pushed through the front door and were quickly seated by the hostess who knew them well. Once they eased into a familiar, comfortable booth, they took stock of the menus.

"You have to order alcohol on our behalf since we're both two knocked-up ladies now," Casey insisted.

Megan's eyes widened. "I didn't know you were pregnant."

Casey grinned. "Yeah, Nate finally wore me down." She then shook her head. "Sometimes I think he's the chick in this relationship."

"He must've done some heavy convincing," Megan said.

With a nod, Casey replied, "He comes from such a large immediate and extended family that he's been itching to have a child. We've been married a year and together eight, so I guess it was just time. And while I wasn't thrilled with the idea of having a baby when his internship was so crazy, his hours will be better by the time the baby gets here."

"When are you due?"

"Around the same time as Emma."

That statement made Emma beam. "Our babies are going to be best friends, too. I just know it."

Casey grinned at the sentiment. "Or boyfriend and girlfriend..."

"That's a thought." Emma jerked her chin up. "I'm not sure I want your son corrupting my little girl."

With her dark eyes widening, Casey huffed, "And what if it's *my* daughter that *your* son is corrupting?"

Emma giggled. "If my son takes after his father, then that would be the case. But I think we also have to consider that if your daughter is anything like you, she'll be the one doing the corrupting."

Casey laughed. "That's true."

"Guess I should keep Mason clear of her too, huh?" Megan asked, with a smile.

"Probably," Emma replied.

After the waitress appeared to take their drink and food orders, Casey pinned Megan with an intense stare. "So," she began, quirking her brow at Megan. "I hear your doing your clinicals under Dr. McDreamy Bollywood."

Megan couldn't help but laugh. "If you mean I'm doing them under Dr. Nadeen, then the answer is yes."

Emma nibbled on her bottom lip before speaking. "Have things been awkward considering what happened the night of Noah's baptism?"

Before Megan could reply, Casey's eyes bulged. "Whoa, whoa. Hold the phone. Something happened between you two?"

Megan felt heat rising in her cheeks. It was almost too mortifying to repeat, but finally, she filled Casey in on each and every embarrassing detail that had happened.

"Man, he's so freakin' honorable, isn't he?" Casey mused.

"Yes, he is," Megan replied, glumly.

Emma shook her head. "There's nothing wrong with his honor. It's what attracted me to him in the first place. There are so few gentlemen left on the planet."

Before she could stop herself, Megan blurted, "But I didn't want a gentleman. I wanted to get laid."

Casey grinned. "Don't we all?"

Emma rolled her eyes. "Just when I think your pregnancy hormones haven't made you even more sex crazed, you go and say something like that," she grumbled.

Megan twirled the straw in her Diet Coke thoughtfully. "What's bizarre is even though he should have been completely and totally turned off by what happened that night, he's still interested in me. I mean, the man is gorgeous and has half of the women in the hospital panting over him, and he still wants me."

"Then what's the problem?" Emma asked.

"He's interested in dating, not sex."

Emma's brows furrowed. "But wouldn't you have sex eventually if you were dating?"

Megan sighed. "We're at a stalemate—I just want straight sex without dinner and a movie, and to quote him, he wants to show me a whole new world through a date."

"How Aladdin of him," Casey quipped to which Emma shot her an exasperated look.

With a shrug, Megan replied, "Basically we're going to stay forever in the friend zone because neither one of us is willing to give in."

"Would it really kill you to go out with the guy?" Casey asked.

Megan widened her eyes in surprise. "You mean, you of all people are actually advocating me giving in to him?" She jerked her thumb over at Emma. "I'd expect that out of her but not you."

Casey dabbed the corners of her lips with her napkin. "It's just a date. I don't think he's going to drug you and drag you to a wedding chapel."

"I'd certainly hope not."

"So what's wrong with having an innocent dinner and maybe a movie?" Casey asked.

"Because that's not fair to him. I'd just be leading him on, and I think we can all agree that he doesn't need that."

"Exactly," Emma agreed.

Cocking her head, Casey eyed Megan thoughtfully. "Deep down, you like him, don't you?"

Megan rolled her eyes. "Of course I do. Everyone likes him."

"No, you really like him. You find yourself thinking about him more than you should. And you're kinda wishing you weren't such a stubborn ass about dating him. Because even though you'd kill to know how well he uses his wang, you're even more intrigued about what being loved by him would be like."

Dumbfounded, Megan could only stare at Casey. She'd certainly hit the nail on the head about her feelings. Finally, she sighed. "Look, it's a no-win situation. I'm a nursing student. I can't get involved with a physician. It just wouldn't look good on my record. That's just one of the many reasons it wouldn't work between us."

"Fine. You just keep telling yourself that."

"Why don't we talk about something else?" Megan suggested.

"Who's up for a movie after we hit the mall?" Emma asked.

Megan chewed her lip. "Oh, I don't know if I should be gone that long. I don't want to take advantage of Ankle's kindness for watching Mason."

Emma shook her head. "He won't mind. He's happy to do it."

As Megan raised her brows skeptically, Casey snorted. "Lemme guess, you bribed him sexually to get him to give up a perfectly good Saturday watching two kids who are under two."

A red flush entered Emma's cheeks. "I don't know what you're talking about."

Casey laughed. "Oh Em, you are so busted!" Leaning forward, she put her elbows on the table and stared straight at Emma. "So what was it? Green lingerie? A blow job? Maybe a blow job while wearing green lingerie?"

Refusing to meet Casey's inquisitive gaze, Emma finally murmured, "It was a blow job in the shower this morning, okay?"

Casey snickered. "I knew you had done something. Hmm, that was fun. It was like solving a sexual game of *Clue*—it was Emma in the shower with a blow job."

Megan brought her hands up to cover her eyes. "Umm, hello? That's my uncle you're talking about."

"Sorry, sorry. I'll refrain from making any more comments about Aidan and Emma's sex life."

"Thank you," Megan and Emma replied in unison.

"Shopping and a movie then?" Casey questioned.

Megan reluctantly agreed. "I'll just blame you two if Ankle gets all pissy."

Casey winked. "Just blame Emma. Then he can take it out on her later…in the bedroom."

"I seriously hate you," Emma grumbled.

Thankfully, the food arrived then and all sex-based conversation was forgotten. At least for the moment.

Chapter Eleven

Brushing his hand across his sweaty brow, Pesh leaned back against the glass door of the trauma area. As the adrenaline began depleting from his system, he needed to prop against something hard for support. Regardless of how physically drained he felt, he was emotionally on cloud nine. A beaming smile lit up his face as he stared across the room at the gurney. On it, a young woman was getting acquainted with her newborn son. She had been brought in just twenty minutes before after a car accident sent her into early labor. The paramedics had gotten her through the roughest patches, but thankfully, they had made it to the hospital in time. Because her labor was so advanced, they hadn't risked getting her up to the Labor and Delivery floor. Instead, they'd wheeled her in, and Pesh had gone to work. It really was an amazing moment considering he'd only delivered three other babies in the history of his medical career. Each one was an experience he treasured.

The woman glanced up at him and smiled. "Thank you so much, Dr. Nadeen."

"You're very welcome. They will be taking you up to maternity in just a few minutes."

As he stepped out of the room, he found himself ambushed by Kara, one of the shift nurses. "Hey there. How's the good doctor doing today?"

The way she spoke was more of a purr, which was a pretty apt summation since she basically acted like she was a cat in heat anytime he was around. He cringed as she ran her hand up his arm. "It's fine, thank you. How are you?" he questioned politely.

"I'm better now that I've seen you," she replied.

"Yes, well, I need to go see about my next case."

Her heavily painted lips turned down in a pout. "Aren't you ever going to want to get a drink again?"

Inwardly, he groaned. In a moment of weakness when he was still reeling after what had happened with Megan, he had allowed her to talk him into getting a drink after work. Once turned into several times, and then he did the unthinkable. He had made out with her in his car under the faded lights of the bar's neon sign. Well, making out didn't quite sum up the fact that she had given him a blow job. Although he had vowed to never let anything like that happen again, he found himself walking a fine line around her whenever they were at work.

"Um, sure. Maybe. Things have been really busy."

"I hope that you'll free up some time. I really, really need a night out with you again." Reaching around him, Kara did the unthinkable. She squeezed one of his ass cheeks. A gasp of shock behind him caused him to whirl around. Of all the people in the world that could have been standing there, it had to be Megan.

Pesh quickly jerked out from Kara's reach. Megan's eyes bulged at the two of them before she quickly looked away. With her head ducked, she started past them. The last thing in the world he needed was for something to be awkward between them. Without another word to Kara, Pesh turned and fell in step beside Megan. "What are you doing?" she asked.

He shrugged. "Nothing. Just walking with you. Is that a problem?"

Glancing over her shoulder at Kara, Megan said, "It looked like you were a little busy back there."

With a grimace, he said, "The conversation and the contact were unwanted by me."

Megan stared up at him. "Why am I not surprised by that?"

He eyed her curiously. "Just what do you mean?"

"You are not the type of man who does public displays of affection...or I should say lust."

"Haven't we already established that you shouldn't try to typecast me? I don't fit into any of the preconceived holes you have tried to put me in."

"There is one hole that you remain firmly lodged in, and that is being a gentleman when it comes to women and sex."

As much as he hated to admit it, she had a point about him being a gentleman. He touched her arm, urging her to stop. "Yes, I am a gentleman both in public and private. But let me address part of your assumption. When I am committed to a woman and she is committed to me, there is never a time I would reject public displays of affection or lust."

Megan's lips curved up in a smile. "So what you're saying is you would actually grab your girlfriend's ass in public?"

"Yes, I would." Glancing around, he found them happily out of anyone's earshot. "When I am truly committed to a woman, I have trouble keeping my hands off her regardless of where we are."

"That's good to know," she replied, with a wink.

He couldn't help the silly grin that filled his face as she hurried down the hall to join up with Kristi. He was making progress with her, wasn't he? Surely Megan had to be seeing how much she enjoyed spending time with him in the hospital and would soon decide that she wanted more. His smile started to fade as he wondered if he was deluding himself.

With a resigned sigh, he made his way over to the reception bay to sign off on some charts. He eased down on a stool and immersed himself in the paperwork, so he didn't have to think about Megan.

"Alpesh!" a voice across the room shouted. He snapped his head up. Without even looking over his shoulder, Pesh knew who the voice belonged to. Few people in his life addressed him by his full name, and no one in the hospital ever called him by his first name.

Slowly, he rose off his stool and turned around. His youngest brother, Dev, stalked toward him with a stormy expression plastered on his face. As the oldest of his three siblings, he had always felt a responsibility to look out for his two brothers and sister. While Arjan and Shveta had never given him any trouble, Dev, as the spoiled baby of the family, had been a challenge for both Pesh and his parents.

After experiencing teenage rebellion and a wayward early adult life, he had managed to get his wild ways under control when he was twenty-five. Dev had set his sights on a beautiful nurse Pesh had befriended when he was still a resident. Mia Martinelli had been through hell with an abusive boyfriend, so Pesh was reluctant to pair the two together. But at Dev's continued insistence, Pesh fixed the two of them up. What followed was a three-year courtship and then engagement. Mia was accepted and loved by all of Pesh's family. And then Dev had gone and thrown it all away by cheating on Mia. In her heartbreak, Mia had stayed close to Pesh, and he wanted her to be happy more than anything else in the world.

Pesh would have liked to have been surprised by his brother's visit, but ever since he had been summoned to console Mia a few days before, he had been anticipating it. Truthfully, he had been bracing himself for his brother's wrath. "Hello Dev," he said, in a calm voice.

Shaking his head furiously, Dev said, "I just got a fucking blow off text from Mia. When I tried calling her back to demand she explain herself, she couldn't talk because she was in Mexico. With AJ."

"Yes, I'm aware of that."

Dev's dark eyes narrowed at Pesh's confirmation. "So it's true that you went to talk to her?"

"Yes, it is."

"I can't believe it." He threw up his hands in frustration. "I didn't want to believe anything Mia said, especially that it was you who helped her see that she shouldn't give me a second chance and take me back—that she should make things work with AJ."

"It's all true. You and I both know Mia would never lie."

"But how could you?" Dev demanded, in a strangled voice.

"I'm sorry, but I had to do what was best for Mia."

Dev's brows shot up. "And what about me? I'm your fucking blood."

With a sigh, Pesh replied, "I'm sorry, my brother, but blood or not, I couldn't stand by and let you hurt her again—she's been through too much."

"I love her!" Dev shouted, which caused several of the nurses to spin around in shock.

"This is not the time nor the place to be having this discussion," Pesh growled.

"I'm not going anywhere, so you better start explaining yourself before I really start a scene."

Pesh shook his head. "Fine. You want the truth? Here is it. You only think you love Mia. You and I both know you cannot be faithful to a woman."

"I could have for Mia."

"You already failed her once. She deserved better."

Dev narrowed his eyes. "What, are you fucking her now?"

He grimaced at his brother's choice of harsh words. "Of course I'm not. There's never been anything amorous between Mia and myself. Thankfully, she's back with the man she loves—the father of her unborn child."

"But I need her," Dev insisted, his voice taking on a plaintive tone.

"I'm sorry, but I think it's best if you moved on. Most of all, baby brother, I think you need to do a lot of soul searching and maturing before you even think about getting in another relationship."

Dev's eyes widened. "You...You fucking bastard!" he shouted. Pesh was debating calling security to remove his unruly brother when he was knocked off his stool by Dev's right hook to his jaw. He tumbled backward and crashed onto the floor. Before Dev could do something like kick him when he was down, Megan appeared and wedged herself between them.

"I think you better leave before I call security," she demanded.

Pesh struggled to his feet as Megan came into Dev's line of fire. He couldn't bear if Dev hurt her in his anger just because she had taken up for him. Dev stared down at Megan with a smirk. "So my brother needs some pint-sized pussy defending him now? Word to the wise, sweetheart, don't waste your time on him. He's only got a boner for his dead wife."

A deep growl erupted in Pesh's throat as he lunged for his brother. But he never made it. Instead, Megan's fist cracked into Dev's jaw. The impact didn't take him off his feet, but he did stagger backwards. Even as she flailed her wrist back and forth from the obvious pain, Megan still managed to bellow, "Get the hell out of here. *Now.*"

Dev stared at her in shock as he rubbed his jaw. "Crazy bitch," he muttered, before stalking off.

When Megan turned to him, her glowering expression faded to one of concern. "You're bleeding!" she cried, rushing for him.

His hand came up to grip his cheek. Surprise flooded him when he felt wetness. Dev must've hit him harder than he thought. He slid his jaw back and forth, causing him to grimace at the popping sound. "Come here," Megan said, grabbing his hand.

She started leading him over to one of the examining rooms, but he jerked back. "I don't need all this fuss."

Megan shook her head. "We need to get you cleaned up."

Resignedly, he followed her into the room. For the first time in a long time, he found himself on the opposite line of care. He eased down onto the examining table. "Really, Megan, this isn't necessary."

As she busied herself taking out gauze, cotton balls, and antiseptic, she replied, "Quit your bitchin'." She glanced over her shoulder at him. At what must have been his incredulous expression at her word choice, she grinned. "That's right. Just shut up and let me take care of you."

"When you put it like that, how can I not?" he teased.

Her laughter warmed his heart. Deep down, he was pleased to find her so attentive to him. She obviously really cared about him if she insisted on cleaning him up. Or was she just attentive because she was a great nurse? But then there was the fact she punched Dev for insulting him. Of course, that was also mortifying. Did that mean she questioned his manhood since he didn't go toe-to-toe with his brother? God, what she must think of him now.

As he allowed Megan to treat his cuts, his thoughts turned to Dev's last verbal punch. He grimaced about Dev's alluding to the fact he was in love with a ghost. Was that what stopped Megan from believing his attraction to her? Was she really hiding her commitment phobia behind a belief that he was still completely in love with his wife?

His feelings gave him away when Megan asked, "Are you hurting?"

"No, I'm fine." When she gave him a skeptical look, he replied, "It's more the fact that I'm angry than I am physically hurt."

"So what exactly was all that about?" she asked, as she dabbed some antiseptic along his jawline.

He winced when the medication hit the broken skin. "My brother is angry with me."

Megan snorted. "No shit." She held the cotton ball frozen as she eyed him curiously. "What I'm wondering is what got him so fired up that he would stomp into a hospital, call you out, and then punch you? You are the last person on earth I would imagine being in a fight."

"The reason is so cliché," he murmured.

"Enlighten me," she urged.

"He's a petulant child who didn't get his way—he's lashing out at me because he thinks it's all my fault."

"I heard the name Mia. Was it all about a woman?"

"Yes, that's why I called it cliché." He sucked in a harsh breath before filling Megan in about what all had transpired between him, Dev, and Mia.

"Wow," she murmured, when he finished.

"I suppose that is all one can say about the situation."

"You were awfully kind to take care of her like you did—I mean, with both her abusive ex-boyfriend and Dev."

He shrugged. "What else was I supposed to do? I cared for her, and I wanted to see her happy." At the look that flashed in Megan's eyes, he quickly added, "There was no amorous love between us. I was happily married at the time, and she desperately needed someone to be strong for her."

Megan cupped his unhurt cheek in her hand. "You really are the most decent man I've ever known."

"I don't know about that," he murmured.

"You truly are." She shook her head. "No wonder women are so crazy about you. It's one thing for you to be so good-looking and a smart doctor, but then when you add in the fact of how sweet, caring, and compassionate you are, it's like you're a triple threat." She turned to throw the cotton ball into the trash can.

His heartbeat thrummed louder and louder at her words while he sat unblinking and unmoving. Part of him wanted to rail at her for not seeing him like all the other women did. If she truly saw what others did, then she would want to date him, wouldn't she? Why couldn't she see how good he could be for her?

When Megan met his tense gaze, she jerked back and momentarily faltered by dropping the piece of gauze in her hand. She quickly deposited the soiled one in the trash and then got another one. "So this Mia chick, she's run off with some drummer, huh?" she asked, clearly trying to change the subject and lighten the mood in the room.

"Not just any drummer. A famous one at that."

"Really? What band?"

Pesh's cocked his head as he tried remembering. "Something train."

Megan gasped. "Not Runaway Train?"

He snapped his fingers. "That's it."

Clapping her hand to her chest, Megan's eyes widened. "You know someone who knows AJ Resendiz?"

Pesh laughed. "I suppose I do if you consider that's Mia's fiancé."

"That is so wild. I *love* that band."

"I'll see if I can get you an autograph."

With a squeal, Megan said, "Really? That would be amazing."

"Anything for the woman who is willing to risk her life for me."

Megan laughed. "It was nothing."

"What about your hand?"

"I'm not going to lie. It hurts. I kinda forgot what punching someone felt like."

Pesh couldn't help his brows from rising in surprise. "Have you done a lot of fighting?"

She grinned. "Not exactly MMA material, am I?" When he merely shook his head, she replied, "I may have thrown a few punches in my early college partying days when a guy overstepped his bounds."

With a smile, Pesh said, "Good for you."

"Yeah, my dad was really big on teaching me self-defense moves. You know, with him being ex-military."

Pesh couldn't help liking Megan's strength and spunk. He hadn't known a lot of women like her. In his world, women were bred to be demure and obedient. Even though Jade wasn't Indian, she would've never dreamed of throwing a punch to defend him against Dev. But Megan, she was so refreshing with her ability to stand up for herself and others—to voice her mind whether it was good or bad.

"You would have made your father very proud today."

"Thank you. I'm sure later on today when my knuckles are bruising, he'll want to know why."

"I'm very sorry." He took her hand in his before bringing it to his lips. "Here's a kiss to make any bruises go away."

She gave him a teasing smile. "Is that the best medicine you can do, Dr. Nadeen?"

His mind went wild with illicit images of all the "medicine" and "healing" he could give her. A chaste kiss to alleviate her pain was all he could really offer. His pager went off before he could reply. "I better go." He hopped off the table and started for the door. As his hand hovered over the doorknob, there were so many things he wanted to say to her. But finally, he just said, "Thanks again for taking care of me."

"You're welcome."

"And you should probably ice your hand during your break tonight."

"Yes sir," she replied, with a mock salute.

He shook his head at her with a smile before heading out the door.

Chapter Twelve

Days melted into weeks as Megan immersed herself in her clinicals. Every day she found a new challenge to conquer. She hadn't imagined how hard it would be, or how exhausted she would be most nights when she crawled into bed. But it was a thrilling exhaustion because she was doing what she felt like she was called to do.

Each day, she spent more and more time with Pesh. She loved working beside him on cases. He had the best bedside manner of all the residents and interns. Patients, both young and old, adored him. And the more she was with him, the more Megan began to adore him as well.

She had just left an examining room where he had charmed a little boy into finally letting them run the tests they needed when Kristi beckoned her from down the hall. After hustling to join Kristi, Megan was quickly ushered inside one of the trauma rooms.

Immediately, her entire body switched gears as she prepared herself for what she might face.

"Female, thirty, car accident," the paramedic began before rattling off her vitals and other information. After Megan had absorbed the information, she turned to the patient. "Hi, I'm Megan. I'm going to get your IV started."

The woman gave Megan a weak smile. "I'm Mary."

"I guess it would be wrong to say it's nice to meet you, huh?" Megan said, trying to talk as normally as she could to put the patient at ease.

"Yeah, I guess so," Mary replied.

When Megan reached for Mary's arm to find a place for the needle, Mary winced. "Ouch."

As Megan surveyed the forearm, she shook her head. "Looks like you've got a break there."

"My arm is broken?" Mary asked in a panic.

"We won't know until we get you into X-ray. I'm going to try this vein here in your wrist." The needle slipped easily into the vein, and Megan started the IV.

Pesh appeared in the doorway then. He smiled at Mary on the gurney. "Hello, Mary, I'm Dr. Nadeen. I understand you had a little accident today?"

She nodded. "This car came out of nowhere and hit me head on."

"I'm so sorry. Why don't we start by you telling me where it hurts?"

"My chest," she said, with a grimace.

Pesh pulled back the hospital gown. "Were you wearing your seat belt?"

"Yes, I always do."

"From the dust in your hair, can I assume the airbag deployed?"

"Yeah, it did."

"Is this where it hurts?" he asked, running his fingers down an angry red whelp. It started at her neck and crossed over her chest. Some of it was hidden by the many leads coming from the heart monitor.

"Yeah."

"It looks like the seat belt and the airbag did a number on you."

Mary winced. "I thought they were supposed to help you, not hurt you."

Pesh smiled. "Trust me. You're much better off with a little burn than if you hadn't been wearing it." After eyeing the monitors Mary was hooked up to, he turned to Megan. "Blood pressure is low. Let's administer some blood products to raise it."

Megan nodded. After checking Mary's chart for her blood type, she grabbed a bag of blood from the coolers. Trading places with Pesh, she started another IV in the crook of Mary's right elbow.

"Besides your chest, are you hurting anywhere else?" Pesh asked, after he finished listening to her heart and lungs.

"My stomach."

Megan's breath hitched. It was never good for a car accident patient to have stomach pains. That usually meant hemorrhaging, which could also attribute the low blood pressure.

Pressing on Mary's abdomen, Pesh asked, "Does this hurt?"

"No."

"Here?"

"No."

"What about here?"

A screech came from the bed. Pesh's brows drew with worry. "I'm going to do a quick ultrasound, Mary. I want to see what's causing the pain."

"Okay."

Megan pulled the machine over to the bedside. She squirted the jelly onto Mary's stomach, and then Pesh began running the wand over the skin.

"I'm feeling a little dizzy, too," Mary said, in a low voice.

Pesh and Megan exchanged a quick look before he shoved the ultrasound machine back. Turning to Kristi, he said, "Call the OR. She's got a ruptured spleen."

After depressing the break on the gurney, Pesh swung it out of the trauma room and started down the hall. "Go with him," Kristi instructed, as she held onto the phone.

Megan jogged down the hall to catch up with Pesh. He smacked the buttons on the elevator before glancing down at Mary. "Stay with me, okay? We're going to get you into surgery, and then you'll be good as new."

"Are you sure?" she asked.

Without hesitation, Pesh replied, "Yes, but you have to stay with me."

The elevator's doors slid open. As Megan helped Pesh push the gurney inside, Mary asked, "Did you turn on more lights?"

Megan creased her brows in worry as she glanced over to Pesh. "We're getting in the elevator to take you to the OR for surgery," she replied.

"But it's so bright," Mary whispered before closing her eyes. Her head lolled to the side just as the alarms on the monitors began screeching in Megan's ears. "Dammit, she's crashing!" Pesh cried.

Ice-cold fear pricked its way from the top of Megan's head all the way down her body. A patient was crashing in the elevator without the crash cart. What the hell were they supposed to do? "Lower the gurney," Pesh ordered.

Megan's jerky hands fumbled with the lever. Once it was flat, Pesh brought his hands to Mary's chest and began compressions. Without having to be told, Megan leaned down, pinched Mary's nose, and began breathing into her mouth. They worked in perfect synchronization.

"Stay with me, Mary!" Pesh barked, as his hands pumped in a manic pace up and down on Mary's chest.

Glancing up from her breathing, Megan eyed the monitors. "No pulse."

When Pesh didn't respond, she continued doing breathing cycles. At the taste of something warm meeting her lips, she jerked back. Blood oozed out of Mary's mouth. "There's more damage than the spleen. She's bleeding from the mouth." Pesh didn't even acknowledge her comment. "The seat belt and airbag could have caused an aortic tear as well. There's nothing we can do."

Instead, he kept right on with his compressions. The elevator doors opened, and Megan met the expectant faces of the surgical team. When one doctor stepped forward, she shook her head. "She's gone."

Pesh growled across from her. "No, she isn't. We have to keep trying. Get a cart in here."

The doctor eyed the stats on the monitors. "I don't think it will help."

Jerking his head up from Mary, Pesh snarled, "Get the fucking cart!"

As one of the nurses scrambled away, two others pulled the gurney from the elevator. Megan stood back, feeling helpless as to what to do. Once the cart arrived, Pesh ripped open Mary's gown. "Charging 260 joules." He rubbed the paddles together. "Clear!"

Mary's chest jolted off the gurney with the force of the electricity. Megan didn't need to look at the monitors. The heart stayed in a flat line. "Charging 360 joules." Megan closed her eyes when Pesh administered the second shock. "Dammit, Jade, don't do this! Try for me!"

Megan couldn't hold back the gasp that escaped her at Pesh calling Mary by his late wife's name. Before Pesh could do another charge, one of the surgeon's stepped forward. After he removed his mask, he put his hand on Pesh's back. "Calling time of death."

Defeated, Pesh dropped his head. Slowly, he eased back from the gurney. A nurse took the paddles from him and put them back on the cart. "I'll go notify the family," Pesh murmured.

The surgeon shook his head and stared pointedly at Megan. "Get a resident to do that. Nadeen, you go take a breather, buddy."

"They deserve to speak to the doctor who was with her when she died."

"You don't need to do this."

Pesh slung away from the surgeon and started for the elevator. Megan knew there was no point in arguing with him or trying to get one of the residents to take his place. She didn't know if she should try to go to him or not. She regretted her decision when he turned to face her in the elevator. His expression was agonizingly broken. As the doors closed, her heart ached for him. She knew any doctor hated to lose a patient, especially a young one, but this went far deeper than that. From his behavior, Megan knew that Mary's death had exposed a raw nerve in Pesh—one that after two years still hadn't healed. Somehow he had seen his wife in Mary, and once again, he wasn't able to save her.

After she had escorted Mary's body back upstairs to wait on the funeral home, Megan went in search of Pesh. She couldn't find him in any of the exam rooms, nor was he in the doctors' lounge or break room. Finally, she went to Kristi for answers. "Did you see where Dr. Nadeen went?"

Kristi gave her a sad smile. "You'll probably find him on the roof."

Megan's brows shot up in surprise. "The roof?"

Kristi nodded. "Whenever he has a really bad day about his wife—" She sucked in a breath when she realized she might have said too much.

At the thought of Pesh's grief, Megan's chest tightened in agony. He was too good of a man to have to suffer like he did. "So he goes up to the roof?" Megan finished for Kristi.

"He likes to be alone to clear his head. Although none of us would say anything, he usually ends up pulling another shift to make up for the time he was gone."

Of course Pesh would do something like that. He was honorable every moment of his life, even after those of immense grief. Even though she knew he probably wanted and needed to be alone, Megan wanted to check on him. She couldn't bear the thoughts of him suffering so much.

"Um, if it's okay, I think I'll go ahead and take my dinner break."

Kristi gave her a knowing look before nodding. "Sure, honey. Go right ahead."

Megan smiled before brushing past Kristi. She bypassed the break room where her purse was. Instead, she kept going. After a brisk walk down the hall, she got to the Authorized Personnel Only stairwell. She didn't dare use the elevator shaft where trauma patients were brought in from being airlifted. Without hesitation, Megan swiped her access card. When the lock clicked, she flung the door open and started up the flights of stairs. She was winded when she reached the top. Cautiously, her hand hovered over the doorknob. She couldn't help wondering what she might find on the other side. Would Pesh be an emotional mess? Would he be angry that she had interrupted his private grieving? Shaking the thoughts from her head, she flung open the door.

As she stepped onto the roof, the air grew cooler. A breeze rippled her scrubs. Her gaze spun around frantically until she found him. Pesh stood at the edge of the roof. His usual ramrod straight posture was slumped, his broad shoulders drawn in. Although she couldn't see his face, his gaze seemed fixed straight ahead into the night sky. To add insult to injury, clouds blotted out the stars, cloaking everything in darkness.

Tentatively, she started over to him. "Hey," she said softly.

He whirled around in surprise. Her heart clenched at the sight of the tears sparkling in his eyes. Even in the darkness, she could see a blood-red flush entering his cheeks. His hands quickly came up to swipe away the moisture from his eyes. "Hello," he finally replied in a hoarse whisper.

They stood in an awkward silence, staring each other down. Finally, Megan took a step forward to close the gap between them. "How did you know I was up here?" he asked.

"Kristi told me."

"Hmm."

Unable to stop herself, she reached out to touch his arm. "I'm so sorry, Pesh."

"It isn't necessary."

She shook her head. "Yes, it is. You're in pain…you've *been* in pain. I can't help but feel sorry for what you're going through."

His usually warm eyes took on a cold look. "You were in that elevator, too. You have every right to be emotional. Maybe you should be more concerned with why you aren't weeping."

"Don't," she murmured.

"Don't what?"

"Don't try to mask your pain by being someone you're not or by pointing fingers at others. That isn't you, and you can't fool me."

With a ragged sigh, Pesh jerked his hand through his dark, wavy hair. "I'm sorry. That was completely uncalled for."

"It's okay."

"No, it's—" She silenced him by bringing her hand up to cover his lips. When she pulled her hand away, he sighed.

"Talk to me," Megan pleaded.

The clouds above them opened up, causing a slight drizzle to fall. "The death of a patient is never easy. Any doctor of worth, or nurse for that matter, must possess compassion. Then it is inevitable that the same compassion you possess will come back to haunt you—it may even cripple you. When death comes, you can't help feeling for the life that has been lost and for the family members left behind." His voice choked off, and Megan drew herself even closer to him. She knew that his last statement held personal meaning for him.

"What exactly happened to your wife?" she questioned softly.

Pesh's eyes closed. "Jade had an undiagnosed clotting condition. She was adopted, so she didn't know anything really about her family history. She'd always been in perfect health—she rarely even went to the doctor with the sniffles. And after we'd been married for three years, we decided it was time to have a baby."

When Pesh remained silent, Megan tentatively asked, "Did she die in childbirth?"

He shook his head. "No, we never got that far. We tried for over a year to get pregnant on our own, and it didn't happen. So we were recommended to a fertility clinic. Once the IUI process didn't work, we started IVF." A ragged sigh came from deep in his chest. "The whole process was physically trying and then emotionally gutting for both of us, but especially for Jade." He met her gaze. "She blamed herself since the testing revealed that everything was fine with me. Although we were labeled as 'non-specific infertility,' she felt that it was all her fault."

"Bless her heart," Megan murmured, as her heart went out to a woman she'd never met. Getting pregnant had been so easy for her. Although Mason wasn't necessarily expected, he had never been unwanted in her eyes. But she knew what infertility did to a woman when she saw it ravage her father's sister. Although her aunt was now the happy and doting mother of two adopted girls, she knew the emotional toil not getting pregnant had taken. Megan, herself, had once been the recipient of her aunt's childless pain when she had announced her pregnancy with Mason.

Still without answers as to how Jade had died, Megan pressed Pesh for more. "So what happened with the IVF?"

"She got pregnant on the first transfer only to miscarry three weeks later. We had just been through another transfer when she died." Pesh's Adam's apple bobbed up and down as he swallowed hard. Megan could only imagine he was trying to keep his emotions in check. Finally, he spoke again. "She had an embolism most likely brought on by the fertility medication. I was in the kitchen making breakfast when I heard a crash in the bedroom." Tears pooled in his eyes. "When I called her name and she didn't answer, I ran back to her. She was crumpled on the bedroom floor. After calling 911, I did CPR over and over again, but I could never revive her."

"Oh Pesh," Megan murmured. The weight of his pain was so heavy that even she found it hard to breathe.

Without looking at her, he continued staring straight ahead. "From what the medical examiner said, I have some peace in knowing she didn't suffer—that she went quickly without any fear or pain. One minute she was getting ready for work, and the next she was gone."

"It's true that there is some peace, especially the fact she didn't know she was going to die. Sometimes I can't imagine what it must be like for terminal patients." She shuddered. "When you wonder if every day is your last, when you have to think about all you're going to miss."

"Yes, that is true," he said, in a hushed whisper. When he finally turned to look at her, he gave her a sad smile. "It's been two years. Every time I think I've moved on, that I've been able to compartmentalize my grief, a case comes through that brings me to my knees."

"I'm so sorry," Megan murmured, bringing her hand up to cup his cheek. He leaned his face into her hand. His head bowed until their foreheads met. "You have to remember that no matter what happened to your wife, and to Mary, it wasn't your fault. You weren't responsible. You need to keep living. You're alive." Tilting her head up, she gazed into his dark brown eyes. "You're *alive,*" she repeated.

The rain began to fall harder. Her eyelids fluttered to keep the moisture out of her eyes as she gazed up at him. His mouth hovered next to hers, his breath warming her cheek. She could barely breathe in that moment. It was like every molecule in her body was pulsing with need. Silently, she pleaded with her eyes for him to kiss her.

And then, after what felt like an eternity, he slid his lips over hers. It wasn't the first time she had kissed him—it was just the first time she was sober and had kissed him. Now her senses were heightened, and she could experience exactly what she was feeling. His lips were tender and soft at first, and then they switched over to desperate and demanding. It was like he was breathing her in with every brush of his lips and stroke of his tongue as if to prove to himself that he truly was alive. His tongue danced along hers, causing her to moan. He brought his hands up to cup her face while her arms went around his chest, pulling him closer to her.

Drops of rain pelted her head and ran down her cheeks while Pesh's white coat grew moist as she ran her hands up and down his back. She realized, in a dizzying flurry, that no man had ever kissed her like this before. This was like lovemaking with their mouths, and she never wanted it to end.

When Pesh finally tore his lips from hers, Megan's breaths came in heaving pants. Her eyes opened to stare up at him. His expression turned from lust to anguish. He shook his head. "I'm sorry."

"Pesh, you don't—"

He held up his hand. "Please, just go." He turned away from her, wrapping his arms around his chest. Torn, Megan didn't know if she should argue with him and stay or leave. "Please," he whispered.

With her heart still beating wildly from their passionate lip-lock, she turned and fled. As she pounded back down the stairs, her emotions yo-yoed to where she felt like a watch that had been wound too tight. After bursting back through the door, Kristi met her in the hallway. Her eyes widened at Megan's appearance.

"I, uh, I went outside on my dinner break, and it started raining," Megan lied.

"Next time you'll have to remember your umbrella," Kristi replied.

Megan nodded. "Yeah, I will."

"Why don't you go to the break room? There's a hair dryer under the sink. When you finish drying off, I could really use you in the supply closet doing inventory. Seems like we always almost run out of everything at once."

"Sure. I can do that." As Megan turned to go down the hallway, Kristi reached out and grabbed her arm.

"Is he okay?"

Megan bit down on her lip to keep a hysterical laugh from escaping. Was Pesh okay? Was she okay? Who the hell knew? One minute he'd been weeping about his wife and losing a patient, and the next he'd been liquid passion dripping on her lips. Regardless of his emotional whiplash, she'd experienced the same. She now found herself wanting more of his kisses when she shouldn't. But it wasn't just the kiss she wanted—she wanted all of him and not just for sex.

"No, he's not. I guess he's just trying to accept the loss, both past and present, as best he can," she finally replied.

Kristi nodded in acknowledgement. When Megan felt she was free from any more questioning, she hurried down the hall to the break room. Thankfully, she found it empty. After grabbing a brush from her purse, she went to the sink to grab the hair dryer. Gazing at her reflection in the mirror, she looked a bedraggled mess. She was practically washed out except for her lips. They were swollen and bright red from Pesh's kisses. Her finger came up to trace her bottom lip. As memories of his kisses filled her mind, she tried desperately to think of anything else.

In the end, she had gone up to the roof to somehow save Pesh, and instead, she had lost herself to him and his emotions.

Chapter Thirteen

Pesh regretfully watched Megan's retreating form. He cursed under his breath as she disappeared into the stairwell. What was his problem? The woman had been merely comforting him, and he had allowed his libido to take over. He had promised her he would keep his distance. Regardless of the flirting and easy banter between them, he had kept things professional. Now she probably felt trapped and harassed by him. She tried to talk to him about it, and he'd dismissed her.

He paced around the rooftop as the rain that had soaked him to the bone began to dissipate. His mind was a jangled mess of thoughts and emotions. One voice argued over and over that Megan had wanted him to kiss her—that the look in her eyes told the truth. But Pesh worried that in his agony he had misread the signals she may or may not have been giving. In the end, he'd made a terrible situation even worse by not being able to control his feelings for Megan.

With a frustrated grunt, he realized he had to make things right with her. He needed to apologize. Casting one last look out over the horizon, he then turned and started for the stairwell. After pounding downstairs, he searched the hallway for any signs of Megan. When he spotted Kristi, he was surprised not to see Megan with her. "Where's Megan?" he asked.

"Oh, since we're kinda slow tonight, I asked her to go work in the storage closet. We're behind on inventory and cataloguing."

"I see."

Kristi eyed him up and down before shaking her head. "You're drenched."

"It's raining outside."

"So I've heard," she said knowingly.

"What does that mean?" he asked.

She waved her hand. "Nothing. Why don't you do us both a favor and go get out of those wet clothes? The last thing we need is you coming down with something."

Pesh knew it was fruitless to argue with her. Instead, he tucked his tail between his legs and made his way to the doctors' lounge. He took a clean pair of pants and shirt out of his locker. After he slid on a new white coat, he strode down the hall to the medicine closet. After swiping his key card, he entered the room. When he closed the door behind him, Megan turned around, gazing expectantly at him. Now that he was in front of her, he didn't know exactly what to say.

He had been on an emotional overload on the roof, and things had escalated far too quickly. "Look, I just want to say how very sorry I am about kissing you."

"Well I'm not," she replied matter-of-factly.

Pesh's neck snapped back in shock. Her response wasn't what he was expecting at all. He had imagined she might be relieved or even embarrassed, but he hadn't imagined that she would be unregretful. He cleared his throat. "Regardless, I shouldn't have done it. I was in an emotionally vulnerable position, and you were merely trying to comfort me. Nothing more." His words were more for his own good than hers.

She shook her head. "Just because I was comforting you, doesn't mean I didn't want you to kiss me. That I *still* don't want to kiss you again."

His brows furrowed in confusion. "But you—"

"Pesh, I've wanted you since the night of Noah's baptism. But you shot me down then, and you still do."

Although his heart wanted to soar at her admission of wanting him, the reality of her words caused his chest to clench instead. "Sexually. You only want me sexually."

"Yes."

He should have been flattered that a young, sexy woman like Megan desired him. But he wasn't. Half of the women in the hospital would be willing for him to drag them to an empty patient's room for a quick and dirty screw. But that's not who he was. He had never been that way with women, and he didn't see how it could be possible to change. All he wanted was for her to really see him and how good he could be for her. How good they would be for each other. He thought that was what she was feeling in the moments before and after he kissed her. But now it seemed it was once again only lust.

Although it was probably pointless, he couldn't help putting everything out there once again. "But when we were up on the roof, there wasn't a moment where you wanted more from me than just sex?" He licked his lips and took a step toward her. "Just a second where you could imagine your life with me in it?"

Megan stared at him, her expression contemplative. For a brief moment, Pesh thought by her hesitation that she had changed her mind about him. But then she shook her head. "How many times are you going to make me hurt you with this? You're too good for me, Pesh. We both know that. I'll remind you again of some of the reasons I'm not the one for you. I'm twenty-five, and you're thirty-seven. You want a wife, and I'm not ready to be married."

Her words cut into his chest the same as if she had taken a sharp blade to him. She may have had to repeat herself this time, but he realized the finality of her words. And then an idea hit him so hard that he shuddered—a true light bulb moment and epiphany. There was only one way he was going to get to have his sweet Megan, and that was if he gave in to her. He would have to become someone else for her, even if it was just for a little while. He could distract her with sex that she both desired and demanded, but at the same time, he would make her fall in love with him. It could work. It had to.

Cocking his head at her, he questioned, "So let me get this straight once and for all. You would let me…"

He paused, fighting the conflict within himself to say what he needed to. He drew in a ragged breath. "You would let me fuck you but not love you?"

Her eyes widened at his word choice. "What's gotten into you?"

He shrugged nonchalantly, feeling slightly empowered in the Dr. Jekyll and Mr. Hyde moment. "I merely asked a simple question."

She snorted exasperatedly. "Yeah, about…" She swallowed hard. "Fucking, of all things."

"Yes."

Megan shook her head wildly back and forth. "I can barely acknowledge hearing you say the word, least of all you doing that."

"You can't imagine me—"

She held up her hand. "You're not the type of man to fuck," she countered.

Crossing his arms over his chest, he countered, "Oh really? I'm too nice of a guy?"

"Something like that."

"I am a *man*, Megan. We all have needs. Isn't fucking one of them?"

Her body trembled slightly at his words. She licked her lips before replying, "S-Stop saying that word—it isn't you."

"So, fucking isn't me? Don't tell me you think I'm totally asexual—that you can't imagine me fucking a woman…fucking *you*." He eased in closer to her. "We both know for a fact that you wanted nothing more than to fuck me the night of Noah's baptism. Given the chance right now, you'd let me strip off your scrubs and fuck you up against the medicine cabinet."

As her chest heaved up and down, she took a step back from him, bumping against the counter. "But you don't say things like that. You're refined. You're a gentleman," she whispered.

"It may have been a while, but even a gentleman like me enjoys fucking." He closed the gap between them.

"What are you doing?" she whispered.

"I'm giving you what you want."

"You're giving in?"

"Yeah, why not?" As he dipped his head, his mouth hovered over hers. "If you really want me to take you, then kiss me."

Without a moment's hesitation, Megan crashed her lips against his. The kiss was hard and desperately seeking more. As his tongue thrust into her mouth, his hand came to her breast. Tenderly, he cupped the flesh, feeling the weight fill his hand. Unsatisfied with the lack of contact, he pulled his hand away and slid it underneath Megan's top. Over her bra, he kneaded her breast again, feeling her nipple harden under his touch. He felt his erection grow at the sound of her whimper. He wanted nothing more than to strip off all her clothes and kiss every inch of her body.

Megan's mouth popped off of his, and she stared up at him with hooded eyes. "What about someone finding us?"

"I'll lock the door," he replied. Reluctantly, he pulled away from her to walk back over to the door. After he turned the lock, he made sure to push a box in front of it as well. They would have enough warning if someone were to try to use their card to come in. With his hands on her shoulders, he steered her behind one of the floor-to-ceiling shelves, concealing them even further from potential prying eyes.

"Now where were we?" he asked, with a smile.

She grinned and wrapped her arms around his neck. "I think you were getting acquainted with second base."

"Yes, I remember now." Instead of his hands going back to her breasts, he pulled her flush against him. As his lips met hers, he slipped his arms around her waist. He grabbed the globes of her ass and squeezed, causing Megan to moan into his mouth. His hands gripped her flesh, urging her upward. Rising on her tiptoes, she allowed him to hoist her up. Her legs wrapped around his waist.

Once he had secured her to him, he rammed them back, until they bumped into the wall. He ground his pelvis into her core, letting her feel how much he truly wanted her.

"Mmm," she murmured, as he continued rubbing against her. One of her hands abandoned his shoulder and slid down his back to squeeze his ass.

His fingers jerked her hair back, pulling her lips back from his. He gazed into her heavy lidded eyes before his mouth dipped to her neck. His tongue slid up her jugular, feeling her racing pulse. "So you'll let me inside your body but not your heart?" he demanded.

"Yes. Please Pesh."

Now that he had her right where he wanted her, it was time to put his plan into motion. "If I give you an orgasm, you'll have to go on a date with me."

Her eyes widened through her panting. "You can't be serious."

"Oh, but I am. Give and take, Megan. I give you what you want—" He paused in his thrusts to let his fingers dip into the waist band of her scrubs. Through the thin scrap of her thong, his hand caressed her, causing her to whimper. "Which is to explode in bliss."

As he continued stroking her, she hissed in a breath as she glared at him. "You want me pretty bad, don't you, Megan?" he asked, as his fingertips felt of her growing moisture.

Her fingernails dug into his shoulders. "Yes. God, yes, I do."

"So let me give you this pleasure. I want nothing more than to see you come apart." He licked his lips. "Then you'll let me take you out."

Her eyelids fluttered, and she bit down on her lip. He could tell she was internally raging war with herself about what to do. As his fingers sped up their tempo against her clit, her head fell back against the wall. "You don't play fair," she groaned.

He momentarily eased his hand off of her. "I don't want to play games with you at all, but you leave me no choice." He lowered his head to kiss her again. "All I want is you," he murmured.

"Fine, fine."

"Fine what?" he questioned, as he looked her in the eye.

"Make me come, and I'll go out on a date with you."

He smiled before easing her back onto her feet. When he sank to his knees before her, Megan's brows furrowed in confusion. He then gripped the waistband of her scrubs. He eased them down, along with her panties, never taking his eyes off hers. When he had them down to her ankles, he rose back up. Grabbing her by the waist, he shifted her to the side where she bumped into the counter. He gripped her hips once again and raised her up to where her butt rested on the cool Formica. He slid her pants and thong over her shoes, letting the drop into floor below him.

He was so far gone with desire that he didn't stop to think how long it had been since he had gone down on a woman. He pushed the voices out of his head when they reminded him of how Jade had teasingly called his tongue a master of orgasms. Instead, he focused on the beautiful, panting woman before him as she widened her legs invitingly for him.

When he slid his tongue slowly up Megan's wet slit, they both shuddered. He took one of her legs and propped her foot on his shoulder, so he could get better access to her while he pushed her other thigh further open. Her pink, glistening center was laid out beautifully before him. As his tongue flicked and teased her swollen clit, Megan threw her head back and moaned. His lips closed over her clit, sucking it hard. Her hips began to rock back and forth. He knew it wasn't going to take him long to make her come—she was too ready for this. It had been a long time for her as well.

He resisted using his fingers. Instead, he spread her apart and then thrust his tongue rhythmically inside her. Megan's cries grew louder to where he brought his hand up and clamped it over her lips. The last thing they needed was someone banging on the door. As he felt her walls tensing, she reached out to twist her fingers in his hair. He welcomed the pain as she went over the edge, convulsing and screaming against his hand. When Megan's walls finishing clenching and pulsing, Pesh removed his tongue from inside her. He placed butterfly kisses against her core and then on the insides of her thighs.

When he finally glanced up, he found Megan staring at him, a combustive mix of emotions swirling in her blue eyes. "That was…"

Smiling, he rose up from the floor. His hands gently came to her waist. He was just about to pull her down when she stopped him. "Don't. I can't even feel my legs right now."

He brushed her hair back from her face. "It has been a long time, hasn't it?"

She shook her head. "How about *never* has it been like that."

He couldn't help staring at her incredulously. "What do you mean?"

"I mean, that I've never gotten off like that." She gave him a sheepish grin. "At least not with a man."

At her insinuation, he felt warmth enter his face. "Are you blushing about me mentioning masturbating?"

"No, I'm not," he protested feebly.

Megan laughed. "You really are something else, you know that?"

"I am?"

"Hell yes. One minute you've got your tongue buried inside me, giving me *the* most intense orgasm of my life, and then the next you're blushing. It's like you became another person a few minutes ago. You were forceful and domineering." A shudder rippled through her as she raised her brows. "Do you always get like that when it comes to sex?"

Pesh felt even more warmth creeping into his cheeks. How she could talk so frankly without any pants on, he had no idea. "We should cover you up."

"You were enjoying the view a few minutes ago." She leaned over and winked at him. "A very up-close and personal view."

He rubbed his hands over his face. "Honestly, I don't know what came over me. I came in here to tell you I was sorry and that you wouldn't have to worry about me coming on to you again." And then all hell had broken loose. It was like he had been fried with the electrical current from the paddles on the crash cart. He'd decided to become another person to win her and damned if he had. Almost too easily for his liking. What had he said to her in the heat of the moment?

He stared intently at her. "All I could think of was how much I wanted you and what it would take to have you."

"You really wanted me that much?" she asked, her brows rising in surprise.

"Yes, I did."

With a coy smile, she scooted to the edge of the counter. She wrapped her legs around his waist and drew him closer to her. "What about you?" she asked, as her hand cupped his erection through his pants.

His hips bucked involuntarily, and he closed his eyes, trying to steady himself. "This wasn't about me," he murmured.

"I can't let you go back on the floor with a hard-on." She licked up the side of his face, causing him to shudder. "I owe you at least a happy ending after those multiple orgasms you just gave me."

His closed eyes popped open. "Multiple did you say?"

She giggled. "Yeah."

"Then that means you owe me multiple dates, right?"

Megan reached around to smack his ass. "You're a bad boy trying to trick me."

"I'm sorry. I play dirty when I have to."

Without another word, Megan unbuttoned and unzipped him. She eased his pants and boxer shorts off his hips. When his erection was freed, she glanced between them. "Hmm, pretty impressive."

He started to laugh at her remark, but when she gripped him in her hand, he gasped. All coherent thoughts flew out of his mind as she stroked his length up and down, alternating from smooth slides to hard tugs. "Would you rather it was my mouth on you than my hand?" she asked.

"Feels good no matter what," he muttered, his head dipping to rest against her shoulder.

Her breath scorched against his ear. "Mmm, I love that you're so hard. Just for me, right?"

"Yes," he panted. "Just for you. Only you."

Flicking her tongue out, she encircled his lobe and the shell of his ear. "Can you imagine what it would be like to bury yourself deep inside me?"

Her words were having too much of an effect on him. The dirty talk, coupled with the way she had her hand on him, caused him to tighten up. He tried to pull away, but she kept hold of him. And then he was coming undone.

When he finally came back to himself, he opened his eyes to see that he'd come on Megan's exposed thighs. "I'm sorry," he said.

"It's okay. It was worth it to see your O face." She smiled dreamily at him. "God, you were beautiful."

Since he'd never had a woman tell him that, he couldn't help flushing. He pulled away from her to search for something to clean her up with. Finally, he found a roll of paper towels. When he returned to her, he gently wiped himself off her skin. After he finished, he helped her down off the counter. "I'll go out first. I need to clean up. And so do you."

He gave a brief nod. He was having trouble processing all the emotions swirling through his mind. "So when it is?" she asked.

"When is what?" he asked dumbly. He was still far too obliterated by a simple hand job to be processing coherent thoughts.

"Our date."

He had almost forgotten what he asked of her. Out of the heat of the moment, he felt guilty for what he had done. He shook his head. "No, I wasn't being fair. You don't owe me a date."

"Yes, I do. I always keep my promises."

"You're really going to go out with me?"

She grinned. "Of course I am."

His heartbeat sped up. "Are you off this Saturday?"

"Yes."

"You don't have plans?"

"No, I don't."

"And you can get someone to watch your son?"

"Yessss," she replied, with a smile.

"Okay, then let's do it Saturday."

"Do what exactly?"

"The date."

She laughed. "Yes, but what *are* we doing?"

"It's a surprise."

Tilting her head, she eyed him suspiciously. "I'm not sure I like the sound of that."

"I promise you'll like it."

"What should I wear for this surprise date?"

Already the wheels had been turning in his head. Since it might be his only chance, he knew he wanted to make the date as special as he could. "Wear something dressy. We might be going somewhere that requires more formal wear than jeans."

"Okay, I think I can do that."

At the sound of his pager, he grimaced. "Guess I'll be the one leaving first." Without hesitating, he bowed his head to kiss her. Just like before, the feel of her mouth against his lit him on fire. Reluctantly, he pulled away.

"Go wash up first." Her breath warmed his cheek before she glanced up into his eyes. "I can taste myself on you."

He closed his eyes as a shudder went through his body. "You're trying to kill me."

She flashed him a wicked grin. "Sorry. It's the truth."

"Behave yourself," he replied, before he headed to the door.

Chapter Fourteen

With less than ten minutes before Pesh was set to arrive for their date, Megan found herself a neurotic mess still holed in the bathroom. She'd changed outfits at least three times before deciding on a black and white lace dress that came just to her knees. It had actually come out of the back of her closet—one of the tamer remnants of her wilder days. Pesh had told her to wear something dressy, and it did fall into the dressy category, although it was probably a little sexier than she would have liked.

While she'd pulled her long hair back into a loose knot at the back of her neck, she was now rethinking her strategy. If she'd left her hair down, it would cover more of the exposed skin that the spaghetti straps and neck of the dress showed. Glancing at her phone one more time, she cringed. "Fuck it," she muttered, before spritzing on some perfume. After the fragrant cloud faded, she headed out of the bathroom. She grabbed her purse and headed upstairs.

When she came into the kitchen, a loud, cat-calling whistle pierced her ear. She scowled at Sean. "Seriously?"

He shrugged. "You look hot, sis."

Gavin, who stood beside Sean at the counter, nodded. "We never see you in anything but scrubs."

Megan couldn't help smiling at her brothers. "Thank you."

Wagging his brows, Gavin asked, "Got a hot date, huh?"

"Not exactly," she replied, as she went to grab her purse.

"Yeah right," he mumbled under his breath.

After slinging her purse on her shoulder, she whirled around to pin him with her stare. "And what's that supposed to mean?"

"It means that chicks don't get dressed up like that for nothing. You obviously want to impress this guy. So, it's obviously a hot date."

"Since when did you become the love guru?" she questioned.

Sean grinned as he elbowed Gavin. "She's getting riled, man. Being irrational about little things usually means love."

Megan opened her mouth to lay into her brothers, but then found herself speechless, so she closed it back up. Without another word to her brothers, she went into the living room. She found her dad lounging in his chair with Mason snuggled to his side. When her dad looked up, he did a double take. "Don't you look beautiful, sweetheart," he said.

She bent down and kissed his cheek. "Thanks, Daddy."

Mason tore his gaze away from the television to look at her. "Mommy, bye-bye?"

This was one question she hadn't anticipated explaining. "Yes, Mommy is going to go see a friend today, and you're going to stay here with Grammy and Granddad."

His tiny brows furrowed. "Mace no go?"

Guilt rocketed through her. How could she spend one of her few off days away from her son? The doorbell rang, and she was forced out of her self-loathing to answer the door. Taking a deep breath, she opened it. Her heart did a funny little flip-flop at the sight of Pesh on the porch. It wasn't just how handsome he looked in his khaki pants, red button-down Polo shirt, and black blazer. It was also the fact he held a dozen red roses in his hand. "Hi," she said shyly, after they had stared at each other for a few seconds.

He smiled. "Hello."

"Would you like to come in?"

As he nodded, she stepped aside to give him room to come in the door. He turned back to her and held out the roses. "These are for you." After the words left his lips, he grimaced, as if what he had said offended him.

"They're beautiful. Thank you."

"Bye-bye kiss, Mommy!" Mason called from the living room.

She smiled apologetically at Pesh. "I'm sorry. I'll just be one minute."

"Take your time."

She hurried across the foyer and into the living room. She deposited the roses onto one of the tables. "I'll be back tonight. You be a good boy, okay?" she said, when she got to her father's chair. She leaned over and kissed both of Mason's cheeks. "Give Mommy a kiss."

He gave her a smacking kiss on the cheek. "Bye, my love," Megan said, before turning and heading out of the room. She'd just reached Pesh's side when he glanced past her. "What?" she asked.

"I think we have a potential stowaway," he replied, with a smile.

She whirled around to see Mason standing in the foyer. "What's wrong, baby?"

"No go," he whimpered.

She glanced up at Pesh. "I'm sorry. He usually is fine about me leaving him." She knelt down beside Mason. "I won't be gone long, and you'll have much more fun here with Grammy and Granddad. Pesh and I are doing boring, big people stuff."

"No go!" he cried, as big tears pooled in his eyes.

Pesh knelt down beside her. "Hey buddy, don't cry. I'm not going to take your mommy away from you."

"Mace go?" he asked hopefully.

Megan shook her head. "No, sweetheart, I told you that we were going to do big people things today."

"That's true," Pesh said. Then he smiled at Mason. "But that doesn't mean we can't take a little detour first."

Megan's widened her eyes in surprise. "What do you mean?"

"Why don't we take Mason to lunch at his favorite place?"

"You don't mean that," Megan argued.

Pesh cut his gaze over to her. "Sure, I do. I can adjust our reservations."

She couldn't help staring at him in shock. How was it possible he was so willing to change his plans simply because Mason didn't want her to leave? She fought the urge to reach out and touch his shoulder to make sure he was real—he was far too good to be true at times.

"Is that okay with you?" Pesh asked her.

"Of course it's all right with me. I was worried about it not being okay with you."

"I wouldn't have suggested it if I didn't mean it." He reached out and ruffled Mason's hair. "All right, buddy, where do you want to go for lunch?"

"Cheese! Cheese!" he cried, as he bobbed up and down.

Megan groaned as Pesh's expression grew confused. "He wants to eat cheese?" he asked.

"No, he wants to go to Chuck E. Cheese—every parent's worst nightmare."

Pesh chuckled as he rose up from the floor. "All right then. Chuck E. Cheese it is."

"Go get your shoes," Megan instructed.

As Mason raced back into the living room, Megan stood up. "You really don't have to do this."

"Honestly, I don't mind. We can go have lunch with Mason, and then we can start our date. I'm sure he'll be worn out and ready for a nap when we get back, right?"

"Yes, he will."

"Good. Then he won't have any reason to miss you if he's asleep."

She smiled at his thoughtfulness. "Thank you. I really mean that."

"You're welcome." He reached out and brushed her cheek. When he started to lean in to kiss her, Mason ran back into the foyer with his shoes. Pesh quickly jerked back.

To combat the awkwardness, Megan busied herself with getting Mason's shoes on. When she finished, Mason bounded over to Pesh and grabbed his hand. "Go! Go!"

Pesh laughed at Mason's enthusiasm. He held his other hand out for Megan. She slid her hand into his and then they started to the car.

As Megan walked through the doors of their local Chuck E. Cheese, she recoiled slightly at both the ear- splintering noise and the stomach-turning smells. She also fought her embarrassment at the looks she and Pesh were getting for their more formal outfits. "I think we're a little overdressed," she said.

He held up his index finger and thumb before pinching them close together. "Just a little bit."

Tugging on Pesh's hand, Mason dragged him over to the toddler area of games. Megan quickly dug in her purse for some money for tickets. After she bought them, she went over to Pesh. "I'll go grab us some pizza." She waved the tickets at him. "Once these are gone, he's done."

"I don't mind getting him more."

She shook her head. "Trust me. He's done."

"Okay then," he replied good-naturedly.

Megan felt completely at ease leaving Pesh to watch Mason. She got them a couple of slices of Mason's favorite, pepperoni, along with some drinks and then made her way over to a table close to the toddler area. When she caught Pesh's eye, she waved them over. After several tense moments, he was finally able to convince Mason to leave the play area to come and eat.

As Mason bounced around in his seat, Megan knew she would be doing good to get four bites of pizza down him before he was raring to go play again. She also had a fear that she, Pesh, or the both of them were going to be wearing tomato sauce before it was all said and done.

"This place is very interesting," Pesh remarked, as he gazed around.

Megan laughed. "Have you never had the pleasure?"

"Sadly no. My brother, Arjan's, and his children live in Florida, so I've really never had a reason to come."

"You've dodged a bullet there. That's for sure."

He smiled before taking a bite of his pizza. His expression turned so sour that Megan couldn't help giggling. "This is terrible," he muttered.

"I should have warned you not to bother eating. It only seems appetizing to small children who are hyped up on adrenaline."

He took a long swig from his Coke and swished the liquid around like he was trying to rid himself of the taste. When he caught Mason looking at him, he put on a fake smile. "Mmm, that's good pizza. You better eat yours before I do."

"Nice save," she murmured.

He winked at her as he threw his napkin on his plate. She couldn't believe when her heart fluttered at his gesture. It was almost impossible to believe that she could be getting feelings for him in the middle of Chuck E. Cheese.

"Done. Go play," Mason announced, bringing her out of her thoughts.

She shook her head. "I don't think so. You need to eat more."

Mason scowled at her before grabbing another bite and shoveling it into his mouth. He managed to clean his plate with a little coaxing from Pesh. Then the two of them went back over to the play area. As Megan watched them, the small ache in her chest began to grow. Pesh was completely hands on, hoisting Mason up where he could reach things and then catching him when he came off the slide. He seemed to genuinely enjoy spending time with Mason. Some guys would have played with Mason only to get on her good side. But Pesh didn't have an agenda when it came to her, unless it was to have her embrace the idea of a relationship with him.

When the last ticket was spent, she rose off her chair. "Okay, time to go."

Mason's face scrunched up, and he looked like at any minute he might throw a tantrum to stay. But Pesh took his hand. "We'll come back another time."

His reply seemed to pacify Mason, and he happily slung his and Pesh's arm back and forth as they walked to the car. When they got buckled up, Megan turned back to Mason. "What do you say to Pesh for bringing you?"

"Tank you, Esh," Mason said.

His words sent a broad grin stretching across Pesh's face. "You're welcome, buddy. I had a good time."

When he glanced over at Megan, she gave him a genuine smile. "I had a good time, too."

Taking one of his hands off the steering wheel, he reached over to take her hand in his. While the gesture was a little too lovey-dovey for her liking, she didn't argue with him. Instead, she just enjoyed his touch.

Once they had deposited a sleepy Mason back home at Megan's, they abandoned her SUV and gotten into Pesh's Jaguar. "So where exactly are we going?" Megan asked, as she buckled her seat belt.

"It's a surprise."

"Seriously? You're still playing coy about it?"

"For just a little while longer."

She shifted in her seat where she could look at him better. "Can I try to guess?"

"I suppose. I'm not sure I'd tell you even if you guess," he teased.

"Are we going to Atlanta?"

He cut his gaze from the road over to her. "Have patience."

Crossing her arms over her chest, she huffed, "I don't have patience for games."

"Okay, I'll give you a little hint. Actually, it's more of a question than it is a hint."

"Yeah?"

"Do you have a fear of heights?"

She snorted. "No, I don't. Why?"

He gave her a sly grin. "I told you. It's a hint."

"I went skydiving when I turned twenty-one, so I'm totally fine with heights. Of course, I seriously doubt we're going sky diving in these clothes."

"No, we're not."

She wrinkled her nose. "Please tell me it's not box seats at the opera or something like that."

His face fell. "You don't like the opera?"

"Never been and never want to."

Pesh appeared almost personally insulted. "I'm going to have to change your mind on that one."

"Why am I not surprised you like opera?"

"Don't knock it until you've tried it."

"A bunch of screeching men and women singing in a language I don't understand? Not my idea of a good time."

"But there is such love and passion in their delivery," he argued.

"Um, I'm just going to have to agree to disagree with you."

"For now at least," he said, with a wink.

When the car started slowing down, Megan peered out the windshield before turning to Pesh. "We're at McCollum?"

"Yes."

"You're taking me flying?"

He smiled. "Yes, I am."

Even though she had known he had a plane from how he'd helped get Aidan to Noah's delivery, she couldn't believe their date included something as unique as flying.

"So let me get this straight. I'm dressed like this," she did a little hand motion over her dress, "to go flying?"

An amused look twinkled in his dark eyes. "You have absolutely no patience, do you?"

"No, I don't."

As he put the car in park outside the hanger, he turned to her. "By your lack of being able to withhold gratification, I'm assuming you've never partaken in any Tantric sex?"

She couldn't stop her mouth from dropping to her chest. "W-What?" she stammered.

Turning in his seat, he pinned her with a hard stare. "Have I managed to shock you again?"

Unable to speak, she merely bobbed her head. Pesh only chuckled at her response. "Come on. Let's get going."

Still in shock, she remained rooted to her seat. When he came around to open her door, she peered up at him. "Tantric sex? Like Sting, Trudie Styler, and Tantric sex?"

"Yes, I suppose so," he replied, as he offered her his hand. Ordinarily, she wouldn't have taken it, but at the declaration that Pesh was actually into something outside the sexual norms, she was too floored to argue with him. "I didn't think you'd like anything…kinky."

Pesh's dark eyes widened. "Tantric isn't kinky. It's about connecting with your lover on a more intimate level. It's about breathing them in and truly being one."

"So it's not about marathon sex that lasts for days?"

He chuckled. "You've gotten the more salacious side confused with what it actually is."

Megan pursed her lips at him as her mind whirled with the possibilities. After all, if Tantric sex with Pesh was anywhere as good as his efforts in going down on her, she was one very lucky lady. "I guess you'll just have to educate me."

They were interrupted by an air traffic controller with a headset. "Hey, Dr. Nadeen, how goes it?"

"Good. Thank you. Everything ready to go, Lewis?" Pesh asked, as he pumped the man's hand.

"Gassed up and checked out. We just need your flight plan."

Pesh's gaze went to Megan before he said, "We'll be flying into Savannah/Hilton Head airport."

"Great. Thanks," Lewis replied, before he started back inside the hanger.

"You're taking me to Savannah?" she asked.

"For dinner and dancing. I had originally intended on more, but we got a later start."

"This is crazy. *You're* crazy."

He gave her a puzzled look. "You don't like Savannah?"

"No, I love it. I just meant taking me four hours away for dinner."

"It's not that long by plane."

Crossing her arms over her chest, she tilted her head at him. "You couldn't just take me somewhere fancy in Atlanta? You have to fly me in your private plane to another city?"

He shrugged. "Why not?"

Although it was probably unattractive, she couldn't help snorting with contempt. "I'm probably going to sound a little like the line from *Pretty Woman* when she says she appreciates the seduction scene, but she's a sure thing." She patted her chest. "I am a sure thing. You don't have to go to all this trouble."

His dark eyes narrowed. "Your way of thinking is precisely why I'm doing what I am."

"What do you mean?"

"You've only been with men who wanted a sure thing—men who didn't even bother trying to imagine a future with you past when they came at the end of the night." She sucked in a breath at his words. With his expression softening, he closed the gap between them. "While you may only want sex from me, I want far more from you. I want your time, but I also want you to understand that you're worthy of something special. And if it takes planes and fancy meals to prove it to you, then I'm going to do it."

After his argument, Megan sat frozen in dumbfounded silence. How was it possible that he knew so much about her? He was right in the fact that she settled for being the 'sure thing' for the guys she dated in the past. She knew she didn't want to make those mistakes again, so why shouldn't she let him try to wine and dine her? "Fine. Take me to Savannah."

He opened the passenger side door. "Here you go. Make sure you buckle your seat belt."

She nodded before she dipped inside the plane. Pesh waited for her to adjust her dress before he closed the door. As he walked around the front of the plane, she got busy finding the seat belt and buckling up. Once he climbed inside, he handed her a headset. "This will help with the cabin noise."

"It's going to mess my hair up," she complained.

He laughed. "I never took you as the type of woman who worried about her hair."

She grinned as she eased the headset on. "Now you know. I worry about my hair, and you get your freak on in the bedroom."

He rolled his eyes at her and turned in his seat. After placing his headset on, he started flipping switches and turning knobs. The propeller on the front of the plane started whirling.

"So what kind of plane is this?" she asked over the noise.

Holding up a finger, he spoke into the mic on the headset. "Ground to Tower, this is Cessna 172 requesting to taxi for takeoff."

Suddenly the sound of the tower came over her headset. "Clearance for taxi and takeoff, Cessna 172."

"Roger that," Pesh replied. The plane lurched forward and then started taxing down the runaway.

"Hmm, I'm guessing a Cessna 172?"

Pesh smiled. "Yes, it is."

"It's nice. I like it."

"I hope you'll be saying that again in a minute."

Megan knew what he meant when the plane started gaining speed down the runaway. Just like when she was on a commercial flight, it was on the ground one minute, and then in the air the next. They soared into the blue sky while zipping through white, fluffy clouds. Once they had gained enough altitude, Pesh eased off on the rudder and glanced over at her. "You okay over there?"

She grinned. "Are you kidding me? This is amazing."

"I'm glad to hear you like it. I didn't know if you were going to take after your Uncle Aidan."

"I hear you gave him drugs to make it."

Pesh laughed. "Yeah, I did. He slept most of the way there."

"Total wuss," she remarked with a smile.

After adjusting one of the controls, Pesh said, "Well, I have to admit that my late wife wasn't a fan, either. She tolerated flying with me because she knew how much I loved it, but most of the time, she'd take a pill to relax."

"So she didn't share your passion?"

"No, she didn't. She always encouraged me to do what I loved. She never was one to make me choose between her or something else. She was that sacrificing."

"That was really amazing of her to be that giving."

When Pesh remained silent, Megan knew it was time for a conversation change. "Now that I know we're going to Savannah, are you going to tell me where we're going for dinner?"

He smiled. "It'll probably be a late lunch when we get there."

"So, where will our late *lunch* be?"

"Do you like the Historic District?"

"I love it."

"Good. I've picked a restaurant there for us."

"Do you come to Savannah often?"

"A couple of times a year, mainly for medical conferences on the Coast."

"And you always fly?"

"I do," he replied, with a smile.

The flight took less time than she thought, and with clear weather, it was totally smooth. As they started making their descent, Pesh glanced over at her. "Are you ready for the landing?"

"Sure. Why wouldn't I be?"

"It can be a little intense for some people. You see a lot more of the ground rushing at you than when you're in a 747."

She cocked her head at him. "I went skydiving, remember?"

"Ah, that's right." With a wink, he added, "You're my little adrenaline junkie."

Megan laughed. "I was. Not anymore."

"What changed all that?"

"Mason. When you're responsible for the health, safety, and happiness of someone else, your entire perspective changes."

"He's a true gift."

She jerked her gaze to him. "Yes, he is."

Pesh gave her a small smile before radioing the tower. Once he had clearance to land, they started rapidly losing altitude. The runway got closer and closer until the plane jolted forward and then began skidding along the pavement. When it finally came to a shuddering stop, Megan exhaled the breath she'd been holding. "Still okay?" Pesh asked.

She grinned. "Never better."

The sound of the tower came in her headset as Pesh listened to the instructions. The plane started rolling toward one of the hangers. Once he had parked and powered down the plane, he got out to help her. After a quick talk with a member of the grounds crew, Pesh took her hand and led her out of the hanger. A cab waited to take them into the city.

She laughed as she slid across the seat. "What?" Pesh asked.

"I'm surprised by the cab. I thought you might really go upscale by having a limo or chauffeur-driven car pick us up."

"I like to stay humble," he replied with a wink.

She shook her head at him before turning to gaze out the window at the scenery. When they began winding through the antebellum homes of the Historic District, Megan felt her stomach growl. She'd been too nervous to eat breakfast, and then she hadn't dared eat at Chuck E. Cheese's.

The cab stopped outside a chic looking restaurant. As Pesh paid the driver, Megan hopped out and took in the sights around her. She loved the old world feel of the city with all its history and charm. Pesh offered her his arm, and then they walked inside. The restaurant's popularity was evident in how crowded it was even at four in the afternoon. They were ushered to a quiet, candlelit table.

"Wine?" Pesh asked.

"Yes please."

"White okay?"

"Sure."

After the waiter left with their drink order, Megan surveyed the menu and sighed. "Everything looks so good."

Glancing over his menu at her, Pesh said, "With the cuisine being Southern, I imagined you would like it."

"I love all types of food. Trust me, as hungry as I am now, I would have eaten anywhere."

The waiter returned with their wine, and Megan knew she needed to make a decision. "I'll have the shrimp and grits, please."

"Very good, ma'am," the waiter replied.

"I'll have the same," Pesh said, handing the waiter his menu. When Megan grinned at him, his brows rose. "What?"

"I'm just surprised to hear you eating something so Southern as shrimp and grits."

He tsked at her. "When will you learn that you can never pigeonhole me as one thing or the other?"

She laughed. "Actually, I like that you're proving me wrong and being unexpected."

"Really?"

She nodded. "Sometimes I feel like people try to do the same thing to me. People have their own assumptions about girls or women who get knocked up. I hope I constantly prove them wrong."

"I'm sure you do." After taking a sip of his wine, he cocked his head at her. "Prove me wrong on this one. Does a Southern girl like you eat Indian food?"

"Oh yes, I love it."

His dark eyes lit up. "What's your favorite dish?"

"Hmm, I love Butter Chicken, but I'm also a fan of Pav Bahaji."

"I'm impressed. Emma had never eaten any Indian food, and I don't think I made a good impression on her." Pesh's chuckle died out, and he immediately grimaced at the mention of Emma's name.

Knowing that they were dancing around the white elephant in the room, Megan reached across the table and patted his hand. "It's okay that you're talking about Emma."

"Speaking of old girlfriends or women you've dated while you're with another woman is never a good idea."

"This is different. Emma is my family." She swirled the wine around in her glass. "I've heard her side of the story, but I don't think I've heard yours."

"You heard a little when you were inebriated the night of Noah's baptism."

Now it was Megan's turn to grimace. "I still would like to know."

Pesh drew in a ragged breath. When the waiter appeared with their salads, it appeared that he might dodge the question entirely. But once they were alone together, he smiled. "Emma came along at a time when I was facing extreme pressure from family and friends to move on from my grief and date again. There was no escape to it—I faced it at the hospital, as well as when I was at home. People seemed to think that once a year went by on the calendar that meant I was through with my mourning. Then one day, there she was in the ER. She was scared out of her mind about your grandfather. Somehow I just connected with her through her grief and pain." He dabbed his mouth with his napkin. "She reminded me so much of Jade that it was easy to try to imagine that what I was feeling for her was romantic. I hadn't been out in so long that I wanted to woo her, just like I wanted to you."

"And Aidan came between you?"

"In a way, both he and Jade did."

"What do you mean?"

Pesh laughed. "Let's just say, during a very heated moment together, she was with Aidan, and I was with Jade."

Megan was surprised by his candor. "I see." There was one item in the Pesh and Emma equation she had always wondered about. "You didn't mind that she was pregnant?"

Shaking his head, Pesh replied, "It just made her even more beautiful to me. I'd been through so much death that I guess I was drawn to her because she had life growing within her."

"That's really beautiful," Megan murmured.

He gave her a mirthless laugh. "One of my worst character faults is having a hero complex. I guess it's one of the reasons I became a doctor. I saw Emma, and I wanted to save her. When she had to go on bed rest, I wanted to be her knight in shining armor."

"Being a hero is not exactly a bad character trait."

"It is when you can't save someone, and you have to constantly live with the guilt."

Megan's heart ached at the pain on his face. Sensing she needed to lighten the mood, she teased, "I'm glad to hear you actually have a bad character trait. I mean, you seemed a little too perfect to me."

A shadow of a smile played on his lips. "Did I mention I'm a terrible slob?"

"You? Never," she replied.

"Oh yes. If I didn't have a housekeeper, I'm pretty sure I might end up on World's Nastiest Houses."

Megan laughed. "I find that hard to believe."

"It's the truth. I also have no athletic ability whatsoever."

After chewing thoughtfully on her bite of salad, Megan said, "But you're built like a football player."

"I'm built because I go to the gym to work off stress. But if you put me on the field, I'd be a serious disappointment."

She shook her head. "That doesn't turn me off at all. I've had my fill of jocks."

"Oh?" he questioned. Although he was trying to be nonchalant about it, she knew he wanted to hear the full story.

"Dating jocks for me is poison, and when I did date one, I made sure to date the ones at the top of their game. My first athlete's influence caused me to ruin my chances at medical school."

"That's horrible."

"Yes, it is. But what's worse is I didn't learn anything from my mistakes because I fell for another one." With a rueful smile, she added, "At least I got Mason out of that one."

Pesh laced his fingers together. "Mason's father is a professional athlete?"

"Yes, he plays football for the Falcons."

"You know I'm friends with the team's sports medicine doctor. I could probably arrange something for him. Maybe a little Icy Hot in his cup?"

At the mischievous twinkle in Pesh's eyes, Megan burst out laughing. "I cannot believe, you of all people, suggested such a thing."

With a shrug, Pesh replied, "It's a harmless prank."

"I realize that. It's just I can't imagine someone like you would even think of doing something like that." When he started to open his mouth to argue, she held up her hand. "I know, I know. Don't pigeon hole you."

"Exactly."

Their main course arrived, and Megan couldn't help digging into the wonderful aromatic food. As they ate, the conversation came easily. That was one of the things she liked most about Pesh—he was so easy to talk to. Because he was older, refined, and a doctor, she could have felt intimidated by him. But he never made her feel that way. He always seemed fascinated by every single thing she had to say, which was quite a change from most of the guys she dated. They were usually half listening to her while glancing over her shoulder at the TV to get the latest score.

After they finished, the waiter took their plates. "Dessert?" Megan asked, as she downed the last of her wine.

Pesh nodded his head toward the small dance floor. "How about a dance instead?"

She wrinkled her nose. "I'm really not much of a dancer." He arched his brows at her as if he knew she was lying. "Okay, fine, I used to dance all the time back in high school and college."

"Then dance with me."

"I'm not good at slow dancing. You'll probably regret asking me the moment we get out there."

Pesh stuffed a wad of bills into the bill envelope. "As Shakespeare would say, the lady do protesth too much. And I think I know the reason."

"Oh, you do?"

He nodded. "Slow dancing is intimate, and you don't want to want to let yourself be intimate with me."

"You went down on me in a supply closet. I think that's pretty intimate," she challenged.

"That was not intimacy. Sexual acts are of the mind where our pleasure center is. Intimacy is of the heart." He held her gaze. "We both know you'll let me into your body but not your heart."

Knowing he was right, she crossed her arms over her chest and scowled at him. She didn't know why she just couldn't get up and go dance like he had asked. She'd slow danced a thousand times at parties. What was the difference here? Somewhere deep down, she knew the answer to that question.

"If you don't want to dance, then let's go and see the city."

Not wanting to let him get the best of her, she rose out of her chair. "Fine. I'll dance with you."

He chuckled. "Don't sound so thrilled."

After he stood up, he took her hand and led her over to the dance floor. She started to wrap her arms around his neck like she was accustomed to, but he put one of her hands on his shoulder and then he took the other hand in his. His other hand slid around to rest at her lower back.

The band finished the jazzier beats of a song and then switched over to another. A lone piano pounded out the opening chords. The lead singer's sultry voice filled the air, "Like a flower waiting to bloom." Megan immediately recognized the song as Norah Jones' *Turn Me On*. The electricity between them shifted, and as Megan stared up into Pesh's eyes, she saw desire and lust flaring in them.

Her gaze dropped down to his full lips, and she couldn't help wanting him to kiss her. As if he read her mind, Pesh's mouth closed over hers. Darting her tongue out, she sought to find his warmth. When she did, he tasted like a mixture of the wine and spices they'd eaten. His tongue pulled back to trace her lips as his hips jerked, pushing him against her. She followed his lead by pressing herself flush against him to where her breasts were rubbing against his chest. She shivered when he groaned into her mouth.

His thumb slid back and forth between her shoulder blades, and she couldn't help arching into his touch. As he pulled away from their kiss, he kept his eyes locked on hers. She'd never had a man stare at her so much. It was like he was trying to see through her to her very soul. It both overwhelmed and inflamed her at the same time. It was all part of his slow seduction plan, and it was working.

"Please take me somewhere—somewhere we can be alone."

His expression became pained. "Megan—"

She brought her hand from his shoulder to cover his lips. "Don't make me beg to be with you anymore."

Shaking his head, he replied, "I can't deny you anymore, not after having a taste of you."

Megan shuddered at the intensity of both his words and the way he delivered them. Taking her by the hand, he led her off the dance floor. They snaked around the tables in the dining area until they reached the exit. Weaving through the people, they went into the hotel that adjoined the restaurant. It was actually more of a historic bed and breakfast than a hotel. As they neared the reception area, Pesh dropped her hand to reach into his coat pocket. Once he retrieved his wallet, he stepped up to the desk. "I need a room please."

"Credit card and identification please," the inn keeper droned. As she sized him up, Megan couldn't help thinking he looked rather pompous—the usual type of person who worked in a high-end place. "Would you prefer queen or—"

"A king please," Pesh requested through clenched teeth.

"Do you need help with your luggage?"

"No, we don't have any."

The man typed something into the computer. "And how long will you be staying with us?"

"As long as we need," Pesh replied, drumming his fingers on the marble counter.

Megan watched as the man's eyes widened and a flush entered his face. He quickly finished the reservation and handed Pesh a key card. "We have you in one of our balcony king suites."

"Thank you." Taking her by the hand, Pesh led her over to the elevators. When Megan dared to glance over her shoulder, she saw the man peering curiously at them. As they stepped onto the car, Megan couldn't help the nervous giggle that escaped her lips. When Pesh looked at her in surprise, she laughed even harder. "What is it?"

"By the way that conversation went down, he probably thinks I'm a prostitute."

Pesh's eyes widened. "You don't seriously think that?"

"Okay, maybe a high-end escort?"

A growl came from low in his throat. "Do not demean yourself like that."

"I'm not demeaning myself. Think about it. We come in during the middle of the day with no luggage, and we want a hotel room with a king sized bed." She tapped her chin with her finger. "Hmm, what could we possibly be doing?"

The corners of his lips turned up in a smile. "I probably should care what the man thinks, but right now, I frankly don't give a shit."

She laughed. "Me either."

The elevator dinged, signaling they had reached their floor. They stepped out and read the signs to find their room. Once Pesh opened the door, Megan walked inside. She took in the cozy décor of the room with its brick fireplace, antiques, and four-poster bed. Going to a hotel could have been sleazy, but this room had such a romantic feel to it.

When he came up behind her and slid his arms around her waist, she couldn't help suddenly feeling shy. "Are you all right?" he asked.

"I'm fine."

His breath warmed against her ear. "You tensed when I touched you."

"I'm sorry. I didn't mean to. I guess I'm just nervous."

Pesh turned her around to face him. "You don't have anything to feel nervous about. If you don't want to do this anymore, we don't have to."

"No, I want to do it," she assured him.

Without another word, his fingers went to her hair. After he undid the clasp, her hair tumbled down over her shoulders. An appreciative shudder rippled through her when he nuzzled his face into the strands at her neck. From there he sought out the zipper at the middle of her back. Slowly, he slid it down. When the back of the dress gaped open, he took the spaghetti straps and eased them over her shoulders and down her arms. Megan felt his breath warming her back as the dress pooled onto the floor. She stepped out of it, and then turned to face him.

The heat of his gaze stoked the fire burning deep inside her. His expression was fierce as he drank in her strapless black bra and panties, along with her heels. "You are so beautiful."

For some reason, she felt the urge to blush at his words. Guys had told her she was beautiful before, but it didn't feel the same or sound the same coming from them as it did Pesh. The way he said she was beautiful, coupled with the way he looked at her, made her tingle in all the right places.

Her hands came to his tie. After she loosened it, she ripped it off him and slung it to the floor. Deftly, her fingers worked the buttons on his shirt. When she opened it, she sucked in a breath at the sight of the dusting of dark hair covering his chest. It trailed down over his washboard abs and down into his pants. "You're pretty beautiful yourself," she said with a smile.

As he shrugged off his shirt, her fingers went to his belt. The entire time she unbuttoned and unzipped him, his burning gaze took in everything she did. "Why do you keep staring at me?" she questioned quietly.

"I'm afraid if I look away, you won't be real." His hand cupped her cheek. "I've wanted this for so long—I've wanted *you* for so long. It's hard to believe that you're really here."

"Touch me," she urged. She took his other hand and brought it to her breast. "Touch me and feel how real I am."

Lowering his head, his mouth hovered over hers. "Breathe me in," he instructed, as he kneaded her breast over her bra.

At the feel of his breath against her lips, she inhaled while his heated gaze almost singed her cheeks. Even if she had wanted to, she couldn't bring herself to look away from his eyes. When she exhaled, he inhaled, and it was like they were doing a dance. It was both relaxing and somewhat erotic. She'd never spent time just breathing and gazing into someone's eyes. "Now you've had your first lesson in Tantra," he murmured against her lips.

She jerked her head back to stare at him in surprise. "Are you going to do more?"

"Maybe." He reached around to undo her bra. "Do you want me to?"

"I think so."

"Then I will. I want to do whatever is pleasing for you."

She wrapped her arms around his neck and kissed him. He eased her over to the four-poster bed. After removing his pants and boxers, he slid her panties down her legs. As Megan sat on the edge of the massive king sized bed, she widened her legs to allow him to step between them. When he brought his hand to stroke between her thighs, she moaned and let her head fall back. Two fingers entered her and began a slow, teasing assault. She began to rock her hips against his hand, adding the friction she desired. When she felt his erection rubbing against her leg, she reached between them to take him in her hand.

Her eyelids fluttered open, and she stared into his face as they worked each other into a sweaty, panting frenzy. When Pesh curled his fingers inside her, she bit down on her lip to keep from screaming out in pleasure. Her orgasm rocketed through her lower half, causing her head to fall forward onto his chest.

When she came back to herself, Pesh was sliding her body up the mattress. Then he was hovering over her, kissing her breasts and licking her nipples into hardened peaks. "Now, Pesh," she urged. "I want you deep inside of me."

Just as his head nudged against her opening, he stopped. "Oh no," he murmured before rocking back to sit on his knees.

Megan propped herself up on her elbows and gazed up at him. "What's wrong?" She hoped that after giving in, he hadn't decided to back out at the last minute.

He rubbed the stubble on his cheeks. "I, uh…we can't do this without a condom, and I don't have one with me."

"Oh," she murmured. In the heat of the moment, she had totally forgotten about that.

"You don't happen to have one?" he asked hopefully.

She shook her head. "Sorry."

"It's me who ought to be sorry for putting you in a position like this without protection." When he started to pull away, she sat up to grab his shoulders, urging him to stop.

"We can still do this. Neither one of us has been with anybody in at least two years—we've had tests for the hospital."

"That's all well and good but what about pregnancy? Are you on the pill?"

"No." She chewed on her bottom lip momentarily. "Wait a minute," she murmured. In her mind, she began counting down the days since her last period. "Twenty."

"Twenty what?"

"I'm on day twenty, so we should be safe."

"I'll still pull out."

"If you say so," she replied. Gripping his biceps, she urged him to cover her again with his body. She loved the feel of his chest hairs rubbing against her nipples. Pesh widened her legs, and then he eased inside her, filling and stretching her walls. It had been so long that she couldn't help feeling a bit of a sting.

"Are you all right?"

"I'm fine."

He withdrew and flexed his hips, thrusting back inside her. This time they both moaned. Setting up a rhythm, he began rocking in and out of her. The pace was slow and sensual, and while he was hitting all the right spots, she wanted more. The entire time he moved in and out of her, he kept his eyes locked firmly on hers. His gaze was so dark with desire that she didn't dare look away. The longer she stared into his eyes, the more connected with him she felt. The old saying was that the eyes were windows to the soul, and she was getting a pretty good glimpse into his. And that scared the hell out of her.

Wanting to make things less sensual, she gripped his biceps. "Harder," she panted.

Rising on his knees, he slid his forearms under the backs of her knees. This enabled him to pull her back against his pounding thrusts. While their connection at first had been so intimate, this was more about lust and desire. She reached up and clasped his face in her hands, bringing his head down to hers. Their mouths and tongues met in frenzied kisses.

When he pulled out of her, Megan whimpered at the loss of feeling. He quickly flipped her over onto her stomach. Pulling on her hips, he raised her up onto her knees. When he reentered her, Megan moaned. With each thrust, he went deeper and deeper. Her fingers fisted the sheets as he leaned over her back, kissing a trail down her spine. She didn't know how he was able to be so many places at once. While his mouth licked her back and teasingly left love bites, his hands were rubbing her thighs and then sliding under her to squeeze her breasts or tease her clit. He was giving her so much that she couldn't stay silent. She moaned, chanted his name, and cried out as the sounds of their wet skin slapped together.

Finally, she couldn't take it anymore. Dropping her head, she screamed into the mattress as she found her release. Once her walls finished clenching, she felt Pesh withdraw from her. As he groaned, Megan felt warmth spurt onto her back and buttocks. After seeing him come before, she hated she couldn't see his face. He was so beautiful when he was finding release.

Once he finished, she eased down onto her stomach and curled a pillow under her head. After a few seconds, Pesh lay down beside her. She turned her head and met his gaze. Exhausted and completely sexually satisfied for the first time in her life, all she could muster to say was, "Wow."

A slow grin spread across his cheeks. "You seem to say that a lot around me after orgasms."

She laughed. "It's because you render me absolutely speechless with your talents."

"Thank you. I could say the same about you." His gaze left her face and trailed down her naked back. "We need to get you cleaned up."

Rolling her shoulder blades, she said, "I kinda like it. Makes me feel marked or something."

He smiled shyly at her. "I like the idea of marking you—making you mine."

He wanted her to be *his*. She didn't know quite what to think about that statement. Did she want to be his? She certainly couldn't imagine belonging to anyone else. Besides the amazing physical chemistry they shared, she was starting to feel such a deep connection to him.

Staring over at him, she couldn't help wondering what was going on in his mind. "We've really done it now, haven't we?"

"Yes, I do believe that was the universal "it" that we just did," he teased.

She smacked his arm playfully. "That's not what I meant."

"I know," he murmured.

"No matter what, this changes everything."

"For the better, I hope."

"I suppose." The truth was she'd never really had casual sex before. There was one time her freshman year that she hooked up with a guy at work. It was the first and only time she'd ever done anything so crazy. In that instance, the sex had been over before she'd known it and without her coming even once. After that fiasco, she had never wanted a repeat performance with him or any other random guy, until she'd found herself in a sex slump after Mason's birth. But with Pesh, the sex had been…she shivered as the remaining echoes washed over her. Before sleeping with Pesh, she could count the number of past sexual partners on one hand, as well as the times she had had even remotely good sex. For Megan, her experience with Pesh was seriously earth shattering and life altering. She couldn't imagine just walking away now.

Pesh sat up and edged to the side of the bed. He held out his hand to her. "Come on. Let's shower."

"If you insist."

She slid over to him before throwing a leg over the side of the mattress. Although she should have felt a little bashful being naked in front of him, she felt surprisingly comfortable.

When she got into the bathroom, she raised her brows in surprise. "A clawfoot tub?" she questioned.

Pesh laughed. "All the old charm but modern conveniences." He pointed to the detachable shower head.

"Nice."

He turned on the water and waited for it to heat up. Once he decided it was warm enough, he took her by the hand and helped her inside. She turned her back to the spray, letting the water clean her up. Pesh didn't seem to think that was enough because after he soaped up his hands, he began to wash off her back and ass. As his magic hands massaged in slow strokes, she couldn't resist asking the question that was plaguing her. "Did I feel different?"

His hands stilled on her lower back. "What do you mean?"

Glancing at him over her shoulder, she replied, "That was the first time I've had sex since I gave birth to Mason. I just wondered if I felt different. You know, inside."

His face came to nuzzle her neck. "You felt amazing."

"Not any different?"

"Did you hear me complaining?"

"No, but I just worried."

"You have nothing to worry about, my love." His hand skimmed over her ribcage to cup her breast. As her nipple hardened beneath his fingers, she sucked in a pleased breath. "I want nothing more than to be back inside you as soon as I can."

"Then why don't you?" she challenged.

"Fine then. Put your hands on the tile," he ordered.

"Yes, sir," she teased before placing her palms on the cool, wet tile.

Pesh slid the gleaming silver shower head between her legs, causing her to gasp at the contact. Then he flicked his wrist to the side, sending the jets of water pounding into her clit. She moaned and threw her head back against his drenched chest. Slowly he started moving the shower head to where it would rub against her. Each time she moved back, the water hit her in just the right spot. She arched her hips as the pressure began to build. Pesh slid his free hand up over her ribcage to cup her breast. He kneaded the flesh, pinching the nipples that were already hardened. She pinched her eyes shut from the sensory overload. Just as she would feel herself about to come, he would shift his wrist so the vibrations hit her in another area, building her again.

"Please, Pesh," she moaned.

"What, baby?"

"Please make me come."

"Have you had enough pleasure yet, or should we continue on?" he asked, moving the shower head away from her.

She groaned at the loss. Rubbing her ass against his hardened erection, she begged, "You let me come, and then I'll make sure you do as well."

With his knee, he nudged her legs even further apart. When he once again brought the shower head between her legs, it reached even more sensitive areas. It took only a few seconds of the water coupled with his rubbing and her grinding to cause her to scream with the pulsing convulsions. She smacked her hands against the walls as wave after wave pulsed through her. When she finally stopped shuddering, she slowly slid around to smile up at Pesh. "Wow?" he said, with a smile.

She teasingly pinched his arm. "I was going to say exquisitely amazing."

"I'm sure you were."

Reaching between them, she took his erection in her hands. "Good thing I'm about to get on my knees because I don't think I could stand after all that," she said, with a teasing wink. Bending her head, she began trailing kisses down his wet chest. As she stroked him, she took time to kiss and then suck on his nipples. His groan told her she was finding some of his most sensitive places. After teasing his nipples to erect points, she continued on down his delicious washboard abs and through the dark hair that crowned his erection.

Sinking down onto the floor of the tub, she stroked him hard from base to tip. When his chest began to heave, she leaned over to slide him into her mouth. "Megan," he groaned, his fingers coming to tangle in the wet strands of her hair. She took him as far back as she could before sliding him out. Her tongue flicked over the sensitive head before she suctioned it. When she released him again, she began long licks up his length. Then she once again slid him in her mouth and began bobbing her head up and down his length. His groans began to echo throughout the bathroom.

"Oh, Megan," Pesh murmured. His grip on her hair tightened as he flexed his hips to go even deeper into her mouth. When he started tightening up, he tried to pull away, but she gripped his thighs and held him in place. He cried out and then came in a rush into her mouth. She swallowed all of him before she glanced up to see him staring down at her with such adoration in his face.

"Thank you."

As he fell free from her mouth, she smiled. "You're welcome."

He helped her up off the tub floor. "We better hurry up before we use all the hot water in these old pipes."

"I think you would probably do a good job keeping me warm."

He smiled. "I feel the same way about you."

Although they were tempted for another round, Megan knew Pesh didn't want to chance it without any condoms. Instead, she tore herself away from him when they finished their shower. She blew her hair dry while he got dressed. Once she finished, he helped her slide back into her dress. Then they left their suite without even turning down the bed.

When they got downstairs, Megan inwardly groaned that the same man was at the reception desk. She knew from his expression that he recognized them as well. As Pesh handed him the key card, Megan decided to make the most of the situation.

She rubbed Pesh's arm. "Thanks again, Mr. Nadeen. Make sure to call me again next time you're in Savannah. I love big spenders like you," she purred.

While the man's eyes bulged, Pesh stared at Megan like she had grown another head. His mouth opened and closed like a fish out of water, but no words of admonishment came out. When he finally, recovered, he tersely replied, "I'll try to remember that, Miss McKenzie."

Truly playing her part, Megan turned on her heels and started walking across the lobby. She didn't get far before Pesh was at her side. After shoving the hotel bill into his suit pocket, he slid his arm around her waist, drawing her close against him. "You are in so much trouble," he growled into her ear.

She giggled as they walked out of the hotel. "Mmm, are you going to punish me by taking me over your knee and spanking me?"

"I just might," he replied.

Tilting her head, she eyed him in the street lights. "You can't seriously expect me to believe that you of all people are into BDSM?"

"No, I'm not."

She snorted. "Once again, that doesn't surprise me."

When he stopped walking right in the middle of the crowded street, she stared up at him in surprise. "A good spanking, some handcuffs, and a blindfold all have possibilities. As far as all that other stuff?" His thumb came up to trail slowly across her bottom lip. "If one truly knows how to fuck, you don't need any accessories and embellishments."

She licked her lips as a little shiver went down her spine. "And you certainly know what you're doing. You just got me wet right here in the middle of the street."

His jaw clenched as he took her by the arm. "Don't say anything else like that. I need to get you home."

"To your bed?" she asked.

"I wish. But you need to go home to your family."

Megan didn't argue with him because she knew he was right. She had a son to think about. Regardless of how tempting it was, she just couldn't go on some pleasure binge when she was a mother. But there was a part of Megan that didn't want the bubble to burst by leaving Pesh and going home to her regular life. She wanted nothing more than go back to his place. Sex with Pesh had been phenomenal.

And despite being a little sore from underuse, she certainly felt ready for more. Sex, that was.

Pesh grabbed them a taxi, and they made the drive back to the airport. Even though they didn't speak, Megan didn't feel awkward around him after what they had done. He sat as close to her as he could with her hand clasped in his.

Once they got back to the plane, she felt exhaustion begin to set in. Leaning back against the headrest, she closed her eyes as Pesh went about getting them ready to take off. She only opened her eyes again when she felt them start racing down the runway. When they got into the air, she couldn't help sitting on the edge of her seat and peering out the windows at the city lights. "It's so beautiful in the dark."

"Sometimes I think I favor flying at night."

"You do?"

He nodded. "For some reason, it seems much more tranquil. There's a vulnerability to it as well. In the day, everything is within your sight distance. But in the dark, you have to rely on your instruments and instincts."

"I'd love to learn how to fly."

"You would?"

She nodded. "I've always thought it would be something amazing to learn."

"Then I'll teach you."

She turned to him in surprise. "Really?"

"Sure. Why not?"

With a shrug, she replied, "You're a busy man, and I don't know how fast a learner I would be."

He smiled. "For you I would make time."

As she stared at him across the small interior of the plane, she knew she was ready to make more time for him as well. Where it would lead them, she couldn't wait to see.

Chapter Fifteen

As the cornflower-blue horizon spread out for miles and miles before her, Megan couldn't help fighting the urge to pinch herself. She was actually up in Pesh's plane during her first flight lesson. From the moment they had taken off, she had been overwhelmed by such a surreal feeling. It must've been something about being in control of the plane as it rocketed down the runway and then took off into the sky. Of course, she really wasn't in total control of the plane. Pesh was able to take over at any moment from his spot in the co-pilot's seat. That made her feel a little better considering she had so little flying experience, and the manual she had read at least twice didn't prepare you for everything.

Now as they coasted along the city skyline, she kept both hands firmly gripping the steering wheel, or yoke as it was called in small plane terminology, as they passed through wispy strands of white clouds. When Pesh had first offered to give her flying lessons, Megan didn't know if she should believe him or not. Looking back, she wasn't sure why she ever doubted him considering he was always a man of his word. And now, just two weeks after their first date in Savannah, they were back up in the air flying around Atlanta on a Thursday afternoon.

It had been quite a week together of having dinner after work or them picking up something on the way to her house. Although, the first day back at work proved both difficult and awkward as they tried to appear as though nothing had changed. But the fact was *everything* had changed, and it wasn't just because they had become physical. As much as Megan tried to fight her growing feelings for Pesh, it was virtually impossible. A man like him made it too hard for any woman not to fall in love with him, and as much as she didn't want to acknowledge it, she could see herself falling for him.

Of course, he was also full of surprises. Like on Monday when he had asked her to see if there was an extra heart monitor in one of the empty patient rooms on the first floor. She had obediently gone to check. While she found the heart monitor, she also found him. The gentleman she had once known became somewhat of a sex fiend when he locked the door and disappeared with her behind the curtain. A mid-day sex session in an empty hospital bed made for quite an experience, especially when the brake on the bed released, and they literally banged into the walls.

But besides the naughty sexcapade, he'd wanted to spend down time with her and Mason. Earlier in the week, Pesh brought Mason to see his plane. Megan had to smile at the image in her mind of

Mason on Pesh's lap in the pilot's seat as he explained the ins and outs of the buttons and knobs. Pesh had shown such patience with Mason by constantly fielding his questions and letting him wear one of the headsets. He'd even gotten the ATC to send a message over the headset so Mason could hear. While it was supposed to be a pre-flying lesson for her, it turned educational for Mason as well. And to make it a day that neither Mason, nor Pesh would forget, they'd gone by McDonald's afterwards so Mason could play on the playground. The fact that Pesh was so willing to do anything to make Mason happy was slowly starting to crack Megan's tough resolve against dating him.

It wasn't just the fact that Pesh was so wonderful with Mason that had her reeling. When they talked, she shared more with him than she ever had with a man. He made it easy to open up to and speak of both the good and the bad in her life. He was such a good listener that she never felt like she was just rattling on and boring him. He truly seemed interested in everything she said. It was an amazing feeling.

"Still doing okay over there?" Pesh asked, bringing her out of her thoughts.

She grinned. "Fine."

"I wish you could see your face," he mused.

"Do I have some dopey expression?" she asked.

"It isn't dopey. It's wide-eyed wonderment like a kid on Christmas morning."

"Oh, I would totally believe it since this certainly feels like a very big and very dangerous toy."

"It's a wonderful sight to see. I'm so glad I get to share this with you." He took one of her hands from the yoke and brought it to his mouth. As his lips kissed over her knuckles, she tensed.

"I need my hand back. I don't feel like I have a good grip on the steering wheel like you said I should," she protested.

Pesh sighed and released her hand. "How I regret telling you that tip now," he lamented.

She smiled. "That's not fair to try and distract me. I need to focus, so we don't crash."

"All right. I'll keep my hands to myself…for now."

A shudder went through her at his words. At that moment if there was any way possible to actually fly the plane and bang him, she would have tried. Shaking her head, she tried ridding herself of her inappropriate thoughts.

"What's that?" she asked, pointing at a dark blip far down on the horizon.

Pesh leaned forward in his seat, peering out the windshield. "Looks like a storm cloud moving in."

"We should head back then."

He chuckled. "I don't think it's going to affect us."

"Yeah, well, I don't like the thought of trying to fly in a storm."

"Then we'll head back."

"Which way should I turn the plane?"

"Let's take a right," Pesh replied.

Megan bobbed her head and then turned the yoke at the same time she pressed on the right rudder pedal with her foot.

"Good. Keep it coming. We're almost turned around." Once they were facing the opposite direction, Pesh said, "Now let's bring up the speed."

She did as she was told and waited for him to give her any further instructions. "We're good to go now. When we're about ten minutes out from McCollum, you need to let the ATC know we're coming in."

"Okay. I can do that."

"Do you have plans for this evening?"

"Not that I know of."

"Would you like to have dinner with me?"

She nibbled on her bottom lip to keep from laughing at his formalness. "I suppose so. Do I get dessert afterwards?"

His body tensed beside her. "Are you implying that I'm dessert, or that after we finish dinner I should get you dessert?"

Megan laughed. "No, I want you for dessert."

"Then you can have me. Always."

Glancing over at him, she said, "I might have to ask for a to-go box since I'm assuming we'll have Mason with us."

"I don't mind. I enjoy spending time with him."

Megan couldn't keep the smile off her face at Pesh's words. "He really likes being with you, too. I've never seen him warm up to a stranger as much as he has to you."

"I'm a likeable guy," he teased.

"Yeah, you are," she murmured, trying not to let the out-of-control fluttering of her heart make her think more than she should about him.

Pesh interrupted her thoughts by motioning to the controls. "Go ahead and start doing your landing checks."

Megan vaguely remembered what knobs and meters she had looked at before they took off. Once she got through the landing checks with Pesh's help, they were getting closer to McCollum. "Now radio ATC."

"Um, okay," Megan replied, nibbling on her lip. After clearing his throat, Megan glanced over at Pesh. He motioned to the yoke. "Oh, duh," she replied. With her thumb, she pressed the push-to-talk button. "This is Cessna 172 coming in for landing."

Before she could ask Pesh if she had done it right, he relayed a different message over his push-to-talk. The ATC's response crackled over her headset. "Cessna 172, this is ground control confirming you are clear to land."

"Now push on the yoke to start the descent," Pesh instructed.

After she did what she was told, her eyes locked on the speedometer. "Should we be picking up this much speed?"

"Yes and no," Pesh replied.

"What the hell does that mean?" she asked, jerking her wild gaze to his.

He chuckled. "See the black knob there labeled 'throttle'?"

"Yeah."

"Look at it this way. You know when you're in a car and you're going downhill, you pick up speed?" Megan nodded. "It's the same thing in a plane. But if you pull on the throttle knob, it reduces the engine power so there won't be an increase in speed."

With her fingers grasping the black knob, Megan asked, "How hard do I need to pull on it?"

"Try pulling back half-way."

After pulling on the knob, Megan eyed the speed. "We're slowing down."

"Good."

"Are we at ninety knots?"

Megan glanced down. "Yeah."

"Okay, then lower the nose just a little bit. That will give us a glide-path or a controlled descent."

Megan eased on the steering wheel until the nose of the plane dipped below the horizon.

"Now put the landing gear in the down position," Pesh instructed.

"Is that the button with the little tire on it?"

"Yep, that's the one."

Megan pressed it. "Got it."

"Using the steering wheel, roll the wings a little to the right, so we're lined back up with the runway."

Megan turned the steering wheel to the right a little too abruptly. "Oops," she replied.

"It's okay. Just level it out. You always want your runway target spot to stay in the same fixed spot on the windshield."

As Megan stared ahead, she realized how close they were getting to the runway, and in turn, the ground. Suddenly she wasn't so sure if she could land the plane. It was one thing taking off, but it seemed like there was so much more that could go wrong when landing. "U-Uh, P-Pesh," she stammered.

"Yeah?" he asked casually.

"I don't think I can do this." She cut her eyes over to him. "I can't land the plane. It's too scary."

"Yes, you can."

Megan shook her head furiously back and forth. "No really. You need to take back the controls. I could cause us to crash."

"But I have faith in you."

"Really?"

"Of course. I wouldn't let you do this if I didn't think you could."

She stole a glance at him, taking in his earnest expression. God, he really and truly believed in her. And it wasn't just about the fact they were banging each other every chance they got alone. No, he saw through to the real her.

After taking a deep breath, she felt herself slowly calming down. "Fine. I'll try, but I'm not making any promises."

"That's my girl," Pesh replied.

"What should I do now?"

"All right, now you need to pull the throttle all the way out as well as pulling back on the wheel to keep the nose from dipping."

Clearing her throat that felt as dry as sandpaper, Megan jerked on the throttle button before pulling on the steering wheel. It was a little harder considering how sweaty her hands were.

"Keep it steady. You're doing great."

As they came closer and closer to the runway, Megan fought the urge to close her eyes, but she realized that would not be the right thing to do. Instead, she braced herself for the impact. The moment the wheels hit the asphalt she shrieked and clutched at the steering wheel.

"Don't fight the bounce. We're fine. *You're* fine."

They skidded along the pavement. "Okay, now ease up on the wheel and push on the tops of both pedals to apply the brakes."

Without thinking, Megan stomped her feet, causing the plane to screech. "Easy," Pesh said.

She let her feet off the brakes, and they began to coast. "Now you're going to bring it back into the hanger."

"Oh, hell no! I would end up mowing out the side of the building or another plane!" Megan cried.

Pesh's amused chuckle died quickly at the death glare she shot him. "Megan, you'll do fine. You just landed a plane. I think you can handle pulling into a hanger."

She scowled at him. "Fine. But when you have to file a huge insurance claim, I'm going to say 'I told you so.'"

"We'll see," he replied. She could tell he was fighting back a smile the way he kept biting down on his lip. "All right, take a right here," he said, pointing to where the runaway split.

She turned the wheel to the right and began easing her foot down on the brake when she saw the hangers come into view. "Which one is yours?"

"I share the third one. Luckily for you, it's pretty much a straight shot in. Just watch out for my dad's plane."

Megan jerked her horrified gaze over to his. "I could be taking out your *dad's* plane?"

Pesh shook his head. "You're not going to take out anyone's plane, Megan. I have faith in you."

She gripped the steering wheel until her knuckles turned white. After taking a deep breath and giving herself a mental pep talk, she started slowly easing the plane inside the hanger. Even though she was far away from the back wall, she hit the brakes. "Is this okay?"

"Looks good to me. Now you want to pull on the red knob."

"The one that says mixture?"

"Yeah, that's the one. It will kill the engine."

When Megan pulled on the knob, the plane shuddered into silence. She couldn't help sitting absolutely frozen for a few moments, processing everything that had happened.

Pesh's hand reached out to rub her shoulder. "You okay over there?" he asked.

Turning her head, she smiled. "I think so."

"You were starting to worry me for a minute."

"I think I was worrying myself."

Pesh's warm laugh made her tingle in parts it shouldn't. With the adrenaline depleting from her system, she knew exactly what she wanted to do. Or maybe the more appropriate word was who she wanted to do.

Frantically, she unbuttoned her seat belt and dove over into his lap. "Megan, what in the hell are you doing?" he demanded.

Her response to his question was to kiss him. Greedily her mouth devoured his lips. As her tongue thrust into his mouth, her hand went between them to cup his growing erection. He groaned while she worked him over his pants. When she rose up on her knees to get a better grip of him, she banged her head against the ceiling of the plane. "Shit!"

"Are you all right?" he asked, bringing his hands up to cup her now aching head.

"I'm fine."

He snickered. "The last thing you need is a concussion. How would we explain that one?"

Megan giggled. "Maybe turbulence during the flight?"

"You're the one creating turbulence," he replied, a wicked gleam in his eyes.

"How are we going to do this?" she asked.

"Backseat," he replied.

With a nod, she began climbing over him into the small two seats in the back. As Pesh unbuckled his seat belt, Megan's fingers furiously worked to get her jeans unzipped and unbuttoned. She was easing them down her thighs when his body came over hers. She once again claimed his mouth as Pesh worked to get his own pants down. "Pocket. Condom," he murmured against her lips. She nodded and then reached her hand down to dig out the foil wrapper.

During high school, she gotten used to having sex in cars, but this was taking it to a whole new level. Somehow without being able to see him in the small confines of the plane's backseat, she rolled the condom down Pesh's length. When she felt his hardness pressing against her core, she widened her legs as far as she could in the cramped quarters. With one quick thrust, he was buried deep inside her. She gripped his shoulders, pushing against him to keep from knocking back into the seat. Considering where they were, there was no time for soft and sweet. Instead, the sounds in the air were of skin slapping together as Pesh's movements were frantic against her. She loved every delicious minute of it, and it wasn't too long before she felt herself going over the edge. Her nails raked over his back as she screamed his name. With her walls milking Pesh's erection, he came with a shout, crushing her body with his.

Just when she thought she couldn't breathe, he jerked back. "Are you okay?"

"I'm fine," she replied. She cupped his cheek. "Really good now, thanks to you."

He gave her the shy smile of his that warmed her all over. "I'm glad to hear that."

"Um, Dr. Nadeen?" someone called outside the plane.

"Oh shit," he muttered, as he slid out of her body. As he went about ridding himself of the condom and jerking his pants up, he called, "Yeah, Trace?"

"I was just concerned about you considering you landed a few minutes ago and hadn't deplaned. And then there was a lot of knocking going on inside the plane."

Megan's hand flew over her mouth as she started giggling uncontrollably. It probably didn't help that as Trace was talking, she had noticed that the windows of the plane were fogged up.

"I appreciate your concern, Trace. I was just checking on some post-flight issues. I'll be out in just a moment."

As Pesh finished and climbed into the front seat, Megan hurried to get her jeans up. Once she had them buttoned and zipped, she smoothed down her hair that had to look like she had just been fucked against an airplane seat. She slid into the passenger seat to find that Pesh had opened the driver's side and was talking to Trace.

Trace's gaze left Pesh's and came to hers. It took only a few seconds for him to put two and two together of what had actually been going on. He slowly started backing away from the plane. "Yeah, well, you two have a nice day then," he said.

"Same to you," Megan called, trying not to start giggling again.

Pesh shook his head as he hopped down out of the plane. "Come on. Let's go before we get in any more trouble."

"But getting in trouble is so much fun," Megan protested, as she opened her door.

He grinned at her as he came around to meet her. "You, my lovely, are a very bad influence." He wrapped his arms around her waist, drawing her close to him. "But I'm grateful for every moment I have with you."

"Mmm, you know just how to flatter a girl," she said, before kissing him.

After a few heated moments, Pesh pulled away. "Considering this hanger has security cameras, let's not totally give them all our secrets today."

Megan squealed and covered her mouth. "Did they…can they…?"

"Not inside the backseat."

She exhaled with relief. "Thank goodness."

He laughed. "Come on, little troublemaker. Let's go get something to eat."

"Sounds good to me." With a wink, she added, "Especially if there's dessert!"

Chapter

Sixteen

A few days after her flying adventure and partial induction in the mile high club, Megan had started to take a few scripts to the pharmacy when she was yanked by the arm and dragged into an examining room. "What the?" she began, as the door was slammed behind her.

Instead of Pesh before her, it was Kristi. "I need to have a word with you."

Anxiety bubbled in Megan's chest, and she had to take a few deep breaths before she could speak. "Have I done something wrong with a patient?"

Kristi shook her head. "Oh no, this has everything to do with Dr. Nadeen."

Megan's brows shot up in surprise. "Pesh? What's wrong with him?"

"It's not what is wrong with *him*. It's what is wrong with *you*."

Megan gulped. "Me?"

Kristi nodded. "I really like you, Megan, but I am worried that you are just playing him. It is cruel. He doesn't deserve it."

"I don't know what you mean."

"Please don't play coy. Not only do I have two daughters around your age, but I've spent enough time working with women to have a pretty good insight into the female mind. So, I'll ask once again, what are you doing?"

Megan squirmed under the heat of Kristi's stare. If anyone found out that she and Pesh were hooking up, it could be very bad for her nursing career. "We're friends. He's my cousin's godfather."

Kristi rolled her eyes. "Fine. Let me speak as freely as I can since you insist on playing dumb. I don't give two shits if you and Pesh are screwing all over this hospital—"

Megan was unable to contain her loud gasp. "Excuse me, but I—"

Now it was Kristi's turn to interrupt. She held up her hands. "Let me finish please."

"Fine," Megan muttered.

"I realize that deep down he's just a man, and after going a long time without sex, it was probably a little easier for him to give in to just a causal relationship with you. But I've worked by his side for seven years, so I have a pretty good handle on what he's truly feeling."

"Oh really?" Megan countered, unable to stop herself from being snarky.

"Yes, I do. That man loves you with every fiber of his being."

Those words caused Megan's steely resolve to fade. She couldn't help staggering a bit on her feet. She knew that Pesh liked her—I mean, any fool could see that. But love? "H-He does?"

"Oh yeah, he does. He's been holding a candle for you since the moment you walked in here. I saw it the first day I introduced you two. I don't know what has happened since that day, but I know something has changed for you, too."

"It's true that I care about him. He's the most amazing man I've ever known."

"Then what the hell is the problem?"

"I wish I could tell you, but I don't even know myself," Megan moaned as tears stung her eyes. "Dammit, stupid PMS hormones."

"Oh honey, you do actually care about him, don't you?"

"Yes," she whispered.

"And you're a wreck about what you're feeling for him, aren't you?" Kristi asked.

Megan couldn't hold back the sobs any longer. They rolled through her, causing her to bend at the waist under the burden. Kristi stepped forward, wrapping her arms around Megan. Even though she knew she should try to fight her emotions considering she was at work, she decided to let herself go and get it all out. When she finally had a hold of herself, she raised her head, wiping what she imagined were the hideous black mascara streaks off her face.

"I'm so sorry. That was so unprofessional of me."

Kristi gave her a sad smile. "Would you stop that, please? This isn't an evaluation. Besides, I'm the one who pulled you in here and provoked you. You always keep your emotions in check out on the floor."

"The truth is I do care for Pesh. How could I not? I'm just not sure I'm the right woman for him."

"But if he loves you, how could you think you're not the right one?"

Megan blurted out all the reasons she'd previously given Pesh about her age and her lack of wanting a committed relationship. When she finally finished unburdening herself of all her doubts and fears, she glanced up at Kristi. There was no judgment in her eyes or anger for that matter. Instead, she merely patted Megan's cheek. "Oh honey, you've got to tune all those negative voices out and go with your heart."

Megan shook head. "But what if I don't know what my heart is telling me to do?"

"You will. Just give it time." Kristi patted her back. "Why don't you go get cleaned up and then take your lunch break?"

"No, I need to make up for the time I've missed."

"You're fine." She motioned to the door. "Go on. See if Dr. Nadeen is on his way to lunch so you can join him."

"But I shouldn't. It won't look right if we're alone together."

Kristi chuckled. "Alone together in a crowded hospital cafeteria? I don't think that's possible."

Megan nibbled on her bottom lip and fought the urge to argue with Kristi. After all, if the very woman who was in charge of her clinical grade didn't give a shit about her and Pesh being seen together, why should she? Finally, she just gave a defeated sigh. "Okay, I'll go see."

"Good girl. And you be listening to your heart now. Okay?"

"I'll try. I promise."

Although she spoke the words with such conviction of character, Megan was afraid it was going to be harder than she thought.

Chapter Seventeen

When Pesh arrived at work the following day, he found Kristi alone in the nurses' station. Gazing around, he asked, "Where's Megan?"

"Oh, she called in sick today."

Both disappointment and concern filled him. She had seemed a little off the night before when they had dinner together in the cafeteria. She was quieter and somewhat withdrawn. He had just chalked it up to the fact that they were sitting with some of the other staff and she was trying not to make things seem weird with them now.

He wondered if he should call her and check to make sure she was okay. They were in such limbo together that even though it sounded like the right thing to do, he wasn't sure. With a resigned sigh, he decided to leave things as they were and vowed to check on her tomorrow when she returned to work.

As much as Pesh hated to admit it, the day dragged mercilessly without Megan. He went from patient to patient with a monotony he hadn't felt in a long time. When his shift ended, he met Kristi in the hallway. "Want me to walk you out?" he suggested.

"Thank you. I'd appreciate that."

"It would be my pleasure."

They started out the mechanized doors to the employee parking lot. To fill the quiet of their shoes echoing on the pavement, he said, "I hated to hear that Megan wasn't feeling well."

"So did I. Poor thing offered to pull a double tomorrow to make up for being gone." Kristi smiled. "She sure is going to make a fine nurse."

"Yes, she is."

"You've taken a special interest in her, haven't you?" Kristi asked.

Pesh's steps momentarily faltered, and he stumbled. "Whatever do you mean?"

Kristi chuckled. "You know exactly what I mean."

"It is true that we know each other outside of the hospital, but when we're in the ER, our relationship is strictly professional."

"I never said it wasn't."

After gazing around the somewhat deserted parking lot, he shook his head. "What you're alluding to between me and Megan? Nothing good can come of those types of rumors."

Patting his arm, Kristi smiled. "There are no rumors—merely an observation by someone who loves and admires you."

His brows rose in surprise. "You don't disapprove?"

"Of course not. I think it's a good match for both you and her."

He remained silent for a few moments, contemplating her words. "Perhaps I should call and check on her."

"I think that would be a very good idea." She took her keys out of her purse and motioned at the Honda they were standing in front of. "Well, this is me."

"Have a good night, Kristi."

"Same to you, Dr. Nadeen. And good luck."

He smiled. "Thank you. I appreciate that."

When he got to his car, he slid inside and took his phone out. He scrolled through his contacts to find Megan's number. After he dialed, he anxiously drummed his fingers on the steering wheel. The call went to her voicemail, leaving him with a defeated feeling. Although he knew it probably wasn't the best idea in the world, he decided to go to her house to check on her.

The moment he rang her parents' doorbell he really regretted making a house call. One of her younger brothers answered. "Hey, what's up?" he asked.

"Hello. I'm Dr. Nadeen. I work with Megan."

Snapping his fingers, he pointed at Pesh. "Wait, I know you. Aren't you Noah's godfather?"

Pesh smiled. "Yes, I am."

"Cool. Listen man, Megan's downstairs. If you go around the side of the house, she has her own door."

"I see. Thank you then."

"No problem."

When the door closed, Pesh debated going straight to his car. But he knew it would look even worse if her brother told her he had been there and then he had left without seeing her. Heaving a frustrated breath, he headed off the porch. He followed the sidewalk around the house to where it sloped down the hill.

At the side door, he knocked loudly. When the door flew open, Megan stared at him in a mixture of both surprise and horror. "What are you doing here?" she demanded.

Pesh shoved his hands in his pockets. "You called in sick today. I was worried."

"I'm fine."

He fought the urge to say that by her disheveled appearance and dark circles under her eyes, she most certainly didn't seem fine. "I tried calling you, but you didn't answer. Kristi and I were worried about you."

Her expression softened a little. "I'm sorry. I must've forgotten to charge my phone."

"Can I get you something to eat? Some soup maybe?"

"Really, I'm fine."

"But you look so pale. Will you let me do an exam? You know the flu is—"

"I don't have the flu."

"How can you be sure if you haven't been checked? Did you get the flu shot at the hospital? Sometimes it can give you a mild case."

She shook her head and smiled. "I don't have the flu. Since you're going to keep on and on, I'm going to go ahead and tell you. I have really horrendous cramps with my period. Usually, I can manage them with birth control, but when I started clinicals and stopped working, I couldn't afford the birth control without health insurance. And it wasn't like I was having sex anyway."

While he appreciated her honesty, he was also slightly mortified. "Oh, I see."

"I'm sorry to have embarrassed you," Megan said.

He waved his hand dismissively. "Listen, when you return to work tomorrow, there will be a script for you for birth control. I don't like the idea of you in pain, so I don't want this to happen next month."

"But the money," she protested.

He shook his head. "It will be discounted through the hospital pharmacy."

"Thank you, Pesh. That's a very decent thing for you to do."

A blonde head peeked around Megan. "Hi Esh. You play?"

He smiled at Mason. "I came to check on your mommy."

Mason tilted his chin to look up at Megan. "Her tummy hurts. She no play. U play?"

"Um, well…" He wanted nothing more than to spend time with Mason, and in the same token, with Megan as well. But he was also walking such a fine line with her that he didn't want to come on too strong and scare her off. "I'm not sure your mommy feels up to company."

Megan smiled. "If you really don't mind staying, we'd love to have you."

"Are you certain?"

"Sure."

"Okay then."

Mason grabbed his hand and led him through the door. Pesh took in the cozy décor of the basement apartment. In one chair, Megan's textbooks and papers were strewn around, while on the floor it looked like a tornado had blown through the living room with all the toys lying around. When he met her gaze, she flushed. "Sorry it's such a mess."

"It's fine."

"Are you hungry?" she asked.

"No, I'm good," he lied, as his stomach rumbled.

Megan cocked her head and shot him a look. "Sit down and let me fix you something."

"Not with you feeling unwell."

"Although I wish I could cook you something, I think I'm up to reheating some of the pizza we ordered today, or there are some homemade enchiladas I made last night," she replied, as she opened the fridge.

"Enchiladas would be lovely."

She smiled and took out a casserole dish. "You hungry, Mace?"

"Mmm, hmm," he murmured, barely looking up at his mother from one of his toys. After spooning out two heaping plates full, along with some rice, she put it in the microwave. She then motioned for him to have a seat at the table.

"You don't need to wait on me."

"Just shut up and let me take care of you for two seconds."

Her words reminded him of when she had cleaned his wounds after Dev's punch. No matter what the situation, she was always ready to be there for him and take care of him.

The microwave beeped and brought him out of his thoughts. Mason hurried over to the table and sat down beside Pesh in his booster seat. When Megan put down the steaming plates, he reached for her hand and kissed it. "Thank you."

A funny look passed in her eyes before she smiled. "You're welcome."

"Won't you sit with us?" he asked.

"Actually, I would love to take a warm bath. You know, to see if it would help relax my muscles."

Pesh smiled. "I'll be happy to keep an eye on Mason while you do that."

"You don't mind?"

"Of course I don't."

"Thanks. I really appreciate it." She kissed the top of Mason's head, and then kissed his cheek. She turned to start into the bedroom before whirling back around. He lowered his fork at the expression on her face. Placing her hands on his cheeks, she leaned in and laid a big one on him. He couldn't hide his surprise. When she pulled away, she grinned at his speechlessness. "I won't be long," she said.

Once the bedroom door closed behind her, Pesh gazed over at Mason. "What do you want to do when we finish eating?"

"Minions," he mumbled through a mouthful of food.

Pesh furrowed his brows in confusion. "What's minions?"

Hopping down off his chair, Mason ran over to the TV. When he returned, he had a DVD box in his hand. He pointed to some yellow blobs on the cover. "Minions."

"Ah, I see. You want to watch this." Mason bobbed his head. "Is it your favorite?" Pesh asked.

"Uh, huh," Mason replied.

"Then I guess we better eat fast so we can watch it."

At Mason's beaming grin, Pesh felt a little tug in his chest. Even though he shouldn't, he already had strong feelings for the little boy. From almost the moment they'd met, Mason had let Pesh into his world.

The sound of a fork clattering on a plate brought Pesh out of his thoughts. "Done!" Mason exclaimed, hopping out of his chair. Although Pesh wasn't finished, Mason grabbed his hand and led him from the table. Instead of arguing with him, Pesh just let himself be dragged over to the TV. Once he got the movie on, they settled down on the couch. He couldn't fight the warmth that spread through his chest when Mason snuggled close to his side. Instead, he just embraced the feeling and let happiness override the doubt that screamed in his mind.

Under the strong, warm jets of the jacuzzi tub, Megan's pain started to fade. Of course, as much as she tried to relax, it was too hard considering that Pesh was in her living room. She couldn't believe that he had shown up out of the blue to check on her. Just when she thought he couldn't be any kinder or more attentive, he did something like that.

Tilting her neck on the foam headrest, she thought about her talk with Kristi the day before. She hated to admit it, but she knew she had a choice to make. She either had to let go of Pesh, or she had to make things official with him. They couldn't just keep dating and hooking up…or was it just hooking up?

With a frustrated groan, she shifted in the tub, sloshing the water around. Closing her eyes, she tried to search her heart for how she truly felt. No man had ever made her feel like felt with Pesh, and that could be said both inside and out of the bedroom. Gazing down at her pruning fingers, she knew it was time to get out of the tub. She could stay there for days and still not have the answer she so desperately sought.

After she toweled off and wrapped herself in her terry cloth robe, she went out into the bedroom. As she threw on a fresh pair of pajama pants and a T-shirt, she noticed it was awfully quiet in the living room. Wondering what Mason and Pesh could be doing, she ducked out of the bedroom. The sight across from her on the couch made her chest clench with emotion. Reaching up, she clutched her T-shirt over her heart, trying to still some of the ache that burned there.

With the strains of *Despicable Me* playing in the background, Pesh lay on his back with Mason on top of him. Her son's face was snuggled into Pesh's chest, and he was sound asleep. They both were. Pesh's face was tilted down, his nose pressed into the strands of Mason's hair.

Before she could harden herself to the emotions coursing through her, tears stung her eyes. In that moment, she allowed herself to fantasize that this was truly her life. She had a loving husband who adored her, and her son had an attentive and doting father. What more could she ask for in life? In those minutes of weakness, she wondered why she had been fighting Pesh so hard about a relationship. Besides her own happiness, there was nothing more in the world that she wanted than for Mason to be safe and happy.

As she came crashing back to reality, she saw things clearly for the first time in a long time. Pesh had been so worried about her that he'd driven over just to check on her. She'd never had a boyfriend who cared about her that much, and no matter how hard she searched in the future, she was probably never going to find another man like Pesh. There were so many things about him that she liked...maybe even loved. He made her want to get up in the mornings, so she could see him at work. She found herself anxiously checking her phone to see if she had a text from him. She loved spending time with him. But it was more than just the feelings that Pesh felt for her or that she felt for him—it was the fact that he cared so much about her son. They were a package deal for any future man, and he had willingly embraced that fact without complaint.

On shaky legs, she walked over to the couch. As she stood over the two of them, she couldn't help reaching out her hand and tenderly touching Pesh's cheek. He stirred at the contact. When his eyelids fluttered open, she smiled at him. "Hi."

His gaze spun around the room like he was trying hard to remember where he was. When he glanced down at Mason, realization washed over his face. "Sorry. I didn't mean to fall asleep."

"It's okay. I'm sure you needed it. Besides, I took too long in the tub."

He smiled. "I would argue that you need it as well."

Bending over, she slid her hand under Mason's stomach while the other went under his legs. She hoisted him up and into her arms. When he whimpered, she murmured, "Shh, Mommy's going to put you to bed."

"Night, night, Pesh," Mason mumbled drowsily.

"Good night, little man," Pesh replied.

Once she had tucked Mason in and kissed his cheek, she closed his bedroom door and returned to the living room. Pesh sat hunched over on the edge of one of the couch cushions, as if he were planning to leave as soon as she came back. "Is he okay?" he asked.

She nodded. "Out like a light the moment I put him down."

"Good." When he started to stand up, she pushed him back down on the couch. Easing down onto his lap, she wrapped her arms around his neck. He brought his hand up to rub lazy circles over her back. She didn't speak for a few minutes. Instead, she just enjoyed being close to him, the feel of his hand on her, his strong, muscled thighs beneath her.

"Thank you for coming over tonight."

His brows rose in surprise. "Are you sure? I was afraid I was overstepping my bounds."

Raking her fingers through his dark hair, she shook her head. "I think we need to talk about our boundaries."

"Oh?"

She nodded. "You coming over here tonight made me realize something very important. What we've been doing has been fun, and I've enjoyed every minute of it. But now—"

Pesh's dark eyes snapped shut, and the expression on his face shifted as if he were in pain. "Please. You don't have to say this. I'll just go."

"But I don't want you to go," she argued.

"Then what are you trying to say?"

"That I need you in my life, and I want more."

His brows shot up. "More? As in more of us together?"

"Yes."

He sucked in a breath. "You want us to be an official couple?"

She smiled. "Yes, I do. Well, everywhere except work."

"I can't believe it," he murmured.

"This isn't exactly the reaction I thought you would have," she teased.

"Oh, I'm happy. Trust me. I'm just shocked, that's all."

She brought her lips to his and gave him a tender kiss. Against his lips, she murmured, "Can you ever forgive me for being so stubborn and so stupid?"

"I can try. But I suppose you're going to have to work very hard to make it up to me."

"Am I?"

He nodded. "Yes, very hard."

"Why do I have the funny feeling that your idea of me making it up to you is entirely different than mine?"

"No more orgasms for dates. Just dates."

"I can handle that."

A wicked gleam flashed in Pesh's eyes. "The first date will be to the Fox to see an opera."

She groaned. "You don't play fair."

He ran his hands up her sides, causing her to shiver. "I would have to argue that you haven't been playing fair all along. Now it's my turn."

"Are you going to punish me?" she questioned in a whisper.

"Mmm, hmm, there will lots of dates and lots of time spent together." He quirked a brow at her. "A true hell on earth."

She couldn't help giggling. "I'll be a good girl and take it."

"I'm glad to hear it."

As they lapsed into silence, Megan's fingers wound through the hair at the base of his neck. "Do you want to stay the night with me?"

Pesh's brows furrowed as if silently questioning her proposal. "But you—"

"No sex. Just sleeping."

"You think that's a good idea with Mason?"

"We're a couple now. He's going to be seeing a lot of you."

Pesh smiled. "Yes, he is."

Staring into his eyes, she asked, "So you'll stay?"

"It would be a pleasure."

Without another word, she rose off his lap. After he got up off the sofa, she took him by the hand and led him to her bedroom. As she sat on the edge of the mattress, she watched as Pesh stripped down to his boxer shorts. When he was finished, he walked slowly over to her. "I'm sorry we can't do anything else."

He brushed the hair out of her face and cupped her cheeks. "I don't mind. I'm happy just to be with you."

In her heart, she was happy as well and not just about him staying the night. But for how everything between them had worked out. "So am I," she murmured before lying back on the bed. "So am I."

Chapter Eighteen

For Megan, the next few weeks flew by. She didn't know if it was because she was so busy at work, or it was because she was so happy being with Pesh. She liked to think it was the latter. Or maybe it was that she was busy being with Pesh. On her off days and his, they spent every second together. Most often, he came to her house. They made dinner together or they went out. Although her parents didn't entirely approve, he slept over as well. What they didn't know is that some nights nothing illicit even happened between them. Exhausted from the day's events, they merely enjoyed lying in each other's arms.

As she came out of a patient's room, she glanced up to see Pesh standing across the hall talking to another doctor. For just a moment, his gaze met hers, and although no one else could have possibly noticed it, she saw the longing and the affection. She gave him a brief nod before walking on to the nurses' station.

Since they had become a couple, their time at work had become almost a game of wills to pretend there was nothing going on between them. Most days, it was harder than Megan could have ever imagined not to burst out in a smile whenever she saw him or to resist the urge not to wrap her arms around him. But somehow they made it work. In the end, the pent up emotions that were suppressed during the day made for a lot of heated fireworks in the evenings.

Megan's thoughts were interrupted at the buzzing of her phone. When she glanced down at it, she grinned. It was Pesh.

It killed me not to be able to kiss you a moment ago.

I know. Me too.

Dinner at my place tonight?

U cooking? She questioned.

Yeah. Indian food.

Mmm, sounds good. What time?"

7. Does Mason like Indian food?

Megan eyed his text thoughtfully. The last three times she had been with Pesh, Mason had been with them as well. Pesh never seemed to mind, but Megan wanted a night with just him. A true date night.

Not sure. Will get my parents or Papa to babysit.

You don't have to do that.

I know. I want to.

Okay. See you at 7.

Bye.

She had just slipped her phone back in her pocket when she was ambushed by Kara. Since the day she'd seen Kara grope Pesh in the hallway, Megan had loathed the sight of her. She had managed to keep her distance from her at work, but lately, she noticed that Kara had been creeping around, staring at her.

"Can I do something for you?" Megan asked politely.

"Yeah, for starters, you can drop the sugar sweet act. I know how you feel about me."

Megan fought the urge to roll her eyes. Instead, she crossed her arms over her chest. "Fine. What do you need Kara?"

Kara glanced around them before she spoke. "I want you to back off of Pesh."

"Excuse me?"

Narrowing her eyes, Kara said, "I know you're into him. I can see it in the way you look at him…it's in the way he looks at you, too. And I don't like it."

"Well, I'm terribly sorry that you don't, but frankly, I don't see how any of that is any of your business."

"Oh, he is very much my business considering we've been together."

"Um, okay. Whatever," Megan replied, feeling slightly shattered by Kara's proclamation. In the rational side of her mind, she knew there was no way Pesh could be involved with Kara. But at the moment, it was the irrational side that seemed to be winning out over whether Pesh was truly hers.

Kara jerked her chin in the air. "Besides the fact of what Pesh and I are to each other, I'm sure it would be very interesting business to your professor. Last time I checked, a nursing candidate wasn't supposed to get involved with a doctor. Bad for one's reputation."

"Are you threatening me?"

After a casual shrug of her shoulders, Kara replied, "Just stating facts. You don't impress me as one of those bimbo girls who likes to be used by a man for sex, which I'm afraid that's exactly what Pesh is doing with you. But more than not wanting to be a sex toy, I imagine you wouldn't want to do anything to harm your future career."

"I'm not discussing this any further," Megan muttered, as she started past her.

"I won't be either as long as you stay away from Pesh."

Without giving Kara a final glance, Megan continued walking down the hallway. She didn't know where she was going, but she knew she wanted to put as much distance as she could between herself and Kara.

The rest of the day she felt haunted by Kara's words. More than anything, she couldn't wait until she could be alone with Pesh to talk to him about it.

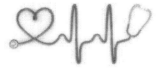

Pesh jerked his head up at the loud bang behind him. The garage door leading into the kitchen was thrown open with such a force that it rattled on its hinges. Megan stalked into the room, her mouth turned down in a determined frown. She threw her purse down onto the floor beside one of the bar stools. With a frustrated breath, she blew back a few errant strands of blonde hair that had escaped the loose knot at the back of her neck.

"Bad day?" he asked, with thinly veiled amusement.

She glared at him. "Yes, as a matter of fact it was."

"What happened?"

"Well, where do I start? When I went to drop Mason off at Papa's house, there was a woman there with him."

Pesh's brows rose in surprise. "Patrick is dating?"

"He claims she's—"Megan paused to make air quotes with her fingers, "just a friend. But I don't buy it."

As he stirred the rice, he glanced at her over his shoulder. "Would it be wrong if he were dating?"

A long sigh escaped Megan's lips. "No, he deserves to be happy. My nana has been dead for six years, so it's not like he raced out the moment he was free and started going through women like Kleenex."

Pesh chuckled at her summation. "Did you not like her?"

Crossing her arms over her chest, Megan replied, "That's the other part. She seemed really nice. And Mason loves her. I guess she's been there before when he stayed with Papa."

After abandoning his place by the stove, Pesh placed his hands on the marble countertop and leaned in close to Megan. "It sounds to me like Patrick has found a good woman who loves him and his family. I don't think you could ask for a better scenario."

She stared into his eyes for a moment before she smiled. "You're right. I don't know why I got so upset about it all."

"Because as much as you love your grandfather, you're still protective of your grandmother's memory."

"You're so wise," she murmured.

"It comes with age," he replied, with a wink.

"Whatever."

He gave her a quick kiss on the lips before returning to the stove. "So besides Patrick's new lady friend, what else happened to get you so upset?"

When Megan didn't reply, Pesh turned around. "What else is it?"

"You need to have a serious discussion with Kara."

His brows rose in surprise. "I do?"

"Yes, you do."

"Megan, you do remember that I'm not in charge of nurses."

She rolled her eyes. "Yes, I realize that. But you are in charge of your dick, are you not?"

"Excuse me?"

Crossing her arms over her chest, Megan said, "Kara seems to think that the two of you are an item."

Pesh chuckled. "Oh that's nonsense. We're just friends from working together."

Megan narrowed her eyes suspiciously at him. "You've never seen her outside of work?"

This was one area of questioning he hadn't bargained on ever having to answer. The truth was something he really didn't want to admit to Megan. Carefully choosing his words, he replied, "We got together for drinks a couple of times after work a few months back. I hardly think that categorizes us as an 'item.'"

"It must be enough for her to think she can tell me that you're only using me for sex."

Pesh winced at the words. He would have never taken Kara for being someone who was jealous. He put down the spatula and turned off the stove. He knew he couldn't go forward without coming clean. "Megan, I haven't been honest with you."

"What do you mean?" she asked.

"I told you that Kara and I had only had drinks a couple of times. But that isn't the whole truth."

Megan's eyes widened. "What are you saying?"

Defeated, his shoulders drooped a little. "After the night of Noah's baptism, I couldn't get you off my mind. I wanted to prove to myself that I wasn't so enamored by you. So after having a couple of drinks one night, Kara and I went to my car and fooled around."

"You got drunk?"

He gave a mirthless laugh. "That is what is most shocking to you in what I just told you?"

"Did you think I would be mad at you for messing around with some woman when we weren't dating?"

"Yes," he answered honestly.

Megan shook her head. "What you did then was your business. I mean, I'm not thrilled to hear that you fooled around with her, especially since you wouldn't sleep with me when I asked you to."

"But don't you see the difference? I cared for you, and I cared nothing for her. We were barely in the car fifteen minutes if that tells you anything."

The corners of her lips tugged up in a small smile. "I really don't need the details of how much you didn't enjoy yourself."

He ducked his head. "I'm sorry. I shouldn't have said that."

"But at the same time, I'm glad to hear that you won't be going back for a repeat performance."

Jerking his gaze up to meet hers, he replied, "Never could I do that."

"And you really were trying to get me off your mind?"

"Yes, I was."

"In a warped way, that's very romantic," she teased.

"I'm glad you think so," he mumbled.

"Look, it's not the fact that she said you were using me for sex that has me so upset."

"It's not?"

"She threatened me."

Pesh's eyes narrowed. "Physically?"

"Not exactly. She said that if I didn't watch my back, she would report me to the dean."

A low growl erupted from Pesh's chest. "She seriously said that?"

"Yes, she did."

"I'm sorry that her jealousy and spitefulness is rearing its head. I never imagined she was such a person when I…well, when I got involved with her. I'll make sure to speak to her. No one should have to work in a hostile environment, and she must understand that just because of her seniority, she is not allowed to harass you." Pesh watched Megan fidget on her feet while nibbling on her bottom lip. "Do you not want me to speak to her?"

"No, that's fine. It's just…"

"Is there something else?"

"You know how much I like you. I mean, the very fact I agreed to date you shows how much I'm committed to you."

Pesh crossed his arms over his chest. "I'm thinking there's a 'but' coming that I'm not going to like."

Megan sighed. "But at the same time, whatever it is that is happening between us…" She swallowed hard. "I've worked really hard in school, Pesh. I don't want anything on my record that could hurt my chances of getting a job."

If she was the crying type, he would have sworn her eyes shimmered with tears. He came around the counter to pull her into his arms. "Hey now, don't you worry one bit about getting into trouble. Anyone who has seen you in action on the floor knows what a talented and gifted nurse you are."

She sniffled. "If there's even a rumor of me having an affair with an attending physician, I could be blacklisted."

Pesh pulled away to grip her chin in his fingers. "After I speak to Kara, you will have nothing to worry about, okay?"

He could tell that even though she wanted to relax and let go of her anxiety, she couldn't. "Come on. Let's fix you up."

She wiped her eyes. "What do you mean?"

With a wink, he went over to the cabinet and got down a wine glass. Then he poured some white wine into the glass before setting it down on the bar. "Take that."

Megan glanced at the glass and then back at him. "Are you trying to ply me with wine?"

"Maybe."

She leaned forward and picked it up. He watched as she couldn't resist the temptation and she took a hearty gulp. Closing her eyes, she murmured, "That's so good."

"I'm glad you like it." He walked around the counter again. This time he took her free hand. "Come on."

"Where are we going?"

"For part two of your relaxation."

Megan smiled at him before he began tugging her down the hall. When he got into the bedroom, he noticed her sigh of frustration when they bypassed the bed for the bathroom. "While I finish dinner for us, you need to soak in a nice, hot bath."

"You spoil me," she protested with a smile.

He gave her a playful wink before turning on the bath water. Once he got the temperature right, he turned back to her. "Bubbles? Bath salt?"

She raised her brows. "Don't tell me you actually have those? I mean, I know you're a metrosexual but really?"

"We all have our secrets," he replied. He didn't have the heart to tell her that he had kept some of Jade's Bath & Body Works stuff. He might've tried to bury them under the bathroom counter to get them out of sight and out of mind, but they were still there. He rummaged around to pull out a vanilla bottle as well as a peach. He held them up to Megan for her approval.

"Hmm, vanilla."

"Good choice." It was the one scent that didn't remind him of Jade since she never used it. He poured a healthy cupful under the water, letting the foam magnify.

"Ready to get in?"

Megan glanced down at herself before looking back at him. "Well, I seem to still be dressed."

Pesh cocked his head at her. "Oh really? I can help you with that." He took the wine glass from her and sat it on the counter. His fingers came to the hem of her shirt. Without taking his eyes off of hers, he jerked it up and over her head. He gazed down at her simple, white bra. She sucked in a breath when his fingers skimmed her abdomen before he gripped the waistband of her scrubs and tugged them down. She stepped out of the pants, standing before him in only her bra and skimpy thong.

Taking her by the shoulders, he gently turned her around. His fingers trailed down her back to the clasp of her bra. Once he unhooked it, he brought his hands up to slide it off her shoulders. Unable to resist the softness of her skin, he bent his head to kiss along her back. As he dropped the bra to the floor, his hands skimmed up her ribcage to cup her breasts. "Mmm," Megan murmured, letting her head fall back against his chest.

"I'm only supposed to be undressing you," he argued, as he let her breasts fall free of his hands.

She immediately picked them up and brought them back to cup her flesh. "I like the way you undress me. It's very relaxing."

Rolling her puckered nipples between his fingers, he was rewarded with her gasp of pleasure. "The water is getting cold," he warned.

"I'm getting so hot, I can warm it up."

He chuckled against her ear before taking his hands away from her. As she whined in protest, his fingers jerked her thong down over her thighs. She raised her feet to step out of the underwear. "All right. Get in."

"Tease," she muttered, before walking over to the tub. He only got to admire her naked backside for a moment before she lowered herself into the tub and disappeared under the foam. Leaning back against the wall, she closed her eyes in bliss. "This feels amazing."

"Good."

"But you know what would feel even better?"

"What?"

Her eyes popped open, and she smiled invitingly up at him. "If you were in here with me."

"Really?"

"Mmm, hmm."

"I should be finishing dinner," he argued, feebly.

Megan eyed the growing bulge in his pants. "I think you should be in here letting me finish you."

He threw his head back and laughed. "Fine. You drive a hard bargain, my lady." He quickly unbuttoned and took off his shirt. Then his fingers went to the button and zipper on his pants. He slid them and his boxers down and stepped out of them, leaving him naked.

Megan didn't take her eyes off him the whole time. He shifted them in the water, bringing Megan up to straddle him, but she was facing away from him. "What are you doing?" she asked.

He brought his hands to her shoulders and started massaging the tense muscles. "Helping you relax."

She ground herself against his erection. "I was hoping a couple of orgasms would do that instead."

He chuckled. "Don't you believe in foreplay?"

"Yes, but not when I'm this horny."

Bending his head, he let his warm breath tickle her outer ear. "You, my love, are never going to be a candidate for Tantric sex. You will never allow yourself to enjoy delayed pleasure and release."

"I want to try—honest, I do."

"But just not this evening, right?" One of his hands abandoned her shoulder to slide down in between her legs. She gasped as his thumb rubbed against her clit. As he continued stroking her with his thumb, he pushed two fingers into her slick passage. Megan whimpered and thrust her hips against him. Pesh kissed and licked her wet neck and back as he pumped his fingers in and out of her. "Does that feel good?"

"Yes, oh yes," she murmured.

He increased the pressure of his thumb, and Megan shrieked, bucking her hips faster and faster against his fingers. When his other hand cupped and kneaded her breast, she cried out and came, her walls clenching against his fingers.

Once she finished shuddering, she collapsed back against him. "Feeling better now?"

"A little." She twisted her body around to where she was facing him. "I want you inside me the next time I come." She rose up and then took his erection in her hand. While keeping her eyes on his, she guided him into her core. Slowly, she sunk inch by inch on him. When she was fully seated, they both moaned at the feeling. At the intensity of what he felt inside her, Pesh was thankful she had taken him up on the birth control script where he didn't have to use condoms anymore.

She brought her hands up to his shoulders, and then she began to ride him. His hands came to grip her waist as his head bent forward to suckle one of her nipples into his mouth. His teeth grazed the bud before his tongue flicked and teased it into a hardened point. Throwing her head back, Megan's walls tensed and convulsed around him. He knew he had a long way to go before he was going to come.

Once she recovered, Megan panted as she started riding him faster, causing the water to slosh around them. As his mouth latched onto her other breast, Megan threw her head back and moaned. "Harder," she urged.

Pesh continued sucking her nipple as he began to thrust his hips up in time to meet her movements. Each time he went a little deeper, and it caused Megan to be more and more vocal. She tugged at the strands of his hair and clawed at his chest as she strove harder and harder for her orgasm. "Please, please," she panted, as her hands came to cup her own breasts. As she pinched and tweaked her own nipples, it was Pesh's undoing. Shoving his hand down between her legs, he flicked her clit, sending her over the edge again. Her movements caused him to jerk once and then come in her.

Once he finished shuddering and came back to himself, Megan stared at him with an utterly satiated expression. "That was…amazing."

"Thank you."

"Where did a nice boy like you learn to fuck?"

Pesh chuckled at her choice of language. "You know, a person's reputation has nothing to do with how they are in the bedroom. I'm sure there are many tough biker dudes out there who wouldn't know a clitoris from a labia—if they even knew that terminology."

"Hmm, I suppose that's true. My ex liked to think he was a ladies man, but half of the time, I had to take matters into my own hands if I was going to finish." She shot him a wicked grin. "Thankfully, I have a lover now who has the most amazing tongue and dick. I never have to worry about coming now."

"And don't you forget how amazing he is."

Her expression turned solemn as she replied, "I could never forget his attributes both in and out of the bedroom."

He smiled. "I'm glad to hear that." After he gave her a somewhat chaste kiss, he asked, "How about we test out my kitchen attributes now?"

"Sounds good. I'm starving," she replied, as she climbed out of the tub. Pesh followed her out, handing her one of his plush towels. After she finished drying off, he gave her a terry cloth robe to put on. She slid it on and tied the front together.

"Wait here. I'll bring it to you."

"Dinner in bed? That would be marvelous."

He winked before heading out of the bedroom. He fixed two heaping platefuls of food. After putting the plates on a tray, he got two bottles of water out of the fridge. When he got back to the bedroom, he found her lounging back against the pillows with an expression of pure relaxation.

After he set the tray down on the bed, he smiled. "I want to try something with you."

"What is it?" she asked.

He undid the ties on his robe, letting it fall open. After shrugging it off his shoulders, he stood naked before her. Megan's eyes widened. "What are you doing?"

Without answering her, he climbed onto the bed. His hands went to the lapels on her robe. He opened them and then pushed the robe open to her waist. "I thought we were eating dinner," she murmured huskily.

"We are." While her brows furrowed in confusion, he passed her a plate and a fork. Then he took his.

"Pesh, why are we eating dinner naked?"

"I want to teach you about delayed gratification."

"The Tantric stuff?"

"Yes."

She eyed him curiously. "Okay."

"Look into my eyes," he commanded. When her blazing blue eyes were trained on his, he brought a forkful of food to her mouth. "Open up," he said.

Her gaze held his as her tongue darted out, tentatively tasting the spicy rice. When she decided that she liked it, her mouth clamped over the fork. As she chewed, she still remained staring at him. "Feed me," he insisted.

She momentarily broke their eye contact to stare down at the plate. She speared a piece of lamb before bringing it to his mouth. After he took in the bite, his tongue slid over his lips, licking up the remaining sauce. Something stirred in her at his action—a slight tremble.

He brought a piece of lamb to her mouth, and she wrinkled her nose. "I don't like lamb." He nodded and then took the bite for himself. He then picked some of the vegetables and brought them to her. This time she took the forkful. "It's very good, Pesh."

"I'm glad you like it."

Each time she took the fork into her mouth, he couldn't help imagining that it was his cock instead. Sitting naked with her in such a close proximity had his juices beginning to flow. When she lowered her gaze to eye her plate for his next bite, she caught sight of his growing erection. Immediately, she started to put her plate down, but he stopped her. "Not yet."

"But you're hard, and I'm getting wet sitting here with you staring at me like you're already buried inside me."

"That's the point, my love. How good do you think it's going to be when I do finally get inside you?"

"Oh," she murmured. As she swept up a forkful of rice, she brought it to his mouth. "So how long do we do this?" she asked.

"Until we clean our plates."

She appeared both disappointed and frustrated at his response. To give her something else to focus on, he brought the fork to her mouth. She took from him, chewing methodically while staring into his eyes. Each time he fed her a bite, he tried conveying through his gaze what he was imagining doing to her. A bite of vegetables had him sucking her breast, his tongue flicking over her nipple. A forkful of rice had his face buried in her wet core as he licked her juices. As she chewed and swallowed, Pesh could tell desire was overtaking her.

"Can I have some water?" she asked.

With a nod, he brought one of the bottles to her lips. She drank in long gulps, her eyes never leaving his. When she finished swallowing, she gave him a grateful smile. Then in a flash, she tackled him, causing his plate to flip over onto the sheets. "Megan!" he cried.

She was too busy kicking out of her robe to care. At the sight of smeared vegetables and rice on the sheet next to him, he began to laugh. His chest shook so hard that he wanted to clutch his stomach, but Megan's body was in the way.

As she gazed down at him, he pushed the long, blonde strands of hair out of her face. "I don't believe we were finished eating," he chastised.

She drew his bottom lip between her teeth, causing him to groan. At the same time, her wet core ground against his cock. "I guess you'll just have to punish me the next time," she replied.

Cupping her buttocks, he sent a resounding smack against one of her cheeks. Her eyes widened. "Pesh Nadeen, did you actually just spank my ass?"

He grinned up at her before smacking the other cheek. "Mmm, I like this side of you," she murmured, before bringing her lips to his.

As their tongues battled against each other, Pesh flipped Megan over onto her back. After spreading her legs, he buried himself deep inside her with one thrust. "Oh God, that feels amazing," she cried.

"See how much better it is when you wait?" he questioned, as he leisurely moved in and out of her.

"Yes, mmm, it's so good. You're right."

Although her body trembled, she wasn't close yet. He continued his pace of slow strokes within her. Then he took her legs and put them on his shoulders to where he could pump deeper inside her. She moaned at the feeling, her hands sliding up above her head to grip the sheets.

Pesh ducked his head to bring his mouth to her breasts, alternating between each one. As he felt her begin to tense up, he increased the pressure of his tongue on her nipples, lightly grazing them with his teeth. And then she came apart beneath him, crying out and clasping her hands onto his shoulders. The sight of her was so alluring he couldn't hold back, and he came in a rush inside her.

When he'd finished shuddering, he raised his head to gaze down at her. Her eyelids fluttered open, and then she smiled sheepishly up at him. "Sorry for being a Tantric sex failure."

He laughed. "Baby, I don't care about that one bit. I like the fact you're aggressive when it comes to fucking."

Her hands feathered over his back and down to his ass. As she squeezed his cheeks, he sucked in a breath. "You're very good at that."

"You think so?"

"Mmm, hmm."

"How good are you at laundry?" he asked, motioning to the leftover dinner that was now staining the sheets.

She swatted his ass playfully. "I was planning on taking care of that."

"Why don't we get dressed and then sit down and really eat?"

"I think that sounds like a good idea."

"Good. I want to make sure you're feeling your best for what I have to ask you."

As he pulled himself off Megan, her brows furrowed. "What is it?"

"Can't it wait until we finish eating?"

Rolling her eyes, Megan said, "You know I can't wait for things."

Pesh sighed as he bent down to pick up his robe. As he slid his arm through the hole, he met Megan's questioning gaze. "I wanted to invite you to dinner at my sister's house this weekend."

"Okay, I think I can do that." Tilting her head, she eyed him suspiciously. "Why did you think I would need to be feeling my best for that?"

"It won't just be my sister and her husband. All of my family will be there, including my parents."

Megan's eyes widened. "You want to introduce me to your parents?"

"Yes, I would."

She nibbled on her bottom lip as she was prone to do when she was nervous. "But that would mean we're pretty serious, right?"

"Yes," he replied, with utter certainty.

Scooting to the edge of the bed, she gripped her gaping robe as best she could. She stared up at him. "You're not the least bit worried what they're going to say about you dating me?"

"No, I'm not."

The corners of her lips tugged up in a smile. "Then I'll go," she said softly.

"Really?"

When she bobbed her head, he rushed forward to wrap her in his arms. "Thank you, my love. You've made me very happy."

"You make me happy every day. It's the least I can do." With her head buried in Pesh's chest, she was finally able to let the smile she had plastered on fade into a frown. While she should have been elated that Pesh wanted to introduce her to his family, she couldn't help feeling overwhelmed. What if they hated her? What if their dislike caused Pesh to not want to see her anymore? She didn't want to think about what it would be like not having him in her life.

At the same time, it was hard processing all the emotions that Pesh's devotion made her feel. Davis had never wanted to introduce her to his parents. She met them by accident after one of his games. Now she had a man who wanted nothing more than to share all aspects of his life with her. It was hard to process.

In the end, she could only hope that everything went well.

Chapter Nineteen

The following day at work when Pesh found a lull in patients, he stepped into the nurses' station. While he said hello to some of the other men and women of the nursing staff, he had a singular focus of getting to Megan. When he joined her at the counter where she was doing paperwork, she jumped like he had tasered her.

"Go away," Megan hissed.

He chuckled. "You know, I think I can be seen back here in the nurses' station without arising any suspicion. After all, I could be discussing a patient with you."

"Then you better start talking in patient codes very soon."

"I wanted to know if it would be all right to pick you up at seven on Friday evening?"

When Megan jerked her gaze off the chart she was working on, her blue eyes bulged in horror at him. In a low voice, she said, "I cannot believe you are talking about a date here at work. Do you care anything about my reputation?"

He held his hands up defensively. "I'm sorry. I don't know what I was thinking besides the fact that I missed you and wanted to talk to you."

Megan's expression softened. "I'm sorry, but we can't be that way here."

Pesh opened his mouth to protest when a voice behind them cut him off. "Don't you two look cozy," Kara mused. Pesh whirled around to find Kara staring at them with venom burning in her eyes.

"Excuse me, but I need to get another chart off the carousel," Megan said, with her head tucked to her chest.

She turned to go, but Kara reached out and grabbed her arm. "If you don't mind, exam room Three needs a clean-up."

"Kristi is the only one authorized to give me orders around here," Megan replied.

Kara pursed her ruby red lips. "Insubordination and sleeping with a doctor—you really have a career death wish, don't you?"

Megan started to protest, but Pesh stopped her. Glaring at Kara, he said, "I want to talk to you. Alone."

After shooting Megan a triumphant look, Kara let Pesh lead her out of the nurses' station and down the hall. "What in the hell do you think you're doing?" he demanded.

"Saving you from making a huge mistake. You don't need a girl like that—you need a woman to take care of you." When her hands started to snake up around his neck, Pesh grabbed them.

"Don't touch me!" he snarled.

A sultry smile spread across her face. "You liked when I touched you before."

"That was one time—a drunken mistake that I regret daily, and I never intend on making again."

She narrowed her eyes at him. "So you're throwing me aside for a young bimbo?"

"Do not speak that way about Megan ever again. Do you hear me?"

"And do you really feel that she thinks you're worth throwing her career away for?"

Pesh closed the gap between them. Looming over Kara, his entire body shuddered in anger. "Listen to me when I say that if you threaten to expose Megan one more time, I will make life a living hell for you. As the supervising physician over the ER, I can have you shipped off to some hellhole far from here." He glared down at her. "Do you understand me?"

She slowly nodded her head as the realization that there was nothing between them finally dawned on her. "If you'll excuse me, I need to go clean my exam room."

As she hurried past him, Pesh exhaled a breath of relief. He never used that tone of voice with women, or men for that matter, unless he was absolutely pushed to do so. But Kara's previous behavior and the way she'd acted today had forced him to become what he wasn't. At the feel of a hand on his back, he whirled around.

Megan gave him a beaming smile. "My hero!"

He laughed at her expression and words. "You don't have to worry about her harassing you or me for that matter. I took care of things."

"I heard you."

He grimaced. "You did?"

She nodded. "It was amazing."

"I'm glad you thought so."

"I've never had a man take up for me like that before."

Pesh shook his head. "That's a shame."

"If we weren't in the middle of the ER's hallway, I'd kiss you to show my gratitude."

He smiled. "I'll gladly take a rain check."

"Oh you will? That's good to know."

Lowering his voice, he said, "I'll expect that kiss later tonight when we're alone. And I don't just want it on the lips." His brows rose. "I want it on several places on my body."

Megan grinned. "I think that can be arranged."

"I'll be looking forward to it."

"Dr. Nadeen?" a nurse called from the top of the hall.

"Yes?"

"You're needed in rxam room Four."

"As soon as I finish this patient consultation, I'll be there," he replied.

At his blatant lie, Megan covered her mouth to hide her giggling. "I have to go. But can I come over tonight?"

"Yep. Let me get Mason fed and bathed, and then I'm yours."

"See you later." He winked at her before he turned and started down the hall.

A few nights later Pesh found himself speeding along the quiet streets of Megan's neighborhood. His phone dinged once again. Slowing down, he took a peek to make sure it wasn't the hospital. He wasn't too surprised to find it was another text from Megan. He could tell from the way she had been frantically texting him that afternoon and evening that she was nervous, which was totally surprising to him. She was so strong and fearless that it was hard for him to imagine her ever feeling nervous. But he supposed that in

Megan's mind she had good cause to be nervous as tonight he was introducing her to his family.

After he picked her up, they were going to his sister, Shveta's, house for dinner. His parents, along with at least one of his brothers, would be there. Although he had spent a lot of time with her family, it hadn't quite meant the same thing as her spending time with his. He didn't know if her nerves stemmed from simply meeting his family or if they were from the fear of how far their relationship had progressed in the last few months.

He turned into the driveway at ten after seven. He didn't even get up the front porch steps before the door flew open, and Megan rushed out. Her diminutive figure wobbled a little on the black high heels she was sporting. She wore black pants, and a dressy red top that had a lot of beading. It reminded him of the kurta, a style that women from his culture wore. He wondered if she had chosen it for that reason.

"You look beautiful," Pesh murmured, leaning in to kiss her tenderly. When she didn't warm to his touch, he gazed down at her. "What's wrong?"

Rolling her eyes, she snapped. "Duh, I'm really nervous."

"You're really that worried about my family's opinion of you?"

She threw up her hands. "Of course, I am. Your family is very important to you. I don't want…" She tore her gaze from his.

"You don't want what?" he pressed.

"I don't want to bring shame to you."

He bit down on his lip to keep from laughing at her. He couldn't believe Megan was so concerned with his family's opinion. His heartbeat accelerated at the thought. It had to mean she really was falling in love with him. He brushed a silky strand of blonde hair out of her face. "Sweetheart, you're not the first American girl I've brought home with me."

"Yes, I'm well aware of that. I'm also aware of the fact of how well your family loved and accepted Jade. It might not be the same way with me." She stared up at him. "I'm not like her, Pesh. I'm not meek and good-hearted."

He shook his head. "That's not true. You are good-hearted. I see that part of you each and every day." Cupping her chin with his fingers, he brought her gaze to his. "You saw my brother, Dev. Through all of his missteps and antics, my parents still love him very much. So I promise you there is nothing you can do to where they won't like you or where you'll bring shame on me. Okay?"

She gave a reluctant nod. "Okay."

Taking her by the hand, he led her off the porch. Once he'd gotten her in the car, he went around and slid into the driver's seat. When Pesh cranked up the car, Megan gasped in horror. "What?" he asked.

She motioned to the clock on the dash. "Oh my God, we're going to be late. Can I make a worse first impression?"

Pesh laughed. "Maybe I should tell you a few things, etiquette wise, so tonight will go a little easier."

"What does that have to do with us being late?"

"Because it's considered good form to arrive thirty minutes late."

"Seriously?"

"Yes."

"Huh, I didn't know that."

"Well, how could you?"

"I tried doing a little research. I even watched *Monsoon Wedding*," she said.

Pesh laughed. "Did you now?"

"Yeah, it was pretty good. I kinda hated there weren't more dance numbers and songs."

"Megan, I'm pretty sure none of my family is going to break out into song like in a Bollywood movie tonight," he said, with amusement ringing in his voice.

She rolled her eyes. "I didn't expect them to, smart-ass."

He tsked at her. "So testy tonight."

After exhaling a long breath, she gave him an apologetic smile. "I'm sorry I'm so bitchy."

"You're not bitchy."

"And you're lying."

"Regardless of your out-of-control emotions, I know that my family is going to love you just as much as I do."

The moment the words left his lips he grimaced. There was the Big L word. They hadn't actually exchanged it yet, and now he'd managed to screw up and say it before he could find the right time.

"Oh God, did you have to say that now? Like I'm not nervous enough!"

"I'm sorry," he murmured.

Burying her head in her hands, she groaned. "This is...you are...I..."

"Look, you don't—"

"I love you, too!" she shouted from behind her hands.

His hands jerked on the wheel, and he sent the car careening onto the emergency lane. When he recovered and got the car back into the right lane, he dared himself to look over at her. She peeked at him through her fingers. "I love you, Pesh. I really fucking do."

"Oh Megan," he whispered.

Pulling her hands away from her face, she gave him a genuine smile. "I love you more than any man I've ever known."

"I love you more—" Suddenly he found himself unable to continue. Did he love her more than he had Jade? He had spent years with Jade and had only months with Megan. If he did love Megan more, what did that say about his relationship with Jade?

She reached over and took one of his hands in hers. "Hey, you don't have to say what I said. Our situations are completely different."

He clenched and unclenched his jaw. "No woman wants half a man's heart," he argued.

"But I know it isn't half your heart. And I wouldn't want you to stop loving me just because I died, so why would I expect you to do the same with Jade?"

"It's not fair to you," he croaked.

"Life's not fair, baby. You have to get used to that one." She squeezed his hand. "Besides, I know what I feel when I feel your love. There's no half about it. You love me with all your heart and soul."

"I do. I honestly do."

Unfastening her seat belt, she lunged over to kiss him. When she started to deepen the kiss, he had to pull away. "Hey now, you gotta stop that or we're not going to make it to my parents."

She giggled and then eased back down into her seat. She managed to behave herself the remaining five minutes. When he pulled into his parents drive, he saw it was already crowded with cars. The sight of so many people set Megan off, and she began tapping her fingers nervously on her leg.

"Ready?" he asked, as he turned to her.

"As I'll ever be," she muttered.

He shook his head as he got out of the car. Like always, he opened her car door and helped her out. As they started up the sidewalk, Megan was a flurry of movement. She smoothed down her hair and then she adjusted her top. Then she fiddled with her purse on her shoulder.

"Quit fidgeting," Pesh whispered, as he rang the doorbell.

"I can't help it. I'm nervous."

He grinned down at her. "Megan, they're going to love you. I promise."

She shook her head. "They're going to hate me because I'm not a submissive Indian woman. Wait until they hear I had a child out of wedlock. They'll be ready to disown you then."

The door flew open, cutting off the rest of their conversation. "Brother, it's so good to see you!" his brother-in-law, Sanjay, cried. After he hugged Pesh, his gaze went to Megan. His eyes widened, and he gasped in surprise. "Uh, hello."

"Hi," Megan said.

Sanjay gave Pesh a curious look. "You didn't tell me you were bringing company."

"This is Megan." With a self-assured tone, he added, "She's my girlfriend."

"Really? Well, what about that?" Sanjay gave Megan a welcoming smile. "We're so glad to have you."

"Thank you," Megan replied.

As Sanjay turned to go into the living room, Megan smacked Pesh's arm. "You didn't tell them you were bringing me?"

He shook his head. "No, I like the element of surprise when it comes to my love life."

"S-Seriously?" she sputtered.

"It's better this way. Trust me."

Before she could say anything else, Pesh started taking off his shoes. Wide-eyed, Megan watched him. Quickly, she stepped out of her heels and put them in the pile next to his. "More etiquette you forgot to tell me?" she hissed.

He patted the small of her back. "You're fine."

As they came into the living room, Pesh felt Megan tense at his side. He supposed that it was overwhelming coming into a room packed full of strangers. His sister, Shveta, came forward first. "Hello brother. You're looking well this evening."

"Thank you. So are you." He hugged her tight. As he pulled away, he glanced down at her swollen belly. "And how is the future prince doing?"

Shveta smiled and brought her hand to her abdomen. "He's busy kicking me at the moment." When she spied Megan behind him, she gasped. "And who is this?"

He drew in a breath and gazed around his family. "Before I go through this with each and every one of you, I might as well get it out of the way. I want to introduce you to someone very special, my girlfriend, Megan."

Deafening silence reverberated around the room after his statement. His mother and father exchanged a glance before staring back at Pesh. Megan tucked herself even closer to his side. Although public displays of affection between men and women were frowned upon in his culture, he wrapped his arm around her waist. "Well, say something," he commanded.

"We're sorry, son. It's just you caught us off guard," his mother said.

His father's bushy brows rose. "So you're really dating, eh?"

"Yes, I am."

At his declaration, his father clapped his hands and grinned. "That is most wonderful to hear!" He came forward to embrace Megan. "You are very welcome here."

"Thank you," she said.

"I'm Charlie," his father introduced.

"Megan," she replied, with a small smile.

Pesh peered past his father where his mother stood chewing her lip. He could tell she wasn't entirely happy that another blonde-haired, blue-eyed woman was standing beside her son. While Shveta and Arjan had both sought out Indian partners to marry, he and Dev were somewhat the black sheep since they hadn't chosen to settle down with women within their culture.

Finally, his mother's manners won out over anything else, and she stepped forward to shake Megan's hand. "I'm Lavani. It's nice to meet you."

"Nice meeting you, too," Megan replied.

The room then fell into an awkward silence. Pesh glanced around, willing someone to say something. His mother cleared her throat. "I'll go and finish up dinner." As she started into the kitchen, Shveta followed her, along with Arjan's wife. Since it was customary for women to be in the kitchen, Pesh found it to be only Megan left with the men.

It didn't go without her notice either. "Should I go and offer to help?" she questioned, in a whisper.

"Sure. That would be nice."

Her expression told him that she really didn't want to leave his side, but she did anyway. Once she was out of earshot, Pesh found everyone's eyes on him. "What?"

Charlie chuckled. "You even have to ask, my son?"

"So ask your questions and get it over with before Megan comes back in here," he replied, as he collapsed onto the couch.

He faced a barrage of questions about where they met, how long they had been seeing each other, and how serious was it. He mustered as much patience as he could to answer them all. When he was finished, the men sat back in surprised silence.

"I never thought I would see the day," his father mused.

Sanjay shook his head. "Oh, I knew the day would come. I saw that when he was out with Emma."

Charlie's brows furrowed. "Emma?"

Pesh pinched his eyes shut and wished his brother-in-law didn't have such a good memory. "Just a friend."

With a snort, Sanjay replied, "You certainly didn't look at her like she was a friend, even if she was pregnant."

"You were with a pregnant woman?" Charlie asked.

"Alpesh how could you?" his mother demanded from the doorway.

"How could I what?" Pesh asked.

Lavani's expression was horror stricken. "Get a woman…in the family way."

Pesh rocketed off the couch. He glanced past his mother to where Megan stood. "You're…?" he couldn't even form the words.

Megan's face flushed blood red. "No! Of course, I'm not!"

Lavani gave him a confused look. "Not her," she replied, pointing at Megan. "This Emma that Sanjay speaks of."

Bringing his hand to his forehead, he rubbed furiously to try to ward off the ache that was starting to pound in his head. Everything was getting shot to hell so fast. "First of all, Emma and I were never intimate. She was pregnant by the man she is now married to. Yes, I took her to the opera with Sanjay and Shveta, but there was nothing really between us." He shook his head and couldn't help wondering if he would ever have to stop explaining what had happened between him and Emma. "Second of all, could everyone just back off for a second? I mean, you're not exactly giving Megan a very good impression of our family."

A nervous laugh erupted from Megan's lips. She covered her mouth with her hand, trying to hide her giggling. He winked at her, and she lowered her hand to smile at him.

"Fine, fine. Now that we've cleared all that up, why don't we eat?" Lavani suggested.

"That sounds wonderful," Charlie replied.

As they made their way into the dining room, Pesh went to Megan's side. "You surviving okay?" he whispered.

"I'm hanging in there. I may need a drink when we leave."

"Just no Silver Tequila for you," he mused.

Without the others catching her, Megan smacked his arm. "Ass," she hissed under her breath.

He chuckled as he held out the chair for Megan. "Thank you," she said before sitting down. He then eased in beside her. As the dishes began making their way around the table, he felt Megan kick him. When he glanced at her in surprise, she whispered, "Where is the silverware?"

"We eat with our hands."

"Seriously?"

"Yes." He leaned over to whisper in her ear. "But don't use your left hand because it's considered rude."

She jerked back to stare wide-eyed at him. "I'm left handed," she protested.

He fought the urge to smile at her horror. He could tell that she would rather die than do something to embarrass him in front of his family. "You'll be fine. They won't expect as much out of you since you're American."

"Alpesh, whatever is it that you're whispering about?" Lavani asked, narrowing her eyes at him.

"I was just telling Megan what a wonderful cook you are. She loves Indian food, so I'm sure she's in for a treat." Pesh squeezed Megan's knee under the table. She cut her eyes over to him and smiled.

Once the plates had been passed around and everyone served, they began to eat. "Mmm, the samosa is delicious," Megan complimented.

"Thank you," Lavani replied, with a beaming smile.

As his mother turned her attention to Shveta, Pesh bowed his head and spoke in a low voice to Megan. "Once I tried bribing Beau with some samosa."

She laughed. "You did? Why?"

"I was at Aidan's house checking on Emma when she was on bed rest. I guess you could say he didn't like me invading his turf."

"Would he not take it from you?"

"Oh, he took it, ate it, and seemed to enjoy it. But I didn't make any friends that night."

Megan grinned. "Good old Beau."

Pesh raised his brows. "You're siding with the dog?"

"In that scenario, yes. He was merely protecting Emma and Noah."

"I see."

Tilting her head at him, she added, "Besides, I don't like any scenario where you and Emma are anything more than friends."

"I was there in a medical capacity," he argued.

She wagged her finger at him. "You brought dinner with you. That fact alone shows you were there for more than just practicing medicine."

When he quickly pushed her finger down, she gave him a look that was a cross between puzzled and infuriated. "Are you trying to silence me?"

"No, I'm just helping you save face. We don't point—it's considered rude."

Megan's eyes widened. "I've done something *else* wrong now?"

"You're fine."

She shook her head. "Next time, you better plan on giving me a crash course in Indian culture before you even think about bringing me around your family."

Across the table from them, Shveta cleared her throat. When Pesh and Megan glanced at her, she smiled. "You're doing fine, Megan. Please don't worry about following all the rules of our culture. We certainly don't expect you to."

Megan returned Shveta's smile. "Thank you. I would never dream of doing anything to offend you."

"Of course you wouldn't," Charlie replied.

Pesh didn't dare sneak a peek at his mother. After all, she was the one who upheld the traditions and customs of their heritage while his father had tried to Americanize himself as much as possible, right down to changing his name.

Charlie dabbed the corners of his mouth with his napkin. "I understand you have a son, Megan."

She smiled. "Yes, Mason is almost two. He's my entire world."

"You should have brought him with you this evening. We would have loved to meet him," Shveta said.

"Maybe next time. Of course, after you see how much energy he has, you might change your mind." As the table laughed, she glanced over at Pesh. "Mason truly adores Pesh, and Pesh is so good with him. His patience is infinite."

Pesh smiled. "He's a good boy. I enjoy spending time with him."

"So it's serious between you two?" Lavani asked.

"Uh, well—" Megan began before she was interrupted by the doorbell.

Sanjay rose out of his chair. "That must be Dev."

"How surprising that he's so late?" Shveta mused with a smile.

Pesh almost laughed at the horrified expression on Megan's face at the mention of Dev. "You didn't tell me he was going to be here!" she hissed.

"I wasn't sure if he was coming or not. But don't worry. Things are fine between us now."

Megan gave him a skeptical look as Dev walked into the dining room. "Hey everybody," he said, throwing up a hand.

At the sight of Megan sitting next to Pesh, Dev's eyes widened. "Well, well, if it isn't Miss Right Hook," he mused with a smirk.

"It's Miss *Left* Hook, actually," she corrected.

Dev grinned. "Good to know."

"You've met Megan, Dev?" Lavani asked curiously.

"We had the pleasure of meeting each other one day when I went by the hospital to see Alpesh." At Megan's sharp intake of breath, Dev winked at her. He then eased down across from them and began piling food on his plate. "So you guys work together and now you're dating, huh?"

"Yes," Pesh replied.

After taking a bite of his samosa, Dev motioned at them while he chewed. "Alpesh is sort of your boss, right?"

Pesh could feel Megan's anger rising. "No, actually he isn't. I have a preceptor, or head nurse, who is my boss. And before you can make it sound any seedier, it isn't against the hospital rules to date each other. Besides, we met each other long before I started working at Wellstar."

"Is that right?" Dev replied.

"Yeah, it is."

A slow grin slunk across his face. "I like you," he said to Megan.

"You have an interesting way of showing it."

Charlie chuckled at the head of the table. "My, my, Alpesh, haven't you picked a feisty one?"

Pesh glanced at Megan, who had flushed the red color of her blouse. She gave Charlie a weak smile. "I apologize."

With a tsk, Charlie replied, "Please don't. It's been rather refreshing to see you putting Dev into his well-deserved place. I understand you punched him, too."

When his mother gasped in horror, Megan fumbled under the table for Pesh's hand. He squeezed it reassuringly as she ducked her head. "Um, well, I'm sorry to say that I did."

"In Megan's defense, I totally deserved it. I punched Alpesh and said some really shitty things."

"Dev!" Lavani cried.

In true Dev fashion, he rolled his eyes at his mother's outrage. "We're fine now. Everyone calm down." He met Pesh's gaze. "I'm happy for you, brother. You've made a good choice." He cut his eyes over to Megan. "I hope you both will be very happy together."

Pesh was taken aback by the sincerity in both Dev's words and his expression. "Thank you."

Megan nodded. "Yes, thank you."

Dev leaned back in his chair, clasping his hands behind his head. "And now to ensure that my news overshadows any excitement brought on by the two of you, I'd like to announce that I'm getting married next month—"

Lavani once again gasped in horror. But Dev wasn't finished. "And I'm going to be a father."

Pesh's mouth gaped open as the table erupted in absolute pandemonium. He wondered if his mother was going to pass out. Turning to Megan, he found her with her napkin over her mouth. From the way her shoulders were moving up and down, he could tell she was laughing. He leaned over to whisper in her ear. "Guess we're off the hook, huh?"

She grinned. "Yeah, I think we're good."

"I love you."

"I love you more."

Chapter Twenty

Now that he and Megan were an official couple who had said the "L" word, Pesh no longer had days off where he had to wonder how to pass the time. He wanted to spend every waking minute with her and with Mason, and she always made sure that they had time together. Today found him at Patrick's house, wedged on the couch between some of Megan's male family members. Just like at his parents, the women were all stationed in the kitchen, putting the finishing touches on Sunday lunch.

As soon as Becky came in the living room and announced it was time to sit down, there was a stampede to the dining room. He followed slowly behind the others, searching for Megan who he felt like was his lifeline in the crowd.

"Where's Aidan and Emma? They're never late," Angie remarked, as she sat a giant platter on the table.

Liz shrugged. "They haven't called. We could go ahead and get started, and then they can start when they get here."

John pulled out a chair. "Good. I'm starving."

Becky rolled her eyes. "You're always starving. Between you and Percy, we're going to be eaten out of house and home."

Pesh hung back as the others started taking their seats at the massive mahogany table. Regardless of how welcoming the Fitzgerald's had been, he still couldn't help feeling like an outsider. Megan came in carrying a plate of ham. After she deposited it on the table, her gaze searched the room for him. When she spotted him, she gave him the smile that always warmed his heart before crooking her finger at him.

As he started to join her, Mason came running in. "Get me, Esh," he urged, holding his hands up. Pesh grinned as he stooped over to pick Mason up.

"Are you hungry?" Pesh asked.

"Uh, huh."

"Are you going to sit with me or Pesh?" Megan asked.

"Esh," he replied.

"Is that okay with you?" Megan asked.

"We'll be fine."

She motioned for him to have a seat. Just as they sat down, Aidan appeared in the doorway of the dining room with Noah in his arms. "Sorry we're late."

"Where's Emma?" Megan asked, as she took Noah from Aidan.

With a grimace, Aidan said, "She isn't feeling well. It seems that with this pregnancy she's having third trimester morning sickness. I told her I would stay home with her, but she insisted I come get a good meal."

"Poor thing. We'll fix her a plate for you to take home to her later on," Megan said.

Aidan smiled. "Thanks. If she can eat it, I know she'll be grateful."

Patrick clicked his fork against his water goblet. "Is everyone here that's supposed to be here?"

A chorus of, "Yes," rang around the room.

"Good. Let's return thanks."

Pesh obediently bowed his head along with the others. When Patrick finished, the dishes were passed around and food was served. It was certainly a lot different than how his family did it, but he still enjoyed being with Megan's family. While Mason ate off his plate, Megan gave Aidan a break by feeding Noah, or more appropriately letting him drape her in food while he fed himself.

"You're a mess," Megan said, into Noah's carrot-and-corn crusted face. His response was to grin at her. "I'm sorry, mister, but that cute little grin isn't going to work for me."

"He's so stubborn," Aidan said.

"A stubborn Fitzgerald? I've never heard of such," Becky joked across the table.

Aidan shook his head. "I'm serious. He refuses to let me or Em feed him, and then he ends up wearing more than he eats."

"Sounds like his father," Angie mused. When Aidan gave her an exasperated look, she said, "You were the exact same way. I don't think you ate a meal until you were two that mother didn't have to hose you off after you finished."

Aidan grunted. "Don't tell Em that story. She already blames me enough for Noah's stubbornness."

Megan smiled. "Let's hope that this next baby has Emma's temperament."

"Like she isn't stubborn," Aidan countered.

"Much less than you are," Megan replied.

Pursing his lips, he appeared to be surveying her words. "You might have a point," he said, with a grin.

After everyone finished eating, the adults lounged around the table talking and laughing while the kids went into the living room.

Both Mason and Noah wanted to go with the bigger kids. "Will you keep an eye on them?" Megan asked Percy.

"Sure," he replied.

"I owe you, Perce," Aidan said, as Percy took the boys by the hand.

As he sat with his arm draped over the back of Megan's chair, Pesh enjoyed listening to the lively conversation around him. Occasionally one of Aidan's sisters would ask him a question or his opinion. He had always been naturally quiet, and when he got in the midst of such a lively bunch, he tended to be even quieter. He realized if he was going to truly fit in, he was going to have to speak up more.

Their conversation was interrupted by a shriek that came from the living room followed by a loud wail. Aidan was out of his chair in a flash while Megan was close on his heels. Mason came running into the dining room. "What happened?" Pesh asked.

"Noah got hurted."

Aidan reappeared in the dining room with Noah in his arms. "He's fine. He just fell down." Taking Noah's hand, Aidan said, "Here Daddy will kiss the booboos away, okay?"

Noah sniffled and bobbed his head. Once Aidan finish with his hand, Noah stuck out his leg. Aidan smiled. "Okay." Once he bent down to Noah's leg and kissed it, he asked, "Are you Daddy's boy?"

"Uh-huh."

Angie chuckled. "That's not fair to do that when Emma isn't here."

As the others laughed, Pesh glanced at Mason. He was staring at Aidan and Noah with a contemplative look on his face. Never in a million years could he have imagined what he would do next. Mason crawled up into his lap and patted Pesh's chest. "Esh Mace's daddy. Mace Daddy's boy."

Conversation in the dining room silenced. Without even looking up, Pesh felt his skin singing under the burn of everyone staring at him and Mason. There was no way he could deny the boy when he wore such an expression of happiness. "Yes, you're Daddy's boy."

A strangled cry caused him to snap his gaze from Mason over to Megan. Wide-eyed and open mouthed, she blinked a few times as if she were trying to believe that what she was seeing was real. Then without another word, she bolted from her chair and fled the room. Pesh sat in a shocked silence for a few seconds trying to decide what to do. Bending over, he whispered into Mason's ear, "Will you go back and play with the others? I need to check on Mommy."

When Mason nodded, Pesh gently sat him back down on the floor. After he raced out of the dining room, Pesh finally glanced at the others. "Excuse me," he said, before rising out of his chair. He made his way down the hallway. He didn't have to look hard for Megan—she was in the one bedroom with the door closed. He rapped lightly on the wood. When she didn't answer, he went ahead and opened the door.

He found her sitting on the edge of the bed with her head in her hands. He went over and sat down next to her. Tentatively, he put his hand on her back. "I'm sorry for not setting Mason straight and telling him I wasn't his daddy. He looked so happy, and I didn't want to hurt him."

With her elbows braced on her knees, Megan turned her head to look at him. Tears streamed down her cheeks. "You think I'm angry at you?" He nodded his head. She hiccupped a cry. "Oh Pesh, you're so naïve sometimes!"

He jerked back at her words. "Excuse me?"

"Just when I think I can't love you more, you go and do something like that." Before he could process her words, she threw herself at him, kissing his cheeks and mouth. She straddled his lap and brought her hands around his neck. "You really love Mason, don't you?"

"Of course I do."

"You could see yourself really being a father to him?"

"Yes, I could. But what—"

She silenced him with a kiss. It was one that was laced with desperate emotions. He wrapped his hands around her waist and drew her closer to him. Just as he was about to deepen the kiss, she pulled away. "You love me too, don't you?"

"You should have no doubts on that one."

"You love me enough to be a husband to me?"

Her question caused him to suck in a harsh breath. He felt like he had been kicked in the gut. "Yes, I could—I always have."

She tilted her head at him and smiled. "Then marry me."

"Excuse me?"

Bringing her lips to his, she murmured against his mouth, "Marry me. Make me your wife."

At that moment, he thanked God he was sitting down because if he hadn't been, he was pretty sure he would've done something totally emasculating like fainting. He also questioned both his hearing and his sanity. Had Megan just proposed to him? Surely, he was hallucinating.

"Did you just ask me to marry you?" he questioned lamely.

Giggling, Megan nodded her head. "I wish you could see your face right now. I should be insulted."

"I'm sorry. It's just you surprised me."

She cupped his face in her hands. "I'm sorry I don't have a ring, and I didn't get down on one knee," she lovingly teased.

He brought his hands up to touch hers. "You're really serious?"

"Yes, I am."

Bowing his head, he tenderly kissed the tops of her hands. "I love you so much, Megan, and I want nothing more than to make you my wife."

"So is that a yes?"

"I just want to make sure you know what you're saying. One minute you're in the dining room, laughing with your family, and then the next you're in here weeping and then proposing to me. And let's not forget how adamant you have been the entire time I've known you about being too young to get married."

Megan's lips turned down in a pout. "Can't a girl change her mind?"

"Yes, of course, but I just want to make sure this is really what you want."

Tears sparkled in her blue eyes. "You are everything I could ever want in a man. You love me, you watch out for me, you want the best for me. While that would be enough to make me want to marry you, you love my son. You watch out for him and you want the best for him. I couldn't ever imagine loving someone more than I do you. I can't imagine wanting to be anyone else's wife but you." She sniffled. "I was so stupid for so long. I couldn't believe that someone like me could truly deserve someone like you. But you never gave up on me. If you give me the chance, I'll spend the rest of my life trying to make you happy."

Pesh couldn't stop the racing of his heart. He was sure both his heart rate and blood pressure were off the charts at this moment. He cupped her cheeks. "Nothing in the world would make me happier than for us to get married."

"So we're engaged?"

"Yes, we are." When a smile lit up Megan's face, he shook his head. "But not formally yet. Not until I put a diamond on your hand."

"But I don't need that to know I'm promised to you and that we're getting married."

"Maybe you don't, but I do."

She rolled her eyes. "Fine, fine. I'll let you buy me a diamond. A great big one, okay?"

He laughed. "I promise to spend a fortune."

"You know I would be happy to wear your ring even if it was a little chip."

"I know you would. But I want to spoil my beautiful future wife."

She grinned. "Okay, I won't argue with you."

Pesh brought his mouth to hers. As their lips moved against each other, he couldn't believe how lucky he was. Megan was *his*— she was really going to be his for the rest of his life. When she flicked her tongue against his, he groaned into her mouth.

Considering they were at Patrick's with all of her family down the hall, he knew the last thing on his mind should've been flipping her over onto her back and pounding into her. But he didn't care. He wanted inside her body. He had finally made it into her heart, mind, and soul, and he once again wanted to be inside her perfection.

When Megan pushed him onto his back, Pesh raised his brows at her. "Mmm, I think my future wife is getting ahead of herself. Usually the consummating comes after the wedding, not the engagement," he teased.

"I think we've consummated enough over the last few months where it doesn't matter."

"I suppose you're right."

As she ground her core against his growing erection, she said, "Looks like I'm not the only one with consummating on the mind."

"You should know *that* has a mind of its own."

She grinned down at him. "Well, right now I think we're both of the same mind."

As she continued to grind against him, his hands swept to her breasts. He cupped and kneaded the flesh over her top. At the sound of the door opening, Pesh tried to pull away, but he didn't make it in time.

"Oh fucking hell!" Aidan's voice boomed from the doorway. Megan quickly scrambled off Pesh, and they both rose up, trying to straighten their clothes and hair.

With a pained expression, Aidan said, "Seriously? This is my old bedroom!"

Pesh chuckled. "I'm sorry, but you of all people should understand that when the mood hits, you act on it."

Megan smacked his arm playfully. "That is not exactly what happened."

Holding up one of his hands, Aidan said, "Frankly, I don't really want to know what happened. I just came back here to make sure Megan was all right. Next time, I'll make sure someone else comes, so I don't need eye bleach to wipe that out of my memory. "

"Ha, ha, very funny," Megan grumbled, as she got off the bed.

"We were only celebrating," Pesh said.

Aidan pinched his eyes shut. "I don't think I even want to know what you were celebrating."

"Our engagement, pervert," Megan replied.

Aidan's blue eyes widened. "Holy shit, you two are engaged?"

Pesh smiled as he rose off the bed and took Megan's hand. "Yes, we are. Well, I mean, I need to go to her father and properly ask for her hand. And there's the fact she doesn't have a ring."

Shaking his head in disbelief, Aidan said, "That's…wow. I'm so happy for you two."

"Thank you. And I do mean that. If it weren't for you and Emma, I never would have met Megan," Pesh said.

Aidan grinned as he clapped Pesh on the back. "You're more than welcome, man. I'm just so glad you two finally realized how good you were for each other." He turned back to the door before motioning them. "Come on, let's go tell the others. I think this calls for a celebration, but just not the kind that you two were partaking in."

Megan shook her head. "We weren't going to tell anybody yet."

Pesh nodded. "She doesn't even have a ring."

Aidan snorted. "Do you really think anyone out there is going to give two shits about whether or not you have a ring?"

"We just want to do it the right way," Pesh replied.

Holding up his hands in surrender, Aidan said, "All right, I'm not going to argue with you anymore. But I will say that there is no right way. Hell, look at me and Em. In the end, you have to go with the flow and appreciate the moments that are bigger than you could ever imagine."

He then turned and strode out of the bedroom. Pesh stole a glance at Megan who appeared to be processing Aidan's words. "Come on, we better get back out there before they send someone else," she finally said.

With a smile, he took her hand and led her down the hall. When they got back to the dining room, everyone glanced expectantly at them. Even though he knew he shouldn't, Pesh blurted, "We're engaged!"

He didn't have time to worry about Megan's anger about him blabbing because he realized she had said it at the same time he had. Cheers went up over the room, and he was hugged and kissed by Megan's aunts. When Megan's father, Paul, stood before him, Pesh felt like he'd been kicked in the groin. "Mr. McKenzie, I apologize. I intended to come to you and ask for Megan's hand—to show respect to you and your wife. I'm so sorry."

Paul shook his head and smiled. "Please don't apologize. I'm just grateful that she's met such a wonderful man who will be a good husband to her and a good father to Mason."

"I swear to you that I will." He and Paul shook hands to seal the vow.

In the absence of champagne, wine was poured to celebrate. At the head of the table, Patrick held up his glass. "To my granddaughter and the good doctor, I give you an Irish marriage blessing. 'May God be with you and bless you. May you see your children's children. May you be poor in misfortunes and rich in blessings. May you know nothing but happiness from this day forward.'" He smiled. "To Megan and Pesh."

The others raised their glasses. Once Pesh tasted the rich bouquet of the wine, he leaned over and kissed Megan. He didn't even mind the cat-calls and whistling—he was too happy to care.

Chapter Twenty-One

Standing in front of the lighted hotel mirror, Megan surmised her appearance. It was the first time she hadn't been encircled by Pesh's mother, sister, and aunts since she had stepped inside the suite an hour ago. When she had agreed to an Indian engagement party, she hadn't quite known what she was getting into. She thought it would just be a great way to get their friends and family together. She didn't know that Pesh's family didn't do anything on a modest scale. Without her input, the Plaza ballroom of the Ritz Carlton in Atlanta had been booked. When she had dared a peek inside earlier, it had been transformed into something out of a Bollywood movie.

She had wanted to honor Pesh's culture by dressing just as a true Indian prospective bride would, so she had gone sari shopping with Lavani and Shveta. What she hadn't bet on was how gorgeously intricate the outfit would be. Now as she gazed at herself in the mirror, she was almost blinded by the glittering stones and beading on the deep purple and gold sari. The outfit put even the blingiest

Miss America pageant dress to shame. The top part was sleeveless, and it ended just below her breasts. While the front part appeared to be plain satin, the back was encrusted in beading and gems. The skirt, with its beaded waistband, started just beneath her belly button and fell to the floor in the most exquisite silky material. It was hard imagining she was going to be baring her mid-drift, as was the fashion of the sari. Thankfully, she had a jewel encrusted drape that slung across one of her shoulders and down one side.

Earlier after one of Pesh's aunts had done her makeup, Lavani and Shveta did her hair. The long strands were swept back and pinned on the side in loose curls. A gorgeous purple orchid adorned the curls. All that was missing from her ensemble was the jewelry that Pesh's family had requested that she wear. Apparently, it was all heirloom pieces and kept in a safe at a bank. Although the necklace and earrings were to come, her arms were heavy laden with bangle bracelets that Lavani and Shveta had put on her.

They both had tears in their eyes when they finished. "You look absolutely breathtaking, my dear," Lavani said.

Megan smiled. "Thank you. And thank you so much for making tonight happen."

Lavani cupped her cheek. "I look forward to seeing many happy years between you and my Alpesh. I'm grateful that you make him so happy. It had been so long since I had seen a light in his eyes. But when you came into his life, you brought back that light."

At Lavani's words, Megan felt tears stinging her eyes. "Thank you," she murmured. When she felt like she could speak without crying, she brought her hands together as if she were praying and then bowed her head as was the sign of respect in Pesh's culture. "I want you to know that before Pesh, I was in darkness, too. He has become my light as well. I can assure you that I will spend the rest of my life honoring him and making him happy. I am very thankful for the amazing man you have raised."

Lavani's dark eyes filled with tears, and she brought a handkerchief up to dab her eyes. "Thank you, my dear."

Shveta stepped into the bathroom, her face lit up in a broad smile. "Alpesh is here."

Gathering up the bottom of her skirt, Megan walked out of the bathroom and into the bedroom. Her heart stopped at the sight of him. She had never seen him in Kurta-Pajama, as they were called. Basically, it was a long, tunic like shirt that came to his knees. Underneath he wore loose cotton-like pants. But his top was made much like hers. It was gold in color and encrusted in gems and beading. She didn't want to begin to imagine how much it cost.

When she brought her gaze back to his, she shivered under his heated stare. "You are a vision of absolute and total perfection," he said.

Doing a little turn, the fabric of her sari twirled around her. "So you like it?"

He smiled. "I love it."

She laughed. "I feel a little like a poser. Like 'you can put the Irish girl in a sari, but you can't take the Irish out of the girl' kinda thing."

"I wouldn't have you any other way," he said, with a serious, yet tender tone.

"Thank you."

Megan eyed the two velvet boxes in his hand. "Ooh, let me see the goodies."

With a bark of a laugh, Pesh sat one of the boxes down on the table before he opened the other. Megan gasped as two enormous earrings glittered back at her. While there was a thick base, the rest flowed down in flourishing designs that would probably touch her shoulders when she put them on. They had a gold overlaying, but all the gems were diamonds and amethysts that would match her sari.

"This is why your mother and Shveta wanted me to pick a purple sari?" she questioned.

Pesh nodded.

"They're breathtaking," she murmured.

"Wait until you see the necklace," he replied, with a smile.

Her shaky hands reached forward to take one of the earrings. She quickly worked the clasp and fastened it to her lobe. Then she did the other. While they were so heavy she felt like they might weigh her down, she glanced up at Pesh and smiled. "Thank you."

"You're welcome, my love."

. He reached for the other box. Megan's eyes widened as the diamonds and deep amethysts sparkled in the light. He took the necklace out and unfastened the clasp. He moved behind her and then lifted the necklace over her head. She closed her eyes at the pleasurable sensation of feeling his closeness.

"There. Now you're ready."

Whirling around to face him, she brought her lips to his. "I love you."

His thumb tenderly rubbed her cheek. "I love you, too."

From the doorway of the bedroom, Lavani tsked disapprovingly at them. "Alpesh, stop mauling her, or you're going to mess up her makeup!"

Pesh chuckled. "I hardly think I was mauling her."

She waved her hand dismissively. "Come now. It's time we went downstairs."

After Pesh held out his arm for her, Megan slid hers through his. "Don't be nervous," he murmured into her ear.

"I'm not," she lied.

"Megan, I know you well enough by now that I know when you're nervous. You fidget and bite your lip."

"Sorry," she muttered, as they got onto the elevator.

Considering it was packed with Pesh's family, Megan kept her mouth shut about her nerves. The last thing she wanted to do was to come off wrong in front of them. When the doors opened, she drew in a couple of deep breaths to still her nerves.

There was a whole lot of pomp and circumstance that she didn't quite understand about how they were all supposed to enter. She just tried not to mess up the part when she came in with her parents. Just like at a wedding reception, she and Pesh sat at a table at the head of the room. Of course, she hadn't quite prepared herself for the golden chairs that looked almost like thrones.

Once everyone was assembled, Pesh's father got up to speak. "We are very grateful that you all could be with us this evening. I know that with Megan's friends and family, as well as some of our son's, there are a lot of you unacquainted with our culture. I will try to explain to you what the proceedings are."

On the table in front of them were two flower wreaths that reminded her of the leis that you would see in Hawaii. They were in colors of white, gold, and purple. The wreaths crisscrossed over the black ring boxes. She knew from what Pesh had told her that they would be giving each other rings tonight to symbolize their future union. It all seemed pretty extreme to her for just an engagement party—it was almost like a wedding.

"It's show-time," Pesh murmured in her ear before he stood up. She quickly followed his lead. He took one of the flower wreaths off the table and brought it over her head. He made sure to adjust her hair so it flowed over the flowers. When he was done, she did the same, although it was a little harder for her to reach up over his head

Then he took one of the platinum bands and put it on her trembling finger. "I love you so very much, Megan. There's not another woman in the world I could love like I do you," he whispered to reassure her.

"I love you so much, too." She then slid the band on his hand. Once it was done, applause went out over the ballroom, and Pesh pulled her to him for a kiss.

"Now what do we do?" she asked.

He smiled at her. "We dance."

After exhaling the breath she had been holding, Megan took Pesh's hand and let him lead her to the dance floor. A song she had never heard before in her life began to play from the DJ.

"So what were you thinking when it came to the wedding?" Pesh asked.

"Something small."

His brows rose in surprise. "Really? I was thinking you would want to go all out."

She shook her head. "I just want something simple with our closest friends and family. I don't have to have something showy to make me happy."

He grinned. "You know that anything 'simple' is not going to set well with my parents."

Megan laughed. "Well, they're just going to have to accept it."

"We could just run off and get married in a cave in Hawaii," he suggested.

"That idea has potential, but I think as my parents' only daughter, they would kill me if they didn't get to plan something."

His expression grew serious. "I don't want us to have to wait much longer."

"I agree. I want to get married in the next couple of months."

He smiled. "Good. I'm glad to hear that."

As Megan glanced over to see her grandfather dancing with his lady friend, an idea popped into her head. "What if we got married in Papa's rose garden?"

"It sounds like a beautiful place, but is there enough room?"

"Only our closest friends and family, remember?" she insisted.

"It could work."

"So you like the idea?"

"I do." With a wink, he said, "It makes sense considering you proposed to me at Patrick's house."

Megan grinned. "That's right. It does."

"Think we can put it all together in two months?"

"I don't see why not."

He brought his warm lips to hers, and Megan shivered in spite of the heat on the dance floor. "I can't wait to make you my wife," he murmured against her lips.

"I'm ready to make an honest man out of you, too."

Pesh threw his head back and chuckled. "Only you would say something like that."

"Hey, the truth is the truth."

The song ended, and Pesh escorted her back to their table. After they finished with the blessings from Pesh's family, dinner was served. Megan couldn't believe all the food that was paraded by her. She lost count on how many plates of delicious Indian food she sampled. By the time the desserts came out, she was thoroughly stuffed and couldn't eat any. "Let's go mingle," she suggested when Pesh also turned down any dessert.

"Sounds good to me," he said, before getting out of his chair.

They made their way through the maze of tables, talking to family and friends. Megan was introduced to so many of Pesh's relatives that she was sure she would never be able to remember them all. When they finally got to the Fitzgerald tables filled with her parents and aunts and uncles, she was thrilled when Pesh took a seat across from Aidan and Emma.

After they had been talking for a while, Emma turned Aidan. "Do you think Noah's okay?"

Aidan smiled. "I'm sure he's fine, babe. The sitter looked very qualified."

Although Emma nodded her head, Megan could tell that she wasn't convinced. Both Mason and Noah were upstairs in the hotel with babysitters outside of their family for the first time in their young lives. Megan shared a bit of Emma's apprehension, but when she had dropped Mason off in the suite, he seemed to get along with the woman they had hired.

"I might just go peek in on him. You know, make sure she got him to sleep," Emma said, rising out of her chair.

Aidan shook his head and stood up. "You need to be off your feet. You said yourself you weren't feeling too well before we left."

Emma shot him a murderous look. "Thanks for saying that in front of Pesh and Megan."

Aidan gave them a sheepish grin. "Sorry guys. I hope it doesn't ruin your fabulous party knowing that Emma, at nine months pregnant and some change, wasn't feeling wonderful."

Megan laughed while Pesh shook his head. "Emma, if you want to go on upstairs and lie down, we won't be hurt. I remember how awful it feels being overdue," Megan said.

"No, I'm fine. I want to stay," Emma replied. When Aidan motioned for her to have a seat, she shook her head. "I need to go to the restroom."

"You want me to go check on Noah?"

Emma sighed. "I'm sure he's fine or the sitter would have texted me. I'm just being overprotective."

Aidan gave her a quick kiss. "Love you, sweetheart."

She smiled at him. "I love you, too."

After she headed through the crowd to the bathroom, Aidan began telling Pesh some wild story from work that had Pesh doubled over with laughter. When Emma returned, she didn't sit back down. Instead, she swayed back and forth on her feet next to her chair.

"Aidan," she said in a strained voice. Megan couldn't help noticing how Emma had paled considerably since her trip to the bathroom just a few minutes before.

He held up his finger. "One second, babe. I gotta finish telling Pesh this story."

"But my water broke."

Without taking his eyes off Pesh, Aidan slid his glass of water over to her. "Here take mine."

If the situation hadn't been dire, Megan would have laughed at how oblivious Aidan was. Pesh leaned forward in his seat. "Um, Aidan, I think—"

He didn't get a chance to finish. Instead, water splashed against the side of Aidan's face. He shot out of his chair before whirling around to Emma. "What the hell, Em?"

"My. Water. Broke," she muttered through gritted teeth.

"Oh shit," he replied. After tossing his napkin back on the table, he held up a hand. "Okay, it's fine. No need to panic. We're not that far from the hospital—"

"Like twenty minutes," Emma argued.

Aidan's hands came to her shoulders. "It'll be fine, babe. I promise."

Emma huffed out a few frustrated breaths as she weighed his words. Then her grim expression softened. "Okay."

Aidan grinned as he turned back to Pesh and Megan. "I hate to cut and run, but it looks like baby Caroline is a big attention whore who wants all the glory tonight."

Megan rose out of her chair. "Don't you worry about it one bit. Since she's a week overdue, I'm going to let her have this one without accusing her of trying to steal the limelight."

"Can we do anything?" Pesh asked.

While Aidan shook his head, Emma said, "Just make sure Noah is okay."

Angie rose out of her chair. "I'll go check on him right now."

Emma smiled. "Thanks."

Aidan dug around in his pocket. When he produced a set of keys, he tossed them at Pesh. "Since I came after work, Em and I are in separate cars. Whoever has Noah overnight will need our SUV to get him to the hospital tomorrow."

Pesh nodded as Megan said, "Good thinking. I'm not sure if Mom is taking him or Becky." At Emma's somewhat apprehensive look that there wasn't a strict plan in place for Noah, Megan said, "It'll be fine. I promise."

"Okay," she said, a little reluctantly.

Sliding his arm around Emma's waist, Aidan said, "Come on, sweetheart. We need to go."

At the feel of Pesh's hand on her back, Megan glanced up at him. "Exciting night for them, eh?"

"Yes, it is."

"How about letting me take you for another spin on the dance floor?"

"I'd love that."

As an Indian love song flowed out from the speakers, Megan wrapped her arms around Pesh's neck. This time he didn't bother dancing more formally like he had in Savannah. Instead, he wrapped his arms around her waist and drew her flush against him. Closing her eyes, she rested her head on his broad chest, loving the gentle beat of his heart beneath his shirt.

When the song finished, they didn't move. They just waited for the next one. Thankfully, it was another slow one. Halfway through, she felt a tug on the bottom of her drape. Glancing down, she saw Georgie peering up at her. "What are you doing, sweetie?" she asked.

He glanced left and right before he spoke. "Mommy told me not to tell anybody, but she needs you to come up to her hotel room."

"Okay. What for?"

"Noah's going crazy wanting Aunt Emma, and she thinks you're the only one that might be able to get him to calm down."

"Ah, I see."

When she turned back to Pesh, he smiled. "You don't even need to apologize. Go see if you can help."

She leaned up and gave him a smacking kiss on the lips. "Thank you for being so amazing each and every moment of the day."

His thumb brushed against her cheek. "You're welcome, my love."

"Be back as soon as I can."

"I'm going to hold you to that."

Taking Georgie's hand, she made her way off the dance floor and out of the ballroom. After getting on one of the elevators, they rode to the sixth floor. She let Georgie lead the way. He stopped halfway down the hall and knocked on the door. By then, she didn't have to guess which room Noah was in. She could hear his screams all the way outside. When Becky flung open the door, she waved Megan through with her hand. "The others didn't want me to interrupt you, but we've been trying the last hour to get him to calm down, and he's just not having it."

Megan found the scene in hotel room somewhat comical. Her mother, along with her aunts Julia and Liz, stood in a circle around one of the beds. Outfitted in a fuzzy, blue footed sleeper, Noah sat in the middle of the mattress, his cheeks streaked and soaked with tears and his face red from crying. "What is the matter?" Megan asked.

Everyone whirled around to look at her. "Nothing. Everything's fine. Go back to your party," Angie said, over Noah's wails.

"Um, I think it's safe to say that it isn't fine. Or at least, *he's* not fine."

Liz fanned her face with her hand. "It's like the moment Emma left the hotel, he freaked out. He woke up out of a dead sleep screaming for his mama. The poor baby-sitter hung in as long as she could before she finally called us."

Megan cocked her head at Noah. "Poor thing." She bypassed her aunts to hold out her arms. Considering he'd spent so much time with her, Noah happily reached for her, and Megan pulled him into her embrace. "Hey buddy, you've got to stop crying."

He was snubbing so hard his breath came in big hiccups as his chest heaved. "Mama. Want mama," he pleaded pitifully.

Megan hugged him tight to her chest. "I know, sweetie. But she's at the hospital having your baby sister."

Her answer didn't satisfy him since he drew in a deep breath to start screaming again. She smiled at him. "You wanna go downstairs to the party?" He appeared thoughtful. "Pesh is downstairs. You wanna see him?"

"Esh?"

Megan laughed. "Yes, he's down there."

"See Esh," he said, kicking his feet as if to tell her to start walking.

"Here. I'll take him," her mother suggested, reaching for Noah.

He shrieked before wrapping his arms tighter around Megan's neck. "I think it's safe to say he's staying with me."

"But it's your engagement party," Julia protested.

"Yes, and I've been enjoying it the last four hours. I don't think watching him is going to take away anything for me."

As she started out the doorway, she asked, "Is Mason okay?"

Her mother nodded. "Thank goodness he's down the hall, or we'd have two toddlers running around at eleven o'clock."

Megan giggled as she walked down the hall. Her necklace and the beaded sari seemed to be holding Noah's interest. "Pretty, huh?" she asked, as they got on the elevator.

"Ooh, pwetty," he mimicked.

When she got back downstairs, Pesh was seated at their table, talking to some of their colleagues. The moment Noah saw him, he reached out for Pesh. "Well hello, little one. Were you really crying because you wanted to come to our party?"

Noah grinned at Pesh behind his pacifier, which caused Pesh to smile. "He looks so much like Aidan when he does that, doesn't he?"

"Yes, he does. I'm sure he's going to use that cute little grin to his advantage when he gets older, just like his daddy did." She eased into the chair beside them.

After spitting out his pacifier, Noah asked, "Daddy?"

"Uh, oh, I shouldn't have said that," Megan muttered under her breath.

"My daddy?"

"He's at the hospital with Mommy. We'll take you there in the morning," she replied.

That statement caused Noah's lip to tremble. Before he could start crying, Pesh rose out of his chair. "Let's go look at all the pretty party decorations."

Megan smiled as she watched Pesh take Noah around the room. Her heart warmed at his thoughtfulness. She couldn't believe there was ever a time when she fought her feelings for him. There wasn't a better man in the whole world, and the fact that he loved her was a true miracle.

By the time Pesh returned, Noah had fallen asleep. He carefully sat back down beside her. "Here," she suggested, taking off her glittering drape. She wrapped the fabric over Noah like a blanket.

"Did I mention how much I loved you in a sari?" Pesh questioned, with a wicked gleam in his eyes.

She glanced down to see the top had her boobs bulging out the front as well as the fact her stomach was now bared. "I'll have to wear one more often for you."

"I would love that."

When her phone beeped, she reached across the table and grabbed it. "Oh my God!"

"What?" Pesh asked.

"That was Aidan. The baby is already here."

"Considering it's a second baby, it isn't too surprising."

"I need to tell my mom and aunts."

He nodded. "Go ahead. We're fine."

Megan smiled at Noah sleeping soundly against Pesh's chest. "Be right back." She made her way over to her family's table. "That was Aidan. Caroline was just born."

A whoop went up around the table. "Is Emma okay?" Becky asked.

Megan nodded. "He said mother and baby are doing great."

Julia shook her head and smiled. "Aidan with a daughter—now that's going to be something to see."

They all laughed. "That's so true," Megan said.

Becky glanced at the group. "Why don't we go see them? I mean, the hospital isn't too far from here."

Angie nodded. "Sounds good to me. I'd personally like to see Aidan in action with his baby girl."

With a snort, Megan added, "I would have liked to have been in the delivery room when she was first born. His expression then would have been priceless."

"I bet he cried," Liz said.

"Oh yeah, he bawled for sure," Angie replied, with a grin.

As her aunts started gathering up their purses and telling their husbands where they were going, Megan said, "I want to go too." Before they could argue, she held up her hand. "It's late. The party is pretty much over, and there's two more next week at some of Pesh's relatives' houses. Besides, I want to see the newest Fitzgerald baby girl."

Her mother frowned. "Are you sure?"

"I'm positive."

"All right. Go tell Pesh, and we'll meet you out front."

She smiled as she went back to their table. "My mom and aunts are going to the hospital to see Aidan and Emma."

"You want to go?"

Her heart warmed at the fact that he already knew what she was feeling. "Do you mind?"

He shook his head. "Of course not. Can I go too or is this just a hen party thing for the women?"

She laughed. "Yes, you can come."

Pesh glanced down at Noah. "He's going to want to see his mother."

"Oh yes. I don't think we could go without him."

As Pesh rose out of the chair, Noah stirred but didn't wake up. "Get Aidan and Emma's keys out of my pocket."

She nodded and reached into his pants. When she accidentally touched his penis through the fabric, he jumped. "Sorry about that," she replied, as she pulled out the keys.

"No problem," he muttered through gritted teeth.

They said a quick goodnight to Pesh's parents and other relatives who remained. Then they headed out to the lobby. After giving the valet Aidan's keys, they waited for the SUV to be brought around. When she caught her reflection in the glass doors of the hotel, she gasped.

"What's wrong?" Pesh inquired.

"The jewelry! I can't go loaded down with this expensive stuff to the hospital!" she cried. She snatched off the earrings and then started working on the necklace. "I'll run go give it to your mother."

"If you insist," Pesh replied.

She kicked off her heels so she could run easier. The necklace and earrings weighed down her hands. She grabbed the first member of Pesh's immediate family she saw, which unfortunately happened to be Dev. "Can you get these to your mother? I've got to get to the hospital."

His dark eyes widened as he took the jewelry from her. "Are you okay?"

"I'm fine. A cousin's baby was just born. Don't let anything happen to that, okay?"

Dev chuckled. "Yeah, I'll be unloading this pronto. The last thing I need is for my ass to be the one to lose the family jewels." With a wink, he added, "They'd be taking my family jewels."

Megan laughed and then gave him a wave before running off. When she got back outside, Aidan and Emma's SUV had just pulled around. Noah began to squirm in Pesh's arms. "Guess where we're going?" Pesh said, before he could start crying.

"Mama?"

Pesh smiled. "Yes, we're taking you to your mama and daddy and new baby sister."

Noah's face lit up at the prospect, and he happily let them buckle him into his car seat. Following her mother's car, they made the drive in almost a caravan of relatives. When they got to the hospital, Pesh pulled up to let her out. "I'll go park and bring him in."

"Okay. I'll see you guys up there."

When she got up to the maternity floor, there was a quite a group waiting for her, including Emma's best friend, Connor.

"Did Casey not feel like coming tonight?" Megan asked, as she hugged him. Casey was just a few weeks shy of her own due date with a little girl.

He chuckled. "Oh, she's here all right. She's just in labor herself. It seems like Caroline and Olivia are going to be true best friends by being born almost the same day."

Megan grinned. "That's wonderful news."

Connor wrinkled his nose. "I think Casey will be appreciating it a little more when her epidural kicks in. She wasn't too happy the last time I went back to see her."

"Oh yes, I remember that feeling well."

Megan's phone dinged, and she quickly read the text. "Aidan says we can come back now," she said to her aunts.

The group made their way through the double doors and down the hall. When they reached Emma's room, Angie knocked on the door. Within a few seconds, Aidan appeared. "Hey guys," he said, with a beaming smile. "The nurse is actually checking on Em, but give me a second." He disappeared back behind the door only to reappear within a few moments. This time he held a tiny bundle wrapped in a pink blanket. "Here she is. Miss Caroline Elizabeth Fitzgerald."

Collective oohs and aahs went up over the group as Aidan held Caroline out for them to see. She didn't seem too interested or impressed by them. She yawned and closed her eyes. "She's absolutely beautiful," Megan said.

"She's something all right," Aidan murmured.

"There it is! I see a tear," Becky teased.

Aidan rolled his eyes at his sister. "Let me guess. You had some kind of bet going about whether I cried or not?"

Liz patted his back. "Something like that."

Pesh appeared then. The moment Noah saw his father he kicked to get down. Once he got his feet on the floor, he ran to Aidan, wrapping his arms around Aidan's leg. "Hey buddy. You want to meet your sister?"

Squatting down, Aidan held Caroline to where Noah could get a good look at her. "Mama's tummy baby?" he questioned.

Aidan laughed. "Yeah, this is your baby sister, Caroline."

Noah eyed his sister with a slight frown, as if he was trying to figure her out. Megan could only imagine what was going on in his head at the moment. He'd spent the last sixteen months being the center of his parents' world, and now there was someone else to share the attention.

When Caroline scrunched up her face and whimpered, Noah patted her arm. "No cwy, baby."

"Aw, he's going to be a good big brother," Angie remarked.

Aidan chuckled. "Yeah, he'll be fine until Caroline needs Emma. Then he's going to be ready to sell her to the gypsies."

A nurse exited Emma's room. "You can go in now." As she gazed around the crowd, she shook her head. "Well, *some* of you can go in."

Rising up off the floor, Aidan took Noah's hand. "Come on, buddy. Mama wants to see you."

Noah didn't bother waiting on Aidan. He barreled through the door. "Mama! Mama!" he cried.

Megan smiled as she watched him climb up on Emma's bed. "There's my baby boy!" Emma cried hoarsely, smothering both his cheeks in kisses. He snuggled up to Emma's side.

"Come on, Meggie. You and Pesh come in first," Aidan suggested.

Megan didn't argue with him. Instead, she took Pesh's hand and followed Aidan inside. Emma glanced up and shook her head. "I'm so sorry for ruining your engagement party."

"You didn't ruin our night," Pesh reassured her.

"That's right. We kept right on partying—it didn't bother us at all," Megan teased.

Emma laughed. "I'm glad to hear that."

Megan smiled and jerked her chin over at Aidan, who sat in the rocker with Caroline. "Congratulations on a beautiful baby girl."

"Thank you," Emma replied, as a beaming smile lit up her face.

"Are you feeling okay?" Pesh asked.

Emma nodded. "It was a little easier this time and a lot quicker." She turned to Aidan. "And this time I didn't have to worry that Aidan might not make it."

Aidan chuckled. "No, you just kept screaming at me to drive faster because you were not going to deliver Caroline on the side of the interstate."

Emma's cheeks flushed. "I guess I was a little panicked."

Pesh took Megan's hand and squeezed it. "We better go and let the others have a turn," he said.

"Do you want us to take Noah back with us?"

Considering he was plastered to his mother's side, Megan wasn't really looking forward to trying to take him. Emma gazed down at her son with love burning in her eyes. "No, I think he can stay here with us a little longer. I might get Connor to take him home. I know he'll be here until Casey delivers."

"Are you sure you won't need your rest?" Megan asked.

"Oh, I'll pawn him off to Aidan and make sure I get plenty of sleep until Miss Caroline needs me," Emma replied, with a sly smile.

Aidan didn't argue with her. He looked perfectly content to lose sleep if it meant being surrounded by his wife and children. After exchanging a few hugs and kisses, she and Pesh headed out into the hallway and let the next group in.

As they walked down the hall hand in hand, Pesh turned to her and smiled. "You know, I never thought I would see the day I would be envious of Aidan again."

"What do you mean?"

He heaved a sigh. "Seeing him with his children makes me envious. One day I hope that's you with my child in your arms."

"Oh," she murmured.

Whether or not they would have children together had never really been discussed. It was almost a given that they would, so it didn't seem necessary to iron out when and how many. She wanted nothing more than to give Pesh a baby of his own. He was truly the father Mason had never had.

"Give me a year," she said softly.

His brows furrowed in confusion. "What?"

"I'd like one year for us to be together as a married couple before we try to have children."

"That only makes me an even older father," he protested.

"You'll be fine. You're awfully spry for your old age."

He laughed. "I just don't want to be on a walker at his or her high school graduation."

She smacked his arm playfully. "One year is not going to make that much a difference."

"Fine. You win. We'll wait one year."

As the elevator doors dinged open, they stepped inside. Gazing down at her, Pesh said, "I couldn't have picked a more amazing mother for my future children."

"Yeah, I gotta agree that you did good, Nadeen. Real good," she teased.

He cupped her face in his hands and gave her a lingering kiss that silenced anymore of her comebacks. When he pulled away, she smiled at him. "Keep kissing me like that, and I might decide to wait even longer for a baby. You'll make me want you, your lips, and your dick all to myself for as long as possible."

"And here I thought my kisses might get you in the mood for baby-making," Pesh mused.

Megan laughed. "Either way, it's a win-win situation. So bring it on, Nadeen. Bring. It. On."

Chapter Twenty-Two

TWO MONTHS LATER

Although her stomach screamed in protest to drop her fork, Megan couldn't resist popping in the last bite of delicious crepe into her mouth. As she chewed, she closed her eyes at the delicious combination of chocolate and strawberries danced along her taste buds. "Good?" a voice asked from across the table.

Her eyelids popped open to take in Pesh, her new husband of three days. He wore an amused smile as he held his cappuccino cup in midair. "Orgasmically good," she replied.

He chuckled. "I'm glad you're enjoying them."

"I'm going to gain ten pounds while we're here," she replied. As she dabbed her mouth with her napkin, she sighed with absolute contentment. Gazing around the tiny Parisian café, she fought the urge to pinch herself. Was she actually in Paris on her honeymoon? When Pesh had asked her where she wanted to go, there was only one place. Although it was somewhat clichéd for a honeymoon destination, she had always wanted to see the city. And because she was marrying a man who loved to spoil her, Pesh had booked them for a week's stay at the Hotel Plaza Athenee. Not only had he chosen the hotel for its gorgeous views of the Eiffel Tower, but it was also where Carrie Bradshaw stayed when she was in Paris. It seems Pesh completely understood Megan's love for *Sex and the City*.

Their first day in the city had been spent in their hotel room. A combination of jetlag and lust had kept them naked and in bed, stopping only for room service and showers. Today they had pried themselves away from the room to go sightseeing.

"Are you ready to go back to the hotel?" Pesh asked.

"Maybe." With a teasing grin, she asked, "Are you tired and want to rest?"

Desire pooled in Pesh's dark eyes. "No, I don't want to rest. I want you to model what you bought this afternoon."

Her gaze left his to go down to the pink and black bag at her feet. Part of their sightseeing had turned into shopping, in which she bought some very racy lingerie. Although she was enjoying her day out in the city, she was also itching to put on the outfit and get back in bed with Pesh. "Then let's go," she said.

Pesh certainly didn't need any more convincing. Digging in his pocket, he took out his wallet and threw a wad of euros on the table. Then he popped out of seat like a jack-in-the-box. She had to snatch up her purse and bag to keep up with him before he sprinted out the door and into the sunshine.

As she passed the colorful flowers in bloom outside the café, they transported her back to her wedding. It had been a perfect, cloudless day when she stood with Pesh in the rose garden at her Papa's house. To her, he had never looked more handsome than in his black tux that fit his built frame like a second skin.

Since she was the master of party planning, Megan had enlisted Emma's help in getting the quickie wedding done. Even with newborn Caroline to tend to, Emma had gone above and beyond any expectations Megan had. Tears had stung her eyes when she first caught sight of the garden as she, on her father's arm, made her way from the house to the ceremony.

White chairs draped with blue silk bunting lined the garden in rows while a tent had been erected to the side of the makeshift altar. Next to the chairs, votive candles lit the way up the aisle that was adorned in multicolored rose petals. Emma, Casey, and two of her best friends from childhood stood at the altar in their cornflower blue bridesmaid dresses. Pesh, along with his brothers and Aidan, wore blue vests with their tuxes. A string quartet struck up the bridal march to herald her arrival.

She would never, ever forget the feeling of walking up the aisle to Pesh. His loving gaze took her in, and she felt like the princess she had always wanted to be on her wedding day. Her dress was almost like what a Disney Princess might wear—a long train, a full ball gown, a bodice encrusted with pearls and sequins, and then a glittering tiara holding her veil in place.

The entire world seemed to evaporate when Pesh took her hand in his. He was her only focus. She barely heard the words the priest spoke or the lyrics of the song that Emma sang. She just stared at her soon-to-be husband—the man who made her believe in romance and true love.

She was so lost in thoughts of her wedding day that she accidentally mowed into a woman. "Excuse me," she apologized.

The woman scowled at her while cursing at Megan in French. Well, Megan imagined it was cursing since she didn't speak French.

"Where is that head of yours?" Pesh asked, with a smile.

"Thinking of our wedding day," she replied.

His smile grew broader at her response, and in the middle of a crowded street, he stopped to kiss her. While it was somewhat chaste and full of more love than lust, it did hold a promise of what was to come later on. He ended it far sooner than she would like. "Let's hurry," he replied.

She giggled before breaking into a slight run towards the hotel. He followed her example. By the time they pushed through the revolving doors into the lobby, they were both breathless. Like two mischievous kids, they raced to the elevators. Once inside, they wrapped their arms around each other and kissed passionately until the door dinged open. They pulled apart long enough to get down the hall and into their suite.

When the door closed behind them, Pesh pulled her to him, bestowing a lingering kiss on her lips. As he ravaged her mouth, his tongue darted inside to tease along hers. When she felt his evident desire poking into her stomach, she broke the kiss. At his groan, she shook her head. "Not yet. I have to get dressed."

"Next time," he muttered.

Pushing out of his arms, she grinned up at him. "I'll be back in just a second. You get ready."

"Oh, I'll be ready. That's a promise."

She laughed and then practically skipped into the bathroom. Once she closed and locked the door, she sat the bag down and dug inside. After she decided what to wear, she laid them out on the counter, and then started taking off her clothes.

When she was naked, she reached for the lingerie. The tight bodice was solid black with pink ribbons that wove through making intricate designs. It pushed her breasts up and over the cups, making her appear to have far more cleavage than she was blessed with. The black and pink panties were lace and practically see through. On her legs, she slid black silk stockings that had pink bows at the tops of her thighs. As she fluffed out her hair, she couldn't help gazing in the mirror. She looked quite the sexpot, which she hoped pleased Pesh. Well, she knew it would please Pesh. The man was ravenous for her, something for which she was very thankful. Not quite the polite gentleman she had expected when she first met him, that was for sure.

Megan opened the bathroom door. Across the room, Pesh stood gazing out the window, stripped down to his boxer shorts. When she cleared her throat, he jerked his head to stare at her. Slowly, she walked out of the bathroom. Her eyes stayed on him. A shiver rippled through her as he tracked her every move. When she finally stood before him, it took less than a second for him to pounce on her. His hands grabbed her by the waist, jerking her flush against him. His mouth bore down on hers in a frantic kiss as he ground his cock between her legs.

Breathless, she pulled away to gaze up at him. "Does this mean you like the lingerie?"

"Oh hell yes, I do. I think we're going to have to go back and get you some more."

She laughed. "More shopping? You won't hear me say no to that."

Bending over, Pesh brought his arm under her knees and then lifted her up. She felt so light in his arms as he walked her over to the bed and gently deposited her on the mattress. As he loomed over her, her heartbeat sped up in anticipation the sensual delicacies she was about to experience.

Tugging on the straps of the bodice, he bared her breasts. His mouth hovered over her nipple, breathing warm air onto the cool tip. It puckered under his attention before his tongue darted out and flicked it. "Mmm," she murmured, her fingers tightening in his hair. Making slow circles around her nipple, Pesh continued his teasing assault. Arching her back, she gripped the strands of his hair tighter, willing him to take her nipple in his whole mouth. Finally, he obliged her, sucking the hardened peak into his mouth. While he gave oral attention to one breast, his hand palmed and stroked the other. As the heat and moisture built in her core, Megan began sawing her legs back and forth. The friction eased her a little, but she wanted Pesh's fingers, tongue, and dick there more than anything.

Over the fabric of her bodice, he kissed down her stomach. Just as he reached the juncture between her legs, he bypassed it and began kissing and licking the exposed skin on her upper thighs. She groaned in protest.

He gazed up at her with a teasing smile. "Did you want me to kiss you somewhere else?"

Raising her hips, she replied, "You know where I want you—where I want *all* of you."

"Patience, my love."

"Oh really?" she muttered. With one quick movement, she was out from underneath him in a flash. Surprise filled his face as she flipped him over onto his back and straddled him once again. Raking her fingernails down his chest, she stopped just at the waistband of his boxers. As his breath hitched, her hands went to his thighs, scraping a trail up the exposed skin to his dick. His hips bucked up, causing her to smile. "Oh, did you want me to touch you somewhere else?"

With a growl, he gripped her by the ass and forced her onto her knees. He slid down the mattress to where her core was right at his mouth. His tongue flicked out, sliding along the thin scrap of her panties. She gasped as he flattened his tongue and rubbed it over her clit. Even through the fabric, it lit her on fire. As he added more pressure, she began to rock her hips against his face. Closing her eyes, she concentrated on the feel of tongue. When he pulled away, she whimpered. His lips came to kiss along her thighs again.

Just as Pesh's teeth dug into one of the bows on her stockings, Megan's ringtone for Mason blared out over her frustrated breaths. Pesh protested the interruption with a grunt, but immediately let the stocking fall from his mouth.

"I'm sorry. It's his bedtime call. I have to take it," Megan said, as she sat up in the bed.

"It's all right, my love. I'm the one with patience, not you," he replied, with a smile.

She rolled her eyes at him as she grabbed the phone off the nightstand and answered it. "Hey baby," she said, trying to catch her breath.

"Hi Mommy. Miss you."

Her heart warmed hearing his tiny voice while an ache filled her chest. "Oh, I miss you too, sweet boy. Are you being good for Grammy?"

"Uh-huh. Pway with Noah today."

"Did you? Did you have fun?"

"Uh-huh. But Caowine cwies."

Megan laughed at his summation of the latest Fitzgerald family member. "I bet she does. She's a little baby, and they do like to cry. You cried a lot when you were that age."

"Where Daddy?"

Glancing at Pesh, Megan smiled. "He's right here. You want to talk to him?"

"Uh-huh."

Megan handed the phone to Pesh. His face lit up as he said, "Hey buddy, how are you?"

As Mason rattled along to Pesh, Megan couldn't help thinking of how happy Mason had been on her wedding day. He had played his part as ring bearer wonderfully. Everyone commented on how handsome he was in small tux and how much he looked like her. He was so excited to have a daddy and to be part of a real family. He didn't even seem to mind that they were moving away from his grandparents into Pesh's house. Of course, Pesh had sweetened the moving angst by having a black Lab puppy, just like Beau, waiting for Mason in his new room. He had squealed so loud that Megan thought her ear drums were going to burst.

"Oh, so Beau Two pee-peed on Grammy's rug, huh?" Pesh asked, throwing Megan an "oh shit" look. While they were away, Angie was in charge of both Mason and the puppy, who Mason had aptly named Beau Two after his first love, Beau. Megan could imagine her mother was fit to be tied with her rugs being christened by puppy piss.

"Okay, you better go to bed now. Mommy and I miss you very, very much. We're bringing you lots of presents home." At Mason's reply, tears shimmered in Pesh's eyes. "I love you, too, buddy," he replied, in a choked voice. "Say goodnight to Mommy," he replied, thrusting the phone at Megan.

A sheepish expression came over Pesh's face as he ground the moisture from his eyes with his fists. Megan took the phone. "Night, night, Mommy!" Mason called.

"Night, night, baby. You have sweet dreams, and I'll talk to you tomorrow."

"Okay. Wuv you!"

She smiled. "I love you, too."

After Megan hung up, she still cradled the phone to her ear as if by doing that, she was able to have Mason a little closer. Pesh's hand came to rest on hers. "He's something, isn't he?" he asked.

"Yes, he is," she murmured.

"I know it makes me a complete pansy, but every time he tells me he loves, I can't help but cry."

Putting her phone back on the nightstand, Megan eased herself over onto Pesh's lap. "Don't you ever worry that I think you're a pansy because of what you feel for Mason. It makes me love you even more." Brushing her hand across his cheek, she added, "A man who isn't afraid of showing his emotions or his vulnerability is very sexy."

"You think so?"

"Mmm, I do."

He smiled. "I'm glad to hear you say that."

"Where were we?"

Glancing down at his crotch, Pesh said, "I think we're starting over from my perspective."

Megan's hand went to cup his now deflated erection. She rubbed him over the boxers before dipping her hand inside to grip him. Pesh hissed in a breath. His head fell back against the headboard as she started stroking his growing length. Sliding down his body, she brought her hand to his lap and took him into her mouth. Her tongue teasingly flicked across the tip. Pesh's hand came to tangle in her hair. She did leisurely strokes up and down his length before bringing him into her mouth. As she began bobbing up and down, Pesh's groans echoed through the room.

As she cut her gaze up to him, he glanced down at her with hooded eyes. "So good, baby. So, so good," he murmured.

When he started tensing up, she let him fall free of her mouth. "I want you to come inside me," she said, as she climbed up his body. Rising up on her knees, she brought Pesh's hands to the elastic band of her underwear. He tore them off her hips and down her thighs. Somehow she managed to get them off and toss them to the floor beside the bed.

Leaving on the bustier, she guided his erection to her core. Slowly, she eased down on him, inch by inch. When he was balls deep inside her, she sat back on his thighs. Raising her knees, she placed both her feet flat on the mattress. From this position, she was giving Pesh quite the view as she rose on and off of him. As the pressure began building inside her, the more frantic her movements became. Harder and harder she bounced, the sound of skin slapping along with grunts and panting echoing through the room. When Pesh's fingers came to tease her clit, she came undone, crying out and collapsing onto his chest. He continued raising his hips to pump into her until he came a few moments later.

Brushing the hair out of her face, Pesh stared up at Megan with a satisfied expression. She brought her lips to his for a gentle kiss. "I love you, Mr. Nadeen."

"Do you?"

She bobbed her head. "I love you and your talented fingers and dick, all of who give me wonderful orgasms."

He barked out a laugh. "I've married such a naughty girl, haven't I?"

"Yes, you have."

"I wouldn't have you any other way, my love."

Megan smiled as he slid free of her body. Easing her onto her side, Pesh spooned up behind her, nuzzling his face in her neck. "Rest now," he said, drowsily.

"Yes, you need your rest. I'm going to want more of you in a little while."

His chuckle made her tingle with love and lust. With the feel of his arm wrapped around her, Megan let her drooping eyes close and drifted off to a contented sleep.

Chapter
Twenty-Three
TWO MONTHS LATER

As they sat outside the courtroom waiting to be called in, Megan adjusted Mason's blue and white striped tie for the hundredth time. "Mommy, no," he pleaded.

She snatched her hands away. "I'm sorry, sweetheart. I'll leave you alone."

"Tank you," he replied, going back to his game on his tablet.

The truth was her nervous hands needed to be doing something. Sensing her need, Pesh reached over and took her hands in his. "Relax. Everything is going to be fine."

Megan wanted to believe him, but she couldn't help feeling anxious. She wouldn't be able to calm down until the ink had dried on the paperwork. Her feet, encased in black heels, tapped anxiously on the floor. The clattering noise echoed around the atrium. As she glanced between Pesh and Mason, Megan had to smile. The two men in her life looked almost identical today in their navy suits and ties. Of course Mason's was considerably smaller than Pesh's.

When the door opened and a clerk poked her head out the door, Megan's heartbeat started thrumming faster and faster. "Megan Nadeen?"

She shot off the bench. "That's us. I mean, I'm Megan Nadeen."

The clerk smiled. "You guys can come in now."

Taking a deep breath, Megan reached for Mason's hand. "This is it, baby."

He grinned and then glanced up at Pesh. "You be my daddy now?"

Pesh smiled. "Yes, I'm going to be your daddy for real now."

They walked through the massive doors of the courtroom. The judge, in his ominous black robe, gazed down at them from his bench. "Good morning," he said, politely.

"G-Good morning," Megan stammered.

"I understand that we're here today to petition for the adoption of the minor child, Mason Patrick McKenzie?"

"Yes," Megan and Pesh replied.

"First, we need to swear you all in," the judge said.

Megan went through the motions of the procedure, trying desperately to calm her nerves. When Pesh had first broached the subject of formally adopting Mason, she initially had been thrilled and honored. But then she had to worry about whether Davis would allow Pesh to adopt Mason or not. Although he still had nothing to do with his son, Davis hadn't shown a lot of enthusiasm about the prospect. The closer they got to the adoption hearing, the more Megan worried that he would refuse.

"Dr. Nadeen, I understand that you wish to adopt the minor child of your wife?"

Pesh nodded enthusiastically. "Yes, your honor, I would."

"I see that you and your wife have been married less than two months, and that you've only known her a year." The judge adjusted his glasses that had slid down his pointy nose. "Do you think it wise to legally bind yourself to this child after such a short time?"

Megan fought the urge to stalk up to the bench and smack the judge. Instead, she took deep breaths and tried to reign in her temper. She glanced over at Pesh who merely smiled pleasantly at the judge. "Your honor, I realize that on paper it might seem as though I am rushing into things. However, I've never been more certain of anything in my life as I am about my love for Megan and in turn, my love for Mason. I've waited a long time to be a father, and I don't want to have to waste another second."

"I see." The judge eyed the folder open before him. "I understand the biological father has had no contact with the child."

"That's correct," Megan replied.

"He has also waved his parental rights so that Dr. Nadeen can adopt his son."

Megan exhaled a relieved breath that Davis had signed the paperwork. "I'm glad to hear that, your honor," she said.

"Do you feel that your husband will make a good father for your son?"

"I never would have dated, least of all married him, if I didn't believe that Pesh would be a good and loving father to Mason."

"So the fact that he is a wealthy doctor had nothing to do with it?"

"How dare you!" Megan cried. When Pesh grabbed her arm to silence her, she slung him away. "You've known us for two minutes and you're making assumptions about me, my husband, and my marriage? If this were about money, I could have used his father for child support considering he is a wealthy NFL player. But I would have sacrificed everything to ensure that my son had a good father!"

"Mrs. Nadeen, I will ask that you control yourself, or I will have to hold you in contempt," the judge said sternly.

Pesh wrapped his arm around her waist, drawing her against him. "Easy," he murmured.

Although she hated to do it, she said, "I'm sorry, your honor."

When he smiled at her, she gasped in surprise. "And I am sorry for rattling you, Mrs. Nadeen. I often say or do unorthodox things to see the true nature of the people who come before me."

"You mean, you said that to get a reaction from me?"

"Yes, I did. And you unwaveringly rose to my challenge. I can see that you are truly concerned with the wellbeing of your son."

Still reeling from the judge's behavior, Megan mumbled, "Thank you."

Peering down over the bench, the judge surmised Mason. "Son, do you know why you're here today?"

"I gettin' 'dopted," Mason replied.

The judge smiled. "Yes, you are. Do you want Pesh to be your daddy?"

"Uh, huh."

"Do you want anyone else to be your daddy?"

"No," Mason replied quickly, shaking his head back and forth.

"Then come up here while I sign the paperwork."

Mason happily ran around the side of the bench to the judge. He climbed up onto the judge's lap. After signing several sets of papers, the judge handed Mason his gavel. "Once you bang that gavel, Pesh is officially your daddy, and you are Mason Nadeen."

With a broad grin, Mason brought the gavel down. Tears stung Megan's eyes, and she gladly let Pesh pull her into his arms. "Thank you, thank you, thank you," she murmured.

"I love you," he replied, squeezing her tight.

"I love you, too."

Their attention was drawn to where Mason kept banging the gavel. The judge chuckled. "Okay, I think that is enough. Why don't you go to your mommy and daddy now?"

"Tell the judge thank you," Megan instructed.

"Tank you," Mason replied, before he hopped off the judge's lap and came running to them. "I 'dopted! I 'dopted!"

Pesh bent down to pick him up. "That's right, buddy. You're my son for now and always."

Megan smiled and patted Mason's back as they started out of the courtroom. "Come on. Let's go to Papa's. We've got a big party for you there."

Mason's face lit up. "Ice cweam?

"Oh yes, there's lots of ice cream just for you."

"Yay!" he cried.

When they drove up at Patrick's, Megan did a double take at the sight of an inflatable bouncy castle out on the lawn. John, Percy, and Georgie were already making good use of it. "Emma, the Party Planning Monster has struck again," she mused.

Pesh chuckled as he got out of the car. He went to get Mason while she started into the house. Balloons and flowers filled the foyer and living room. Over the dining room archway, there was a giant CONGRATULATIONS MASON sign.

When she got to the kitchen, she sucked in a breath at the sight of all the catering pans. "Emma Fitzgerald, what have you done?" she questioned.

At the sound of Megan's voice, Emma jumped. Clutching her chest, she whirled around. "Okay, so maybe I found a really excellent deal on the bouncy castle. Like ridiculously cheap."

Megan crossed her arms over her chest. "The food? I thought Mom and my aunts were cooking."

Holding up one hand, Emma replied, "Just Williamson Brothers BBQ. Nothing fancy."

"Anything else I need to know about? Live band or celebrity bursting out of a cake?"

Emma giggled. "Nope. That's it."

Megan watched Emma bustle around the kitchen, setting up the plates and cutlery. "Um, is there anything I can do? I mean, I feel pretty shitty considering this is my son's adoption party," Megan said, with a smile.

Pink tinged Emma's cheeks. "I'm sorry."

Megan threw her arms around Emma and squeezed her tight. "Don't be sorry. You're amazing to do all of this for us."

Emma smiled. "You're more than welcome. I'm so happy for you and Pesh and for Mason."

"Thank you."

When Megan pulled away, Emma said, "Oh, there is something you can do. Go tell Aidan we're about to start. He went to get Caroline up from her nap."

"Sure. I'll be happy to." As Megan started down the familiar hallway, she stopped outside of Aidan's boyhood bedroom. Through the crack in the door, she could see him walking around the room, bouncing Caroline in his arms. At the sound of his singing, she had to stifle a laugh. Ankle was many things, but a singer wasn't one of them.

"Sweet Caroline, dum, dum, dum. Good times never seemed so good," he crooned off-key.

When Megan pushed open the door, Aidan jumped. "Um, hey," he said, a flush entering his cheeks.

"I never really pictured you as a Neil Diamond fan," she said, with a smile.

"Yeah, well, *Sweet Caroline* seems like the right thing to sing to her." He cleared his throat. "What are you doing in here?"

"Emma wanted me to come get you."

"Oh," he said. In his arms, Caroline began to whimper, her little fists flailed. "Shh, it's okay, sweet pea. Where was I?"

"I've been inclined," Megan answered him.

"Right," he said, over Caroline's cries.

When he picked back up with the song, Megan said, "That's really unfair to torture her like that."

As Aidan scowled at Megan, Caroline began to quiet. Aidan's expression then turned triumphant. "See? She likes it when I sing to her."

"But you *can't* sing," Megan protested.

Aidan shrugged. "It doesn't matter to her."

Megan laughed. "She has a mother with a killer voice, yet she likes to listen to you?"

Flashing his signature cocky grin, Aidan replied, "What can I say? All women love me."

With a roll of her eyes, Megan said, "Give me a break."

Glancing down at Caroline, Aidan said in a sing-song voice, "Don't you have the sweetest, handsomest, and most wonderful daddy in the whole wide world?" Caroline cooed at his question and kicked her legs. "She's a smart girl because she knows how lucky she is."

"You're terrible," Megan said, with a grin.

Aidan looked from his daughter over to Megan. "You want to hold my most perfect little princess?"

"I would love to." She held out her arms as Aidan passed Caroline to her. Outfitted in a frilly purple dress and purple bow, Caroline looked like she could be modeling baby wear. Unlike Noah's strawberry blond hair, hers was a deep auburn. She had also inherited her mother's green eyes. "I have to agree that you're a lucky girl because you look just like your mother," Megan said.

Aidan laughed. "Yeah, she is a little mini-Emma, isn't she?"

"She is. Boy, she's going to give you hell when she's a teenager," Megan teased.

"I know. Trust me, I know."

As Caroline smiled up at her, Megan couldn't help sighing. "You're a bad influence, missy. You make me want to have another baby."

"Is that a bad thing?" Aidan asked.

"No, it's just…"

"Just what?"

"I asked Pesh to give me a year of marriage before we start trying. I know he's ready right now, but I just want this time with him. You know, just the two of us."

"That's understandable."

"But holding her…" Megan shook her head. "You're just bad for business, Miss Caroline."

Aidan laughed. "Tell me about it. Whenever I hold her or Noah, I think how much I'm going to miss it when they're not babies anymore. It nags at me enough that I think I'll be okay if we have more."

"No vasectomy on the horizon?"

He grinned. "No yet. Still not ruling it out though. And as far as you and more babies, you'll know when the time is right. And if anyone is patient and understanding, it's Pesh."

"That's true," Megan murmured.

Mason appeared in the doorway then. "'Mon, Mommy. Want ice cweam!"

Megan laughed. "Okay, let me give your little bad influence back to you," she said, handing Caroline to Aidan. She then took Mason's hand and started out of the bedroom.

"Daddy says I have ice cweam first."

"Did he?" Megan said, as she planned to strangle Pesh.

"Uh huh. 'Cause it's my 'doption day."

When she met Pesh's eye, she raised her brows. Immediately, his face flushed. "Spoiling him rotten already, aren't you?" she questioned in a low voice.

"I couldn't help it. It's a special day."

"Mmm, hmm, and when this special day turns into an all nighter because he's hyped on sugar, you're going to deal with him."

Pesh grinned. "I will. I promise."

Megan leaned up to kiss him. "You're too sweet for your own good. You're always going to have me playing bad cop when it comes to discipline."

"But you love me anyway, right?" he murmured against her lips.

"So much I was almost ready to reconsider our plan about when we're starting a family."

His eyes bulged at her response. It took him a few moments to speak. "That means a lot that you would do that, but deep down I know how you really feel. So, I'm going to be good and patiently wait ten more months before confiscating your birth control."

"It's a deal," she replied, before kissing him again.

Epilogue

As soon as he finished with his last patient, Pesh practically sprinted from the exam room. He hustled into the doctors' lounge, trying hard to keep his head down and not call any attention to himself. He wanted to be able to get out the door without anyone calling him back for a consult or to pull a longer shift. Once he had retrieved his things, he started for the parking lot.

"Dr. Nadeen!" Kristi called.

Inwardly, he groaned. "Yes?" he questioned, as he turned around.

"You weren't leaving, were you?" she asked.

He exhaled a defeated breath. "I was planning on it. Does someone need me to cover for them?"

Kristi winked at him. "Thought you were screwed there for a minute, didn't you?"

A relieved laugh escaped his lips. "I did."

She smiled. "I have something for Megan."

"Honestly Kristi, you didn't need to do anything else for us."

Waving her hand dismissively, she handed a pink gift bag to him. "I wanted to do this."

After peeking inside, Pesh smiled before he leaned down to hug Kristi. "Thank you. I'm sure she'll love it."

"You tell her we miss her around here."

"I will."

She patted his back. "Now go on home to your girls."

He nodded and then hurried out the door. Today had been his first day back after taking both paternity leave and some of his many amassed sick days. As he slid into the seat of his Jaguar, he felt a rush of embarrassment at how he had actually gotten teary on the way to work that morning after leaving Megan. It had been the longest shift of his entire life. He thought he would never be through so he could get home to her.

Even now, the usual ten-minute drive home seemed to take an eternity. He anxiously drummed his fingers on the steering wheel. He'd tried not to pester Megan with too many calls and texts, but after the tenth, "How are you guys?" text, she'd told him to lighten up and get his head in the game at work.

That's why he didn't even bother telling her he was on his way home. As he pulled into the driveway, he noticed Emma's SUV. He was glad to know that Megan hadn't been alone without him. When he pushed through the garage door into the kitchen, Emma was at the stove. "Hello," he called pleasantly.

Whirling around, she gave him a beaming smile. "Hello to you, too."

"How are my girls?"

"Good. They've slept most of the day."

Pesh nodded. Noticing how quiet the house was, he asked, "Where's Mason?"

"Patrick came by and got him, along with Noah and Caroline, a little while ago." She cocked her head at Pesh and grinned. "Although he swore to me that he wouldn't ruin their dinner, I have a feeling they're having ice cream right now."

Pesh smiled at the mention of his son. Although he wasn't Mason's biological father, the love he felt for him was just as strong as if he had been a part of his conception. From the moment he'd been able to adopt him, he had felt an even stronger bond than before, especially whenever he saw "Mason Nadeen" written on his pre-school paperwork.

More than anything, he relished being a father. He had been forced to wait so long, while desiring it so hard, that it made it all the more sweeter. Because Mason adored baseball, Pesh had bought season tickets to the Braves, rather than the opera. Even though Pesh had never been athletically inclined, he signed up to help coach Mason's Little League team as well. Every time he heard Mason say

"Daddy," it warmed his heart the same as it did to hear Megan say "I love you."

Pesh eyed the dishes on the stove. "It's awfully kind of you to come stay with Megan on my first day back. But we certainly didn't expect for you to cook."

"It's my pleasure. Besides, it kills two birds with one stone—I can feed my family and yours. Aidan's coming by after work."

"Good. I'll be glad to see him."

As his gaze swept toward the living room, Emma laughed. "Go on. You don't have to stay here with me. I know you want to see your girls."

He smiled. "Thank you. I have missed them terribly today." After giving Emma a quick kiss on the cheek, he made his way into the living room. At the sight of Megan sleeping on the couch next to a frilly pink Pack N Play, his chest swelled with so much love and pride he felt like it might explode. Peeking over the side of the Pack N Play, he eyed his dark-haired daughters.

After waiting so long to become a father, he had been doubly blessed when they found out they were having twins. While Aidan liked to claim that his fear of the twin gene in his family had bypassed him, and instead, it had found its way to Megan, that wasn't entirely true. His girls were identical twins, which had nothing to do with old wives' tales. The two of them looked so much alike that Megan put different colored socks on them to tell them apart.

Although it had freaked Megan out a little at the prospect of two babies to care for along with Mason, Pesh was thrilled. Every aspect of the pregnancy and birth had been special to him. Thankfully, Megan had been blessed with great health, although she had been advised to take early maternity leave to stay off her feet. After her clinicals, she had accepted a job in the ER at Wellstar, where they sometimes were on similar shifts. The girls arrived only a few weeks short of their due date and were both healthy five pounders. Six weeks later, they were thriving and were the greatest joy in his life.

Sucking relentlessly on her pacifier, Maya's wide eyes took in her surroundings. She stretched and flailed her arms. If she wasn't careful, she was going to hit her sister. Since Sara remained sleeping soundly, Pesh bent over and picked Maya up. He kissed her cheek before drawing her close to his chest. As he stared into her tiny face, he couldn't help the surge of love that overtook him. For all the years of struggle and heartache he had endured, it was moments like these that made him feel as though he was finally complete. His heart was full, and he was so thankful.

Once they learned they were having girls, he and Megan had decided to give them both Indian and Irish names to represent their combined heritages. Maya, which meant princess and honorable in Indian, was coupled with Katherine, to honor Emma, whose middle name was Katherine. Without Emma, he and Megan never would have met. Sara, which meant 'soul', was given her mother's real name, Margaret, as her middle name.

At the sound of Megan's gentle snores, he smiled. "Did you wear your mommy out today?" he asked Maya. She opened her tiny mouth like she wished she could respond to him. "Let's wake her up."

After he swept a strand of Megan's long blonde hair out of her face, Pesh leaned down to kiss her cheek. She stirred as her eyes fluttered opened. "Hey," she said with a lazy smile.

"Hello, my love," he replied.

"How was your first day back?" she asked, as she stretched her arms over her head.

He grimaced. "Absolutely miserable without you and the girls."

Megan smiled. "We missed you, too." She jerked her chin up at Maya. "She cried for thirty minutes straight after you left. I think we have a serious Daddy's girl on our hands."

"Really?" he asked, gazing down at Maya. He couldn't help the warm glow that spread through his chest at Megan's words. At just six weeks old, his girls were already showing distinct and different personalities. Maya was inquisitive and fought sleep to be awake to see what all was going on. He'd ended up holding her more than Sara simply because Maya often exhausted Megan by not going to sleep. Sara, on the other hand, was already very sweet tempered and a natural snuggler. She probably represented his more laid-back, quiet personality where Maya was likely to be a little firecracker, just like her mom.

Maya stared up at him, her dark eyes peering intently at him. "Did you miss me, my little princess?" A fleeting smile appeared on her face.

"Oh my God, she smiled at you!" Megan cried.

"But babies don't respond with smiling until later. It must be gas or something," he argued.

Megan nudged his leg with her knee. "She most definitely smiled at you, Pesh." She rose off the couch to rub Maya's cheek. "You smiled at your daddy, didn't you?"

Without taking her eyes off of Pesh, Maya flashed another smile and waved her fist. The sight caused tears to sting his eyes. He blinked fast, trying to clear them. He didn't like feeling emotionally weak in front of Megan. But he knew he was busted the moment Megan murmured, "Oh baby."

She slid her arm around his waist, leaning up on her tiptoes to burrow her face in his neck. "Do you know how much my love for you grows because you just got teary over your daughter?"

He glanced down at her in surprise. "Really?"

"Mmm, hmm." She gave him a brief kiss. "After Davis, all I ever wanted was for my children to have a father who loved and adored them." She smiled. "You make that dream come true every day."

He brought his lips to hers. His mouth worked frantically to illustrate all that he was feeling inside—the intense love that he felt would burst from him. "I love you," he murmured against her lips.

"I love you, too."

Just as he started to kiss her again, a loud commotion in the kitchen drew them apart. Megan rubbed his cheek tenderly before bestowing a kiss on Maya's head. She then jerked her chin towards the kitchen, and he followed her. Patrick had just burst through the backdoor with all the kids in tow.

"We're back!" Mason called, as he bobbed around the kitchen. Three-year-old Noah and his two-year-old sister, Caroline, made a beeline for their mother. They began chattering non-stop to Emma while their bodies shook with unspent energy.

Pesh watched with amusement as Emma's hand came to her hip and she pointed her stirring spoon at Patrick. "You gave them ice cream, didn't you?"

Patrick shrugged. "I'm a grandfather. Spoiling them is what I'm supposed to do."

Emma rolled her eyes. "Yeah, and then you bring them home to detox on my watch."

"Mommy, I hungwy!" Caroline protested, stomping her foot. With her auburn hair swept back in pigtails and her emerald eyes narrowing in determination, she looked just like her mother. Well, her expression was pure Aidan.

"Caroline Fitzgerald, you get one ice cream cone in you, and you start acting like you have no manners. We do not stomp our feet to get what we want."

She appeared thoughtful for a moment before saying, "Pwease Mommy, I vewy hungwy."

Emma grinned. "Go wash up and then have a seat at the table in the dining room."

"Come on guys," Mason said. At almost four-and-a-half, he was always the caretaker of his younger cousins. Noah and Caroline followed him into the half bathroom off the kitchen.

Cradling Maya in his arms, Pesh joined Emma at the stove. "Something sure smells good."

"Thank you. It's Megan's favorite chicken casserole. Then there's broccoli and cheese casserole, green beans, and some cornbread, extra crispy on the edges just like Megan loves it." The corners of her mouth turned down in a frown. "I'm sorry it's not Indian food."

He grinned. "I would have been very surprised if it had been considering how much you didn't appreciate it many years ago."

Patrick nodded in agreement. "That's quite a spread you've fixed for us."

Emma smiled. "I was happy to do it."

"Are you feeling all right?" Pesh asked, motioning to her expanding belly.

Emma patted her bump lovingly before responding. "I think I've felt the best this pregnancy out of all the others. You would think with a three and two-year-old, I would be exhausted all the time, but it's amazing how good I've felt."

Patrick gave a beaming smile. "I can't tell you how thrilled I am to be having yet *another* grandson to carry on the family name." With a wink, he added, "Not to mention the fact he's been given fine Irish names."

Aidan and Emma had found out the sex of their third, and final child, the week before. They had decided on the name Connor Liam, which was a double representation of Irish names. While Emma's best friend, Connor, was thrilled at the namesake, he also wanted them to call the baby Connor as well. In the end, it would be Liam Fitzgerald joining the rest of the crew in four and a half months.

"And is Aidan still feeling okay?" Pesh asked.

Emma opened her mouth to answer him, but Aidan chose that moment to walk in the door. "Me and my soon to be non-swimmers are just fine," he replied, with a grin. A week before he had gone under the laser for a vasectomy. While Caroline had been a surprise, Liam had not. With Emma nearing thirty-four, they thought it best to finish out their family while they were still young. And while Emma was pregnant and there were no worries about conception, Aidan thought it was the best time to get his vasectomy and let it take effect.

"Daddy!" Caroline squealed, as she came bounding around the corner. Aidan's grin grew wider as he took his daughter in his arms.

"Hi sweet pea."

She kissed both of his cheeks before she started wiggling, wanting down. Noah ran to him next, and he got to hold his son a little longer as Noah told him all about his day helping out with the babies. A cry from the living room snapped Pesh's attention away from Aidan and Emma.

Megan was bending over the Pack N Play, picking up Sara. "Aw, what's wrong, sweetheart?" she cooed, as she took Sara into her arms. As Megan rocked her back and forth, Sara continued wailing, which caused Maya's face to crumple up as well. "You must be hungry."

"I'll get their bottles," Pesh called, over the twin's loud cries.

"Thank you."

As Emma worked to gather the kids, along with Patrick and Aidan, around the dining room table, Pesh got busy heating up the formula. Once he had the two bottles fixed, he grabbed them and then went to the dining room. Megan was already seated with Mason trying to entertain Sara to stop crying her crying. He passed a bottle to Megan before sitting down himself. He'd barely gotten the bottle in her mouth before Maya started sucking greedily at the formula.

As Aidan reached to start spooning some chicken casserole onto his plate, Patrick shot him a disapproving look. With a sigh, Aidan dropped the serving spoon. "You gonna say grace even though it's not your house, Pop?"

"Why yes, I am. It's good for all these children to learn," he replied, motioning to Noah and Caroline who sat between their parents, and then over to Mason.

"It should be up to Pesh and Megan whether it's said or not," Aidan grumbled.

Pesh held up his free hand that wasn't holding Maya. "It's fine. Truly, I don't mind."

Aidan mouthed "suck up" at him before grinning. Pesh merely shook his head at Aidan's antics. "Then let's return thanks," Patrick said.

With Maya still taking long pulls at her bottle, Pesh bowed his head. As Patrick recited the blessing, Pesh couldn't help feeling so very blessed himself. Three years ago, the dining room would have been empty. Most likely, he would have been grabbing something on the way home or finishing some leftover takeout. But now, he had a beautiful, loving wife by his side—one he fell a little more in love with each and every day. Across from him, he had a son who was strong and healthy. In his arms and his wife's, he had two daughters who he couldn't wait to see what the future held for them. He also had the love and support of good friends and family. At the end of the day, true love in its many forms was all you could really hope for and cling to.

- THE END -

VICIOUS CYCLE
SYNOPSIS

<u>Add to Goodreads</u>

David aka 'Deacon' Malloy has devoted his adult life to the Hell's Raiders motorcycle club. Plucked off the streets as a teenager for his fighting ability, he willing embraces the violent life-style of his new family. After his adoptive father's murder during the last club war, he slid into the vacated role of Sergeant at Arms. His world is thrown for a loop when a former club whore dies, and the five year old daughter he had no idea he had fathered is deposited on the club steps.

Alexandra Evans followed in her parents' footsteps by going into education. As a Kindergarten teacher, she loves helping her young students learn to read and write. At the start of the school year, one little girl stands out to her above all the rest. With an aura of sadness about her, Willow Malloy is someone who needs all the tender loving care Alexandra can give. When she suddenly stops coming to school, Alexandra goes in search of her. What she finds is a clubhouse full of bikers, and a father hell bent on keeping his daughter always within his sight during a turf war.

The moment Deacon lays eyes on Alexandra he knows he has to have her. He doesn't give two shits about the fact she's a naïve civilian or that she has no desire to become another one of his conquests. He's never found a woman he couldn't have, and he wants nothing more to persuade Alexandra into changing her mind.

Will Deacon seduce Alexandra into his dark world, or will she help him embrace a brighter future for himself and his daughter?

Aidan's 7th Ring of Hell or Emma's Baby Shower:

A deleted scene from The Proposal

At the shrill sounds of feminine squealing, Aidan grabbed his beer and tipped up the bottle. With two long pulls, he downed the foamy liquid. A loud burp escaped his lips. As a practicing Catholic, he was well acquainted with the idea of Purgatory. However, he never imagined he would have to experience it while on earth, nor could he imagine he would be hiding out in his sister, Becky's, bonus room from the gaggle of females attending Noah's baby shower.

One thing was certain about his son. He was already attracting hoards of female love and attention, and he wasn't even born yet. Almost fifty women had converged on Becky's house. They had arrived with ornately wrapped packages and bulging gift-bags coupled with non-stop conversation. Once the crowd had gathered, he had slunk away to seek out refuge with the other men.

When Aidan went to grab another beer out of the mini-fridge, his father shook his head. "You better watch it. Emma will have your hide if you go out there drunk," Patrick warned.

Aidan grimaced. "How else am I supposed to endure this?"

His brother-in-law, Tate, snorted. "I feel for ya, man. But if you don't shape up and act right, you'll incur the wrath of not only Emma, but all the Fitzgerald girls."

A shudder went through Aidan at the thought of five angry females. Emma's fury was enough to scare the hell out of him, but if you combined that with all his older sisters, it was an estrogen shit-storm of epic proportions. "Fine, fine," he grumbled, putting the beer back.

For the last half hour while inane shower games were played and the feast of food was consumed, Aidan had stationed himself in the bonus room with Patrick and Tate along with his other brothers-in-law, Tim, Jack, and Barry. A play-off game on the big screen captivated the other men, along with John and Percy, but Aidan was too anxious to unwind.

He knew when it came time to start opening the overflowing table of gifts, Emma would want him at her side, and he really, really didn't want to do that. All of the oohing and ahhing and giggling…it was a nightmare.

Georgie came running into the room. "Come on, Uncle Aidan! It's time to open presents!" he cried.

Aidan couldn't help grinning at Georgie's excitement. He had refused to leave Emma's side the entire day and couldn't wait to see what Baby Noah was getting for his "pre-birthday". Aidan was glad that in Emma's thoughtfulness she had brought gifts for all of the boys since the shower was being hosted at their home and uprooting them for an afternoon. But deep down, he knew she was mainly looking out for Georgie.

He bounced up and down as Aidan remained rooted on the bar stool. "Whaddya waitin' for?" Georgie questioned impatiently.

Aidan drew in a deep breath. Glancing over at Patrick, he said, "Wish me luck."

Patrick thumped Aidan on the back. "Come on, son. I'll go out there with you."

"You will?"

"For Emma's sake, not yours," Patrick replied, with a wink.

"Figures," Aidan grumbled.

Georgie grabbed Aidan's hand and jerked him off the stool. With a tug, he pulled Aidan out the door and down the hallway. As Georgie led him around the corner, Aidan saw an empty chair waiting on one side of Emma while on the other side was a mountain of wrapped boxes and gift bags.

When she met his gaze, her pleased smile warmed his heart. He knew she had waited all her life to get to have a baby shower, and from the flush on her alabaster cheeks, he knew how thrilled and excited she was. And for him, there was nothing better than seeing Emma truly happy.

Impulsively, he leaned over and kissed her tenderly on the lips. "Have I told you how beautiful you look today?"

He wasn't just flattering her either. The emerald maternity dress, cream colored leggings, and brown knee boots made her absolutely stunning. He loved how she could appear both trendy, graceful, and sexy as hell in what she wore, even eight months pregnant.

Pink tinged her cheeks at his compliments. "Thank you." Her hand came up to cup his cheek. "Baby, are you sure you don't mind helping me open gifts?"

He furrowed his brows and held his breath. This had to be some sort of trick question, right? She couldn't possibly be giving him an out from Baby Shower Hell. And just like that, he saw the flicker in her eyes, and he knew how much she wanted him beside her.

"Of course I'm sure."

At her wide smile, he reluctantly plopped down in his chair. Gazing out at the sea of faces, he recognized a few friendly ones. Casey and Connor were both in attendance along with Virginia, Emma's grandmother. Although he couldn't name them all, there were a bunch of Emma's female cousins who had come down for the day from the mountains. If he survived this baby shower, he had to make it through another one the following weekend with all of Emma's relatives.

"Okay, let's get started," Becky said, handing a large box to Aidan.

He glanced from Becky to Emma. "You want me to open it?"

"Sure, go ahead," Emma said.

Sucking in a breath, Aidan tore into the pastel blue wrapping paper. He peered down at the box. "What the hell…"

Emma giggled at his side. "It's a breast pump, babe."

"A what?"

"It's so I can pump my milk for Noah to take while I'm at work or when I can't breastfeed him."

He jerked his gaze over to hers. "You mean, you're actually going to hook yourself up to that?" he asked incredulously.

Women's laughter rang in his ears, and it was his turn to blush. "It looks painful," he muttered.

"It'll be fine," Emma reassured him.

With one last skeptical look, he passed the box back to Becky. After a few minutes, he felt like a robot on an assembly line. A box or bag was given to him to open. Emma and others would ooh and ahh over it—sometimes Emma would even get teary like with the quilt Virginia presented her with—and then the process would be repeated all over again.

He rubbed his temples at the sight of so many clothes, blankets, bibs, pacifiers, and toys. It made his head swim, especially the thoughts of getting it all back to their house. He couldn't imagine they would need to buy anything else for Noah for a long, long time.

When the last gift was unwrapped and Emma, through her tears, had thanked everyone profusely, she eased her chair closer to his. "Thank you for helping me." She slung one arm over his shoulder and leaned in to nuzzle his neck. "I know you how much you hated doing this, but I really appreciate it."

"Are you kidding? I just had the time of my life," he argued.

Emma pulled away to grin at him. "You're such a liar."

"Okay, so that was a little bit of hell on earth for me."

"I thought as much." She took his hand in hers—the one that now glittered with her platinum engagement ring along with her wedding band— and brought it to her belly. "Noah says thanks to."

At his son's movements beneath his hand, Aidan smiled. "He likes having his old man around, huh?"

Emma gazed up at him with a dreamy smile. "Yes, he does. And so does his mom." Her lips hovered close to his. "I love you, Aidan. I love you for giving me today and every day that we're together."

His chest welled with emotion, and his only response was to kiss Emma passionately. He didn't care that they were in a room full of other women or surrounded by breast pumps and diaper genies. He just wanted to show her how much he loved her.

And he did.

Guess Whose Hopping Down the Bunny Trail?

A Proposition/Proposal Easter Story

A high-pitched squeal broke through the layers of Aidan Fitzgerald's subconscious. As the wailing persisted, his senses slowly came awake. "Em?" he murmured drowsily. With his eyes still pinched shut, he rolled over in bed to find it empty. Craning his neck, he heard the unmistakable sound of the shower running. Well, he barely heard it over his four-and-a half-week old son's screams.

"Okay, okay, I'm coming, Noah," Aidan muttered as he pulled himself into a sitting position.

As he hurried around the side of the bed, Aidan dug the sleep out of his eyes with his fists. By the time he reached the bassinet, Noah was in full-on, pissed-off fit mode. He drew his tiny legs to his stomach while flailing his fists. His face was crimson from his exertions. "Easy Little Man," Aidan said as he reached over to pick Noah up. While all of their family members loved telling Aidan and Emma that they had been blessed that Noah had such an easy temperament, he could really let you have it when he got going. Of course, the only time he really wailed was when he was hungry or had a dirty diaper.

Kissing Noah's cheek, Aidan then snuggled him against his chest. When Noah's tiny brows furrowed in confusion, Aidan grinned down at him. "I know, I know. I'm a poor substitute for Mommy, especially if you're hungry." At the sound of Aidan's voice, Noah popped open his eyes. "Hmm, feels like you've got a wet diaper. Let's get you changed."

Aidan's once bacheloresque master bedroom had become baby central. With the nursery upstairs, Emma didn't want Noah that far from her when he was so small, so he slept in Pack and Play in the bedroom. Aidan wondered with all of Noah's shit in their bedroom why he needed his own room. But when it came down to it, Aidan actually liked having him close too. Even though he adored and loved Emma with all his body and soul, the love for his son was far greater than anything he could have ever imagined. From the moment Noah had been placed in his arms, Aidan had felt the most amazing, life-altering bond. He hated spending any time away from Noah. He had even taken two weeks Paternity Leave to be with Emma when Noah came home from the hospital, but he'd been forced with a heavy heart to return to work the last week.

Laying Noah back down on the Pack and Play, Aidan then undid his onesie and diaper. It had taken one epic dousing of piss to the face for Aidan to remember to take the proper precautions when changing Noah. While Emma had found it hilarious, he had not been so amused. After he put a fresh diaper on, Aidan tenderly kissed along Noah's exposed belly, inhaling of the sweet essence that was baby, before snapping his onsie back together. He then popped Noah's pacifier back into his mouth just in case he wanted to get fussy again before Emma got out of the shower.

He sat down in the glider and began to do one of his new favorite things—rock Noah. He couldn't get enough of the feeling of Noah in his arms. Emma had teased him that he was going to spoil Noah by holding him so much, but the truth was neither one of them could keep their hands off of their sweet son for long. Aidan loved the way Noah felt nestled against his chest along with the way he would stare intently up at him, as if he were memorizing Aidan's face.

Emma appeared in the bathroom doorway outfitted in her green silk robe. Just the sight of her wet, tangled Auburn hair and flushed alabaster cheeks from the shower got Aidan's juices up and running. But they were still two weeks shy of getting back to clockwork in the bedroom, so Aidan quickly doused the fire growing below his waist. He smiled at Emma from his seat in the glider. "Someone woke up while you were gone."

"Oh, I'm sorry. I thought I better slip into the shower while I could."

Shaking his head, Aidan rose out of his seat. "I don't mind getting up with him, babe." He kissed Emma's cheek. "I just don't have what all you have to offer him."

Emma laughed at his insinuation. "He just ate three hours ago."

Aidan chuckled. "Yeah, well, he's got that 'this pacifier ain't gonna hold me much longer' gleam in his eyes."

"Here I'll take him," Emma said. Aidan gently passed Noah over to her. "Is Mommy's angel hungry again?" she cooed.

Just the sound of her voice made Noah come alive as he waved his fists and snuggled closer to her. She beamed at him as she eased down in the glider. He unceremoniously spit out his pacifier out as Emma pushed open one side of her robe. Once he was nursing heartily, Emma turned her attention back to Aidan. "Are you ready for a full day in the mountains?"

"Of course I am. You know I love being with your family."

"Ah, but you've never experienced one of our Anderson Easter Egg hunts."

Aidan quirked his brows at her. "Should I be afraid?"

Emma giggled. "Trust me, it's intense. There are probably over a hundred people with a thousand eggs hidden."

"Holy shit! A thousand?"

"Why do you think I've been dying eggs like crazy the past few days?"

"I thought you had an Easter egg fetish. Who was I to judge?"

With a laugh, Emma replied, "Nope, it's a tradition, not a fetish."

"If you say so."

"Oh, we need to leave as early as we can."

Aidan lifted his brows in surprise. "Don't tell me you volunteered my services for the massive egg hiding undertaking?"

Emma grinned. "No, it's more about me helping Grammy. She keeps being so stubborn and insisting that she's not too old to do lunch all by herself. But then she's wiped out for days after she does it."

Aidan smirked at her. "Hmm, so that's where you and now Noah get the stubbornness."

"Hey now. There's plenty of stubbornness floating around in your Fitzgerald DNA," Emma countered as she propped Noah on her shoulder to burp him.

"If you say so. I better go hop in the shower then."

"You do that, stubborn ass," Emma replied, with smile.

He winked at her before ducking into the bathroom. He showered at a lightning quick pace before getting out to shave at record speed. After he wrapped a towel around his waist, Aidan stepped out of bathroom and into the bedroom. Wearing a beautiful green sundress that made Aidan's heartbeat accelerate, Emma had Noah on the bed, easing him into his clothes. At the sight of the outfit, Aidan did a double take. "What the hell is he wearing?"

Emma glanced up at him in surprise. "His Easter outfit."

Aidan shook his head wildly back and forth. "It has pink in it."

"And blue and green." When he continued giving her a skeptical look, Emma huffed, "These are pastel, Easter colors, Aidan."

"I don't want my son in pink."

Emma rolled her eyes. "Seriously?

"Yeah, I am."

Lifting Noah into her arms, she pinned Aidan with a hard stare. "You wear pink shirts."

Aidan scratched the back of his neck. "That's different. I'm a man."

"And he's a little man. There isn't any difference. Besides, look how adorable he is." She held Noah out for Aidan to inspect him.

As much as he hated to admit it, Noah looked cute as hell in his gingham outfit. He even had a hat to match that bunny ears sewn on. He exhaled noisily. "Fine, you win."

Emma grinned. "I win in more ways than one. Patrick picked this out for him."

Aidan groaned. "Jesus, not Pop?"

"Yes, your father." With Noah in one arm, she reached over to playfully smack his ass. "Now hurry up and get ready. We need to be on the road in half an hour."

Later that afternoon, Aidan lounged around the giant mahogany table in Grammy and Granddaddy's dining room. He fought the urge to undo his pants since like always, he had eaten way too much. Between Grammy and Emma's combined efforts, the meal had been delicious. He was debating eating another piece of cake when Emma crooked her finger at him from the dining room doorway. His brows furrowed in confusion as he rose out of his chair. At the head of the table, Noah slept peacefully in Earl's arms, so he couldn't help but ask, "What's wrong?"

"Come with me," she said, taking him by the hand and leading him down the hallway. She closed them into Grammy and Granddaddy's bedroom before she spoke again. "I need to ask you to do something for me."

Her intense stare caused him to swallow hard several times. "Um, Em, are you asking what I think you're asking?"

It took her a moment before her eyes bulged, and she shook her head wildly back and forth. "Oh God no! How could you think I brought you into my grandparent's bedroom for sex?"

Aidan exhaled a defeated breath. "Maybe because I've been without sex for years now."

Emma laughed. "It has not been years. It's been exactly four weeks and five days."

"You have it down to a science?"

"Well, it's all based on Noah's birthday since I gave you that going away present that sent me into early labor."

Aidan grinned at the memory. "Oh yeah."

"Anyway, I brought you in here because we're in sort of a crisis—an Easter Bunny crisis."

"Excuse me?"

Emma motioned to the bed. Draped across it was a furry, adult sized Easter Bunny costume. "You see every year Henry, the neighbor from down the road, plays the Easter Bunny during the egg hunt. But we just got a call from his wife that he's in the ER passing a kidney stone." Emma drew in a ragged breath. "Aidan, we need you to play the Easter Bunny."

A hysterical laugh escaped his lips. "You're shitting me, right?"

Emma nibbled her bottom lip nervously before replying. "I wish I was, but we're in desperate need here."

Aidan stared at her for several long seconds, expecting that at any minute she would say it was a joke. When she didn't, he shook his head. "There are about a thousand other men in your family. Why does it have to be me?" he protested.

"All the other men who are your size and could fit into the costume have children in the Easter egg hunt."

Aidan shrugged. "So?"

"Don't you see? If their dads are missing, they're going to think something is up." Emma tilted her head at him. "You don't want to ruin the mystery of the Easter Bunny for them, do you?"

"Um, if it means keeping my ass out of a furry bunny suit, then hell yes I do!"

Emma swept her hands to her hips and pursed her lips at him. "So in a couple of years, you would want someone ruining it for Noah?"

Aidan opened his mouth to protest, but the closed it. Deep down the truth was he wouldn't want some selfish bastard ruining Easter for his kid. "No," he grumbled.

"So does that mean you'll do it?"

"I guess."

The corners of Emma's lips turned up in a pleased smile. "You know, it'll make me very happy if you do this."

He lifted his brows questioningly at her. "Just how happy?" As she closed the gap between them, Aidan's breath hitched. She didn't just walk over to him. She slunk. Her full hips sashayed to and fro in the dress.

"Although we still have a week to go before I'm fully operational again in the bedroom department—" He scowled causing her to pause. "Now Mr. Fitzgerald, I'm not finished."

"Okay, fine."

"As I was saying, although we still have a week left, I'm sure I could find several ways to reward you for your good deeds."

"Just what did you have in mind?"

She tapped her finger against her chin in thought. "Maybe lots of oral attention and tender loving care to your most prized possession?"

He couldn't help the grin that spread across his face. "Hmm, I like the sound of that. But I think I need some further convincing." Snaking his arms around her waist, he said, "Paint me a more vivid picture."

Emma laughed. "Do you remember the furry green handcuffs and whipped cream from our honeymoon?"

Aidan's eyes rolled back in his head as he groaned. "Oh fuck yes."

"Then I guarantee if you put you on that bunny costume, we'll reenact that scene tonight when Noah is asleep."

"Then bring on the fur and bunny ears!" Aidan exclaimed.

"See, I knew you'd see reason when I made you an offer you couldn't refuse." Emma kissed him with just enough passion to leave them both breathless. "Okay, we better get you ready."

Aidan glanced warily at the costume on the bed. "So how do we do this?"

"First, I think you should take your clothes off."

Aidan couldn't help the cocky smirk that formed on his face. "You don't have to ask me to do that twice."

Emma rolled her eyes. "I'm just thinking that it's going to be hot enough outside as it is. We don't want to add to it by keeping on a layer of clothes."

"Fine," Aidan murmured. He quickly slipped out of his dress shirt and khaki pants but left his briefs on. Holding out the body of the costume, Emma helped him step inside. When she zipped him up, Aidan couldn't help the momentary feeling of panic wash over him that he was trapped in the costume. Great, if he was freaking out now, what would it feel like when the giant head was put over him? He drew in a few calming breaths before Emma covered him with the bunny head.

"How's that?"

Surprisingly he could see better than he thought out of the mesh eyes, and he was getting plenty of oxygen. "Not bad."

"Good." Rubbing his furry chest, she asked, "Ready to go wow the kids?"

"As ready as I'll ever be."

When she guided him into the hallway, Grammy was waiting on them. "How did you ever talk him into it?" she asked.

"I just appealed to his sense of duty as a father," Emma replied.

Virginia glanced between Aidan and Emma before crossing her arms over her chest. "Uh, huh..." she murmured skeptically.

Earl appeared in the hallway with Noah in his arms. At the sight of Aidan in the costume, he began snickering. It wasn't too long before he was howling with laugher. "Wow, son, I do believe you just totally lost your man card!"

Aidan sighed inside the costume. "Fine, fine. Laugh all you want. I'm the one who'll be reaping the benefits

tonight."

Emma's eyes widened before she smacked his bunny arm. "Watch it!"

Grammy giggled behind them. "Like we didn't know some sort of favors had to be promised to get him into that costume."

As Emma died of mortification next to him, Aidan waved his furry paw at Earl. "Bring Noah over here, so he can see me—I mean, the bunny."

Earl closed the gap between them. Noah peered around, happily sucking on his pacifier. But the moment

Aidan leaned over Earl, Noah's tiny face crumpled. He began screaming in what could only be fear.

"I'd say he's not a fan of the Bunny," Earl mused over the wailing.

"Great, now I've scarred my kid for life," Aidan moaned.

Emma took Noah from Earl. After kissing his cheek reassuringly and rocking him back and forth, he began to quiet. "It's all right, sweetheart. Mommy won't let that mean bunny get you."

"Babe, that's so not funny," Aidan muttered through his bunny head.

"All right then." She grinned at him before glancing down at Noah. "You should be very proud of your daddy today. Although he was swayed by the idea of getting something he really wants, he made a great sacrifice because of you. He loves you enough to make an absolute fool out of himself. So don't be afraid of the bunny, sweetheart. Love him as much as he loves you."

Although she couldn't see it, Aidan beamed inside the costume. "That sounds much better."

Emma leaned up and kissed the cheek on his bunny head. Happy shrieks and children's laughter came from out in the yard. "Well, I think that's your cue," she said.

"Let's get this show on the road."

And with that he waddled down the front door and out into the sunshine.

Halloween with The Fitzgeralds

It's the Great Pumpkin, Aidan Fitzgerald

Tapping out the song's rhythm with his thumbs on the steering wheel, Aidan Fitzgerald eased his Mercedes convertible through the streets of his subdivision. The crisp October air rippled through the strands of his blonde hair. He loved fall days like these when it wasn't too cold to ride with the top down. Although there was a Volvo SUV in one side of his garage to highlight his new family man status, he had managed to keep his toy, aka the convertible, after Noah had been born. Instead, Emma's reliable, but older model Camry, had been traded in for a more family practical SUV. Although Emma had thought it was pretentious, Aidan had insisted on the Volvo for its safety record. He wanted to pull out all the stops to keep the loves of his life safe and protected.

As he neared 401 Ansley Park Drive, he did a double take. Actually, he drove straight past his house before realizing it. Although he'd been living there for over five years, nothing in the yard was familiar to him. Throwing the car into reverse, he peered wide-eyed and open mouthed at the spectacle before him. His yard and two-story Cape Cod had somehow been transformed into a Halloweenapoolza.

When he had left for work that morning, there was only a decorative fall wreath hanging from the front door and two pumpkins on the porch that had been bought at Burt's Pumpkin Patch when he and Emma had taken Noah the week before. Now there were orange and black twinkling lights adorning the rails on the porch. A witch was ass-up in the yard to give the appearance she'd flown straight into the grass. Another was smushed up against the side of the porch along with her broom. Tombstones and hay bales also filled the yard while ghosts flitted in the oak trees.

"Christ almighty," he muttered, as he eased the car into the driveway. Although his house looked like a lot of the other ones in the neighborhood, it was a completely foreign concept to him. After parking the car, he jerked out the keys and hopped out.

As Aidan threw open the door from the garage leading into the house, delicious aromas assaulted his senses. Wait, was that Grammy's BBQ cooking? Surely not. That shit took a lot of time and effort. At the same time, Aidan's stomach rumbled in hopes that it was actually some homemade BBQ.

His gaze flickered around the kitchen before honing in on Emma. She stood at the stove, humming along with the radio. Close by her, Noah sat in his bouncing saucer. A grin stretched on Aidan's face at the sight of the cackling baby. With Beau standing in front of him, Noah tried desperately to catch Beau's tail that was thawping him in his face. Noah was laughing so hard he could barely catch his breath.

"I'm home," Aidan called.

Beau barked happily as Emma whirled around. "Hey baby," she said, a genuine grin spreading across her cheeks.

Aidan stooped over to pick up Noah who was holding his arms outs out patiently for his father. "Hey Little Man," he said before bestowing a kiss on Noah's cheek. He then turned his attention to his wife. Emma beamed as he leaned in for a kiss. Tightening his arms around her, his lips found hers warm and inviting. Just as he thrust his tongue inside, Noah's gurgle interrupted them.

"Have a good day?" Emma questioned breathlessly.

"Pretty good. You?"

"Yeah. Busy, but it was great."

Thinking of his now Thrilleresque yard, he blurted, "Em, what the hell happened outside?"

She grinned. "Patrick came over today and helped me decorate. Isn't it amazing?"

"Oh it's something all right. I'm just not sure it's amazing."

The corners of Emma's lips turned down in a frown, and Aidan braced himself for some pregnancy mood-swings. "Don't you like it?"

Aidan exhaled a wary breath. He desperately tried to decide what the best way to answer her question was without putting himself in the dog house. "It just seems like a lot when Noah isn't even a year old."

"Oh, but you should have seen him when we were decorating. He was grinning the entire time. And your dad had so much fun, too. Most of it was his idea."

Great. If the other two Fitzgerald men that Emma loved most in the world were happy with the lawn debauchery, there was no point in arguing. He'd just have to suck it up and smile. He just hoped none of his bachelor friends caught sight of it, or they would demand his man card be revoked.

Needing to change the subject, he sniffed the air. "Hmm, that is Grammy's BBQ I smell, isn't it?"

Emma smiled. "Yep, I made her recipe just for you. Having Patrick here to watch Noah really helped to free up more cooking time. Oh, there's some apple pie, too."

Adjusting Noah on his shoulder, Aidan eyed Emma suspiciously. "Okay, what's going on?"

"What do you mean?" Emma asked innocently.

Aidan chuckled. "Oh no, don't play coy with me, Em. You went through a helluva lot of trouble to do homemade BBQ. So what's the deal?"

Nibbling her lip, she bent over to take out the steaming Dutch Apple pie, which happened to be Aidan's favorite in the whole wide world, out of the oven. She'd made it from scratch, which was no easy feat. When she sat down the pie, she sighed. "Fine. There is something I wanted to ask you."

With a smirk, he replied, "I knew it. You always try to win over my stomach or my dick when you want something."

She rolled her eyes. "I wanted to see if you would dress up for Halloween with me. You know, kinda like a couple's costume thing, but a theme for the whole family."

"You're shitting me, right?" He had never been a huge fan of the holiday. During high school and college, he enjoyed the parties that featured free flowing booze and chicks in scantily clad costumes. After he'd moved into his house, he had discovered with dismay that his subdivision attracted Trick or Treaters by the droves. Usually, he hung out at O'Malley's on Halloween night, drinking beer and waiting for the pandemonium to die down before he went home. Then just when he thought it was safe, Becky would arrive with her boys. He would usually have to give them granola bars or money because he didn't have any candy in the house.

Putting on her best pouty face, Emma said, "It's just I really, really wanted us to dress up as a family this year."

"Babe, this all seems a little ridiculous considering Noah's only eight months old. He has no idea about any of this hoopla, and he certainly won't be eating the candy from Trick or Treating." When she opened her mouth to protest, Aidan added, "And don't even try to guilt me into this. I don't think years later when Noah looks back, the fact his father refused to dress up for Halloween will not send him to therapy."

"So you really won't do it?" Her pouty face had disappeared and a more determined expression appeared.

He knew that when Emma set her mind to something, she usually got her way. She had tried appealing to him with extreme kindness, and he knew from her fiery disposition, that his dick would be feeling the next repercussions of his actions. She might be pregnant again and in sex craved hormone city, but she wouldn't let that stop her from giving him the cold shoulder.

Aidan exhaled nosily. "If, and that's a big if, I said yes, I would have to approve of the costume. No tights under any circumstances."

Emma grinned. "Okay, I think I can work with that."

"But before your imagination runs wild with what costumes you're going to stick us in, I want to be fed this magnificent meal you went to the trouble to bribe me with."

"I'll be happy to." She wrapped her arms around his neck and then bestowed a warm, inviting kiss on his lips. "I'd planned to appeal to your dick later on, but now that you've consented, I'll save that for another time."

Aidan shook his head furiously from side to side. "Oh no, you can pull out all the stops. I won't argue with you."

She laughed before kissing him again. "All right. Once Noah is asleep, I'm at your mercy."

"Mmm, I like the sound of that."

"I thought you would." She pulled away and smiled at him. "Now sit down and we'll eat."

After he'd inhaled two BBQ sandwiches and eaten a large piece of pie, Aidan sat back and rubbed his full belly. "Okay, Em, hit me with the costumes."

She smiled and rose up from the table. After handing Noah off to him, she dug in one of the kitchen drawers. She returned with a thick catalogue full of couples and family costumes. Tapping her finger on one of the pages, Emma asked, "How about this Star Wars one? You'd look very sexy as Han Solo while Noah would look pretty cute with some Yoda ears."

While he had to admit that the "Baby Yoda" costume was pretty freakin' cute, Aidan eyed the Han Solo and Princess Leia costumes contemptuously. He was still not onboard with this ridiculous couples costume thing. "Hmm, I'd much prefer you sporting the Leia Slave Girl costume to this one," Aidan mused, with a wink.

Emma snorted before gazing down at her abdomen. "I don't think with this belly it's happening."

Aidan reached out to rub Emma's barely protruding bump. "Like you're even showing yet."

Shaking her head, Emma replied, "Oh whatever. With this baby, I practically started showing at conception." She nudged him playfully. "Which confirms yet again that this baby is a girl."

Aidan felt the familiar kick in the gut whenever the baby's sex was mentioned. It wasn't that he didn't want a little girl—he loved all his nieces, especially his oldest one, Megan. It was just he knew that girls were trouble—the young ones and especially the older ones. Hell, with four older sisters, he more than knew what he was talking about. Then of course, there was the red-headed beauty sitting next to him who continued to mystify him daily.

"Did you hear me, Aidan?"

"Hmm, what?"

Emma smiled. "I asked you what you thought of naming the baby, Caroline, after your mother?"

"That would be beautiful," he murmured, his chest overcome with emotions. He couldn't imagine a more perfect name for his daughter than the one that had belonged to his late mother. Just like Emma always knew him better than he knew himself, she reached over and squeezed his hand. When Aidan gazed up at her, she gave him a reassuring smile. "I love you."

He leaned in to bestow a tender kiss on her lips. "I love you more."

"Mmm!" Noah grunted between them.

Aidan laughed as he gazed down at his son. "What Little Man? Are you jealous that I'm giving mommy some loving?"

Noah grinned and waved his fist. Aidan lifted him up to blow raspberries on his tummy. Noah giggled and kicked his legs. Bringing Noah back down to face him, Aidan quirked his brows at his son. "You know, Little Man, if I hadn't given mommy some loving, you wouldn't be here."

"Aidan!" Emma admonished, a red flush filling her cheeks.

He laughed. "It's the truth." With a wink to Emma, he added, "And I plan on giving her lots of loving after you're in bed."

She rolled her eyes. "You're impossible," she huffed.

"Mmm, and you're the sexiest woman in the entire world when you're flustered."

Emma's eyes stayed locked on his while her chest rose and fell in harsh pants. "W-We need to pick a c-costume," she stammered.

Aidan shook his head. "That can wait. Let's give Noah a bath and get him ready for bed."

A shudder ran through Emma's body, causing Aidan to shift in his chair. "If you insist," she said, with a teasing lilt in her voice.

"Oh yes, I do."

As she rose out of her chair, she pinned him with a look. "I guess this means I'll pick the costume, and you'll go along for the ride?"

"Oh, I'll give you a real good ride—"

Emma shook her head. "Say it. I pick the costumes, and you'll go along with it."

Aidan held up his right hand as if he were swearing an oath. "Yeah. Fine. Whatever."

"Good, I'm glad to hear it." She reached and took Noah out of his arms. Glancing at him over her shoulder, she then proceeded to walk towards the stairs with an extra bounce and swish in her hips. When she threw him an expectant glance over her shoulder, he scrambled out of his seat and hurried to her side.

Two Weeks Later
Halloween

Aidan was just putting the finishing touches on a proposal when his buddy, Mike, stuck his head in the door. "Hey man. Wanna grab a beer at O'Malley's?"

"Uh, no, I gotta get home."

A knowing look came over Mike's face. "Oh yeah, Trick or Treating with Noah, huh?"

"Something like that," Aidan grumbled.

Mike gave him a mischievous grin. "Have fun. I'll make sure to drink a beer or two in your absence."

"Thanks a lot."

With a laugh, Mike closed the office door back. Knowing that Emma was expecting him home a little earlier than usual, Aidan saved his documents and then turned off the computer. He put the pedal to the metal on the way home and managed to get home with time to spare. The sun was just beginning to set, and he knew it wouldn't be long until the doorbell began ringing with candy seekers.

When Aidan trudged down the hallway, he found Beau lying outside the bedroom door. He sucked in a pained breath. Beau was outfitted in a Tin Man's costume complete with tin cup hat on his furry, black head.

"Not you too, buddy?"

Beau appeared to be resigned to his fate and wasn't trying to chew off the costume. Instead, he just gazed up at Aidan with an expression like, What was I going to do? I love her, and for reasons my doggy brain can't comprehend, this shit makes her happy, so there.

Bending over, Aidan patted Beau. "You're a damn good dog, you know that?"

Beau thumped his tail in response. With a sigh, Aidan stepped over Beau to walk into the bedroom. Dread washed over him at the sight of the Scarecrow's costume that was draped over the bed. Somehow among all the choices, Emma had decided on The Wizard of Oz since it was her favorite movie since she was a kid. She'd even played Dorothy in a high school production. And while there were worse things she could have picked, making him the scarecrow? Honestly.

"Aidan is that you?" Emma questioned from the bathroom.

"Yeah," he mumbled.

She stepped to the doorway with Noah in her arms. Aidan's heart melted at the sight of Noah's Cowardly Lion costume. While most of the body was golden brown, the mane was varying shades of dark and light. A puffy tail trailed down Emma's leg. Noah's face peeked out from the mane to grin at him. "Looks like he's enjoying his costume," Aidan mused.

Emma laughed. "He is. I thought he might pitch a Fitzgerald fit when I got him inside it, but he's been perfectly fine." Gazing down at her son with a beaming smile, Emma said in a sing-song voice, "He's Mommy's sweetest and best tempered boy in the whole wide world. Aren't you Noah?"

At that moment, Aidan's gaze left Noah's to take in his wife's appearance. Damn, she even made a Dorothy costume sexy. Her long, auburn hair was swept back in the identical hair style of Judy

Garland's. Her blue and white checked dress pulled tight across her breasts, making Aidan's mouth run dry. While the dress came down a little longer than he would have preferred, he still got an eye-full of her fabulous legs down to where the ruby slippers glittered on her feet.

"Like what you see?" she teased.

His gaze snapped to meet hers. He gave her a seductive smile. "Yes, I do." He took a step towards them. "I know what treat I want tonight."

She giggled. "You're impossible." Leaning in, she bestowed a kiss on his lips. When she pulled away, she cocked her head, surmising him. "If you make it through tonight with whining or having that bored borderline pissed off expression of yours, I promise to come to bed tonight wearing nothing but these heels."

Aidan snaked one of his arms around Emma's waist. "Mmm, I'll make sure to keep saying in my mind, 'There's no place like home, there's no place like home!'"

Acknowledgements

First and foremost thanks goes to **God** for all of his amazing blessing in my life the past year.

To Karleigh Brewster: Thank you so much for all of your ER medical expertise. I appreciate you going through several different scenarios with me to make sure the scene turned out right. *While she lay the foundation, I took on the story-telling, so if there are issues with poetic license that is all me.*

To my readers: I cannot thank you enough for your support and your love of my books. You are the most amazing blessing I have had in this business. Big, big hugs and love from me!

To Marion Archer—editor and plot magician extraordinaire—I couldn't make it without you. You bring so much to my books and make me a better writer and story-teller.

To Marilyn Medina: Your "eagle eyes" know no bounds, and I'm so thankful for getting to work with you, as well as your friendship. Golden Girls 4-Ever!

To Kim Bias: I can't thank you enough for talking me down from the ledge as well as making my books the best they can be. Thanks for the plot/blurb sessions. You do rock my socks!

To Shannon Fuhrman, Tamara Debbaut, Jen Gerchick, Jen Oreto, and Brandi Money: Thank you so much for being my "sluts" and working so hard to promote and support me. I can't tell you how much I appreciate it.

To my street team, Ashley's Angels, thank you so much for your support of me and my books.

To Raine Miller and RK Lilley: SCOLS 4-EVER! Thanks for your unfailing love and support in all areas personally and professionally. I couldn't ask for better friends and travel partners!

To the ladies of the Hot Ones: Karen Lawson, Amy Lineaweaver, Marion Archer, and Merci Arellano, thank you all for the laughter, the friendship, and the support. You're all amazing!!

About the Author

Katie Ashley is the New York Times, USA Today, and Amazon Best-Selling author of The Proposition. She lives outside of Atlanta, Georgia with her two very spoiled dogs and one outnumbered cat. She has a slight obsession with Pinterest, The Golden Girls, Harry Potter, Shakespeare, Supernatural, Designing Women, and Scooby-Doo.

She spent 11 1/2 years educating the Youth of America aka teaching MS and HS English until she left to write full time in December 2012.

She also writes Young Adult fiction under the name Krista Ashe.

Follow Katie Ashley

Website

Facebook

Twitter

Goodreads

Other Works of Katie Ashley

The Proposition | The Proposal | The Party

Music of the Heart | Beat of the Heart | Music of the Soul

Search Me | Don't Hate the Player...Hate the Game

Nets and Lies | Jules, the Bounty Hunter

The Guardians | Testament

Made in the USA
Lexington, KY
08 April 2014